"I need to bite you, Marisa," he said.

That was the last thing she'd expected him to say. She was shocked.

"No, no, do not struggle. 'Tis for your own good."

"For my own good," she sputtered. "You are crazy. Let go of me, at once, or I'm going to scream my head off."

She opened her mouth to do just that, but he laid his lips over hers to halt her protests. And any inclination she had to struggle died a quick death of molten, wet heat, emanating from their joined lips and ricocheting to all her extremities and some interesting places in between.

A groan of raw hunger, low in his throat, caused a mirroring groan from deep inside her, and she wrapped her arms around his wide shoulders.

Never, in all her life, had she been so aroused by a man. Not so quickly. Not so strongly.

The kiss seemed to go on forever as he slanted his open mouth over hers, this way and that, seeking the perfect fit. And when he found it, his tongue teased hers w
out forays of taste.

VAMPIRE IN PARADISE

A DEADLY ANGELS BOOK

SANDRA HILL

AVON

An Imprint of HarperCollinsPublishers

AVON BOOKS
An Imprint of HarperCollins*Publishers*
195 Broadway
New York, New York 10007

First Avon Books mass market printing: December 2014

Avon Trademark Reg. U.S. Pat. Off. and in Other Countries, Marca Registrada, Hecho en U.S.A.
HarperCollins® is a registered trademark of HarperCollins Publishers.

Printed in the U.S.A.

10 9 8 7 6 5 4 3 2 1

This book is dedicated to Trish Jensen, writer extraordinaire, critique partner, and best friend, who passed away, way too young and unexpectedly, during the writing of this book.

Trish and I shared a sometimes warped sense of humor. She loved the stories of my four sons and their antics (think boxers that glow in the dark saying, "Yes, yes, yes!"); my husband, who had been known to bring golf buddies home to get one of my books because they heard romance novels turn women on; and my cleaning lady, who thought there were aliens living in my freezer.

My books were funnier because of Trish's input during hundreds of sometimes hilarious critique sessions. Folks at the restaurants where we met often looked our way with yearning, somewhat like that Billy Crystal/Meg Ryan scene.

I told Trish before she died that when she got to the Other Side, she must be my muse, my forever source of humor and good romance writing.

So here's to you, Ms. Muse. I will miss you forever.

VAMPIRE IN PARADISE

Prologue

The Norselands, A.D. 850 . . .

Only the strongest survived in that harsh land . . .

Sigurd Sigurdsson sat near the high table of King Haakon's yule feast, sipping at the fine ale from his own jewel-encrusted silver horn. (Many of those "above the salt" held gold vessels, he noted.) Tuns of ale and rare Frisian wine flowed. (His mead tasted rather weak, but mayhap that was his imagination.)

Favored guests at the royal feast (he was mildly favored) had their choice among spit-roasted wild boar, venison and mushroom stew, game birds stuffed with chestnuts, a swordfish the size of a small longboat, eels swimming in spiced cream sauce, and all the vegetable side dishes one could imagine, including the hated neeps. (Hated by Sigurd, leastways. He had a particular antipathy to turnips due to some youthling insanity to determine which lackwit could eat the most of the root vegetables without vomiting or falling over dead as a stump. He lost.) Honey oat cakes and dried fruit trifles finished off the meal for those not filled to overflowing. (Peaches, on the other hand, were fruit of the gods, in Sigurd's opinion.) Entertainment was provided by a quartet of lute players who could scarce be heard over the animated conversation and laughter. (Which was just as well; they harmonized like a herd of screech owls. Again, in Sigurd's opinion.) Good cheer abounded. (Except for . . .)

In the midst of the loud, joyous celebration, Sigurd's demeanor was quiet and sad.

But that was nothing new. Sigurd had been known as a dark, brooding Viking for many of his twenty and seven years. Darker and more brooding as the years marched on. And he wasn't even *drukkinn*.

Some said the reason for Sigurd's discontent was the conflict betwixt two warring sides of his nature. A fierce warrior in battle and, at the same time, a noted physician with innate healing skills inherited from and honed by his grandmother afore her passing to the Other World when he'd been a boyling.

Sigurd knew better. He had a secret sickness of the soul, and its name was envy. Never truly happy, never satisfied, he always wanted what he didn't have, whether it be a chest of gold; the latest, fastest longship; a prosperous estate; the finest sword. A woman. And he did whatever necessary to attain that new best thing. *Whatever*.

'Twas like a gigantic worm he'd found years past in the bowels of a dying man. Egolf the Farrier had been a giant of a burly man in his prime, but at his death when he was only thirty he'd been little more than a skeleton, with no fat and scant flesh to cover his bones. The malady had no doubt started years before innocently enough, with a tiny worm in an apple or some spoiled meat, but over the years, attached to his innards like a ravenous babe, the slimy creature devoured the food Egolf ate, and Egolf had a huge appetite, in essence starving the man to death.

"Sig, my friend!" A giant hand clapped him on the shoulder, and his close friend and *hersir* Bertim sat down on the bench beside him. Beneath his massive red beard, the Irish Viking's face was florid with drink. "You are sitting upright," Bertim accused him. "Is that still your first horn of ale that you nurse like a babe at teat?"

"What an image!" Sigurd shook his head with amusement. "I must needs stay sober. The queen may yet produce a new son for Haakon this night."

"Her timing is inconvenient, but then a yule child brings good luck." Bertim raised his bushy eyebrows as a sudden thought struck him. "Dost act as midwife now?"

"When it is the king's whelp, I do."

Bertim laughed heartily.

"In truth, Elfrida has been laboring for a day and night so far with no result. The delivery promises to be difficult."

Bertim nodded. 'Twas the way of nature. "What has the king promised you for your assistance?"

"Naught much," Sigurd replied with a shrug. "Friendship. Lot of good that friendship does me, though. Dost notice I am not sitting at the high table?"

"And yet that arse licker Svein One-Ear sits near the king," Bertim commiserated.

I should be up there. Ah, well. Mayhap if I do the king this one new favor . . . He shrugged. The seating was a small slight, actually.

A serving maid interrupted them, leaning over the table to replenish their beverages. The way her breasts brushed against each of their shoulders gave clear signal that she would be a willing bed partner to either or both of them. Bertim was too far gone in the drink and too fearful of the wrath of his new Norse wife, and Sigurd lacked interest in services offered so easily. The maid shrugged and made her way to the next hopefully willing male.

Picking up on their conversation, Bertim said, "The friendship of a king is naught to minimize. It can be priceless."

Sigurd had reason to recall Bertim's ale-wise words later that night, rather in the wee hours of the morning, when Queen Elfrida, despite Sigurd's best efforts, delivered a deformed, puny babe, a girl, and Sigurd was asked by the king, in the name of friendship, to take the infant away and cut off its whispery breath.

It was not an unusual request. In this harsh land, only the strongest survived, and the practice of infanticide was ofttimes an act of kindness. Or so the beleaguered parents believed.

But Sigurd did not fulfill the king's wishes. Leastways, not right away. Visions of another night and another life-or-death decision plagued Sigurd as he carried the swaddled babe in his arms, its cries little more than the mewls of a weakling kitten.

Despite his full-length, hooded fur cloak, the wind and cold air combined to chill him to the bone. He tucked the babe closer to his chest and imagined he felt her heart beat steady and true. Approaching the cliff that hung over the angry sea, where he would drop the child after pinching its tiny nose, Sigurd kept murmuring, " 'Tis for the best, 'tis for the best." His eyes misted over, but that was probably due to the snowflakes that began to flutter heavily in front of him.

He would do as the king asked. Of course he would. But betimes it was not such a gift having royal friends.

Just then, he heard a loud voice bellow, *"Sigurd!* Halt! At once!"

He turned to see the strangest thing. Despite the blistering cold, a dark-haired man wearing naught but a long, white, rope-belted gown in the Arab style approached with hands extended.

Without words, Sigurd knew that the man wanted the child. To his surprise, Sigurd handed over the bundle that carried his body heat to the stranger.

"Take her, Caleb," the man said to yet another man in a white robe who appeared at his side.

"Yes, Michael." Caleb bowed as if the first man were a king or some important personage.

More kings! That is all I need!

The Michael person passed the no-longer-crying infant to Caleb, who enfolded the babe in what appeared to be wings, but was probably a white fur cloak, and walked off, disappearing into the now heavy snowfall.

"Will you kill the child?" Sigurd asked, realizing for the first time that he might not have been able to do it himself. Not this time.

"Viking, will you never learn?" Michael asked.

He said "Viking" as if it were a bad word. Sigurd was too stunned by this tableau to be affronted.

"Who are you? *What* are you?" Sigurd asked as he noticed the massive white wings spreading out behind the man.

"Michael. An archangel."

Sigurd had heard of angels before and seen images on wall paintings in a Byzantium church. "Did you say arse angel?"

"You know I did not. Thou art a fool."

No sense of humor at all. Sigurd assumed that an *arch*angel was a special angel. "Am I dead?"

"Not yet."

That did not sound promising. "But soon?"

"Sooner than thou could imagine," he said without the least bit of sympathy.

Can I fight him? Somehow, Sigurd did not think that was possible.

"You are a grave sinner, Sigurd."

He knows my name. "That I freely admit."

"And yet you do not repent. And yet you would have taken another life tonight."

"Another?" Sigurd inquired, although he knew for a certainty what Michael referred to, and it was not some enemy he had covered with sword dew in righteous battle. But how could the man—rather angel—possibly know what had been Sigurd's closely held secret all these years? No one else knew.

"There are no secrets, Viking," Michael informed him.

Holy Thor! Now he is reading my mind!

Before Sigurd could reply, the snow betwixt them swirled, then cleared to reveal a picture of himself as a boyling of ten years or so bent over his little ailing brother Aslak, a five-year-old of immense beauty, even for a male child. Pale white hair, perfect features, a bubbling, happy personality. Everyone loved Aslak, and Aslak loved everyone in return.

Sigurd had hated his little brother, despite the fact that Aslak followed him about like an adoring puppy. Aslak was everything that Sigurd was not. Sigurd's dull brown hair only turned blond when he got older and the tresses had been sun-bleached on sea voyages. His facial features had been marred by the pimples of a youthling. He had an unpleasant, betimes surly, disposition. In other words, unlikable, or so Sigurd had thought.

Being the youngest of the Sigurdsson boys, before Aslak, and the only one still home, Sigurd had been more aware of his little brother's overwhelming popularity. In truth, in later years, when others referred to the seven Sigurdsson brothers, they failed to recall that at one time there had been eight.

Sigurd blinked and peered again into the swirling snow picture of that fateful night. His little brother's wheezing lungs laboring for life through the long predawn hours. His mother, Lady Elsa, had begged Sigurd to help because, even at ten years of age, he had healing hands. Sigurd had pretended to help, but in truth he had not employed the steam tenting or special herb teas that might have cured his dying brother. Aslak had died, of course, and Sigurd knew it was his fault.

Looking up to see Michael staring at him, Sigurd said, "I was jealous."

Michael shook his head. "Nay, jealousy is a less than admirable trait. Your sin was the more grievous, envy."

"Envy. Jealousy. Same thing."

"Lackwit!" Michael declared, his wings bristling wide like those of a riled goose. "Jealousy is a foolish emotion, but envy destroys the peace of the soul. When was the last time you were at peace, Viking?"

Sigurd thought for a long moment. "Never, that I recall."

"Envy stirs hatred in a person, causing one to wish evil on another. That was certainly the case with your brother Aslak. And with so many others you have maligned or injured over the years."

Sigurd hung his head. 'Twas true.

"Envy causes a person to engage in immoderate quests for wealth or power or relationships that betimes defy loyalty and justice."

Sigurd nodded. The archangel was painting a clear picture of him and his sorry life.

"The worst thing is that you were given a treasured talent. The gift of healing. Much like the saint physician Luke. But you have disdained it. Abused it. And failed to nourish it for a greater good."

"A saint?" Sigurd was not a Christian, but he was familiar with tales from their Bible. "You would have me be as pure as a saint? I am a Viking."

"Idiots! I am forced to work with idiots." Michael rolled his eyes. "Nay, no one expects purity from such as you. Enough! For your grave sins, and those of your six brothers . . . in fact, all the Vikings as a whole . . . the Lord is sorely disappointed. You must be punished. In the future, centuries from now, there will be no Viking nation, as such. Thus sayeth the Lord," Michael pronounced. "And as for you Sigurdsson miscreants . . . your time on earth is measured."

"By death?"

Michael nodded. "Thou art already dead inside, Sigurd. Now your body will be, as well."

So be it. It was a fate all men must face, though he had not expected it to come so soon. "You mention my brothers. They will die, too?"

"They will. If they have not already passed."

Seven brothers dying in the same year? This was the fodder of sagas. Skalds would be speaking of them forevermore. "Will I be going to Valhalla, or the Christian Heaven, or that other place?" He shivered inwardly at the thought of that last fiery fate.

"None of those. You are being given a second chance."

"To live?" This was good news.

Michael shook his head. "To die and come back to serve your Heavenly Father in a new role."

"As an angel?" Sigurd asked with incredulity.

"Hardly," Michael scoffed. "Well, actually, you

would be a vangel. A Viking vampire angel put back on earth to fight Satan's demon vampires, Lucipires. For seven hundred years, your penance would be to redeem your sins by serving in God's army under my mentorship."

Sigurd could tell that Michael wasn't very happy with that mentorship role, but he could not dwell on that. It was the amazing ideas the archangel was putting forth.

"Do you agree?" Michael asked.

Huh? What choice did he have? The fires of Hell, or centuries of living as some kind of soldier. "I agree, but what exactly is a vampire?"

He soon found out. With a raised hand, Michael pointed a finger at Sigurd and unimaginable pain wracked his body, including his mouth where the jawbones seemed to crack and realign themselves, emerging with fangs, like a wolf. He fell to his knees as his shoulder blades also seem to explode as if struck with a broadsword.

"Fangs? Was that necessary?" he gasped, glancing upward at the celestial being whose arms were folded across his chest, staring down at him.

"You'll need them for sucking blood."

"From what?"

"What do you think? From a peach? Idiot! From people . . . or demons."

"*What? Eeew!*" *He expects me to drink blood? From living persons? Or demons? I do not know about this bargain.*

"Thou can still change thy mind, Viking," Michael said.

Reading my mind again! Damn! "And go to Hell?"

"Thou sayest it."

Sigurd thought about negotiating with the angel,

but knew instinctively that it would do no good. He nodded. "It will be as you say."

Moments later, when the pain subsided somewhat, the angel raised him up and studied him with icy contempt, or was it pity? "Go! And do better this time, vangel."

On those words, Sigurd fell backward and over the cliff. Falling, falling, falling toward the black, roiling sea. He discovered in that instant that there was one thing a vangel didn't have. Wings.

Chapter 1

Florida, 2015

**Sometimes life throws you a lifeline,
sometimes a lead sinker . . .**

No one watching Marisa Lopez emerge from the medical center in downtown Miami would have guessed that she'd just been delivered a death blow. Not for herself, but for her five-year-old daughter, Isobel.

Marisa had become a master at hiding her emotions. When she'd found out she was pregnant midway through her junior year at Florida State and her scumbag boyfriend Chip Dougherty skipped campus faster than his two-hundred-dollar running shoes could carry him. When her hopes for a career in physical therapy went down the tubes. When she'd found out two years ago that her sweet baby girl had an inoperable brain tumor. When the blasted tumor kept growing, and Izzie got sicker and sicker. When Marisa had lost her third job in a row because of missing so many days for Izzie's appointments. And now . . . well, she refused to break down now, either, not where others could see.

And there *were* people watching. Looking like a young Sophia Loren, not to mention being five-eleven in her three-inch heels, she often got double takes, and the occasional wolf whistle. And she knew how to work it, especially when tips were involved at the Palms Health Spa, where she was now employed as a certified massage therapist, as well as the salsa bar where she worked nights at a second job. Was she burning the candle at both ends? Hell, yes. She wished she could do more.

Slinging her knockoff Coach bag over one shoulder, she donned a pair of oversize, fake Dior sunglasses. Her scoop-necked, white silk blouse was tucked into a black pencil skirt, belted at her small waist with a counterfeit red Gucci belt. Walking briskly on pleather Jimmy Choo knockoffs, she made her way down the street to her car parked on a side street—a ten-year-old Ford Focus. Not quite the vehicle to go with her seemingly expensive attire, a carefully manufactured image. Little did folks know that hidden in her parents' garage was a fortune in counterfeit items, from Rolex watches to Victoria's Secret lingerie, thanks to her jailbird brother, Steve. A fortune that could not be tapped because someone besides her brother would end up in jail. *Probably me, considering the bad-luck cloud that seems to be hanging over my head.*

It wasn't against the law to wear the stuff, just so long as she didn't sell it. To her shame, she'd been tempted on more than one occasion this past year to do just that. Desperation trumps morality on occasion. So far, she hadn't succumbed, though all her friends knew where to come when they needed something "special."

Her parents had no idea what was in the green-lidded bins that had been taped shut with duct tape. They probably thought it was Steve's clothes and other worldly goods. Hah!

Once inside her car, with the air conditioner on full blast, Marisa put her forehead on the steering wheel and wept. Soul-searing sobs and gasps for breath as she cried out her misery. Marisa knew that she had to get it all out before she went home, where she would have to pretend optimism before Izzie, who was way too perceptive for her age. Marisa's parents, on the other hand, would need to know the prognosis. They would be crushed, as she was.

A short time later, by midafternoon, with her emotions under control and her makeup retouched, Marisa walked up the sidewalk to her parents' house. She noticed that the Lopez Plumbing van wasn't in the driveway, so her father must still be at work. Good. Marisa didn't need the double whammy of both parents' reaction to the latest news. One at a time would be easier.

Marisa had moved into her parents' house, actually the apartment over the infamous garage, after Izzie's initial diagnosis two years ago—to save money and take advantage of her parents' generous offer to babysit while Marisa worked. Her older brother, Steve, who had been the apartment's prior occupant, was already in jail by that time, serving a two-to-six for armed robbery. The idiot had carried an old Boy Scout knife in his pocket when he'd stolen the cash register receipts at the 7-Eleven. Ironically, he'd never been nabbed for selling counterfeit goods—his side job, so to speak.

Unfortunately, this wasn't Steve's first stint in the slammer, although it was his first felony. She hoped he learned something this time, but she was doubtful.

Marisa used her key to enter the thankfully air-conditioned house. Immediately, her mood lightened somewhat in the home's cozy atmosphere. Over-stuffed sofa and chair. Her dad's worn leather recliner that bore the imprint of his behind from long years of use. And the smell . . . ah! The air was permeated with the scent of olive oil, onions, and green peppers, along with dark, rich Cuban coffee. It was Monday, so it must be *ropa vieja*, or shredded beef, her father's favorite, which would be served over rice with freshly toasted Cuban bread with warm butter. Knowing her mother, there would be *natilla* for dessert.

Izzie was asleep on the couch where she'd been watching cartoons on the television that had been turned to a low volume. *Mima* was a stickler for the afternoon siesta. The pretty, soft, pink and lavender afghan her grandmother had crocheted covered her from shoulders to bare feet, but her thin frame was still apparent. There were dark smudges beneath her eyes. Even so, she was cute as a button with her ski-jump nose and rosebud mouth, thanks to her father. But then, she'd inherited a Latin complexion, dark dancing eyes, and a frame that promised to be tall from Marisa, who was no slouch in the good looks department, if she did say so herself. No doubt about it, Izzie was destined to be a beauty when she grew up. If she ever did.

Marisa put her bag on the coffee table and leaned down to kiss the black curls that capped her little girl's head. She and her daughter shared the same coal-black hair, but Marisa's was thick and straight as a pin. At one time, Izzie had sported a wild mass of dark cork-screw curls, all of which had been lost in her first bout of radiation. A wasted effort, the radiation had turned out. To everyone's surprise, especially Izzie's, the shorter hairdo suited her better.

With a deep sigh, Marisa entered the kitchen.

Her mother was standing at the counter, shredding with a fork the flank steak she'd slow cooked in special seasonings all day. She wore her standard day-time "uniform": a richly embroidered apron covered a blouse tucked into stretchy waist slacks, and curlers on her head. Soon she would shower with her favorite soap from Spain, "Maja," and change to a dress, control-top panty hose, and medium pumps, her black hair all fluffed out, lipstick and a little makeup applied, to greet Daddy when he got home. It was a ritual she had followed every single day since her marriage thirty-two years ago. Just as she maintained her trim, attractive figure at fifty-nine. To please Daddy, as much as herself.

As for her father . . . even with the little paunch he'd put on a few years back and a receding hairline, when he walked into the house wearing his plumbing coveralls, Marisa's mother had been known to sigh and murmur, "Men in uniform!"

Marisa's mother must have sensed her presence because she turned abruptly. At first glance, she gasped and put a hand to her heart. No hiding anything from a mother.

"Oh, Marisa, honey!" her mother said. Making the sign of the cross, she sat down at the kitchen table and motioned for Marisa to sit, too.

First-generation Cuban Americans, they'd named their firstborn child Estefan Lopez. He became known as Steve. Marisa Angelica, who came five years later—a "miracle baby" for the couple who'd been told there would be no more children—was named after Abuela Lopez "back home," and Tia Angelica, who was a nun serving some special order in the Philippines.

"Tell me," her mother insisted.

"Dr. Stern says the tumor has grown, only slightly, in the past two months, but her brain and other tissue are increasing like any normal growing child and pressing against . . ." Tears welled in her eyes, despite her best efforts. "Oy, Mima! He says, without that experimental surgery, she only has a year to live. And even with the surgery, it might not work."

Izzie's only hope, and it was a slim one at best, was some new procedure being tried in Switzerland. Because it was experimental and in a foreign country, insurance would not cover the expense. Marisa had managed to raise an amazing hundred thousand dollars through various charitable endeavors, but she still needed another seventy thousand dollars. That seventy thou might just as well be a hundred million, considering Marisa's empty bank account, as well as that of her parents, who'd second-mortgaged their house when Steve got into so much trouble.

She and her mother both bawled then. What else could they do? Well, her mother had ideas, of course.

After drying Marisa's tears with a handkerchief she always kept in her bra, her mother poured them both cups of café con leches, her special brewed coffee with steamed milk. No fancy-pancy (her mother's words) Keurig or other modern devices for the old-fashioned lady. They both put one packet of diet sugar and a dollop of milk in their cups before taking the first sip. A small plate of galletas completed the picture.

"First off, we will pray," her mother declared. "And we will ask Angelica to pray for Izzie, too."

"Mima! With the hurricane that hit the Philippines last year, Tia Angelica has way too much on her prayer schedule."

"Tsk, tsk!" her mother said. "A nun always has time for more prayers. And I will ask my rosary and altar society ladies to start a novena. A miracle, that is what we need."

Marisa rolled her eyes before she could catch herself.

Her mother wagged a forefinger at her. "Nothing is impossible with prayer."

It couldn't hurt, Marisa supposed, although she was beginning to lose faith, despite being raised in a strict Catholic household. Hah! Look how much good that moral upbringing had done Steve.

That wasn't fair, she immediately chastised herself. Steve brought on his problems, and was not the issue today. Izzie was. Besides, who was she to talk. Having a baby without marriage. "Okay, Mima, we'll pray," she conceded. *If I still can.*

She let the peaceful ambience of the kitchen fill her then. To Cubans, the kitchen was the heart of the home, and this little portion of the fifty-year-old ranch-style house was indeed that. The oak kitchen cabinets were original to the house, but the way her mother cleaned, they gleamed with a golden patina, like new. Curtains with embroidered roses framed the double window over the sink. In the middle of the room was an old aluminum table that could seat six, in the center of which was a single red rose in a slim crystal vase, the sentimental weekly gift from her father to her mother. The red leather on the chair seats had been reupholstered twice now by her father's hands in his tool room off the garage. A Tiffany-style fruited lamp hung over the table.

A shuffling sound alerted them to Izzie coming toward the kitchen. Trailing the afghan in one hand and her favorite stuffed animal, a ratty, floppy-eared rabbit named Lucky, in the other, she didn't notice at first that her mother was home.

Marisa stood. "Well, if it isn't Sleeping Beauty!"

"Mima!" Dropping the afghan and Lucky, she raced into Marisa's open arms. Marisa twirled Izzie around in her arms until they were both dizzy. She dropped down to the chair again, with Izzie on her lap, both of them laughing. "Dizzy Izzie!" her daughter squealed, like she always did.

"For you, Isobella." Her mother placed before Izzie a plastic Barbie plate of chocolate-sprinkled sugar cookies and a matching teacup of chocolate milk. Her mother would have already crushed some of the hated pills into the milk.

"I'm not hungry, Buelita," Izzie whined, burying her face against Marisa's chest.

"You have to eat something, honey. At least drink the milk," Marisa coaxed.

After a good half hour of bribing, teasing, singing, and game playing, she and her mother got Izzie to eat two of the cookies and drink all of the milk.

"What did the doctor say?" Izzie asked suddenly.

Uh-oh! Izzie knew that Marisa had gone to the medical center to discuss her latest test results. "Dr. Stern said you are growing like a weed. No, he said you are growing faster than Jack and the Beanstalk's magic beans." At least that was true. She was growing, despite her loss of weight.

Izzie giggled. "I'm a big girl now."

"Yes, you are, sweetie," Marisa said, hugging her little girl warmly.

Somehow, someway, I am going to get the money for Izzie, Marisa vowed silently. *It might take one of my mother's miracles, but I am not going to let my precious little girl die. But how? That is the question.*

The answer came to her that evening when she was at La Cucaracha, the salsa bar where she worked a second job as a waitress and occasional bartender. Well, a possible answer.

"A porno convention?" she exclaimed, at first disbelieving that her best friend, Inga Johanssen, would make such a suggestion.

"More than that. The first ever International Conference on Freedom of Expression," Inga told her.

"Bull!" Marisa opined.

They were in a back room of the restaurant, talking a break. They wore the one-shouldered, knee-length black salsa dresses with ragged hems, La Cucaracha's uniform for women (the men wore slim black pants and white shirts). They were both roughly five foot eight, but otherwise completely different. Where Marisa was dark and olive-skinned, Inga was blond and Nordic. Where Marisa's figure was what might be called voluptuous, Inga's was slim and boy-like, except for the boobs she bought last year. The garments they wore were not meant to be revealing but to accommodate the restaurant's grueling heat due to the energetic dancing. They needed a break occasionally just to cool off.

Inga waved a newspaper article at her and read aloud, *"All the movers and shakers in the freedom of expression industry will be there. Multibillion-dollar investors, movie producers, Internet gurus, actors and actresses, store owners, franchisees—"*

"Franchisees of what?" Marisa interrupted. "Smut?"

Inga made a tsking sound and continued, *"—sex toy manufacturers, instructors on DIY home videos—"*

"What's DIY?" Marisa interrupted again.

"Do it yourself."

"Oh good Lord!"

"Martin Vanderfelt—"

"A made-up name if I ever heard one."

"Please, Marisa, give me a chance."

Marisa made a motion of zipping her lips.

"Martin Vanderfelt, the conference organizer, told the Daily Buzz *reporter, 'Our aim is to remove the sleaze factor from pornography and gain recognition as a legitimate professional enterprise serving the public. Freedom of Expression. FOE.'"*

Marisa rolled her eyes but said nothing.

"This is the best part. It's being held for one week

on a tropical island off the Florida Keys. Grand Keys, a plush special events convention center, offers all the amenities of a four-star hotel, including indoor and outdoor pools, snorkeling and boating services, beauty salons and health spas, numerous restaurants with world-class cuisines, nightclubs, tennis courts—"

"I'd like to see some of those overendowed porno queens bouncing around on a tennis court," Marisa had to interject.

Inga smiled.

"I thought they always held the pornography thing every year in Las Vegas."

"The expo is held there, but that's more for public show. They have booths and stuff and even an awards show like the Oscars. This is more for industry insiders."

"Inside, all right," she said with lame humor.

"So cynical! Becky Bliss will be there. You know who she is, don't you?"

Even Marisa knew Becky Bliss. She was the porno princess famous for being able to twerk while on top, having sex. "Are you suggesting we might learn how to do *that*?"

"It wouldn't hurt. Maybe it would enhance your nonexistent sex life."

"Not like *that*!"

"Okay. Besides, Lance Rocket will be there, too."

Marisa had no idea who Lance Rocket was, but she could guess.

"Anyhow, this conference isn't for your everyday Joe, the porn aficionado. It costs five thousand dollars to attend. The only access to the island is by water. They expect to see lots of yachts and seaplanes."

Marisa was vaguely aware of the private islands comprising the Florida Keys: an unbelievable seventeen hundred islands, some inhabited, others little more than mangrove and limestone masses. The islands lie along the Florida Straits dividing the Atlantic Ocean from the Gulf of Mexico.

"Okay, I give up. Why would you or I even consider something like this? Oh my God! You're not suggesting I make porno films to raise money for Izzie, are you?"

"Of course not. Look. This article says they're looking to hire employees for up to two weeks at above-scale wages, all expenses paid, including transportation. Everything from waiters and waitresses to beauticians to diving instructors . . . even a doctor and nurse. Waiters and waitresses can expect to earn at least ten thousand dollars, and that doesn't include tips, which could add another twenty K or more. Upper-scale professions, much more."

"Why would a hotel have to hire so many employees for just one event? Wouldn't they have a staff in place?"

"The company that owns the island went bankrupt last year, and the property is in foreclosure. In the meantime, until it is sold, the bank rents it out at an exorbitant amount. You know how abandoned properties deteriorate or get vandalized. Plus, the bank probably hopes one of the wealthy dudes or dudettes who attend this thing might fall in love with the place."

"You know an awful lot about Grand Keys Island."

Inga shrugged. "I checked it out on the Internet. Hey, here's an idea. You could even work as a massage therapist. Betcha lots of these porno stars need to work out the kinks. The *big* ones would leave hundred-dollar tips." She grinned impishly at Marisa.

Marisa couldn't be offended at Inga's teasing her about the popular misconception of professional masseurs and masseuses. "Kinks . . . that about says it all. Pfff! Can you imagine what they would expect of a massage therapist at one of these events?" She lowered her voice to a deep baritone and added, "'My shoulders are really tight, honey, and while you're at it, check out down yonder.'"

Inga laughed. "I'm just saying. If you worked as many hours there, let's say double shifting between waitressing and therapy, you might very well earn close to thirty thousand dollars. In less than two weeks! When opportunity comes down the street, honey, jump on the bus."

"You say opportunity, I say bad idea. Honestly, Inga, I can't see us doing something like this."

"Why not? We don't have to like all the people that come to the salsa bar, but we still serve them food and drinks."

"I don't know," Marisa said.

"There's something else to consider."

"If you're going to suggest that I might find a sugar daddy to pay for Izzie's operation, forget about it." *But don't think that idea hasn't occurred to me.*

"No, but there will be lots of Internet types there. Maybe you could find someone with the technical ability to set up a website for Izzie to raise funds."

"I already tried that, but every company I contacted said it has been overdone. There's no profit for them."

"Maybe you've made the wrong contacts. Maybe if you met someone one-on-one . . . I don't know, Marisa, isn't it worth a try?" Inga was serious now.

"I'll think about it," Marisa said, to her own surprise.

"Applications and interviews for employment are being held at the Purple Palm Hotel in Key West next Friday," Inga pointed out. "Don't think too long."

"Don't push."

They heard the salsa band break out in a lively instrumental with a rich Latin American beat. A prelude to the beginning of another set of dance music.

As they headed back to work, Inga said, "I'll drive."

Chapter 2

Transylvania, Pennsylvania, 2015

It was a male fantasy assignment . . . or was it? . . .

Sigurd was late arriving at the castle for the conclave called by St. Michael the Archangel.

He'd run into a traffic pile-up on the Beltway when he left his job as a physician at Johns Hopkins. Then he'd gotten behind a vampire parade in this wack-job touristy town that celebrated . . . guess what? Yep. Dracula wannabes.

Hah! If they knew how inconvenient fangs actually are, Sigurd thought, running his tongue under his own pointy set, *they would keep their fool mouths shut and take up a saner hobby, like sword fighting. Try kissing a maid when the incisors are out. Or drinking a cold beer, modern man's wonderful invention that surely rivals our ancient Viking favorite beverage . . . warm mead. I scare even myself when I happen upon a mirror and see how I look.*

He could have teletransported, but vangels were warned to use that talent only on special occasions. Like when they were needed quickly to back up one of their fellow Viking vampire angels. (He still shuddered after all these years to consider himself one of those.) Or when a Lucipire was about to gobble them up.

He pressed the code numbers into the remote on his SUV dashboard and watched as the gates opened onto the massive property where his oldest brother, Vikar, was converting an old, run-down castle into one of the headquarters for all the vangels. Vikar was three years into the project, and the progress was slow, as evidenced by scaffolding around one of the towers. Sigurd parked his vehicle in the back courtyard, rather than going down into the underground parking garage. He didn't expect to be staying long.

He entered the kitchen, about the size of most longhouses "back in the day," a modern expression he was embarrassed to find himself using way too much lately. He wasn't that old. Well, actually he was. Twenty-seven human years, but a mind-boggling one thousand, one hundred, and sixty-five vampire angel years. His original sentence . . . uh, assignment as a vangel had somehow been extended, and extended, by a few transgressions he was unable to avoid over the years. Or a lot. But, really, did Mike (the rude name Sigurd and his six brothers had given their heavenly mentor) expect virile Viking men to remain celibate for decades, let alone centuries?

Sigurd shook his head to clear it. His mind seemed to be wandering so much today. Probably overwork on his latest medical project, not to mention having gone on a vangel mission in Baltimore over the weekend where a Lucie horde had been nesting in one of the slums, preying on drug addicts. Lucies was a nickname he and his brothers had given to demon vampires.

The scent of cooking food hit Sigurd first, and he noticed one of the vangels, their cook, Lizzie Borden (yes, *that* Lizzie Borden) hacking away at what appeared to be the hind quarter of a cow, then tossing the pieces to brown in a huge, sizzling iron skillet.

"Good morning, Miss Borden," he said.

"Pfff! What is good about feeding fifty ravenous Vikings?" Lizzie always complained about her cooking chores, but she guarded her domain like a Norseman protecting his longship.

Sigurd opened the commercial-size fridge to get a bottle of Fake-O, the blood substitute he had invented several years ago to supplement the vangels' supply when it had been too long since they saved sinners or annihilated Lucies. Blood caused a vangel's skin to have a nice suntanned hue. Without it, their skin turned lighter and lighter until it was almost transparent.

"Where is everyone?" he asked Lizzie after quaffing down the thick beverage in one long swallow, then wiping his mouth with the back of a hand, fighting a shiver of disgust. One of these days, when he had more time, he would have to do something about the taste.

"In the front parlor. They started an hour ago," Lizzie pointed out with relish. She did not care overmuch for men.

"Thanks, Liz," he said, just to annoy her.

She said something very unangelic as he walked away. Not that any of them were angels. More like fallen angels.

On the way down the long corridor he ran into Regina, who had been a witch back in the thirteenth-century Norselands. A real witch, the kind who brewed potions in a boiling cauldron and issued curses hither and yon. She was always threatening to do unsavory things to the manparts of the various VIK when they displeased her, which was all the time. VIK was the name given to the seven brothers as the rulers of the vangel society.

"Why aren't you in the meeting?" he asked, in a very polite manner, if he did say so himself.

Despite his good manners, she sneered at him. "Mike was done with us peons hours ago. He is dealing with the sins of you VIK now." She cackled. She actually cackled, and added, "Someone is about to have his arse chewed up good and well."

"Me?" he inquired with mock innocence, and made a rude gesture at the hissing black cat that followed on Regina's heels.

The cat tried to piss on his boot but he managed to get away, unscathed. Regina was muttering something behind him, probably a curse. He would have to get a codpiece to protect himself when he left here today. Where did one buy a codpiece, anyhow?

He tried to enter the parlor unobtrusively, to no avail.

His six brothers turned as one, eyebrows arched, lips twitching with humor at his expense. They sat in a semicircle before Mike, who was sprawled lazily in a throne-like, wingback chair, jeans-clad legs crossed at the ankles over a pair of athletic shoes. The latest, very expensive Nike ones. He probably thought the swoosh emblem represented an angel wing, but then Mike had a fascination with modern footwear. A large gold cross hung on a thick chain around his neck, nestling on his pure white T-shirt. The only other indication of his saintliness was a rather halo-like glow about his long, black hair. No wings today.

As Sigurd passed behind his brothers' chairs, each had a special greeting for him.

Vikar, the oldest of his brothers, the VIK assigned to man the Transylvania castle headquarters, grinned and said, "Welcome home, Dr. Sig. Did you lose your watch?"

Ivak, an Angola Prison chaplain, who fashioned

himself the most handsome Viking dead or alive, said, "You look like death warmed over, Sig. I hope those bags under your eyes are due to something pleasant."

"And he smells like Saxon shit. Can you not invent a new Fake-O that does not reek?" asked Trond, a Viking Navy SEAL, of all things, especially considering how lazy Trond was known to be. And, really, those Navy SEALs worked so hard in senseless exercise that Trond knew better than anyone what reeked. Like himself. Of body odor. Not today, of course, but when he'd jogged five miles in heavy boots and monstrous backpack, whew!

Mordr just scowled. Wrath had been Mordr's sin, and his demeanor was ofttimes grim, though he was not so bad since he'd married and taken on five . . . yes, five . . . children.

Cnut, a security expert just returned from some Pentagon secret training program, winked at him, as if he knew a secret that Sigurd did not.

Finally, he came to Harek, their technology guru, who was tapping away on a laptop with fingerless gloves. He was huddled in a massive fur cloak. Ever since Harek had returned from Siberia, a penance assignment if there ever was one, he claimed to be unable to get warm again. Mike was not sympathetic.

No more brothers. Sigurd sank down into the empty chair. The one closest to Mike, unfortunately.

"Ah! The prodigal vangel deigns to honor us with his presence," Mike said. Sarcasm was a favorite tool of Mike's, and it was usually directed at the VIK. None of them was immune.

"Sorry. There was a—"

Mike waved a hand, uninterested in his explanation. "Vikar, recap for the tardy one what we have been discussing."

Vikar winked at Sigurd. "It appears that Jasper and

his demon vampires are growing in number. Well over two thousand, at last count. Whereas the number of vangels is closer to five hundred." Jasper was the king of the demon vampires, one of the fallen angels who had been kicked out of Heaven along with Lucifer. It was the job of the vangels to kill Lucipires . . . not just kill them but annihilate them through the heart with swords or bullets symbolically treated with the blood of Christ. Just killing them resulted in their coming back again as demon vampires. In addition, vangels attempted to save sinners, especially those who had been fanged by a Lucipire, clearly identified by their lemon scents. A lemony human was on the fast track to becoming a Lucipire . . . a worse fate than going to Hell.

"We are going to add more new vangels to our ranks . . . one hundred at a time, under the training of Cnut and Mordr," Michael continued. "And there is a big event being planned by Jasper for next month."

Sigurd tilted his head in question.

"Let Harek show you," Mike directed.

Harek sat in the chair on Sigurd's other side. He was the computer guru in their ranks. He slid the laptop from his knees to Sigurd's and pointed to the screen. "Grand Keys Island."

"And is that not an appropriate name?" Mike interrupted.

Sigurd saw a picture of a lush, tropical island with what appeared to be a massive hotel complex from which bungalows stemmed out like the spokes of a wheel. Luxury yachts and sailing vessels were anchored in the clear blue waters.

"It is an island in the Florida Keys. That large structure there is a special events hotel. And, whoo boy, is there a special event being planned there." This from a grinning Harek.

"One which Jasper hopes to infiltrate where he

will harvest more souls for his evil legions," Mike told Sigurd.

"The first ever International Conference on Pornography." Harek grinned at him. He must have finally warmed up, enough to tweak him, leastways. "Well, they don't call it that. The new word for pornography is FOE, Freedom of Expression."

Sigurd frowned and turned to Mike. "What has this to do with me? I am a physician at Johns Hopkins."

"Not anymore," Mike said. "Thou art about to tender thy resignation."

"Why? I enjoy working there."

"Ah, and that is your goal as a vangel, is it not? Pleasure?" More Mike sarcasm.

Well, I opened myself up for that one. "I do good work there," Sigurd protested.

"You do."

"I'm supposed to be finding a cure for cancer."

"Someone else will."

That put Sigurd in his place, good and well.

"Thou hast been in one place for twenty years, and you do not age, Sigurd. 'Tis time for a change."

Sigurd understood. "Then another hospital?"

Mike shook his head. "Thou art about to start a new . . . job. Thou will be the resident physician on Grand Keys Island for the duration of this vile affair."

Thou, thou, thou! I am getting sick of Mike's thous. Usually they are followed by some unpalatable assignment. As this island is sure to be. Sigurd almost choked on his tongue, so stunned was he by the prospect of doctoring on some remote island inhabited by scurvy pornographers. His brothers barely stifled their snickers.

"Me? I am going to a porno convention?"

"Thus sayeth the Lord," Mike pronounced.

Bullshit! Sigurd thought. *Thus sayeth Michael the Irksome Archangel.*

Sigurd wondered briefly what his sin of envy had to do with this assignment. Usually Mike assigned them penances—or, rather, missions—to places or duties related to their weaknesses. What envy had to do with pornography was a puzzle to Sigurd.

"Thou wilt know when the time is right," Mike told him.

Sometimes Sigurd forgot that Mike could read minds.

That was how Sigurd found himself the following week in Key West, Florida, applying for a new, unenviable position.

For the love of a troll! He was a fierce fighting warrior, a practicing healer and physician, a Viking vampire angel. He'd thought he could not be shocked anymore.

He was wrong.

It takes all kinds! . . .

Marisa and Inga arrived at the Purple Palm Hotel at eight a.m. Interviews were to start at nine, but already the line ran out the door and down half a block.

It wasn't just the numbers that amazed. What a crowd it was lined up in front of them!

"Good Lord!" Marisa said.

Inga agreed. "Every crazy in the Sunshine State must have gotten up at dawn."

Men and women alike had bimboed themselves up—or was that down?—in outfits designed to accentuate their assets, the emphasis being on *assets*. Tights pants, cleavage down to the belly buttons in front and butt cracks in back, male junk sticking out like torpedoes, female butts that would make Beyoncé blush, boobs that defied gravity. And the tattoos! And the piercings!

This was the third of five days of on-site, open applications for employment at the conference. Marisa had no idea how many people had been hired thus far, considering the turnout today, but the number of employees they were supposedly hiring was supposed to be four hundred for the ten-to-twenty-day period, which included both setup duties and cleanup afterward. Plus people had been hired already to prepare the hotel for the incoming rush and serve the early arrivals.

To be honest, there were a lot of normal-looking people here, too, like she and Inga. Probably half of the two hundred or so in line so far. Still . . .

"The ick factor here is off the chart," Marisa remarked. "No way am I standing around for hours in this crowd in the heat to apply for a job I'm not sure I want."

"Y'all won't hafta wait long, honey," the girl in front of them said in a heavy Southern accent. "Mr. Vanderfelt, the darlin' man, came out a bit ago and said once the doors open we'll be movin' faster'n a greased pig on a spit slide. Besides, lots of the folks in line are just fans."

Fans? Of what? Sleaze?

Marisa and Inga just gaped.

The short, slim girl, who on closer inspection was probably over twenty-one, wore a red spandex jumpsuit, which called attention to her impressive double-Ds, with matching sparkly stilettos. Her hair was blonde, and big. A teased fluff of sexy waves. Makeup completed the picture with false eyelashes and pouty crimson lips. She wore enough Shalimar to choke a goat.

It was hard to tell if she was here for a job, or was one of the "fans."

Compared to Bimbo Barbie, Marisa and Inga looked like nuns. Well, not exactly nuns. Inga, her long blonde hair in a single braid down her back, wore a sheer tunic blouse over a darker blue tank top, with white capris, and a pair of Valentino "Rockstud" triple-ankle-strap pumps. Marisa was more subtle in a sleeveless, rose-colored Donna Karan dress that was nicely belted (thank you, Alexander McQueen) at the waist and came to just above the knees. The only thing that could be construed as sexy about her attire was her strappy, high-heeled, Prada gladiator sandals. Her hair was upswept and held to the top of her head with a tortoiseshell claw.

"Hi! Mah name is Tiffany."

Sure it is.

"I'm Inga, and this is my friend Marisa. Have you been standing here long?" asked Inga, a regular Miss Congeniality today.

Unlike me, who is more Miss Grinchiality.

"Only an hour. Where are y'all from?"

The insane asylum. Or we will be if we actually go through with this insanity.

"Miami," Inga replied. "We drove in this morning."

"Ah came all the way from Georg-ah."

No kidding.

"Ah took a bus yesdidday and stayed overnight at the Holiday Inn." She tossed her blonde mane over one shoulder or tried to. The hair was so heavily lacquered it didn't move. "Ah'm a hairstylist, y'know—"

Could have fooled me.

"—but Ah aim ta be a sensuality star like Becky Bliss. Ah prefer the word *sensuality* to *pornography*. Much more classy."

That answered the question of job seeker versus fan. And, yes, Marisa noticed Tiffany's distinction between "sensuality star" and "porno star." She hadn't yet learned that no matter if you called a fake Rolex a Rolex, it was still a Timex at heart.

"Truth ta tell, mah real name is Helen Biggers, but Ah cain't see Helen Biggers on a movie marquee, kin you?" Tiffany sighed, and continued without waiting for a response, though what they could say to that, Marisa couldn't imagine. "Did y'all know that Becky made a million dollars las' year, an' she has a mansion in Hollywood with a Jacuzzi and everythin'?"

Un-be-liev-able! "I thought these jobs were supposed to be legitimate . . . I mean, regular jobs for regular people," Marisa said, shooting Inga a dirty look.

Inga elbowed her. "Stop being so negative."

"They *are* reg'lar jobs," Tiffany insisted. "Ah'm applyin' fer one of the hair salons, but Ah figure this will be mah opportunity ta get discovered. Becky Bliss got discovered in a Dairy Queen, y'know."

"She probably practiced her twerking while making Blizzards. All that shivering, *y'know*," Marisa commented.

"Huh?" Tiffany said.

Inga smacked Marisa lightly on the arm. "Keep frowning like that, and you'll be able to plant rice in the furrows in your forehead."

"Ah have the best wrinkle cream. Insta-Smooth by Luxor," Tiffany announced. "It's expensive, but Ah get a discount at the beauty shop where Ah work. Ah could get y'all some."

"Gee, thanks."

The sarcasm passed right over Tiffany's head as she smiled at Marisa.

I'm getting way too cynical. And mean.

Having a sick child does that to a person. Living in a world where some bimbo twerking her ass earns big bucks, and a hardworking woman like me can't afford a measly Swiss operation for a sick child just isn't fair.

But it's not this twit's fault.

"Sorry," Marisa murmured.

"Thass okay, sug-ah. Actually, Ah'm havin' trouble with mah twerkin'," she confessed. "Maybe you gals could help me practice while we're on the island. We could be roomies and everythin'. Mr. Vanderfelt said four people are assigned to each bungalow, y'know."

Roommates? What next? "That is just great," Marisa said before she had a chance to bite her loose tongue.

"Ooh, ooh, ooh! Lookee there! Betcha that's Lance Rocket."

A stretch limousine had just pulled up, and the line in front of them swarmed forward in a cluster, like bees. Four big, burly men in wraparound sunglasses jumped out of the limo—bodyguards, Marisa presumed—and held back the crowd as a tall man emerged, smiling at the screaming women. He wore a lavender silk shirt unbuttoned to the waist of his form-hugging pants. Tights, for heaven's sake! And, yep, the guy had a rocket in his pocket, if that bulge was actually all him. He adjusted himself, causing more screams, and proceeded to sign autographs for his fans, on DVDs, grocery receipts, handbags, even on bare skin.

Inga and Tiffany moved closer to get a better look, but Marisa stayed behind, holding their place in line. She'd seen enough.

"What a bunch of lackwit women!" someone muttered behind Marisa. "And the men! If you can call them that! They have overstuffed their codpieces to compensate for their size. Clearly, none of them are Vikings. Remember the time Trond put an actual live cod in his codpiece? Convinced Dala the dairymaid that he had magic in his wand when it started to move."

Marisa pretended to look over her shoulder at something in the distance to the right, but out of the corner of her eye she surreptitiously studied the tall man speaking on a cell phone. A very tall man. She was six feet tall today in her three-inch heels and upswept hairdo, and he was at least four inches taller than that. Dark blond hair was pulled off his face and tied in a low ponytail at his nape. He wore an unbuttoned, short-sleeved black silk shirt over a black T-shirt tucked into black straight-legged jeans with black athletic shoes, the latest Adidas that cost more than most people's car payments. His face was a work of art with the high cheekbones and sculpted planes of the Nordic race.

He and Inga could be brother and sister, except Inga was an only child.

Marisa turned to see if Inga had got a gander at this dude, but Inga and Tiffany were both captivated by the scene unfolding before them. Apparently, Becky Bliss emerged from the limo, too. Becky resembled a young Dolly Parton. Enough said! Turning back, still looking at something at the end of the block, Marisa saw that the dude in black hadn't even noticed her yet. He was staring off in the other direction while talking on the phone pressed to one ear.

"Harlots and whoresons, that is what I am surrounded by. No, Vikar, that is not a good thing. No, I am not tempted even a little bit. Can't you intercede with Mike on my behalf and . . ." His words trailed off as he saw Marisa staring at him, arms folded under her breasts, tapping the toe of a Prada high-heeled sandal impatiently on the sidewalk. "Uh, I will talk with you later." He pressed the off button and placed the phone in the clip on his belt, which had a strange gold buckle with an angel wing design on it.

Lowering his Ray-Bans down his nose, he peered at her through brown-lashed, startlingly clear blue eyes. "Do you have a problem, m'lady?" he inquired.

"I'm trying to figure if you're going for a role as Zorro with Attitude in that all-black attire, or Rodeo Star, with the oversize belt buckle."

"My belt buckle is not oversize," he said, glancing downward, then glowering.

Cranky!

Which caused her to look even lower, and, yes, he had some junk in his trunk. Not huge, like the Rocket Man, but definitely impressive.

He noticed the direction of her glance and glowered even more. His disgust with the crowd obviously included her.

Marisa felt herself blushing, and she hardly ever blushed anymore.

"I repeat, do you have a problem? Other than ogling my body parts?" He pushed his sunglasses back up his nose.

The jerk! "I heard you talking on the cell phone. Just for your information, not every woman is a whore. Not here or anywhere else."

"Is that a fact?" He couldn't look more bored.

"Absolutely."

"I believe the words I used were *harlots* and *whoresons*. Who else would be applying for a job with pornographers?" He shrugged. "People who eavesdrop rarely hear good things about themselves."

"You self-important, condescending jackass! Guess that means you're one of the, uh, what did you call the men . . . whoresons?"

"I have been called that on occasion," he replied, apparently not at all offended by the insult.

"Not that it's any of your business, but I'm applying for a job as a waitress. Or maybe a massage therapist." She shouldn't have mentioned that second possibility, she realized immediately.

He arched a brow. The usual reaction.

"Not that kind of a massage therapist. I'm a licensed . . . Oh, what's the use!"

He smiled.

"Oh my God!"

"Please do not use the Lord's name in vain. A simple 'Oh fuck!' will do."

"Huh?" She was beginning to sound like Tiffany the Clueless. Then she noticed something interesting. "You have fangs," she accused him.

A rosy blush filled his stark cheeks. "Not really," he said, and ran his tongue underneath his upper teeth. He was right. They were more like pointy incisors.

"Are you with that erotic vampire movie that's sweeping the cable networks? Are you Eric Northman?"

"Alexander Skarsgård? Hardly."

"I heard rumors of a new porno flick series called *Sucked!*" She'd read about it in a *People* magazine article last month in the oncologist's waiting room. "Are you part of that deal?"

"I am not an actor, nor do I aspire to be such. I am a physician."

She could tell that he also immediately regretted his hasty words. He probably felt she was baiting him. More like he was baiting her.

"A physician, huh? Yeah, right. And I'm Joan of Arc."

"I have met Joan of Arc, and you are not she." He gave her a head-to-toe survey that was not complimentary.

Marisa was not used to such disdain from men. That's probably why she said, "How many doctors does it take to screw in a light bulb?" When he didn't react, she continued, "It all depends on their health plan."

He didn't even crack a smile. Instead, just muttered something about politics and lackwit women.

"Don't take that attitude with me. You're no different than all the other men in line. You aspire to be like that rooster up there." She waved a hand toward Lance Rocket. "All cock and nothing between his ears." Marisa had no idea why she was making such assumptions about a stranger. And sharing them! It was as bad as him making sweeping generalizations about women.

Behind his shades, she imagined his intense blue eyes widening with shock. "I do not," he sputtered. "I am not."

"A little penis envy," she remarked, widening her own eyes back at him.

"Envy? Did you say envy? I swear, did Mike send you to plague me?"

"You're a condescending jackass."

"So turn around, and mind your own business. You're starting to bore me."

"Bite me!"

"Where?"

"What?"

He took off his sunglasses and slid them in a shirt pocket. Only then did he bare his little fangs at her. "I will gladly take a nip at you. Where shall I start? Your neck? Your belly? Your arse?"

"Just try and I'll Mace your ass off. I've got a can in my purse."

He eyed her Cartier envelope shoulder bag.

"It's a small can."

Marisa was having serious reservations about this whole bizarre job idea, not just because of the ick factor, but because she really should be home with her daughter.

On the other hand, her being with Izzie wouldn't move her any closer to Switzerland and a life-saving operation.

Just then a dapper little man, all of five foot five, wearing a white plantation suit with a black shirt and red cravat—a cravat, for heaven's sake—walked up to them. Although he was probably only in his mid-forties, his thick hair and mustache were a pristine white, neatly trimmed. His name tag identified him as Martin Vanderfelt. "Dr. Sigurdsson? Is that you? Why are you standing in line? Come along with me. We have drinks and goodies set up in the VIP lounge."

The blue-eyed creep winked at her before he walked away, a clear in-your-face gesture of *I told you so!* She was surprised he hadn't given her the finger, as well.

So he really was a doctor. He probably got his degree on the Internet. Whatever! It took all kinds, she supposed. Even educated men aspired to be porno studs.

Chapter 3

Lemonade, anyone? . . .

Sigurd sat in the VIP lounge of the Purple Palm Hotel discussing his duties as Grand Keys physician for the next few weeks with Martin Vanderfelt, the CEO of this bizarre event. A short rooster of a man—he never sat still for more than a minute, always prancing about, pecking here and there—he wore a ridiculous white suit with white shoes. You'd think he was a virgin or something, an aberration much lacking in this gathering.

Sigurd had been offered a champagne breakfast, complete with fresh fruit, truffled eggs, and French croissants, hand-squeezed orange juice, and a long list of coffees, flavored lattes, or espressos, all of which he'd declined, graciously. He planned on stopping at McDonald's for a bacon cheeseburger and a chocolate milk shake later this morning. If it were later, he would opt for some red meat and beer, a man's meal.

Sigurd was not surprised by the special treatment, and it wasn't just because he was vain. All Vikings were. No, he knew sure as sin that Vanderfelt was falling over himself in an attempt to please because Sigurd was the only doctor dumb enough to apply for the job.

It was humiliating, really. All those years of studying the medical arts, all those years of perfecting his skills, and he was reduced to being a token doctor on an island of sleaze. Mike could just as well have assigned him to a brothel and it would be no less demeaning.

In his head, he heard the words, *Humility is next to godliness.*

I thought that was cleanliness.

That, too.

Sigurd did a mental roll of the eyes.

As Vanderfelt tried to explain the conference and what would be expected of the physician-in-residence, they kept getting interrupted.

First, by Vanderfelt's underlings. A big brawny fellow, probably a security guard, said, "Reporters from the *Miami Herald* and the *Key West Tribune* are trying to get in."

And that is a surprise . . . why?

A second muscle-bound guy who accompanied him added, "And a local TV network is interviewing applicants still in line outside. They got one chick on tape saying that Satan sent her here to breed little demons on the island."

He would if he could.

Between the two of them, these men were so pumped they could bench-press a longship, just like he'd seen the twins Egor and Egolf do one time ages ago, and they hadn't even had the benefit of steroids.

"Was it the bimbo in the purple flowered minidress with chains hanging down between her legs?" Big and Brawny grinned before explaining to Sigurd and

Vanderfelt, "Chains that are attached to her chastity belt. She says she ain't unlockin' her honey pot 'til a devil comes up with the key. Devils that she says are gonna be congregatin' at our porno convention."

Chastity belts do not work worth a Saxon damn. I know from experience that—

"We do not call it a porno convention," Vanderfelt said through gritted teeth. "How many times do I have to remind people? It's FOE, Freedom of Expression. Not pornography."

Are they really so thickheaded? Must be. Obviously they have never heard of that old Norse saying: No matter how many times you call a pig a prince, it still stinks like shit.

"FOE, or smut, or whatever the hell you wanna call it, will be on the six o'clock news, guaranteed," Muscle-Bound pronounced.

"Oh crap! Where's our press secretary?"

"Takin' a crap." Big and Brawny must have been waiting for an opening to say that. "Jamison ate some bad fish last night, and he has the diarrhea real bad."

Vanderfelt rolled his eyes.

I am actually beginning to enjoy myself, Sigurd realized. *So sue me,* he said silently to that ever-present thorn in his backside before he got a heavenly reminder of why he was there, and it wasn't to amuse himself.

"One more thing," Muscle-Bound said, holding up a huge paw to get Vanderfelt's attention. "One of the reporters mentioned that picketers were going to be here at noon. Apparently some women's organization is busing them in."

"Great! That is just great! I was hoping the ASLU would be here to counter any picketers, but apparently they couldn't round up enough folks on short order."

"Don't you mean the ACLU?" Sigurd couldn't help himself from asking.

Vanderfelt shook his head. "No. This is the American Sexual Liberties Union. I started the organization myself." By the way Vanderfelt preened, you'd think he had invented something important, like beer.

"Tell the reporters that we'll hold a press conference at noon. In the meantime, herd them into the pressroom and keep them satisfied with booze and food. We need to get control of our message."

Good luck with that.

The two guards turned to leave, whispering to each other, before Big and Brawny asked, "Um, where's the pressroom?"

"I don't know," Vanderfelt whined as if he were overburdened with questions. "Over by the atrium, I think. And tell Jamison to take an Imodium and get his ass in gear, or he's fired."

"Ass in gear. Ha, ha, ha," Muscle-Bound said.

His partner laughed. Vanderfelt did not.

"Oh, I should have asked you, Doc. What do you recommend for diarrhea?"

"Imodium would be fine." *Now I am reduced to diagnosing running bowels.*

Sigurd was beginning to think he'd fallen into some garden hole like that Alice in Wonderland that Vikar's children enjoyed reading about. He was pretty sure he was the Mad Hatter in this scenario.

No sooner had the two security guards left than a group of three well-dressed men walked in. Their suits, chains, and Rolex watches bespoke wealth and bad taste. Vanderfelt introduced them one at a time. Vincent Lampano, the producer of the Becky Bliss and Lance Rocket videos, was about forty years old, but the lines of dissipation on his face made him look twenty years older. Harry Goldman, a sixtysomething billionaire investor, had apparently made his early fortune in brass toilet fittings but his latest millions in porno-graphic movies. And Seth Williams, a young man no more than twenty-five, was a computer genius and the owner of a dozen websites catering to the most per-verted sexual tastes.

The one thing all three had in common? They reeked to high heaven of lemons. Whether they had been bitten by Lucies wasn't immediately apparent, but they were evil to the bone, Sigurd concluded. If they got within a mile of Jasper's horde, they would be demon vampire bait. And Sigurd was fairly certain he'd detected the scent of sulfur—the Lucipire parfum du jour—amongst the applicants outside vying for jobs on the island.

In the midst of talking about the upcoming con-vention, which caused all four of the men, aside from Sigurd, to salivate with anticipation, Goldman men-tioned a woman he was interested in having for a love interest while on the island. In truth, his words were, "I plan to fuck her ass off."

Vanderfelt frowned at first, uncertain which woman Goldman referred to.

"She was standing in line outside to apply for a job just now when we walked through the hotel." Gold-man licked his thick lips. "Pink dress, screw-me-silly high heels, black hair on top of her head. I think she's Italian or Spanish or something. She looks like a young Sophia Loren. Uhm-um!"

Sigurd almost burst out laughing. The woman he'd been talking to earlier was a head taller and thirty years younger than this old fart. Money or not, she would cut him off at the knees if he tried to approach her. On the other hand, wealth was known to be a great thigh opener. You never could predict what a woman would do.

Actually, he could see why the codger would be interested. She was a gorgeous woman, but she had a tongue sharp as a serpent. Not to Sigurd's taste at all.

Besides, she wasn't his problem.

Take this job, and love it? ...

Inga and Tiffany came back, and the line began to move quickly now that the doors had opened. Into the large conference room off the lobby with its enormous banner, "International Conference on Freedom of Expression," they saw clearly marked tables with interviewers seated behind them, each identifying particular job opportunities.

The fans in the crowd were soon culled out by the security guards, and the rest of them went to designated tables. Housekeeping. Restaurant and bar staff. Lifeguards. Medical. Hospitality. Retail clerks. Cooks. Health spa. Electronic technicians. Photographers. Computer programmers. And so on. There was also a table for private individuals who wanted to pay the huge fee just to attend the conference and schmooze with the porno elite. Dr. Snide was nowhere in sight. Still in the VIP lounge, Marisa presumed.

Tiffany toddled off to the beauty salon table, blowing an air kiss their way. Marisa and Inga headed for the restaurant and bar staff line. Marisa went first.

A chic, middle-aged woman in a pearl-gray Chanel business suit over a white silk Dior blouse motioned for her to sit in the chair across the folding table from her. She wore minimal makeup, but tastefully done. Erno Laszlo, by the tone of her skin, Marisa guessed. Her short salt-and-pepper hair was expertly cut. Her name tag said: "Eleanor Allen, Human Resources." Pecking away at a small laptop, she said, "Name?"

"Marisa Lopez."

"Your application form?"

Marisa removed the completed paperwork from her purse and handed it over. The forms had been available on the conference's website.

Ms. Allen scanned the document. "And you're applying for a job as a waitress?'"

"Yes."

"We have five restaurants on site. Buster's, Steak Alley, The Hub, Calloways, and the Phoenix."

"I prefer the Phoenix." It was an upscale bar/restaurant where Marisa believed the tips would be best. Not too rowdy, like Buster's, but not too luxurious, like Calloways. Sometimes the wealthiest diners were the worst tippers.

"Your background experience is more than satisfactory. I don't see any reason for you not to be hired or to get your pick of restaurants."

Marisa didn't know whether to be pleased or dismayed by that news.

The lady discussed the pay and potential for tips. Rules for employment, including no photographs or tweeting of news from the conference.

Marisa hadn't even thought about that. She probably could have made a bundle sneaking cell phone shots of Lance or Becky and selling them to the *Star* or some Internet pseudo-news site.

"Salary will be withheld for any infraction," Ms. Allen emphasized. "Employees are required to sign a confidentiality agreement not to disclose private information about individuals at this affair, prominent or otherwise."

Marisa couldn't imagine how they would enforce such a rule. And, yes, she tucked that idea for raising extra cash away in a folder called "Only If I'm Desperate." As if she weren't already desperate, as evidenced by her being here to begin with.

"What happens on Grand Keys Island stays on Grand Keys Island," Marisa joked.

Ms. Allen's thin lips didn't even twitch with a smile. "That goes without saying."

Okaaay! I lost a point with that one.

"I notice that you have a child. We have a strict rule of no children under twelve being allowed on the island."

Marisa wondered about those children aged thirteen or fourteen, but brushed the lurid speculation aside. "My daughter will be cared for at home by my parents."

Ms. Allen nodded. Tenting her fingertips against her chin, she stared at Marisa for a long moment. "I'm curious, Ms. Lopez. You already have a job, two jobs in fact. You're a very attractive woman. You could probably get other jobs on the mainland, if you are dissatisfied with your current employment. I don't see any evidence of interest in the pornography industry on your part. Your clothing bespeaks couture. Why are you here?"

Marisa could have made a snide remark, her MO of late, but Ms. Allen's face had softened, almost maternal now. She arched a brow at Ms. Allen's smart suit. "I could ask you the same thing. That's a Chanel suit, I believe."

"Touché!" she replied. "But five years old."

Marisa glanced down at her own designer attire and admitted, "Knockoff."

They grinned at each other, conspirators in the silly game of designer importance.

Then Ms. Allen revealed, "My husband of thirty years, a stockbroker, emptied our bank account . . ."

Marisa almost rolled her eyes, expecting the same old/same old story. Older man runs off with young bimbo, probably his secretary, blah, blah, blah.

But, instead, Ms. Allen said, "The idiot donated it

all to a wacky religious order that is opposed to government, the pope, George Clooney, and bathing. He's living in a hut in some commune in the Himalayas, hiding from the IRS, last I heard. For all I know, or care, the fleas have eaten him alive. I've been taking any work I can get to stay off welfare."

Ms. Allen gave her explanation in such a matter-of-fact manner that Marisa couldn't help but smile.

"I have a sick child," she said.

"Ah," Ms. Allen replied. "Let me make a few suggestions then, my dear. Be very careful. Don't turn your back on that island. Don't trust anyone. These are not nice people. They will . . ." She let her words trail off. "I shouldn't be telling you this. You could get me fired."

Marisa shook her head and patted Ms. Allen's folded hands that rested on the table. "Just between us."

"Now, let me make another suggestion. If you are really in need of money, why don't you go over to the health spa table and see if you can get additional work as a massage therapist. I noticed in your application that you're a licensed therapist."

In need of money? More like desperate.

"I understand why you would be hesitant, but if you spell out your conditions ahead of time, you should be able to bring in a significant amount of tips there. They are understaffed and not getting the number of applications they need. Besides, I know the lady who is running the spa. Hedwig Meyer. Hedy is a good, no-nonsense German woman." She grinned and added, "Her husband fell in love with a clown. Apparently clown sex is the new politically correct perversion."

Marisa was beyond being shocked. So she wasn't about to ask what clown sex involved, other than appearance.

Guessing her question, her interviewer said,

"Mostly it involves fake noses in unaccustomed places. Or so I've been told."

"Holy crap!"

"You have no idea."

"By the way, will you be working on the island at this conference, Ms. Allen?"

"Call me Eleanor," she said. Then, "God help me, yes." They both laughed.

An hour later, Marisa had locked in jobs with both the Phoenix Restaurant and Grand Keys Oasis Spa, while Inga would be working at the Phoenix and Buster's, both of them maxing out the numbers of hours to earn the most in salary and tips. They carried envelopes with the job descriptions, regulations, and tickets for ferry passage to the island a week from Monday. They would get their uniforms when they arrived. When she'd asked what the uniforms looked like, Eleanor had just rolled her eyes.

As they walked through the lobby, a group of suited men walked out of one of the conference rooms. The movers and shakers of this whole shebang, Marisa surmised.

She noticed the oddest thing then. The smell of lemons permeated the air. In the midst of them all was Dr. Grumpy, who gave her the oddest look. It said loud and clear:

Go away! Run as fast as you can. Danger!

She put her fingertips to her lips in seeming dismay. The middle finger might have been raised slightly higher.

His clear blue eyes widened in surprise. Then he scowled.

She did, too. It had been that kind of day.

Chapter 4

Heigh-ho, heigh-ho, it's off to work they go . . .

When Sigurd arrived on Grand Keys Island by seaplane a week later, he was well-tanned and ready for this new assignment. So was his medical assistant, Karl Mortensen, a young vangel who remained a perpetual twenty-two after dying in Vietnam more than forty years ago.

Five other vangels, already on the island, had been hired for various jobs at the conference, everything from snorkeling instructor to desk clerk. Among them was Armod, who fashioned himself a reincarnation of Michael Jackson. Yes, a moonwalking vampire angel. Enough on that subject! The boy from Iceland was only sixteen human years old, but he carried fake identification proclaiming him to be twenty-one, or he would not have been permitted to work on the island.

This would be Armod's first mission, and his undercover job would be as a dancer in one of the nightclub acts. It better not be lewd dancing, Sigurd had warned, and Armod had pointed out that most modern dancing did cross the line at times. At least it would not be stripper-type dancing. That's all Sigurd would need to explain to Mike. A Viking vampire angel shimmying his braies off!

Armod, nigh shivering with excitement when Sigurd had left him back at the hotel this morning, kept asking, "Are you sure I'm tan enough, Sig? I could drink more Fake-O."

The boy had already drunk so much Fake-O, he'd be pissing buckets all day.

Sigurd had been out on a mission to the Rocky Mountains with his brothers and their troops for several days, saving sinners who were being hunted by Lucies at some wild orgy-like music festival. Thus, his skin sported a deep tan, allowing him to blend in with the sunbathing crowd. For some reason, modern folks considered leathery skin attractive.

When saving a human, even the small amount of blood taken was like heavenly vitamin C to a vangel. Same was true of destroying a Lucipire. Lack of a saved's blood, or lack of celestial points for taking down a demon vampire, over time turned the skin white and then transparent. What better way to announce to humans they encountered, *Hey, I'm a vampire. Wanna get sucked?* Sigurd recalled a time, soon after being turned, that his skin became so light, all the veins in his body stood out, like a blinkin' Etch A Sketch.

In an emergency, vangels used blood ceorls in their community or the unsatisfactory Fake-O. Or, as his married brothers had discovered recently, they could flourish off the occasional feeding on their life mates, or eternity mates in their society.

But the best way remained the drinking blood of a person they had saved from Satan's vampires, or annihilating Lucipires. Sigurd expected to have numerous opportunities to do both on Grand Keys Island.

"Wow!" Karl said as they approached the island, and the pilot landed them neatly in the water, close to one of the docks. "This is paradise."

"Yes, but remember Eden. There's always a snake in the garden," Sigurd reminded him.

"More than one in this case," Karl agreed, rubbing a hand over the flat-top haircut that he maintained, though it had gone out of style many years ago.

The island *was* beautiful. A paradise of stately palm trees and lush flowers flourishing in the semi-tropical climate. The island itself was probably only eight square miles, big enough to handle the massive hotel that rose from its center and the private bungalows that were situated along the rungs of a half pinwheel stemming from the back and two sides. Several yachts, expensive sailboats, and more seaplanes dotted the clear blue water, most of them about a quarter mile out from shore. There were no deep water docks on either the ocean or gulf sides of the island, just wharves to cater to smaller craft.

Sigurd's brothers and about a hundred vangel soldiers were on call to come to his aid if it was discovered that there was a large Lucie presence on the island. Last he heard, they were arguing about what kind of boat to purchase as an off-island headquarters for their operation. Vikings did love their boats!

Vikar was pushing for a longship. *Like that wouldn't be conspicuous!*

Cnut suggested a blimp that could sort of float over the island. *Really? Sort of float? Had none of them heard of the* Hindenburg?

Ivak wanted a large speedboat, but was voted down when the size limitations were pointed out. *Not to mention, the Coast Guard would probably be on their tails for speeding or reckless boat driving.* Ivak already had a dozen traffic tickets for speeding down the Louisiana highways. Sigurd had no doubt Ivak's behavior would be the same on the high seas.

Trond, a Navy SEAL, knew someone who knew someone in the military who could get them a used submarine. *I think I have a headache,* Sigurd had thought when that subject was brought up. *A big one!*

In the end, they'd decided to let Harek investigate buying a yacht on the Internet. There was a listing for what Harek described as a "big-ass cruiser," that once belonged to an Arab sheik. *What happened to the days when sheiks confined themselves to desert tents?* "It even has special suites for his harem."

"That will go over big with Mike," Sigurd had pointed out, to no avail. No one listened to reason when Vikings were on a roll discussing their favorite subjects. Ships and women. Well, beer, too, but that was a given, no matter what vessel they decided upon.

"And what are you going to do with a yacht once this mission is over?" Sigurd had asked.

"Sell it on eBay," Harek said.

Of course. Why didn't I think of that?

"Or we could keep it out on Colyer Lake," Vikar had suggested.

Sigurd doubted that the lake near the castle in Transylvania, Pennsylvania, was deep enough to hold a seagoing yacht, and how they would get the yacht there posed another problem. But the biggest problem was that Mike would never allow it. Too much fun!

In any case, he and Karl and the other six vangels were now on the island, and the others would come, when and if he summoned them. *How* was something his brothers could work out without his input.

Workers were emptying boxes of supplies off the more mundane-looking vessels and piling them onto wheeled carts, which they pushed up the inclined path toward the hotel. All-terrain vehicles were also used to transport goods. A ferry was offloading passengers, probably employees, like themselves. The conference wouldn't officially start for another day.

That's when Sigurd saw the woman he'd spoken to in line before the Purple Palm last week. Karl was off in the bushes sneaking a cigarette, a filthy habit he'd picked up while in Vietnam and which he claimed "can't kill me now." Though, come to think on it, Sigurd had rarely seen Karl smoke since his recent marriage. He was probably checking in with his wife.

Should he ignore her, as he was inclined to do? Do not get involved with anyone at this lackwit conference. Get his job done. Save a sinner or five. Destroy a legion of Lucies. Then maybe Mike would let him return to medicine . . . legitimate medicine. Something with prestige.

Hah! Not bloody likely. He would have to do a lot of groveling before that happened. Prove that he could be humble, lacking in envy, like the next guy.

So Sigurd rushed to catch up with the woman to apologize for his rudeness and perhaps offer a warning to her about that lecherous Goldman's interest in her. That should earn him some points with the big guy.

"Greetings!" he said. "My name is Sigurd. We met before."

She gave him a sideways glance. "You again!"

Not a promising start! "And your name is . . . ?"

She hesitated. "Marisa Lopez. Shouldn't you be off doctoring or something in the VIP lounge?"

He gritted his teeth. If there was anything that annoyed him, it was a woman with an irksome attitude. "I do not start my doctoring, or something, until tomorrow. Shouldn't you be off massaging something?"

Tipping her head at him in acknowledgment of his riposte, she replied, "I start tomorrow, too."

She really was a gorgeous woman. Skin a natural

olive. Full, unpainted mouth, which was a natural rose color. Hair black and shiny that spilled out in a thick straight swath onto the bare shoulders of her strapless, form-hugging top. The stretchy red material hugged her breasts and abdomen, leaving naught to the imagination . . . his imagination, leastways. Same for the tight white braies, which ended mid-calf, calling attention to her long legs and rounded buttocks. On her feet were white, high-wedged, backless shoes with big red flowers, the same color as her top. Peeking out of the shoes were oddly sexy, clear, glossy toenails.

Not that he was paying that much attention to her physical attributes. Who was he kidding? Sigurd felt a lurch low down on his body. He was not easily aroused these days, and it surprised him, for a moment.

"Wouldst care to share a drink with me later?" he found himself suggesting.

"Why?" she asked, narrowing her eyes with suspicion. She'd obviously noticed his appreciative perusal.

"There are some things you need to know to protect yourself whilst on this island." *And I want to touch your skin.*

She laughed. "From you?"

He shrugged. "And others, who would not take no for an answer."

"And you would . . . take no for an answer?"

"I would do a damn good job of convincing you to change your mind." He smiled. But then he caught himself. What was he doing, engaging in senseless banter with a woman? He had no business suggesting that he would consider seduction, especially of a woman dim-witted enough to hire herself out at an event celebrating lewdness.

She fanned a hand in front of her face. "Good heavens! When you smile like that, I believe you could."

Well, mayhap not so dim-witted after all. "Even

with my little fangy teeth?" He recalled her remarking on his incisors that other day.

She waggled her eyebrows at him. "Especially with those cute little pointy teeth." She frowned then. "Which don't seem to be pointy at all today."

Cute? That is a not a word a Viking likes to hear. "The points come and go." He waved a hand dismissively.

"Like magic?"

He shrugged. "I am a Viking. We are known for extraordinary . . . things." He was the one waggling his eyebrows now.

"A doctor with a sense of humor. Amazing!"

He laughed. It had been a long time since he'd flirted with a woman. A looooong time. He concentrated on tamping down his pleasure, before someone else did it for him, someone *up there.* "What I was trying to say was, there are evil men on this island. You could be in danger." Really, he was saying more than he should. He forced himself to scowl, instead of grinning like a loopy lackwit.

"Listen, Sigurd—" she started, pronouncing his name like *cigar.*

"Call me Sig," he said.

"Listen, Sig. I've been taking care of myself for years. I don't need your advice. Or whatever else you're offering."

He bristled. "I was not offering *that.*" *Yet. Or never. Or probably never.*

They'd been walking while they talked, each with a carry bag in hand, his in his left hand, hers in her right, but just then a man stepped in front of them as they approached the crushed shell clearing in front of the hotel, a massive white, colonial island plantation–type structure with pillars and wide covered verandahs. "Dr. Sigurdsson! How nice to meet you again! And who is this lovely lady?"

Harry Goldman was wearing a pale green Palm

Beach Golf Club shirt tucked into a pair of white shorts, leaving his hairy legs bare down to leather sandals. His clearly dyed, evenly brown hair was slicked wetly off his face, as if he'd just come from the pool. He sucked in his stomach, but the paunch was still prominent. When he smiled, his capped teeth gleamed against his ruddy complexion. He had either bathed in some citrusy cologne, or the man's pores were oozing lemon scent. Sigurd was betting on the latter.

Without thinking, Sigurd yanked Marisa to his side with an arm over her shoulder and said, "Marisa, this is Harry Goldman, the man I told you about. He invests heavily in certain, uh, movies. Mr. Goldman, this is my betrothed, Marisa Lopez."

"Mar-is-a. What a beautiful name!" Then understanding hit, and Mr. Goldman sputtered, "Be-betrothed?"

"Fiancée," Sigurd elaborated.

"What?" Marisa squeaked.

Goldman gave Sigurd an evil look. "You didn't mention she was your fiancée last week when I pointed her out." He glanced at Marisa's ringless left hand.

Marisa, still in his tight embrace, turned her head to Sigurd, her eyebrows arched. "You talked about me with another man? Last week?" The silent message was, *You didn't even know me last week. Or hardly.*

"We just made it official last night. Didn't we, sweetling?" He kissed her lightly on the lips. Only lightly, for fear she might bite him. But even that little kiss sent a zing through his body so powerful he would be thinking about it later. A lot. "Won't you congratulate us on our engagement, Mr. Goldman?"

"You're overdoing it," Marisa warned in a whisper that tickled his ear, deliciously. And more zinging.

Goldman said something under his breath that sounded like "Fuck you, Sigurdsson. Engagements can be broken." Then the little guy spun on his small feet and turned to Martin Vanderfelt, who had just stepped up and had nervously witnessed the exchange. "In my suite, Vanderfelt. Now!"

"Was that necessary?" Marisa sniped at Sigurd then, shrugging out of his embrace.

That was all the thanks he got! "Only if you want to avoid lecherous old billionaires with evil intents."

She cocked her head to the side and homed in on the most irrelevant thing he'd said, "Billionaire? As in ten-figures billionaire?"

He made a spectacle of counting on his fingers, then nodded. Something else caught his attention then. For just a flit of a second, Sigurd thought he smelled lemons. But maybe it was just the residual fog left by Goldman.

"Besides, I think you exaggerate his *evil* intentions. It's more like *lustful* intentions. And all men have those." She clearly included him in that lot.

Then she was gone, and he berated himself for caring what trouble a dim-witted female would find herself in. He had enough trouble in his own sorry life.

Still, he couldn't help but stare at said dim-witted female's arse as she climbed the steps in front of the hotel. Up, down, up, down, the curvy buttocks went.

Karl came up to him then. "Ready?"

Bloody hell, yes, he was ready. But enough of that!

Sigurd waved a hand in front of his face. "Your breath smells like cigarettes."

"So don't kiss me."

"Ha, ha, ha." Sigurd continued to watch Marisa's progress, and never once did she turn to give him a second look. He was unaccustomed to being dismissed so easily.

"What are you gaping at?" Karl asked.

"My mission," he said. Where that thought came from, he had no idea.

Karl raised his brows as he focused in on Marisa, who was talking with a hotel doorman. "I thought our mission was to save sinners and wipe out Lucies."

"This is my personal mission."

"Uh-oh. Sounds like trouble to me."

"Trouble, challenge . . . same thing to a Viking."

Sigurd realized too late that Northmen throughout the ages had been getting into trouble by making similar lackwitted pronouncements.

His favorite drink: Sin on the Rocks . . .

Jasper and fifty of his favorite Lucipires were on their way to Grand Keys Island off the Florida Keys for what he jokingly called a "working vacation." Unfortunately, demon vampires didn't have much of a sense of humor, and none of them understood the joke.

Or mayhap they were just a grouchy lot today. That was probably the case. Demons didn't consider the extreme heat of an island to be their idea of paradise, despite the legends about Satan rollicking in the fires of Hell. Hah! Satan relished air-conditioning as much as the next guy.

It didn't help matters that his hired boat had stalled halfway between Miami and the island destination. Who knew that a hundred-foot yacht could stall? A mechanic was down in the engine room now fixing the problem. Luckily, the Lucipires had harvested a cruise ship's captain and some of the crew on a mission last year, and they were now full-fledged demon vampires. Unluckily, a gaggle of imps and hordlings had tried to solve the problem first and created nothing but chaos.

Jasper was lying on a chaise longue in the glassed-in salon when his French hordling assistant, Beltane, came in.

"Master," Beltane said, "I brought you some refreshments." Beltane carried a tray of tall glasses of iced pink lemonade.

Jasper did so love the scent of lemons, and the pink color came from the generous dollops of human blood added for flavor. One of the Lucipires had drained a quart from a teenage prostitute last night, so it was especially fresh. There was also a small bowl of caviar sprinkled with hard-boiled egg crumbles with pita bread triangles for dipping. His favorite snack. Blood and caviar. Yum!

Beltane was thoughtful that way, mainly because the young Creole truly adored Jasper. Lots of Lucipires, from imps to haakai, pretended affection for Jasper, but he was not fooled. Ingratiating maggots, most of them. Unlike Beltane, who had been sorely abused growing up in antebellum New Orleans before the demon vampires took him into their fold. He appreciated his new life.

"Thank you, Beltane. Is the mechanic making any progress?"

Beltane rolled his red eyes. "The man curses every other word, in both Spanish and English, but I believe we will be under way within the hour."

"Good, good! You look very nice today, Beltane."

Beltane was dressed for island living, wearing a gaudily bright floral shirt over white shorts leading down to those rubber shoes known as flip-flops. And they did indeed flip and flop as he shuffled around the room tidying any objects left lying about. Jasper doubted that Beltane would ever leave the ship, though. His warrior skills left much to be desired. Plus, being only a hundred and fifty years old as a Lucipire and only twenty before that, he still had trouble controlling his fangs and demon tendencies in public places.

Like Jasper and all the other Lucipires on board, he was in humanoid form for the time being. Until they found a prime sinner. Only then did they morph into demonoid form.

"You look good, too, master," Beltane said. "The hat is a nice touch."

Jasper was dressed for island living as well, but his attire was more formal since he would be going into the hotel disguised as a potential investor in pornographic movies. Hell and damnation, but you had to give humans credit for inventing new kinds of sin. He wore a cream linen suit, with a chocolate-brown shirt and a white tie. On his feet were cream and brown "saddle" shoes, and he had a short-brimmed, straw planter's hat hanging from the back of his chaise, ready to don. His humanoid persona today was a fortyish version of Clark Gable, right down to the trim black mustache. He looked dapper if he did say so himself.

Not so dapper was Zebulan, a high haakai and one of his four elite council members, who walked in, without knocking. One of these days Jasper had to get around to adding another haakai to high command status, to replace Dominique Fontaine, who had the misfortune of being vanquished by the vangel forces a few years ago. No great loss to Jasper, who had despised the woman.

Zebulan wore faded blue denim pants, a tight black T-shirt, ratty athletic shoes, and a Blue Devils baseball cap. Sometimes Jasper wondered why he favored the former Hebrew soldier so much.

"It's hotter than Hades out there," Zebulan remarked.

"You ought to know," Jasper sniped. All Lucipires had visited Satan's lair at one time or another.

Without invitation, Zebulan walked over and picked up one of the glasses, sniffed it, wrinkled his nose with distaste, then quaffed it down all in one long swallow. Wiping his mouth with the back of his hand, he sank down into a chair next to Jasper's chaise, also without invitation. You had to admire the demon's balls. Jasper had squashed others for less lack of deference. And, yes, he did mean squashed ballocks.

"News?" Jasper inquired with arched brows.

Zebulan nodded. "I took a dozen mungs and hordlings with me last night and this morning. We trolled every bit of the island along with several of the ships anchored off shore."

"And?"

"It's teeming with some of the most vile sinners I've encountered since the days of the Roman Colosseum."

Jasper wrung his scaly hands with glee. Idly, he made note to himself to borrow some of Beltane's hand cream before going ashore. "Tell me more."

"Three hundred employees, more or less. Two thousand conference attendees. The event will last one week, but employees will stay an extra few days for cleanup."

"And prospects . . . for us?"

Zebulan shrugged. "One hundred."

"That is all?" Jasper's shoulders sank with disappointment. "One hundred is nothing compared to some of our other missions."

"Yes, but remember, we decided to lay low for a while. Not to call attention to ourselves with the more high-profile harvests. That was a close call in Vegas."

"You are right, of course. I cannot be too greedy."

"And there may be more. Rumors are that a boat or airplane will be bringing in young girls and boys, no more than fourteen, to cater to certain tastes."

Jasper clapped his hands together with delight.

"I love it. Child molesters are among my favorite victims . . . uh, converts."

He could swear Zebulan cringed a little, but then, when Jasper studied him closer, he noticed nothing amiss. "You will come to my party tonight," Jasper decided.

That was a definite cringe he saw now.

"Too much work to do," Zebulan protested. "I will send some of my Lucipires."

The Hebrew almost never socialized with Jasper and the other demon vampires, and, frankly, Jasper was a mite offended. "You will come," he insisted. "And dress appropriately."

"Yes, master." Zebulan saluted him with obvious sarcasm.

"And bring a date. How about that new hordling? Wanda something or other?"

Zebulan's eyes went wide. "The Witch of Wall Street?"

"That is the one! I hear she knows fifty ways to raise a man's Dow. Ha, ha, ha."

"My Dow is just fine, thank you very much." Zebulan grinned then, and Jasper recalled why he liked the man so much. His sense of humor. And he wasn't always fawning for his favors. Fawning could be just as annoying as lack of deference. "I will come to your frickin' party, and I will wear appropriate attire, but I will be damned if I go willingly within fifty feet of Wanda the Bitch . . . Witch."

"That is all I ever wanted," Jasper said with satisfaction. "Oooh, oooh, oooh, I have a better idea. You could bring Becky Bliss. What a demon vampire that woman would make!"

Zebulan made a sound of impatience. "Number one, I cannot just 'bring' the woman."

"Why not?"

"That is not the way civilized men act today."

"Hmpfh! Men have become such wussies."

"Do you mean pussies?"

"Wussies, pussies, same thing," he said with irritation at Zebulan's contrariness. "Ask her for a date then. Is that not how humans do it?"

"A man has to know a woman first before he can ask her for a date."

"Oh." Jasper tapped his chin with a forefinger, pretending to think on the subject. "Here is an idea. Get to know her first."

"Second," Zebulan went on, as if Jasper hadn't even spoken. "The woman is not sinful enough to be turned Lucipire."

"Really? A woman who bares her body and performs sex acts with numerous men before millions of people? That is not sinful enough?"

"She is more dumb than evil," Zebulan contended.

"I can think of things she could do in her sex acts that would make her sin rankings go off the radar," Jasper said. "For example, she could . . ." Jasper cited several particularly perverted ideas. "You could plant those ideas in her head. Mayhap even initiate her in some of them."

"Enough!" Zebulan put his hands over both ears so he couldn't hear any more of Jasper's very vile suggestions. What kind of demon vampire was he that he didn't enjoy vileness? "I will come to your party, but I come alone. I operate best that way."

"You do as I say," Jasper roared, rising up off the chaise to stand at his full seven-foot height, his demonoid features popping out like pimples as his fury simmered and boiled over.

"Sorry I am, master. I did not mean to give offense," Zebulan said, recognizing that he'd pushed his superior too far. But it was too late for apologies. Lessons must be learned.

Pointing a clawed finger at the difficult demon, Jasper caused him to shoot up off his feet and out the open door, over the railing. Last he heard was a curse, followed by a loud splash. He smiled then at Beltane, who was cowering in the corner, fearful that he would be next.

"Damn but it is good to be me!"

Chapter 5

Was this Fantasy Island, or what? . . .

Marisa and Inga were settling into one of the two bedrooms in their assigned bungalow when their other two roommates arrived.

"Hi, y'all," trilled Tiffany, aka Helen Biggers, from the communal living room separating the bedrooms. "Oooh, this heah cottage is so cute! Lak a dollhouse!"

Marisa wouldn't go that far. Though it was small.

The hundred or so bungalows stemming out along paths from the back and sides of the hotel all the way to the ocean were designed to ensure privacy, with their heavy cloaks of tropical trees and bushes, but some were luxurious and bigger than others. She would have expected no more than this for employees. And it really was nice and sunny with white wicker furniture made comfy by bright floral cushions and overhead ceiling fans. There was a tiny kitchenette, just enough for a coffeemaker, a small mini fridge, and a counter with two stools. And one bathroom, though spacious, to be shared by four women! If it weren't for this being serious business to earn money for her daughter, Marisa would have considered it a wonderful vacation spot.

Tiffany, wearing a pink halter top, white short-shorts, and high white wedgie sandals, fast-walked with mincing steps over to her and Inga, who stood in the bedroom doorway. She gave them both warm hugs, as if they were longtime friends.

Good heavens! Does she buy Shalimar by the gallon?

Marisa realized suddenly that despite the bimbo attire, Tiffany resembled no more than a girl trying to appear grown-up. Like one of those kids dolled up in a grotesque fashion in child beauty pageants. Really, Tiffany was to be pitied more than criticized. Marisa vowed to be more tolerant and to try to steer Tiffany on a different path.

"This is Doris Hunter," Tiffany said as another woman, who'd been standing out on the small patio admiring the view, came inside. "Doris, these are mah friends, Marisa Lopez and Inga Johanssen. Marisa and Inga will be waitressin' in the Phoenix Restaurant, Inga will also waitress in Buster's, and Marisa will work as a massage therapist in the health spa, too." Marisa had to give Tiffany credit for remembering their names and jobs. *Maybe she isn't as dumb as she appears to be.*

Doris, a short, plain, thirtysomething woman in a tan T-shirt and cargo shorts with leather docksiders, stared at them for a long moment, as if taking mental notes, or something. "Hello."

"Are you a hairstylist, too?" Marisa asked, without thinking. If she was, Doris, with her short butch haircut, clearly a barbershop creation, was a walking advertisement for why not to use her services.

"No, I'm going to be a maid. No, not the French maid kind."

Marisa and Inga exchanged looks. That was the last

thing they'd expect this woman to do. Marisa would wager her best Louis Vuitton knockoff that Doris was gay. Not that lesbians couldn't be French maids, she self-corrected herself.

"I'll be cleaning rooms," Doris continued. "And that's all."

Okaaay. That's emphatic enough. Tiffany must have given her the Becky Bliss pitch. Millions to be made just from lying down, legs to Manhattan and L.A., knees to the sun, dollar signs dancing in her head. Mansions, Jacuzzis, blah, blah.

"Hope you don't mind my barging in. Tiff said you needed a foursome, and—"

"Whoa, whoa, whoa," Inga spoke up now. "I might look like a tart at times, but I'm hardly past the two-some stage."

Doris laughed, a deep, husky guffaw.

Tiffany's brow furrowed for a moment before she giggled. "Oh you!" She playfully jabbed Inga in the upper arm with a fist. "That's not what Doris meant. Besides, mah boyfriend Tee-Beau would have a fit."

"Holy moly! Your boyfriend is Tebow? Tim Tebow?" Inga gasped out.

"You are such a kidder, Inga." Tiffany pursed her crimson lips into a fake moue of chiding. "Beau is from Loo-zee-anna. To the Cajuns, Tee-Beau means Little Beau. Not that Beau is little now, but he was when he was a chile."

Marisa homed in on something else. "Doesn't your boyfriend mind you trying to break into adult films?"

Tiffany shook her head, causing the blonde curls to bob. "Thass jist bizness. Ah wouldn't be enjoyin' myself or anythin'. Ah'm good at fakin' it. All women are at one time or another, right?"

"Absolutely!" Doris piped in.

Something about Doris seemed off to Marisa, and it

wasn't her sexual orientation. Marisa wasn't quite sure what it was. Maybe it was her eyes, behind rimless glasses that she kept pushing up her nose. Her hazel eyes seemed far too intelligent to be satisfied with cleaning services. *Not that being a hotel maid isn't a noble profession. Well, maybe not noble, but satisfactory. Jeesh! Dig a hole lately, Marisa? Good thing I didn't say all this out loud. The political correctness police would be on my tail faster than I could say Cher. Hole. Getting. Deeper.*

Tiffany smiled brightly. "Ah'll be workin' in the beauty salon, Good Looks. It's right next ta the spa, Risa. You don't mind mah callin' ya Risa, do ya? We'll be seeing oodles of each other. Isn't this fun?"

Marisa barely restrained herself from rolling her eyes. "A barrel of laughs, *Tiff.*"

"And, Inga, Ah'm dyin' ta clip yer dead ends, sugah. Not that your blonde hair isn't beautiful, but just a little layering would make you a knockout."

Inga, who already considered herself a knockout, wasn't so self-controlled. She said, "Just super!"

"And I could give you highlights," she offered Doris, as well.

Doris was clearly taken aback. "Thanks, but I have my own beautician back home. Pierre would have a fit if I let anyone else touch my locks." Doris patted her short hair and winked at Marisa and Inga. At least she had a sense of humor.

"Well, I'm going to finish unpacking," Marisa said before Tiffany could start on her.

It was hard to be mean to Tiffany, though. She was so clearly clueless.

Tiffany raised her huge, wheeled, shocking-pink luggage and was about to go into the other bedroom. Marisa and Inga had brought only small Gucci carry-on bags, figuring they'd be wearing uniforms most of the time, and Doris had only a rolling duffel bag.

Clearly, none of them was as prepared as Tiffany to be "discovered."

"Ah'm gonna put on mah bikini and head fer the pool. Mebbe Ah'll be discovered on my first day here, please God."

God would want nothing to do with that kind of helping hand, Marisa was pretty sure.

"Will y'all join me?"

"Sure," Inga said. In an aside to Marisa, she whispered, "I wouldn't miss this for the world."

Doris rolled her eyes. "I think I'll just relax on the patio with a book."

"I have to make a phone call, but I'll be there in a half hour or so," Marisa promised.

She put away her belongings and went into the kitchenette, where she poured herself a glass of iced tea. Tiffany claimed she couldn't go anywhere without her sweet tea and therefore carried tea bags and diet sugar packets with her. Before she left, she had made the iced tea in a hotel ice bucket, there being no pitcher available.

Sitting down in one of the cushy chairs, Marisa picked up her cell phone and pressed home.

"Hi, Mommy," her daughter answered immediately, then corrected herself, as she'd been taught. "I mean, hello, this is the Lopez rezdance."

"Hello, sweetheart. How are you feeling today?" Izzie had been sleeping when Marisa had left the house at dawn.

"Buelita says this is one of my good days. We're goin' to the pool with PopPop this afternoon. He's takin' off work jist for me."

"That's nice. Don't forget the sunscreen."

"I won't. Are you havin' fun, Mommy?"

"Not yet."

"You should relax and enjoy yourself," her daughter

advised, clearly parroting something she'd heard her grandmother or grandfather say.

"I'm going to be working hard most of the time, but I'm going to a pool now, too."

"Will you swim?"

"If it's not too crowded, sure." Marisa loved to swim. Had been on the swim team in high school. In fact, had gone to college on a partial sports scholarship. But she hadn't been swimming in ages, not with Izzie's problems and Marisa's workload. "Can I talk to Buelita?"

"Buelita!" Izzie yelled.

Marisa winced. Another lesson she would have to teach her daughter. Put your hand over the phone before yelling. Or, better yet, don't yell at all. She hoped she would get the chance for these and all the other little-girl lessons.

Tears filled her eyes immediately, but she blinked them away.

"Love you bunches, Mommy," Izzie said before handing over the phone.

"Love you more, peanut," she countered.

After Marisa spoke with her mother and gave her all the instructions for Izzie's care that she'd already given her a dozen times that week, her mother said, "Relax and enjoy yourself, Marisa." The unspoken words were *While you can.*

Marisa smiled. Like minds, and all that. "I will, and call me immediately if there's a problem."

After donning a white, one-piece, structured maillot swim suit, a 2005 Hermès knockoff, which was cut high on the hips, with detachable straps, and an oversize Garfield T-shirt as a cover up (Izzie had a matching one, no knockoffs with these Wal-Mart specials), she grabbed her Dior sunglasses and shuffled into a pair of flip-flops. When Marisa went out onto the patio, she saw Doris tapping away on an iPad, which she immediately tucked into a canvas bag at her side and took out a hardback book, John Grisham's latest mystery, *Sycamore Row*.

More contradictions. A maid who was fluent on an expensive iPad? And while John Grisham's books hardly qualified as literary fiction, they were not the usual choice for women of a lower education level. Assuming this woman was of a lower education level.

Marisa mentally chastised herself for once again judging someone by appearances. Hadn't people been doing that to her all her life? She should know better.

"Is the book any good?"

Doris shrugged. "I liked the prequel better. *A Time to Kill.*"

"What's not to like about Jake Brigance, aka Matthew McConaughey?"

"Or Ashley Judd, aka Carla Brigance."

Well, that certainly laid the question of Doris's sexual preference to rest. They both laughed.

"No second thoughts about the pool?" Marisa asked.

"Nah. I'll read a little bit, then maybe take a nap. I didn't sleep much last night, and I had to get to Dulles by five a.m."

"Don't forget the employee meeting at four o'clock."

Everyone would be starting work tomorrow, even though the conference didn't officially start until the next day. Last-minute instructions would be doled out today. On-site training tomorrow.

"See you later then."

Bypassing the outdoor pool, which was as crowded as Marisa had expected, mostly with sunbathers, not swimmers, she headed toward the more functional indoor pool. Her hunch had been right. There were only a few people here, and they appeared to be done, if their wet suits were any indication. Nodding a greeting to two men and a woman, she took off her shirt, placing it, her sunglasses, and her flip-flops on a poolside chair. No worry about leaving her oversize Dior sunglasses. Anyone who stole them would be disappointed to learn they weren't worth their weight in plastic.

Without any toe testing, she dived off one end of the pool, pleased to find the temperature cool, but not too cold. She began to do laps, starting with a slow crawl, arm over arm, face half lying in the water, one side, then the other, as she moved smoothly toward the other side. She'd done four laps before she started breaststrokes, alternated with underwater swimming and backstrokes, ending on the eighth lap with a crawl once again. Swimming tended to energize, rather than tire her. It always had. The endorphin rush that some joggers got. When she emerged at the end of the pool, tossing her hair back off her face, she saw a pair of lightly furred legs. Following the mile-long, muscled legs upward, she immediately recognized the man standing there watching her.

Oh great! "Dr. Cigar," she said.

"Sigurd," he corrected. "Or, as I told you before, you can call me Sig."

"For some reason, I don't see you as a Sig. Gurd maybe."

He scowled at her. He did that a lot, she noticed. Dr. McGrumpy, for sure.

For some immature reason, she delighted in annoying the man. So, of course, she asked, "Why aren't you off at some hoity-toity VIP pool, complete with pool boys and scantily clad girls to cater to your every whim?"

"Whore-tee tart-tee?"

"You know very well I said hoy-tee toy-tee. It means exclusive. For snooty folks only."

He shook his head at her teasing. And scowled some more. "I could not find a VIP pool, and I hear all the pool boys and scantily clad girls are on strike. What thorn do you have up your arse over my being of some VIP status?"

Not just grumpy. Rude, too. But then, I haven't been Miss Pleasing Personality, either. "No thorns, and that *was* rude of me. Sorry. It's been a long day, and it's only one o'clock."

He nodded his head in acceptance of her apology. "Likewise. A word of advice, though. Envy is not an attractive feature, as I well know."

"Huh?" *He well knows . . . what? Is he saying that he is an envious person? Of what? And wait a minute. Is he accusing me of being envious of him?* She'd like to pull the lout down into the pool and dunk him a time or twenty. Whatever! He was twice her size. She knew who would be licking the bottom of the pool, and it wouldn't be him.

When she raised herself on straightened arms, he held out a hand to assist her out of the pool. She hesitated, but not because she was actually considering yanking him into the water. Well, considering . . . maybe. Doing? She didn't really have the nerve. She would have liked to, though.

No, it was the idea of her alone in this pool area, both of them wearing nothing but swimming attire. It seemed rather intimate. But then she figured that her bathing suit was modest by many standards today. So she let him help her up out of the water and to her feet on the tiled surround. Where she soon discovered that her bathing suit, when wet, left little to the imagination. And by Sigurd's quick survey, she could tell that the man was doing a lot of imagining.

"Don't look at me like that," she ordered, going over

to get a towel and drying her long hair, then wrapping it turban-like around her head.

"Like what?" He didn't even try to hide the fact that he was imagining her naked.

"Like I am a snack being offered to you on a silver tray."

"I am a Viking. We like to look. Among other things. Besides, looking is not a sin."

Good thing it wasn't because, if he wasn't watching her so closely through crystal-blue eyes, she would like to devour this huge hunk of man candy with her own eyes. His long blond hair hung loose to his shoulders. He wore only a pair of black swimming trunks low on his hips, exposing wide shoulders, a narrow waist, really long legs, and the cutest belly button.

She cleared her throat and asked, "A Viking, huh? Are you from Norway?"

"Not anymore."

She arched her brows in question.

He hesitated and his face flushed before he revealed, "Transylvania. I come from Transylvania."

"Romania?" For some reason, that surprised her. "You were a doctor in Romania?" *I was right about the medical degree from some underdeveloped country.*

Stop it, Marisa. Stop being so damn judgmental.

Medical degrees from Romania are probably just as good as those from the good ol' USA.

She gave herself a mental snort of disbelief.

"Transylvania, Pennsylvania," he elaborated, as if reading her mind. "And most recently I was a doctor at Johns Hopkins."

That raised more than a few questions, which she was about to toss at him, like why would a doctor with the credentials to practice at that elite hospital be working at a porno conference, but he chose that moment to dive into the pool, creating a huge splash that doused her head to toe. Deliberately, she was sure. Good thing she'd already been wet, or she would have a thing or two to say to the jerk. She still would.

But later.

She could swear she heard laughter as she walked away. He was probably staring at her butt.

Chapter 6

*Scent of a woman, scent of a Viking ... a
double whammy of temptation! ...*

She paused at the doorway and waited for him to
emerge from the pool, wanting to give him a piece of
her mind, but he just ignored her, completing lap after
lap of powerful strokes. Finally, she combed her fingers through her hair and went out to join Inga and
Tiffany at the outdoor pool.

What she saw almost made her turn on her heels.
She'd never seen so many Speedos in all her life. Or
bikinis the size of Band-Aids.

Really, what were men thinking? Even the most
physically fit guys looked ridiculous in those little
bulge-revealing bits of fabric. As for the women, they
might as well be naked.

She waved at Eleanor and Hedy, who were on the far
side of the pool, half reclining on lounge chairs in the
shade. They wore matching black Bermuda shorts and
white blouses with some insignia on the one side. Prob-

ably hotel uniforms of some sort. Marisa had half expected the conference uniforms to be slutty, but maybe the hotel office staff, like Doris, or those in supervisory positions, like Hedy at the health spa, weren't expected to follow the regular dress code. If there was one. Or maybe this was just the casual uniform. Marisa had run into Eleanor a short time ago, and Eleanor told her that she and Hedy would be rooming together inside the hotel, rather than one of the bungalows.

Marisa sat down in the limited shade of an umbrella-covered, poolside table next to Inga. Already perspiration popped out on her forehead and underarms. The temperature must be close to ninety. Inga's blonde hair was brushed sleekly off her face, and her bikini was still wet from a recent swim. "The suit looks good on you," Marisa commented.

"Yeah, I like it."

She and Inga had raided Steve's garage boxes yesterday, and Inga had discovered the vintage red-and-white polka dot number, a classic Chanel design from around 2000.

"Your brother has good taste," Inga went on.

Marisa gave her friend a rueful shake of the head. "Too bad he didn't use that good taste for a real job once in a while."

"When's he getting out?"

"Next year, if he's lucky." Marisa loved her brother, but with all the other stress in her life, she couldn't allow herself the luxury of worrying about him. He was thirty-one years old, for heaven's sake! Who was she kidding? Of course she worried about him. "He's studying graphic design in prison."

Inga rolled her eyes. "Oh Lord! He wouldn't dare print counterfeit money when he gets out, would he?"

"What do you think?"

Marisa accepted a small beaded bottle of icy water

from a passing waiter (the core hotel staff was still working), and drank deeply. Then she sat back in her chair and looked around at the several dozen people walking or sitting around the pool. "So what's new?"

"Well, our friend Tiff is networkin' her little Dixie ass off, dontcha know, darlin'," Inga said in an exaggerated Southern drawl.

"That's mean," Marisa said, knowing she was equally guilty. "It's like beating a cute little puppy dog."

"She's already met two film producers who want to give her an audition and Madeline something or other, who sells discreet sex toys through her mail order company, My Ladies Boudoir. Madeline will be giving out samples this afternoon at the employees' meeting. She highly recommends The Bobber, according to Tiffany. Oh, and there's the editor of some skin magazine who might consider doing a layout on Tiffany if—"

"Let me guess. If she auditions for him?"

"Bingo! From what I can tell, it's a mixed bag of folks here . . . so far, anyway. There are the porno wannabes, like Tiffany, but not an overwhelming number. Mainly because it's so expensive to attend. Five thou minimum. The industry biggies are here, of course. Company owners. Wealthy men and women who are either looking for action or new investments, probably both. Lobbyists . . . yeah, some of these companies know the power of having politicians on their side. PR experts to hype pornography as the ultimate freedom of expression. By the way, we're going to be told in the employee meeting not to use the word *pornography*. It's FOE now, baby. Freedom of Expression, not forwarding order expired. Art films, not skin flicks. Sensual literature, not erotica. Yada, yada."

"What a crock!" Marisa said.

"Watch for the Internet types who are riding the

electronic smut waves. You can easily identify them. They look nerdy. And mostly they're young and full of themselves. In a way, these are the most dangerous. They're smart. Really smart. And they know how to access millions of people at the click of a key, as in computer keyboard, and profit from that talent."

"I'd like to meet some of them. All I need is one good guy, or girl, who knows code to help me set up an Internet campaign for Izzie."

As if she hadn't spoken, Inga continued, "Sometimes it's hard to tell the working actors and actresses from the aspiring ones. Except the celebrity ones have fans trailing after them, including—you won't believe this—a celebrity dog named Mr. Big after that *Sex and the City* stud."

"Holy Toledo! A dog? I'm afraid to ask."

"Don't."

They both burst out laughing.

"One guy asked me if I'd like to try out for his upcoming film, *Thor and His Really Big Sword*. Not because I'm built like a brick shithouse, his words, not mine, but because I look like a Norse goddess." Inga smiled. "Shall I go on?"

"Enough said!"

"And then there's a bunch of folks just like us, trying to earn some extra cash while holding our noses."

"Uh-oh," Marisa murmured.

"What?"

Marisa was staring over Inga's shoulder. "Don't turn around. It's Mr. Goldman, that billionaire I met earlier today."

Marisa had told Inga this morning on the way to their bungalow about the meeting with both the wealthy man and the Viking doctor. Inga had declared "no contest" over which one she'd choose.

"I still say you should prime this rich guy's pump."

"That's disgusting!"

"I don't know. It could be like that movie *Indecent Proposal*, where Robert Redford offers Demi Moore a million dollars to sleep with him for one night only, even though she's married to Woody Harrelson. Sort of a devil's bargain, but, hell, it's a million freakin' dollars."

"Pfff! Believe me, this guy is no Robert Redford."

Although I have to admit, if it means Izzie having the operation or not, I would probably do it.

No, I wouldn't. No, no, no way! Dis-gust-ing!

And immoral. What kind of message is that for my daughter?

"He's looking our way," Marisa warned. "Behave yourself."

Marisa studied the man, dressed more sedately this afternoon, compared to the rest of the crowd, anyway, in a polo shirt, neatly pressed khaki slacks, and loafers. The bling was still there, though, in the flashy gold chains and Rolex (no knockoffs here, Marisa noted). He seemed to be making excuses to his entourage, which included a couple of security-type fellows and Mr. Vanderfelt. Then he headed her way.

"Goldfinger, did you say?" Inga asked.

"Tsk, tsk. Not Goldfinger. Goldman. Jeesh, Inga, first you mention Robert Redford, now Sean Connery, who next? George Clooney? Okay, that's getting too tempting."

Marisa put a smile on her face as he approached. Really, she thought Sigurd's warning about the old guy being evil was off-base. Mr. Goldman looked like a harmless, pudgy senior citizen, probably a grandfather. He was about the same age as her father.

"Mar-is-a," he drawled out. "It is so nice to see you again. Do you mind if I join you?"

"Uh, no. I mean, sure, sit down. This is my friend Inga Johanssen. Inga, this is Henry Goldman."

"Harry," he corrected with annoyance, which he immediately masked by smiling, displaying an impressive set of porcelain veneers. At least thirty thousand dollars' worth of dental work. "An easy mistake."

"What do you do, Harry?" Inga asked. Blunt, as usual.

"Do?"

"For a living."

"Oh. Right. Well, I like to say I flushed my first million down the toilet, ha, ha, ha. Before getting involved in other ventures. Gold and diamonds. The stock market. Cattle. A restaurant chain. Real estate development. And now, investing in films. Art films."

Yeah, there's a lot of art in "Oooh, oooh, oooh, you are so big, Bruce. Can you do it harder? Maybe up my butt, please?"

"Now I like to say that I deal in laying pipes, not cleaning them," Harry continued, "ha, ha, ha."

When they didn't laugh, not getting the joke, he explained, "I started a company that made brass balls . . . ha, ha, ha . . . for toilets."

Marisa smiled, though she didn't think it was that funny. "My father is a plumber. I'll bet he uses your balls." *Oh Lord! Did I really say something so crude? My mind is degenerating. Must be all the Speedos.*

Harry thought that was hilarious and laughed heartily, wiping his eyes with a pure white handkerchief he pulled from his back pocket.

His laugh is starting to annoy me.

"So where is your fiancé?" he asked suddenly, glancing at her ringless fingers, as he'd done earlier today.

His too obvious interest is starting to annoy me.

She thought about telling him that she had no fiancé, but for some reason she said, "Swimming."

Fiancé? Inga mouthed to Marisa.

Marisa fluttered her fingertips to indicate she would explain later. In relating her meeting with Mr. Goldman and the doctor, Marisa might have forgotten to mention the fiancé part.

"Has anyone ever told you that you look like Sophia Loren?" Harry asked suddenly. "When she was young."

Now I am really annoyed.

"A few people."

"I met her one time in Italy."

Sure you did.

"Must have been thirty years ago."

It would have to be.

"A gorgeous woman! What a body!"

I swear, if I've heard this line once, I've heard it a hundred times. Not original, Harry. Not at all.

"I always wanted . . ."

Here it comes.

" . . . are you by any chance Italian, Mar-is-a?" He licked his lips and stared at her breasts for a brief moment before he caught himself. *As in, Would you like to have sex with me, mi amore?*

She shook her head. "Cuban."

"I do love a good Cuban cigar." He licked his lips.

Un-be-freakin'-lievable! The things men say and think they're being cool! At least he didn't ask if I'd ever been Lewinskied, like that idiot in Starbucks did last month.

"Did you ever meet that kid Elian Gonzalez?"

It wasn't the first time she'd been asked that question. It was like asking an Australian if he'd ever met Crocodile Dundee.

She shook her head. "I was born in Miami. Never been to Cuba. But both of my parents were born there."

"Ah. I keep one of my yachts in Miami."

One of his yachts!

Okay, so he's rich, I already knew that.

Here's my chance. Hook up with the rich guy. He pays for Izzie's operation. I ride off into the sunset.

I probably wouldn't even have to do anything.
Yeah, right.

Inga kept nudging Marisa under the table, encouraging her to do just that. Make some kind of connection with this guy. But Marisa just couldn't take that step. Not yet. Probably never. Even though he wasn't any more lascivious than the next guy, he annoyed her. She found the idea of being close to him repulsive. No Robert Redford, young or old, that was for sure.

"Listen, ladies, I'm holding a welcome party on my yacht tonight. I hope you'll both come. Champagne, caviar, music, dancing. I promise you'll have a good time."

"I don't know—" Marisa started to say.

"I'm in," Inga said. This time her nudge was a full-fledged kick.

Both Goldman and Inga looked at her. Finally, she gave in with a nod. "Oh, sure, thanks for inviting us. We'll have to leave early, though, because—"

"Wonderful!" Goldman didn't even wait for her to finish. He smiled widely and squeezed her hand.

His hand felt damp and soft. She cringed, trying to imagine that hand . . . No, she was not going to imagine any such thing.

"Just come down to Dock B at seven, and there'll be a boat to pick you up." His attention was diverted for a moment by one of his security men who pulled him aside to talk to him about some supplies—caviar, to be specific—that hadn't arrived.

"Oh. My. God!" Inga said. "Be still my heart!"

Marisa tilted her head in question, not understanding Inga's exclamation. Was she referring to Harry's offering a boat to pick them up? Or Harry having ordered caviar? But then Marisa realized that it was someone behind her that drew her friend's comment.

She turned and said the same thing, but to herself. *Oh. My. God!*

Coming out of the hotel onto the terrace were five men. Five big, tall men. All wearing black swimming trunks with unbuttoned black shirts and black, oddly archaic, cross-gartered sandals. All Nordic in appearance, with high cheekbones and sharply sculpted features. Mostly blond, although one of them had black hair arranged Michael Jackson–style, and one of them had an old-fashioned crew cut. Even though the men wore sunglasses, Marisa would bet they all had clear blue eyes. Like the leader of this outrageous pack. Sigurd.

Dr. Viking and his crew were headed her way, purpose in their wide strides, much like that movie clip for *Men in Black*. She almost giggled at the image. Marisa was pretty sure Sigurd was glaring at her, oblivious to the stares he was getting from practically everyone at the pool. Especially the women. Becky Bliss, for example, looked like she was having one of her famous Triple O's.

For one blip of an insane moment, Marisa admitted that she would probably succumb if Sigurd was the one offering an indecent proposal. She felt a lurch of excitement down yonder that she hadn't felt in a long time.

What did it mean?

Probably that I'm suffering from a bout of lust, and I need some special care from the love doctor. Oh, that was awful. Corny and crude.

The closer they got, a strange scent permeated the area, swirling around Marisa like a fog.

What did it mean?

Does lust have an odor? If so, the lust seems to be coming off Sigurd, but he's not looking lustful to me. In fact, just the opposite. The only place he wants to lay me down is in the deep end of that pool over there. "Can you smell that?" she whispered to Inga.

"Smell what?"

"That odor. Woodsy. Maybe evergreen mixed with oranges. But mostly evergreen."

"How can you smell anything over the pool chlorine and the saltwater sea scent?

"It's subtle."

"Maybe it's Harry's cologne, but that's not subtle. More like overpowering." Harry was still engaged in conversation with his employee.

"No. Harry's wearing Aramis. Can't you tell?" Just as she'd become an expert on designer clothing and accessories, Marisa could recognize designer fragrances at twenty paces. A necessary talent when dealing with a larcenous brother who would knock off the pope's shoes if there was a market for them.

"I guess so."

"Then what is that scent? Where's it coming from? It's like a wispy cocoon of pines surrounding us."

"I don't smell it, honey, and I doubt there are evergreen trees on a tropical island. Besides, who can think about smells when faced with five luscious men? And I didn't think I could be attracted to any men in the porno industry."

"Huh? Oh, I don't think they're porno actors or anything. At least one of them is a doctor. I met him earlier. Remember, I told you about him."

Inga turned slowly to look at her. "You mentioned meeting a doctor, but you failed to mention that he looks like Eric Be-Still-My-Heart Northman."

"Who?"

"That actor Alexander Skarsgård from *True Blood*. Girl, you must be missing a few hormones."

Actually, Marisa had made the same observation to Sigurd when she first met him. Her brain was just a bit fuzzy now with all that pine scent filling her nostrils.

"Oh shit!" she heard Harry say after his employee

left and he noticed Sigurd and his "posse" for the first time. "Ladies, I'll see you this evening. I have a business meeting to attend." He practically scurried away on his short legs.

Sigurd glared after Harry as he stepped closer to the table, and the other four men moved to stand in line behind him. Pointing a forefinger at Marisa, he said, "Did I not warn you about that man? Did I not tell you he could be dangerous? Are you so lackwitted that you be must be at cross wills with me just for the sake of stubbornness?"

"Why don't you say what you really mean, Seegar?" she said. "And keep on pointing that finger at me and I'm going to take a bite out of it."

The pine scent was stronger now, and the orange undertones more pronounced, but it wasn't overpowering like some men's colognes, like Harry's. More tempting than nauseating. *How odd!* She felt a strange compulsion to learn closer and sniff, maybe even lick his skin. *Even odder.*

Sigurd straightened, taken aback at her retort, and withdrew his offending finger. Several of his men chuckled, though they maintained straight faces. Inga gave her a you-go-girl grin.

But then Inga suggested to Sigurd, "Let's start over again, Mr. Pointy Finger. Hi, I'm Inga Johanssen. It would appear we're the same nationality. And you are . . . ?"

Inhaling and exhaling several times for patience, Sigurd said, "I am Dr. Sigurd Sigurdsson, and—"

"But you can call him Sig," Marisa interrupted.

"I thought you called him cigar."

"She thinks she is being cute," Sigurd pointed out.

"I am cute," Marisa said.

Sigurd ignored her flip remark and continued speaking to Inga, "And, for my sins, this irksome, half-witted, mulish, pain-in-the-arse woman"—he waved a hand toward Marisa with disgust—"is my betrothed . . . rather, my fiancée."

Inga was momentarily speechless.

"You sweet talker, you," Marisa said flippantly to Sigurd, but a strange voice said in her head, *He could be the answer to your prayers.*

Not unless he's rich, or a doctor who specializes in Izzie's type of brain tumors who just happens to own a clinic where he could do the operation, for free. She realized with dismay that she was not only hearing voices in her head, but she was arguing with them. *It must be the heat, or the evergreen aura, or testosterone overload flooding the area.*

Tiffany hobbled up then, wearing her itty-bitty thong bikini, high-heeled wedgie sandals, and a sheer cover-up that did little covering. "Hey, roomies," she drawled to Marisa and Inga. Meanwhile, all the men appeared to be ogling her behind their shades. "Ah heah we're all gonna party t'night on Harry's yacht."

"Over my dead body," Sigurd muttered.

"Isn't Harry just the sweetest man?" Tiffany continued.

Sigurd didn't even try to hide his snort.

Tiffany suddenly seemed to notice Sigurd and his men. That's how clueless the bimbo was. "Oh. Hi! Y'all mus' be the actors in that new movie, *Thor and His Really Big Sword*. Mah name is Tiffany. Ah'm gonna audition for the part of Princess Solveig. Isn't that cool?"

Sigurd looked liked he just swallowed . . . a really big sword.

Chapter 7

A posse of Vikings? Yum! . . .

Sigurd turned to Marisa, then did a double take. That is what modern folks called a physical reaction of great surprise to something one saw. For a long moment, he just stared at her, speechless.

She wore a long white shirt with a silly cat on the front. Her black hair hung in a wet swath off her face. Her lashes were thick and uptilted slightly. As far as he could tell, there were no store-bought enhancements on her face. Or other even more important places, from a male point of view. And yet, he could say in all honesty, she was the most beautiful woman he'd encountered in centuries.

Why was she having this effect on him now when he'd been in her presence on three other occasions with no great rise in his male appreciation, other than the usual "She's comely. Ho-hum"?

Mayhap it was the subtle odor that seemed to emanate from her. Magnolias or hibiscus. With something tart. Green apples? No, the island was abounding with flowers and fruit. That had to be it.

To his embarrassment, he blurted out like an untried youthling, "You are so beautiful."

"Pfff! If you tell me I look like Sophia Loren, I'm going to double dunk you in that pool over there."

He glanced from her to the nearby pool and back again, giving her a "just-try!" look. He'd changed into dry clothing and was not inclined to get wet again. "Sophie who?"

For some reason, his answer pleased her.

Taking that as his cue, Sigurd sank down into the chair next to her.

She arched her brows at him and said, "Why don't you join us, Sigurd?" with her usual sarcasm, considering he'd already sat down. She shuffled her chair slightly away from him with obvious distaste.

He didn't usually have that effect on women.

"I already have," he pointed out, and moved his chair closer so they were practically rubbing shoulders, just to annoy her. Immature. He was behaving immaturely. She had that effect on him.

Tiffany, the lackwit Norse princess hopeful, shimmied her bare butt cheeks with exaggerated wiggles onto the chair next to Inga, who was a real Norsewoman if he ever saw one. Inga resembled Princess Solveig, whom he had met, more than the simpering maid. On the other hand, Solveig would fuck a goat if it gained her the ends she so ambitiously sought. Four husbands she had gone through at last count. Inga was seated on Marisa's other side.

Sigurd removed his sunglasses, not to get a better look, but just because it seemed the polite thing to do. To his chagrin, his fellow vangels followed suit and took chairs from the surrounding tables, pulling them up to complete a circle at Marisa's table. He'd whispered to Karl a few moments ago, right after announcing that Marisa was his fiancée, "You and the men, sit over there." He'd pointed to several nearby benches.

"Not a chance, master!" Karl had replied in a whisper back at him. Karl knew how much he hated that name. Even though Sigurd was a member of the VIK, he in no way considered himself above others, except perhaps his medical colleagues. "I wouldn't miss this for the world."

"I knew it!" Marisa said. "You all have blue eyes."

Uh-oh! "And that is remarkable . . . why?"

"No reason. Just an observation," the sly woman told him. "Are you all related?"

"You could say that."

"Brothers?"

He shook his head. "I have six brothers, but they are not here."

She narrowed her eyes, studying them all. Thank the heavens, their fangs were all retracted or she would surely have something to say about that, too. He would have to be very careful around her. She was too observant by half.

"Aren't you going to introduce us to your friends?" Marisa prodded, looking toward the other men.

"If I have to," he muttered under his breath.

"This short-haired young man is Karl Mortensen." Karl hated when he called him a young man. Tit for tat in Sigurd's increasingly immature personality. "Karl was a soldier in Vietnam. He will be my medical assistant at this conference."

"Hi, Karl." Tiffany gave Karl a little wave, which caused him to blush right up to his scalp exposed by the short haircut.

Inga and Marisa nodded at Karl, as well.

"You don't look old enough to have been in Vietnam," Marisa remarked.

Oops. My mistake! Another one! It's what happens when we try to walk in two worlds. Careful, Sigurd, careful! "Must have been some other war," Sigurd immediately corrected.

"Iraq," Karl said. "I was a Navy SEAL."

That impressed the spit out of all three women, and was only half a lie. Karl had started Navy SEAL training with Sigurd's brother Trond, but while Trond continued to completion, Karl had dropped out. Karl's human wife had been dying at the time, as Sigurd recalled. A very trying experience for the vangel who had never aged beyond age twenty-two to watch his sixty-year-old wife pass to the Other Side. Karl had recently been permitted to wed a human who'd lived in a trailer in a small town near Transylvania, Pennsylvania, where their vangel castle was located. And wasn't that a whole other story!

But Sigurd had no time for distraction. He had to continue with the introductions. "These two men are Svein and Jogeir. They will be part of the island's security force." The two men with light blond hair and fair skin that was already fading from their blood-tans in this bright sunlight, nodded but said nothing.

"And the young man over there"—he waved toward the other side of the table—"is Armod. He is a great admirer of the late Michael Jackson, as you can probably tell." The lackwit not only had his hair styled like the singer, but was wearing one sparkly white glove. With a swimsuit! In this heat! "Armod will be dancing in the nightclub program."

"Really?" Inga asked. "Marisa and I are salsa dancers back in Miami."

Sigurd turned to Marisa. "I thought you were a waitress and a massager."

Her dark eyes nigh sparked at him with irritation. "Massage therapist," she gritted out.

"Same thing." He waved a hand airily.

"Not even close. In any case, Inga and I dance *and* waitress some nights in a Miami nightclub, La Cucaracha."

He arched a brow at her. "Cockroach?"

"Yeah. You have a problem with that?"

He put both hands up in surrender. "Not a bit."

"So you understand Spanish?"

"I understand and speak many languages."

"Braggart!"

"I am what I am."

"I am what I am," she mimicked.

"Are you always so rude?"

"I am what I am," she repeated, and smiled at him in the most irksome manner.

"So you like Michael Jackson's music?" Inga asked Armod, no doubt to end his and Marisa's bickering.

"Definitely," Armod replied. "He was the king . . . of music."

"Y'all are so cute," Tiffany said. "And ya do look jist lak him, darlin'. Bet yer dancin' is good, too."

Spare me, Lord, Sigurd prayed. If there was anything that could get Armod talking, it was the subject of music . . . and dancing. Give him the slightest encouragement and he would be moonwalking around the pool. He got the crowd at a Philadelphia airport mob dancing spontaneously one time just by breaking into the song "Thriller," which hadn't thrilled his brother Vikar at all.

Immediately, an active conversation started between Tiffany, Inga, and Armod. A waiter stopped by their table, and the men ordered beers, except for Armod, who had been warned to avoid alcohol. He might be pretending to be twenty-one, but he was only sixteen (plus fifty vangel years, give or take), and not yet accustomed to the effects of hard brews. Marisa and Inga ordered bottled waters, and Tiffany got some tall, pink concoction with an umbrella on top. Armod looked longingly at the drink, but Sigurd gave him a warning look. Instead, Armod opted for a cola.

In the midst of the drinks delivery and the music conversation, Sigurd heard Tiffany ask Armod, "Can ya twerk, honey?"

Oh. My. Sorry. Soul! Sigurd felt as if he were in a minefield, never knowing where the next bomb was planted.

"Sure," Armod said.

Four sets of men's eyes turned as one to gawk at Armod. They'd all seen that Miley Cyrus singer twerking on the television set. Many times, truth to tell. Twerking involved some convoluted arse vibrating nonsense. Vangels watched a lot of television, and movies. Between missions, there wasn't much else to do when one was supposed to be leading a sinless lifestyle. Bor-ing! To a Viking, leastwise.

But he'd never seen Armod do *that*. Sigurd must have scowled his way.

"What? Anyone can twerk if they practice," Armod said defensively.

"Can ya teach me how?" Tiffany begged. "Ah have gotta learn how before mah first audition."

Sigurd wasn't about to ask why a Norse princess would have been twerking. Unless she got a bug up her arse.

"Me too," Inga said. When the men looked at her in question, she added, "Not for an audition. I just want to know how."

When Marisa didn't join in, Sigurd arched his eyebrows at her. She blushed, raised her stubborn chin, and said, "Me too."

Then she turned the tables on him, "How about you? Don't you want to learn to twerk?"

Karl, Svein, and Jogeir snickered.

"Not even a little," he responded.

"Sigurd does not like to dance, at all," Armod offered, then ducked his head when Sigurd scowled, again. The boy talked too much.

Time for a change of subject.

"So tell me about this party Harry is holding tonight," Sigurd said to Marisa.

But it was Tiffany who answered. "It's being held on Mr. Goldman's yacht. A really big yacht named *Brass Balls*." Giggle, giggle. "Everyone who's anyone at this conference will be there." Giggle, giggle. "Y'all hafta come. Do ya want me ta talk ta Harry, and see if he'll invite y'all?"

"No thank you. I don't need a special invitation."

"Party crashing?" Marisa snarked.

He shrugged. "If necessary. Why are you going to this event, Marisa? Have I not told you to avoid the man like a foul fjord flatfish."

"You are not my protector, Sigurd. You aren't even—"

"Yes, I am. I am your fiancé. Remember. We should get a ring."

She said a nasty word rarely uttered by women in his acquaintance. At least she didn't tell him what he could do with a ring. He could tell that she wanted to. "Why don't you go do some doctoring stuff?" she suggested.

"I've been working since I got here. I have done enough STD tests for a lifetime. Did you know some people put tattoos down . . . Never mind. STDs are sexually transmitted diseases."

"I know what STDs are," she groused.

He tilted his head in question.

"Not from personal experience." More blushes.

"I've treated two sunstrokes and three second-degree sunburns. Gave a pain pill to a woman with an abscessed tooth. Refused pain pills for five others who figured I would be their drug supplier while they buzzed through the conference. I also splinted a broken ankle for some lackwit trying to impress the ladies on a high diving board. And removed a fish-hook from a woman's breast. Don't ask."

"Ah got a crawfish bite on my butt one time," Tiffany offered. When everyone looked at her in question, she explained. "Mah ex-boyfriend Bubba and me was catchin' mudbugs on the bayou. In the nude. Ah slipped, and one them critters just took a big ol' bite. Bubba laughed and tol' all his friends. Dumb as a bayou stump, Bubba was, bless his ol' redneck heart, but Ah dumped his sorry behind faster'n he could say Dixie, and that was the las' time Ah went crawfishin', nude, anyways."

She smiled at them all as if this happened to everyone once in a while.

Not so much! Marisa turned back to Sigurd. "Why don't you just go back to Johns Hopkins?"

"I can't."

"Fired, huh?"

"I go where I am sent," he said. Another slip on his part.

Suddenly suspicious, she leaned closer, and Sigurd gasped with dismay. No longer was she perspiring the scent of honey and tart ginger. There was another scent altogether. Lemons!

"Marisa! What have you done?"

She frowned in confusion.

"Either you have committed some great sin, or are about to," he declared.

A rosy color seeped into her cheeks once again, and she raised her chin defiantly. He liked that he could make her blush.

"I don't know what you're talking about."

She knew, all right. "Liar," he whispered.

And more alarming, it meant there was a Lucie presence somewhere on the island. He tilted her chin to the side. Yes, there was a small bite mark there. She had to have already been contemplating some mortal sin, or a Lucie wouldn't have bothered biting her. Demon vampires were not interested in pure humans, not worth the effort. But the Lucie must have been interrupted. He would be back, though, probably at the moment of her surrender to the great sin.

"You've been fa—, uh, bitten," he said. "Come back to my office in the hotel, and I will ... uh, treat it."

"It's only a mosquito bite. Jeesh!"

"Even mosquito bites can get infected."

"I am not going to your office." She laughed. "Next you'll be suggesting that you do an STD test on me."

A slow grin crept over his lips. He couldn't help himself.

"You aren't getting within touching distance of ..." The rose in her cheeks got rosier. " ... my girl parts."

We shall see, he thought, then immediately gazed upward. *Just jesting*.

But that settled it. He would have to stick to her like glue—celestial glue—until he either redeemed her, or she went to the other side. He shuttered to think what a prize she would be for Jasper and his minions.

But then, she asked the oddest things.

"I don't suppose you own a yacht?"

He shook his head slowly.

"An airplane?"

He shook his head more, frowning at her question.

"Have your own medical clinic?"

If he did, he would hardly be on this wacky island at this wacky conference.

She had both hands folded, prayer-like, under her chin. "Are you a billionaire? Or even a millionaire?"

Ah! He saw where she was going now. Wealth was her forbidden fruit.

"No," he said bluntly, although he could gain riches in a trice, if he wanted to, or Mike allowed him to.

"Too bad," she said, and stood. "Too damn bad," she repeated before walking away.

The scent of lemons was almost overpowering in her wake. Tiffany hobbled after her in her high shoes, and his men left to prepare for a conference call with his brothers.

"Don't be so hard on Marisa," Inga said to him when they were alone. "She's under a lot of stress."

"Are we not all?"

"Not like her. She has a daughter with a growing brain tumor who will die without a certain operation."

An oddly unpleasant thought occurred to him. "I did not know she was married."

"She's not." Inga glared at him as if he was making a judgment about Marisa's morals.

"I am not the moral police," he said. *Just an angel on the lookout for immoral folks.* "I am just trying to gather all the facts."

"Why?"

"Truth to tell, I am not certain." He considered what Inga had told him and conjectured, "Her daughter is dying and needs an operation. Let me guess. It is a very expensive operation. How much?"

"One hundred and seventy thousand. In a hurry. Well, she's already raised almost a hundred thousand through various fund-raising projects. Another seventy thousand is needed."

"And she expects to earn that much waitressing and massaging for a week or so on this island?"

"It's a start," Inga said, her eyes not meeting his.

"Ah!" Now he understood. This island was like a

Garden of Eden, and Marisa's apple had a name. Harry Goldman.

Not if he could help it!

The only question was, what role did Sigurd play in that garden? Adam or the snake?

But then, an ever more troubling question entered his mind. What if Marisa was the apple, and Sigurd was the one being tempted? It would be just like Mike to try to trip him up.

Hah! He was stronger than that.

He hoped.

Chapter 8

Zing went her heart again . . .

Marisa, Inga, Tiffany, and Doris were sitting in the large hotel ballroom, along with two hundred or so new employees, listening to an indoctrination lecture.

And indoctrination it surely was.

Banners and badges proclaimed the conference theme: "FOE Proud!" Sample TV spots ran on video monitors along the sides. There was even a music video that was loud if nothing else.

"I wonder if they realize that the public will think FOE stands for the postal service's 'forwarding order expired,'" Marisa whispered to Inga.

"Hah! These folks are delusional," Inga whispered back. "The PR director, Mitzi Dolan, told me that the pornography movement will go down in history comparable to the civil rights movement."

"They better not mention that to the NAACP."

A woman sitting in front of them turned and said, "Shh!" She was taking notes, for heaven's sake. But then Doris, on Marisa's other side, was taking notes, too.

When Marisa tried to read what she'd written, Doris glared at her and covered her words with a forearm.

Touch-y!

Martin Vanderfelt, dressed to the gills in white slacks, a Hawaiian shirt, and docksiders, stood at the podium, where he had been lecturing them for almost an hour. His pristine white hair and mustache gleamed against his already deeply tanned face. He was an impressive cheerleader for pornography, even though they weren't supposed to use that word.

"You will find two 'FOE Proud!' badges in your folders. Wear them proudly . . . ha, ha, ha . . . at all times. The second one is a replacement in the event you lose the first one. Some folks have done that already."

More like lost them deliberately.

"You'll want to wear them when you get home, too, or give them to friends as souvenirs." Harry smiled winningly.

Does he really believe his own hype?

Probably.

"Folks, sexual freedom is alive and flourishing," Vanderfelt announced. "Last year there were more than four million websites catering to men's, and women's, freedom-to-choose sexual palates. In fact, almost a hundred million people visited adult sites last year. That's half of all the superhighway travelers. Who says adult entertainment is dead?"

Loud applause greeted his words.

Like smut cheerleaders, they all were.

"We have Larry Flynt of *Hustler* magazine to thank for all this," Vanderfelt said with dubious reverence, waving a hand to encompass the crowd and the hotel gathering. "Larry was pioneering for freedom of expression in adult entertainment before anyone ever heard of the phrase. And he suffered for his efforts." Vanderfelt bowed his head for emphasis.

Murmurs of agreement rippled through the sheep-like crowd.

He was referring to Flynt having taken a bullet from some nutcase outside a courthouse in Georgia where he'd been fighting one of his numerous battles and had been wheelchair bound ever since. St. Larry of Smut.

"Now, on to the agenda."

Marisa and Inga weren't the only ones to groan.

"No one, and I repeat no one, is to speak to the press. If you are approached by a reporter, direct them to Mitzi." He nodded to the young woman sitting behind him on the dais. Mitzi, who resembled a young Rosie O'Donnell, looked as if she would like to punch Harry a good one. Marisa suspected he'd been passing off any uncomfortable problems on her.

"I thought there weren't supposed to be any news media here on the island," one man yelled out.

"There aren't," Harry said, "but they're sneaky bastards . . . excuse my language. I don't doubt that some will try to slither in. They might even be sitting amongst us now. And you just know they'll portray us as less than the professionals we are."

Marisa glanced quickly at Doris, who said emphatically, "Not me."

"Another thing," Harry said, followed by more groans. "Please give our celebrities here some space." He nodded toward the front row where Becky, Lance, and a dozen other actors and actresses sat.

"Don't ask them for autographs, or approach them about your own careers. Same is true of the directors and producers," Vanderfelt went on.

He is delusional. That's why half the folks are here.

"There will be plenty of opportunity for that the last day of the conference when they can sign videos or posters for you."

Or body parts.

Tiffany raised her hand, and Marisa and Inga sank down in their seats. She asked in her pure Southern accent, "Mistah Vanderfelt, suh, what if they approach us?"

"That would be different," Harry conceded as his face turned red. Clearly, he wasn't going to ask Tiffany what she meant by "approach."

"Imagine that," Inga said. "Someone in the porno industry blushing."

"Now who's being sarcastic?" Marisa whispered to Inga, who had been harping at her for being so cynical all the time.

"If you'll check over the schedule of workshops and events in your folders," Harry continued, "you will get an idea of the times when your particular jobs may begin and end. For example, breakfast in the communal dining room begins at seven a.m. and ends at eight-thirty, with workshops starting at nine. Lunch from noon to one, followed by more workshops and conference events until four. Dinner from five to midnight."

Marisa read over some of the workshop titles: "How to Profit from Erotic Home Videos."

Apparently, erotic is okay. Porno is not.

"Is Anything Taboo?"

God, I hope so.

"So You've Invented a New Sex Toy?"

Marisa tried to picture some dumb everyday guy trying to talk his wife into experimenting with his crazy device on her sensitive parts, and cringed.

"Investing in Sensual Entertainment."

Add sensual to the list of okay words for porno.

If Marisa had the cash, pornography was the last place she would put it.

"To Wax or Not to Wax. (Demonstrations Optional)."

Okay, this is really going too far.

"Fifty Shades of New Sex."

Enough with the Fifty Shades already!

"Bondage in the Bedroom."

Marisa's mind had been wandering. Harry had been continuing to talk. He said now, "You all can break up into your separate groups now, by employment. Good luck and have fun."

The crowd applauded and began to stand and stretch, looking around for signs proclaiming their particular work descriptions. Household maintenance. Landscaping. Restaurant services. Lifeguards. Security. Electronics. Health spa. Beauty salon. Etc.

"See you later," she and Inga said to Tiffany and Doris, who went off in opposite directions.

"I'll go with you to the restaurant group, then head over to the spa one," Marisa told Inga, who couldn't stop giggling at everything they heard and saw.

As they passed the medical group, Marisa burst out laughing.

Sigurd appeared to be arguing with a nurse. Whether she was an actual nurse, or someone hoping to get a video role as a nurse, she had dressed to fit both parts. A white nurse's uniform cut so high on her thighs that Never Never Land would be exposed if she bent over even a little bit. Her well-endowed bosom was barely contained, with the top unbuttoned down to her abdomen. An old-fashioned nurse's cap sat on mile-high, teased blonde hair. She wore five-inch, white, stripper high heels. Bloodred lips matched her bloodred nails. She had piercings in her eyebrows, nose, lip, and God only knew where else.

"I can so give shots," she heard the woman whine.

"With those nails? You would pierce a patient's skin from twenty paces."

"I'll have you know, these sculptured nails cost me five hundred dollars. No way am I cutting them!"

"They breed germs, you lackwit."

"Do not! I'm gonna tell Mr. Vanderfelt on you."

"Feel free."

Sigurd was dressed for the part, too. Blue scrubs enhanced his clear blue eyes. *Had he been in surgery? Or was he just playing a part?* His blond hair was held off his face with a rubber band at the nape. He had both hands on slim hips, and white bootied feet covered his shoes.

The man was drop-dead, be-still-my-heart gorgeous.

An old rock tune bounced in Marisa's brain and she thought with what was probably hysterical irrelevance, *This "Doctor, Doctor" can give me "the news" anytime he wants.*

What news? This is silly. When was the last time Marisa had felt such an overwhelming attraction to a man?

Probably when she'd succumbed to Chip's pleas in college and ended up pregnant. No, even then, when her hormones had been humming like drunken bees, Marisa hadn't felt like this. The sensation of her blood heating and zinging to all the intimate parts of her body both frightened and exhilarated her.

Oooh, I am in big trouble.

Sigurd glanced up at that moment, noticed her perusal, and shrugged.

Zing!

The news was not good. Not for a woman with a sick child who needed to focus.

He winked at her then.

Double zing.

The zings stopped when she got her first look at the Phoenix waitress uniforms. Little black nylon, form-fitting dresses that ended high on the thigh and were unbuttoned on top practically down to the wide red belt. Worn with red high heels. Even worse was the white tank-top bodysuits that spa employees were expected to wear. Also worn with the red high heels, which seemed to be standard issue foot attire for the women employees at the conference!

When she protested, the restaurant manager said, cold as ice, "Wear it or go home."

The spa director, Hedwig or Hedy Meyer as Eleanor had mentioned on her initial interview, was a little kinder. Hedy was a no-nonsense, business-like, burgundy-haired (dyed, of course) German woman of middle years. With the shoulders of a linebacker and a flat-chested, muscled body (her biceps were remarkable for a woman), the bodysuit made her look more like an oversize gymnast than a masseuse.

"Wear Band-Aids and a G-string and no one will know you're not completely naked under the silly thing."

If this was what it took to earn extra money for her daughter's operation, Marisa was beginning to think that Harry Goldman was looking better and better.

There was a definite stink in the air, and it wasn't the ocean breeze . . .

Sigurd had called for a meeting in his hotel office late that afternoon. His five men sat in folding chairs around the small room, and he had Vikar on the speakerphone.

Sigurd gave Vikar a description of this bizarre event and its bizarre attendees, including his last patient of the day. A man who had an industrial-size bolt in his scrotum.

The men in the room winced and Vikar asked, "How could that happen? Was he working on some construction job? No, I cannot imagine any circumstance where that could occur. Although . . . remember Olaf Dimwit who managed to get a splinter the size of a lance stuck in his buttocks one time when he was swiving an energetic maid on his longship?"

"Remember? Remember? I was called to remove it. He bled like a stuck pig and cried like a babe for fear my knife would slip and cut his favorite body bits."

They all smiled at that.

"A man asked me today if I ever use my bristly haircut to enhance my sex partner's pleasure," Karl told them then.

"Have you?" Jogeir asked.

Karl gave Jogeir a jab in the upper arm. Being newly re-wed after an exceedingly long period of celibacy, Karl would likely do just about anything. "No, but I am always open to new ideas."

"That is nothing," interjected Svein. "When I was patrolling the beach, a woman was sunbathing. Nude. As I got closer, she spread her legs wide, and I saw that she was bare as a plucked chicken down there."

"Waxing. Modern women do that. Betimes with unusual patterns," Armod explained. "A landing strip. Stars. Half moons. Diamonds."

All four of them gaped at Armod, whom Sigurd could swear hadn't seen a woman's private parts in fifty years.

"There was a special on one of those women's cable television shows. I was flipping channels looking for music programs."

"Special?" Sigurd choked out.

"On the history of female waxing. Truth to tell, it started in the 1960s with the beginning of pornographic videos," Armod elaborated, "when, for the first time, female private parts were being seen up close like."

"How come I don't ever see those shows?" Jogeir complained.

"Because you much prefer war movies," Armod pointed out.

Vikar made a coughing noise over the speakerphone. You could be sure he would be repeating this conversation to his wife, Alex. Not to mention his brothers. "We're getting off the subject here. Give me an update, Sig, and I'll pass it on to the others. Mike is bugging me to find out what you have accomplished thus far."

"*What?* I've been here less than a day. What does he expect me to . . . ?" He inhaled and exhaled for patience and gave his report. "There are evil men and women on this island. Whether that is due to Lucie influence or their own bad acts, I cannot say for sure. Perhaps it is just that this type of sordid event attracts sordid people."

"And Lucies?" Vikar prodded.

Sigurd nodded, as if his brother could see him. "They are here. I smelled and saw evidence on one human, and where there is one Lucie there are bound to be others."

"At the least, you five can attempt to redeem those sinners who make the choice to repent, whilst searching out Jasper's minions," Vikar mused.

Actually, vangels didn't go out seeking sinners in general to save. That was a job for priests and theologians. If they did approach any sinner they came upon, that's all they would ever have time to do. Suffice it to say, sinners flourished in this new world. No, vangels were to go after those who had been targeted by the Lucies.

"I will send more vangels when needed," Vikar added. "Hmm. Now that I think on it, I will send them, anyway. For a certainty, if there is such an aura of evil as you describe, the Lucies will consider it prime hunting ground."

Sigurd agreed.

"I heard an alarming rumor," Jogeir interjected. "There is a boat coming tomorrow with prostitutes. Sex trafficking. They will be provided to sate the perverted tastes of some of the men . . . and women, I suppose."

Sigurd frowned. "I cannot imagine why they would do that with the news media watching their activities."

"They will probably keep them out on the water, on one of yachts," Jogeir guessed. "International waters, no laws being broken. Pimps, especially these big-scale operators, find ways to avoid arrest, especially of clients with money and a preference for children."

"That is a vile practice," Karl said, summing up the opinion of them all.

Armod looked particularly disturbed, having been subject to just such evil as a young boy. Karl reached over and squeezed his forearm in understanding.

"I will kill them with my bare hands," Armod vowed, his fangs emerging long and deadly.

"No, Armod, you will follow my directions. No hasty actions that will call attention to us vangels," Sigurd said, then softened his tone. "Do not worry. You will have your opportunity to avenge yourself on these miscreants, but only in the proper vangel manner."

Armod nodded reluctantly.

After they concluded their meeting, Sigurd said to the others, "So, anyone want to party tonight?" He explained about Harry Goldman and the yacht festivities.

Armod had dance rehearsals. The others claimed job duties as well.

Thus it was that Sigurd was alone when he teletransported himself that evening out to the yacht. For a while, he just prowled about, admiring the fine workmanship. Teak woods. Brass fittings. Sleek lines. Sigurd loved boats. All kinds, but especially oceangoing vessels.

Sigurd had to admit, he envied Harry this fine specimen. Why did evil men such as Harry get such prizes while he worked away, endlessly, for a greater good? It wasn't fair. It just wasn't.

It was a useless question, the type he avoided under normal circumstances. Envy would ever be his bane.

His distraction caused him to miss the fact that he was not alone on the lower deck. And the first "person" he encountered was one of Jasper's mungs. No one else was about.

It didn't look like a mung, at first. Instead, Sigurd saw a tall, handsome man in white dinner jacket, silk shirt, bow tie, and black pants. Immediately, they sensed each other for what they were, and with a hiss the mung morphed into its true demonic form.

There was a hierarchy in the Lucipire society: the elite haakai, mungs, and then Jasper's foot soldiers, the imps and hordlings. Mungs were big creatures, often more than seven feet tall, and like the other demons, had scales, claw-like hands, red eyes, fangs, and a whopping big tail, which they could swish like a deadly weapon. In addition, mungs oozed poisonous slime, or mung; thus they were aptly named. This character was all that and more. Sometimes mungs were mute. Not so in this case.

"Vangel!" it hissed and gnashed its teeth. "You are mine!"

"I do not think so, beast!"

Lucies hated to be called "beast," and this one growled with outrage, rising even taller. "Sinner!" it howled.

Vangels hated to be called sinners, although that was precisely what they were. Why else would they be vangels? But somehow, being called "sinner" by a Lucipire put them in the same repulsive class.

Sigurd's fangs elongated with a shssshing sound, and he could feel the bloodlust of a warrior race through his body, giving him extra-human strength. One of the vangels back at the Transylvania castle was an experienced tailor. Sigurd was wearing one of Calvin's specially designed sports coats with unique, hidden interior pockets and loops. Vangels almost always wore jackets, or loose-layered shirts, or even cloaks to hide their arsenals, everything from knives to guns.

Faster than a blink he had a throwing star in one hand and a long-bladed knife in the other. At the press of a button, the knife became a sword, a switchblade sword, to be precise, that had been invented by a vangel who'd been a blacksmith in another lifetime. Both weapons had been treated with the symbolic blood of the Lord. They'd been hidden under his jacket.

The mung lunged for him with its own weapon raised high—a heavy broadsword like those once used by Vikings and Saxon knights alike. Sigurd side-stepped and the mung's blade cut deep into a wood railing. If the demon had managed to hit Sigurd, he would have been cleaved from head to belly.

Vangels felt the same physical pains as humans did, but they could recover almost miraculously from the most dire wounds, ones that would prove fatal to humans. But some injuries could not be reversed, such as a split skull. Those vangels who died before their time went to Tranquility, which was a holding place similar to Purgatory, where they would await the final Judgment Day.

While the mung attempted to yank the sword up

and out of the wood, Sigurd aimed a sharp-pointed star for the back of its head. A blow that would render it dead, if not immediately, eventually, but that was not good enough. Unless Sigurd pierced its heart, the demon would resurrect itself later and come back in Lucipire form.

Angry at having been thwarted, the Mung abandoned the broadsword and went for Sigurd with outstretched claws and fangs that were at least four inches long, oozing mung.

A mistake, thank the Lord! That position gave Sigurd the opportunity to thrust his sword up and into the beast's heart, but not before it had swiped the side of Sigurd's face. Immediately, the Lucipire began to dissolve into a pool of slime, leaving behind only its clothing and a shiny, expensive-looking watch that had no doubt been pilfered from one of the party guests.

"Hey, what's going on here?" a voice yelled from behind Sigurd.

Immediately, he retracted his sword and tucked it and the throwing star into his hidden, interior jacket pockets. And he made sure his fangs were retracted before turning to see what must be one of the waiters coming toward him. He wore black pants, a white shirt, and a red bow tie. His name tag said "Barry Hinton."

"Some dude just hurled his guts out. You better not get too close," Sigurd warned.

"Phew! That stinks. I'll have to get maintenance. I'm not touching that crap."

Sigurd nodded and stepped away from the mess.

Barry frowned. "Why are those clothes sitting in the middle of the barf?"

"The idiot was knee-walking drunk. Said something about being hot. Took off his clothes and then hurled. I couldn't get around him."

"Where is he now? Oh no! Did he go overboard? These drunks are a hazard to themselves. Oh shit, shit, shit!" The waiter looked as if he might very well do just that in his own pants.

Quickly, Sigurd told him, "No! He ran away . . . rather staggered away . . . in that direction." He pointed to the area opposite from which the waiter had approached. "He said something about needing to piss."

"Why didn't he just piss over the railing? Never mind. I'll let security take over." Hinton narrowed his eyes at Sigurd. "What are you doing down here? It's for employees only."

"I was looking for a men's room. The one on the upper deck had a line outside."

"That's what happens when the booze flows. There's a men's room over there." He pointed to the left. "Then you better get back to the party."

"Right."

"Hey, bud, your face is bleeding. Did you know that?" Barry was looking suspicious again.

"Cat scratched me," Sigurd lied.

"Here? On the boat?" Barry asked incredulously.

"No. Back on the island. I thought it had stopped bleeding." He put a hand to his cheek and shivered. "I hate cats."

"Me too." Barry grinned and waved him off.

With a sigh of relief, Sigurd went into the small room, locked the door, and washed his face and hands. The scratches on his face were not deep. In fact, they would be healed before the night was over. But he had to make sure there was no poisonous mung in the cuts.

He called his brother Vikar on his secure cell then. "Hey, Vikar! Sigurd here. I just erased a Lucie."

"What was it?"

"A young mung."

"Only one?"

"So far."

"They are definitely on the island then."

"Yes, but this was out on a yacht called *Brass Balls*."

Vikar laughed at that name. "Those idiots definitely have that."

"I'm going to the upper deck now. I'll investigate and let you know if I see more. Still, you better send backup."

Sigurd had an alarming thought then. If there were Lucies on board, and if Marisa had been fanged even slightly as he suspected, her scent would lure the demon to complete the job. A fate worse than death because the human sinner would then go not to Heaven or Hell, or those other holding places, like Purgatory or Limbo or Tranquility, but become a Lucipire for eternity.

Ending his call, Sigurd was on the upper deck in a flash and found Marisa almost immediately. Talking to that evil person, Harry Goldman. She was wearing a red strapless dress.

How is the damn thing being held up? Oh. Oh!

The dress ended mid-thigh . . .

I am not thinking about what is only a few inches higher. No, I am not. But I am imagining.

. . . leaving miles of legs and shoulders exposed.

Is her skin actually sparkling? Yes! She must have sprinkled herself with crystal dust. I wonder if it is edible.

Her hair was upswept, baring her nape, like a Lucie, or vangel, target.

Mayhap she would not notice if I just dropped a fly-by lick on the curve where shoulder meets neck. And just the tiniest bite.

She wore black strappy high-heeled shoes, making her a half head taller than Goldman.

A perfect fit for me. For talking. I do not have to crick my neck to speak with her. That is the only fit I was imagin-

ing, just in case someone up there is listening to me. Not that someone up there ever listens, when I want someone up there to listen. Aaarrgh!.

On her lips was crimson lip paint, which should have appeared garish but was not.

More like licksome. I wonder if it tastes like cherries, or strawberries. Or, God forbid, sweet apples.

In essence, she looked like sin on a silver platter.

And he was a sinner.

Alas and alack, the voice in his head said, *She is not on your menu, Viking.*

Chapter 9

Hobnobbing with the in crowd . . .

Despite the circumstances, Marisa was having a good time.

The boat was luxurious.

Okay, revision here. Remember, do not call a yacht a boat. I've been corrected on that point enough already. Like it matters! Men and their . . . boats!

The champagne fizzed cool and delicious on the tongue.

It's wasted on me, though. I would be just as happy with an icy diet soda.

Waiters carrying gold-plated trays offered appetizers, everything from mini black truffle bruschettas to beluga caviar on toast points.

Can anyone say "doggie bag"?

The music played by a small jazz combo provided a soft backdrop.

Salsa, people! Haven't you ever heard of salsa?

She hadn't expected such a sophisticated gathering of roughly seventy-five guests. The movers and shakers of the porn industry. Even Harry, whom she'd been talking to as he networked among the crowd, was looking nice in what had to be a hand-tailored tux.

Nice, but still old. For me, she thought. *Well, age doesn't matter . . . shouldn't matter . . . if it gains me my daughter Izzie's life-saving operation.*

I am not really considering this . . . thing.

Oh yes, I am.

She had to give Harry credit. He was acting super polite toward her. Host-like. Not at all pushy as he'd been earlier. *Maybe I misinterpreted his actions. Maybe he's not even interested in me* that way.

"Nice party," she told him.

"I'm glad you're enjoying yourself. Shall I introduce you to some of my guests?"

"No, I'd rather just mingle on my own." She glanced around at the teak walls and crystal chandelier. "I love your b— yacht."

His eyes lit up, then drifted half closed in a slow, deliberate perusal of her body. He probably thought he looked sexy doing so. "Would you like a tour?"

Tour, schmore! He's interested, all right. The devious old pervert is up to something. Although I suppose old man/ young woman isn't really a perversion. It's been going on forever. Even in the Bible, for heaven's sake. Though, for the sake of accuracy, the Good Book doesn't condone illicit, out-of-wedlock activities. Jeesh! My brain is splintering apart with all these speculations. "Maybe some other time. I can't stay much longer. Got to get up early for work tomorrow." They'd been at the party for more than an hour already. Boats were available to take anyone back to the hotel at any time.

"Do you have to? Work, I mean?"

"Definitely."

"I could help . . ." His words trailed off as he seemed to realize it was too soon for what he might have been going to propose. "How about dinner tomorrow night?"

"I work at the Phoenix Restaurant during the dinner hour."

He barely controlled a twitch of frustration. "A late dinner? Here on my yacht?"

"Not tomorrow."

The expression on his face was almost hostile before he masked it over with a shrug of acceptance.

"Perhaps another night?" she suggested. By then, she might have made up her mind to do . . . whatever.

"Definitely," he said, leaning up to kiss her on the cheek before moving on to talk to a man she recognized as a famous Hollywood movie director. Clinton Farentino. Maybe he was considering a move to "art" films.

The hot topic of conversation throughout was how the porn industry was moving its physical operations, lock, stock, and beds, from California to Las Vegas because of a new Los Angeles voter-approved regulation requiring male actors to wear condoms. Supposedly the number of permits to make porn films in Los Angeles County had declined by more than ninety-five percent since the law was passed.

Someone, she couldn't recall who, had told her tonight that there were four thousand to eleven thousand porn films made in the U.S. every year. *Yikes!* And despite the decline in the sale of home videos, almost fifty million people watched porn on the Internet on a regular basis. *Double yikes!* Obviously, if she hadn't known it before, she did now: Porn was big business. No wonder people like Harry with legitimate business success were turning to smut.

She scanned the room and noticed Dr. Sig chatting with Becky Bliss and some outrageously good-looking guy wearing a tuxedo with a Blue Devils baseball cap.

Was the brown-haired stud yet another adult film actor? If he wasn't, he could be. In fact, he would be a hit in regular films, as well, based on his appearance alone. Both men could. Brad Pitt and Alexander Skarsgård had nothing on them.

She'd seen the two men arrive with Becky earlier. She wasn't sure if Sigurd or Blue Devil was her date. *Maybe they all came together. A threesome?* In this crowd, she shouldn't be surprised, but she was.

Becky was talking a mile a minute, and both men were just listening, bored expressions on their faces. How bored could any man be with the queen, rather princess of erotica as his date? Especially wearing that white silk gown that showed her lack of underwear every time she moved. Well, it was none of Marisa's business.

Inga was in a group with Tiffany and Lance. They'd practically had to use a shoehorn to help Tiffany get into the pink rhinestone, deep-cleavaged sheath. In fact, Tiffany had lain down on the bed, face first, while Doris straddled her hips and held the sides together so that Marisa and Inga could tug up the zipper. If Tiffany was planning on getting lucky with Lance, he'd have to cut the dress off.

Though luck was in the eyes of the beholder, Marisa mused, finding the male porn star's sexuality too blatant. The torpedo he sported between his legs, even in a tux, was alarming, especially if it was in a relaxed state. *I cannot believe I am thinking about the guy's anatomy. On the other hand, someone else's anatomy, that I could understand. And I don't mean Harry Goldman. Vikings and longboats came to mind.*

Shaking her head to rid it of such unwelcome thoughts, Marisa watched Inga, who was holding her own in a knockoff Valentino beaded peacock chiffon dress and color-coordinated Jimmy Choo stilettos.

Truth to tell, Inga was in her element. The quintessential party girl.

Marisa, not looking too shabby herself in a simple red Alexander McQueen sheath, made deliberate eye contact with her friend. She and Inga had long had an agreement that when they went to parties together, they always stayed within eye contract. It was a nasty fact of life that drinks could be spiked, even in the safest groups.

Indicating with a hand motion that she was stepping outside for a moment, Marisa set her champagne glass down on a table and walked out onto the open deck where the evening air was balmy and sweet. The sound of the combo, which had moved on to old classics of the Frank Sinatra era, became fainter. Off in the distance, she heard a splash. Probably some fish jumping for a quick meal of bugs or smaller fish. Or maybe it was a shark. Nah. The only sharks in these waters were the ones inside the yacht.

Leaning against the rail, she was startled when Sigurd came up to stand beside her. "You" was all she said.

"Me."

"Did you crash or were you invited?"

"What do you think?"

What she thought was this man was too good-looking for her well-being. He wore black slacks, a white shirt unbuttoned at the collar, and a black sport coat. His blond hair hung loose to his shoulders, except for two thin braids that framed either side of his face . . . braids that were interwoven with blue crystal beads the exact color of his pale eyes. And he smelled wonderful . . . that scent she'd noticed before, evergreen with oranges. He couldn't convince her that it wasn't his cologne.

"I think you came riding on Becky Bliss's coattails."

"Coat?" He shook his head. "Tail, yes. Though I wouldn't quite say 'riding.'"

"That was crude."

"Yes, it was. Sinners have that effect on me."

"Sinners? Aren't you being a bit judgmental?"

He shrugged and idly ran a fingertip along her shoulder. Well, not so idle. He put that fingertip between his lips and sucked.

Holy hormones! She would have smacked his hand, but his action had been so unexpected and quickly over, and her lady parts were jumpstarting into gear. Va-room, va-room.

He made a face of distaste, and licked his lips to rid them of the remaining sparkles, then rubbed a forefinger over his bottom lip to see if it was all gone. They weren't.

"Are you crazy?"

"'Twould seem so."

"Why did you do that?"

"Do what?"

"Lick my Sparkle Sprinkles."

"You . . . they . . . looked edible. Call it curiosity!"

"Call it disgusting. What if these Sparkle Sprinkles are poisonous?"

"Why would you wear something poisonous?" He was looking at his sparkled forefinger as if it might explode.

"What would you do if I . . ." She'd been going to ask what he'd do if she licked his finger . . . or his lips where there were indeed still a few sparkles. *Slow down, girl. We are not off to the races today.* She stopped herself from completing the sentence just in time.

Somehow, he knew, though.

"I would probably swoon with delight," he said. Then added that odd expression that she'd noticed him use before, "For my sins. I wonder if Satan invented Sparking Sprinkles to tempt sinners, such as me?"

"Sparkle Sprinkles," she corrected.

"Whatever." He sniffed the air, then leaned closer and sniffed some more.

As if she smelled! *Is it my perfume? No, I forgot to bring perfume.*

With a grunt of disgust, he took her by the hand and dragged over to a dark corner of the deck, under an overhang.

"Let me go!" she protested, but he had her backed up against a wall and not with any lascivious intent, either. The expression on his face was stone-cold serious.

"I need to bite you, Marisa," he said.

That was the last thing she'd expected him to say. She was shocked.

"No, no, do not struggle. 'Tis for your own good."

"For my own good," she sputtered. "You *are* crazy. Let go of me, at once, or I'm going to scream my head off."

She opened her mouth to do just that, but he laid his lips over hers to halt her protests. And any inclination she had to struggle died a quick death of molten, wet heat, emanating from their joined lips and ricocheting to all her extremities and some interesting places in between.

A groan of raw hunger, low in his throat, caused a mirroring groan from deep inside her, and she wrapped her arms around his wide shoulders. Needing no further invitation, he tugged her even closer, one hand behind her neck, the other under her butt, moving himself into the cradle of her hips, giving her a message, loud and clear, or was that hard and insistent, of just how much he wanted her. And, oh my goodness, did she want him, too!

Never, in all her life, had she been so aroused by a man. Not so quickly. Not so strongly.

The kiss seemed to go on forever as he slanted his

open mouth over hers, this way and that, seeking the perfect fit. And when he found it, his tongue teased hers with slow, sensuous, in-and-out forays of taste.

At one point, he whispered into her ear, "You have done something bad, Marisa."

"No," she whimpered, too mindless to be annoyed at his suggestion.

"Then you are contemplating something bad." He wet the side of her neck with a wide swath of his tongue and placed his teeth against the moist skin.

She could swear she felt the imprint of his fangy incisors. "Just contemplating," she admitted. "Not decided yet."

"Let me take a little of your blood," he murmured seductively, even as his left palm massaged her buttocks . . . *Thank heavens, I'm wearing a thong* . . . and the right hand caressed the skin of one arm, from one ear, over shoulder, to elbow and back again, causing all the fine hairs on her exposed flesh to stand on end. Wanting more. Much more.

Then he gave it to her.

The right hand homed in on her breasts. Just a brush of his knuckles. *Thank heavens, I'm not wearing a bra.* Any blood left in her head shot down to her chest, and she felt her knees buckle.

He caught her, promising in a sexy whisper against her ear, accompanied by a nip of the lobe, "I can remove the temptation."

"I bet you could," she murmured, arching her body even closer to his, "but I like the temptation."

He chuckled, and pinched her behind. "Not *that* temptation."

"Aren't you tempted?" She tipped her head back, still in his tight embrace, to see his expression.

He made a deliberate attempt to close his lips—lips that were bruised from her kisses, she noted with inordinate pleasure—over his teeth where those two fangy incisors were prominent once again. How was it that they came and went? "If you only knew, sweetling! If you only knew!" he said on a moan.

He leaned in then and proved just how much he was tempted. With a growl, he kissed her deeply, so deeply she could barely breathe, and didn't want to. He seemed to be taking in enough oxygen for them both.

Is he actually breathing into my mouth even as he deep kisses me? Talk about multitasking!

Did I just suck on his tongue?

Through her lust-infused brain blur, she heard a male voice call out, "Hey, buddy!"

Sigurd went immediately stiff. No, not that kind of stiff, which he'd already been. Stiff all over.

"Where you hiding, Sig my friend? Do not think you can schluff that blonde lackbrain off on me."

"Schluff?" Sigurd groaned against her ear.

"Schluff, as in 'take her off your hands.' She actually asked me the size of my . . ." The man in the tux and Blue Devils baseball cap walked closer, then halted when he saw Marisa. "Whoa!"

Sigurd didn't turn around, but pressed himself tighter against her, as if in protection.

From what? First, he wants to keep me away from Dirty Harry, and now from a tuxedo-clad guy in a baseball cap.

"Get lost, Zeb," Sigurd gritted out.

"Not a chance! I did not know vangels were allowed to do *that*. All the more incentive for me to join the good team!" Instead of leaving, the man propped himself against a nearby rail, arms folded, ankles crossed, and smiled. He, too, had little pointy incisors.

Is it a club they all belong to where everyone has to file down their teeth? Hey, men do dumber things than that all the time. Think tattoos and bolts in unlikely places. And women are just as dumb. Can anyone say "Brazil wax"?

*Has to be a man who thought up that one, but women were
brain dead enough to agree.*

Just then, there was a female scream from inside the
party room, followed by a male voice, probably Harry
Goldman, yes, it was Harry, shouting, "Doctor! Where
the hell's that doctor?" Everyone seemed to be talking
or yelling at the same time.

Sigurd immediately rushed away from her, heading toward the commotion, but he stopped at the door
and pointed a finger at Blue Devil. "Do not dare lay a
finger on her."

Blue Devil—Zeb, Sigurd had called him—tipped
his hat at Sigurd, then held out a hand for Marisa so
that they could go inside and see what was happening. She ignored the hand but did follow after him.
There was something about him that made her uncomfortable. And not in the same way that lots of
men at this conference made her feel. He was kind of
woo-woo scary.

A man was lying on the floor, either dead or unconscious. It was Clinton Farentino, the Hollywood producer. She heard someone say, "A heart attack."

Dropping to his knees, Sigurd checked the man's
pulse and put his ear to the unconscious man's chest.
"Does anyone have a friggin' aspirin?" he hollered,
probably figuring someone should have thought
of that before. One of the women dug in her silver
purse and took out a tiny pill box, handing him one
tablet.

He immediately pried Farentino's mouth open and
stuck the aspirin under his tongue.

Nothing happened.

"Goldman! Get me the ship's medical kit," Sigurd
yelled once again.

Normally, Goldman would have scoffed at taking
orders from anyone, especially with that tone, Marisa

could tell, but he promptly gave a message to a gaping waiter, "In the supply room."

"Uh, what does a medical kit look like?"

"It has a red cross on it, idiot," snapped Goldman, who was clearly losing his patience with this calamity.

Sigurd, still not looking up, yelled again, "Clear this damn room! Everybody! Out!" He spoke softly to Farentino then, with no response, before he called to her, "Marisa, get a phone, and connect us to the nearest medevac hospital." At least he hadn't yelled at her.

People began to amble out, pushed by Goldman, who was telling them, "The party's not over yet, folks. We can go to the theater room. Mr. Farentino is in good hands now." Eventually, everyone was gone except her, Blue Dev—, uh, Zeb, and Sigurd. Inga had offered to stay, but Marisa told her to go on, she would be okay.

She had no idea why Sigurd had singled her out, but she knew how to act in an emergency, having had numerous ones with Izzie. Taking the cell phone that Zeb offered, she called 911 and was eventually connected to Holy Trinity Hospital in Key West. She clicked on the speakerphone and held it out so that Sigurd could communicate directly with a triage nurse.

Meanwhile, the waiter returned with the medical kit, and Zeb opened it, taking out a small vial, showing it to Sigurd, who nodded.

"Dr. Sigurd Sigurdsson here," he said into the phone.

"A medical doctor?"

"Yes. Most recently, Johns Hopkins oncology. I have a patient here on a yacht anchored off Grand Keys Island. The man has suffered an apparent heart attack. His pulse is faint, and he did not respond to aspirin. I am about to administer nitro." He did. "Again, no response."

"Is there a helipad?"

Sigurd glanced over at Zeb, who nodded.

"Yes, there is a helipad. I am about to begin CPR." He looked up at her and Zeb. "I need one of you to do artificial respiration while I do chest compressions."

"I can do it," she said before Zeb was able to respond. Zeb just shrugged and helped her to kneel down opposite Sigurd. Not an easy task in her short, tight dress.

Sigurd placed the heel of one hand over Farentino's chest and the heel of the other hand atop that, interlocking fingers. Immediately he began pumping and calling out numbers, "One." Pause. "Two." Pause. "Three." Until he got to thirty, then he nodded at Marisa, who leaned down and over the unconscious man. Pinching his nose, she lifted his chin, sealing her mouth over his, and breathed. Once. Twice.

Three times they went through the procedure. Midway through the fourth, Sigurd announced, "I've got a heartbeat." He glanced at Marisa and smiled, and she smiled back.

"Good job, folks. Chopper should be there within fifteen minutes. Make the patient comfortable. I'll stay on the line."

Marisa was still slightly bent over Farentino when Sigurd said, "Stop looking at her ass, Zeb."

She realized then that her dress had ridden up, exposing God only knew what. Shooting upright and then standing to shrug the dress down, she glared at Zeb.

He winked at her. "I get my kicks any way I can these days."

"Why are you still here, anyway?" Sigurd asked him rudely, even as he laid a blanket over Farentino, which Zeb had found somewhere.

Not at all offended by Sigurd's rudeness, Zeb replied, "You know why."

Marisa could swear Zeb's eyes looked red in this light. Were they bloodshot? She hadn't noticed it before.

Sigurd shook his head at Zeb. "He is not a candidate," he said enigmatically.

"Damn!" Zeb said and licked his lips.

A candidate for what? Marisa wanted to ask, but she was suddenly very tired from all the emotion and just wanted to go back to the island and crawl into bed.

"You better go give Goldman an update," Sigurd told Zeb. "Have him make sure that the signal lights are on and the helipad is secure for a landing."

Zeb nodded and left.

Sigurd stood then and just stared at her, a questioning tilt to his head.

"You really are a doctor," she said dumbly.

"Apparently so. You doubted me?"

She nodded. "You just don't look like most doctors."

"Know a lot of doctors, do you?"

"More than you can imagine."

Again, the head tilt as he studied her. "You've done artificial respiration a time or two, haven't you?"

"More than you can imagine," she repeated. In the early days, before Izzie's final diagnosis, she had fainted a lot. Marisa had needed to know how to do artificial respiration and lots more emergency care.

Harry came in then and asked, "Is he going to be all right?"

"I think so," Sigurd said.

"Why isn't he awake?"

"It's his body's way of handling the trauma. It's normal."

"I . . . uh, have to thank you for your service, Dr. Sigurdsson," Harry said grudgingly. "You can send me a bill."

Sigurd bristled. "There is no charge."

Harry scowled. He did not like feeling beholden to Sigurd, whom he obviously disliked, for good reason. Sigurd goaded him every chance he got. "Well, then, thank you." The faint sound of the approaching helicopter could be heard overhead. *Whup, whup, whup.* Harry glanced upward. "I'll bring the EMTs down here."

She and Sigurd were alone again, except for Clinton Farentino, whose breathing was shallow but even.

"Will he really make it?" she asked.

"He will, unless he has another attack."

"I was impressed with how you handled the emergency."

He arched his brows. "How impressed?"

She knew what he referred to. "That was a mistake out there."

"A definite mistake."

For some reason, she didn't like his agreeing with her. "I can't explain it."

"Neither can I."

"Getting involved is out of the question for me right now. I have . . . issues that need my full concentration."

"Your daughter?"

"You know about Izzie?"

He nodded. "Inga told me. A little. No details."

Now was not the time for an explanation.

"Back to that . . . um, what happened out there." She waved a hand toward the open door.

He arched a brow.

"The kiss."

He made a snorting sound of disagreement. "It was much more than a kiss, and we both know it."

"It can't happen again."

He ran a fingertip, just a fingertip, over her lips, and in a husky voice, informed her, "For my sins, do not count on that."

There was a fine line separating good and bad . . .

Several hours later, well past midnight, Sigurd sat on the deserted beach with Zeb, drinking beers and watching the surf. There was no sharp dividing line between the black ink of the ocean and the white foam of its breakers. Like him and Zeb. Like good and evil.

The air was thick with the scent of pure salt water and the cloying perfume of myriad tropical flowers. Innocence and seduction.

What a night! For thinking. And other things.

Jogeir had passed them once on a security patrol of the island, and he reported that Svein was walking the halls of the mostly quiet hotel and Armod was asleep with dreams of new dance steps floating in his fool head. Tomorrow, crowds of attendees would arrive for this week-long perversion excursion.

Zeb had already told him that Jasper's yacht would be arriving in a few hours, fifty Lucies with him. They'd both learned of another ship coming in with the vilest of procurers . . . those dealing with the most perverted of sex acts. These folks were not affiliated with the conference, but they hoped to benefit from the jaded appetites of the attendees.

"You could have let me turn the man," Zeb complained, referring to the heart attack victim.

"He didn't carry a sin taint, and his soul was not Lucie material . . . yet. Now, one of the pornographic film producers . . . that would have been a different case altogether. Some of them are . . . what do they say . . . bad to the bone."

Zeb laughed and took a long draw on his beer. "You are becoming too modern by half, my friend."

Sigurd would have bristled with offense, but he knew Zeb only called him that to annoy him. He and Zeb were not friends, and might not ever be, even if by some miracle Mike turned him into a vangel fifty years from now. His brother Trond was closer to Zeb than any of them; they shared the same warped sense of humor. "Needs must," Sigurd replied, quoting another modern expression.

"I have to show Jasper something of a devil nature for the night's work, or he will suspect me. Let me have the woman, then." Zeb did not need to name Marisa for Sigurd to know which woman.

"No!" Sigurd's response was quick and final. *Bloody damn not-a-chance in hell no!*

"Why? Unlike the man, she does have a sin taint."

"Only a slight one." *Just the teeny tiniest scent of lemon, but then Lucies can sense that odor at fifty pace buried in a ton of concrete. I should have known Zeb would smell her lure.* A sudden thought occurred to him. "Was it you? Did you fang Marisa?"

"If I had, she would be salsa dancing her way to Horror by now. I do not do a slight bite."

Rhyming now? A rhyming demon? And he knows of her salsa dancing back in Miami. Why? Why would he know or care to know about Marisa? She is a venial sinner, thus far. Insignificant. Unless . . . oh, why didn't I think of this before? "It's me they want, isn't it? And Jasper hopes to get me through her?"

Zeb shrugged. "Who knows the workings of the deviant mind? But no, this has naught to do with Jasper. Not yet. He has not yet learned of the connection. But he will. A satanic bloodhound he is when sin is in the air."

"Well, forget about it. I am about to remove her sin taint." *I hope.* "Virtue will be her second name." *But not too virtuous.*

"She has agreed to a rescue fanging?"

"She will." *I hope.*

"Sig, Sig, Sig! You cannot let emotion enter into the turning or not turning of a human, let alone the saving or not saving. If you do, you will not be able to endure all that you must do."

Lectured by a devil? I really am sinking to new depths. "Are you speaking of me, or yourself?"

"Both."

It was true. If a vangel let himself care about every sinful person out there, he would drive himself insane. Or more insane than he already was betimes. He supposed the same was true of Lucies, but he'd assumed they'd lost all sense of caring long ago. Zeb was probably the oddball in the crowd.

Another modern phrase! Zeb is right. I am becoming too acclimated to this time period. Mike best not send me traveling back in time again. I can hear myself telling some knight in William the Conqueror's army, "You better toe the line, dude, or you are dead meat."

"You are smiling," Zeb observed. "I thought you were the serious one of the brothers, the one always unsatisfied and yearning for more."

I am, I am. "You know too damn much about us."

"Needs must," Zeb repeated Sigurd's own words back at him.

They sat in companionable silence for a short while before Zeb drank the remainder of the beer in his can and crushed it with one hand. "Beer is good, but blood is better," he said. "I have developed a taste for the body dew and increasingly have to curb my appetite for more and more. Does that mean I am too far gone as a devil?"

Sigurd could have said yes. Why should he attempt to soothe one of the dark ones? But he found himself admitting, "I like it, too. Truth to tell, neither of us could do our jobs if we were not tempted by the heady beverage." *Marisa's blood drew me tonight like the strongest temptation, and not just to cure her inclination to sin.*

I know how Adam felt about that bloody Garden of Eden apple. It would taste rich and sweet and. . .

Zeb nodded. " 'Tis like sex, I suppose. God created it so that men and women would want to procreate."

Sex now? First I get a lecture from one of Satan's followers on emotional detachment and now a philosophy lesson on sex. Still, Sigurd contributed to the discussion by saying, "And then He put limitations on sexual activity, forbidding that which becomes such a powerful urge."

Zeb gave him a sideways glance. "Not getting any lately, hmm?"

"Hah! Lately is an understatement. More like thirty years ago, and then I had another hundred years added to my penance for the lapse."

"I would not mind those extra years if I could live them as a vangel," Zeb said on a sigh. "Or even dead. I could even handle eternal celibacy to escape this horror of vampire deviltry."

Do not ask. It is none of your business. You are not a boyling sharing secrets. He couldn't help himself. He asked anyhow, "What did you do to land yourself in Jasper's camp?"

Zeb remained silent for several minutes, and Sigurd could tell that it was a subject he rarely, if ever discussed. Finally, Zeb told him, "I lived in the Holy Land long, long ago with a wife and two children that I adored. My small vineyard was prosperous, but I wanted more. And so I joined the Roman army, intending it to be only a temporary assignment. I had been promised additional lands adjoining mine if I committed to serve for five years." The sorrow in his voice was palpable and almost heartrending.

Sigurd wished he'd obeyed his initial inclination not to ask. He did not need to know of another's pain and regret. He had enough of his own.

"One time, we—me and the soldiers under my command—were ordered to fire an entire village. Everyone—man, woman, and child—was to perish for some transgression or other. The Romans were easily offended. I did not want to do it, but my five years were almost up, and they were common folks, I was told, little more than beasts of burden. Only later did I realize that another Roman legion had raided the lands of my birth and herded those living there to this village. I killed my wife and children, among hundreds of others."

There was nothing Sigurd could say to that, nothing that would appease the man's sorrow. In the end, he shared his own secret, "I murdered my little brother."

Silence followed.

Finally, Sigurd remarked, "I do not understand the ways of the Lord. I have always questioned, 'Why me?' when thinking on my sorry fate as a vangel. True, I have sinned, as have my brothers, in a most heinous way. But so have many others. Why not give us a chance to repent while we were still alive?"

"At least you were not condemned to be Lucipires."

"There is that."

"And I agree about the questioning. Why could I have not been given a second chance as a vangel?"

"Because you are not a Viking?" Sigurd offered. Thus far, all vangels were of Norse descent.

"I could become a Viking."

"You can't just *become* a Viking. Same as I could not just *become* a Jew."

"Actually, you could convert to Judaism."

"Well, you can't convert to Viking-ism. There is no such thing."

They were both chuckling when Sigurd concluded, "These are moot questions we raise. Beer conversation.

We are what we are, for our sins, and ours is not to reason why."

Enough of this male bonding, or whatever the hell it is. Sigurd tossed his empty can into a nearby receptacle, a neat pitch if he did say so himself, and stood. "I need to get a few hours' sleep. Mayhap I will find a sinner to repent on the way back to my room."

"And mayhap I will find a sinner who does not want to repent."

Thus the line was drawn back in place, the line that separated them both.

Chapter 10

Work 'til you drop, or something . . .

The Grand Keys Health and Beauty Oasis, located in the center of the hotel, was a first-rate facility, with all the accouterments, despite the hotel having been closed for the past year.

The Oasis included a cluster of facilities catering to all sorts of body enhancement. And, despite the expensive charges, not to mention the generous tips expected, all services were booked solid the first day. Beauty and self-indulgence apparently held no price tag with this crowd.

The Good Looks salon, where Tiffany worked, did hair and a whole lot more; it also provided facials, manicures, pedicures, waxing, exfoliation, and mans-caping. Last night Tiffany had mentioned a sign in the waxing room, which not so subtly read, "We do cities. You want the suburbs, expect to pay extra."

At first, Marisa hadn't understood, though Inga and Doris chuckled.

"Darlin'," Tiffany had explained, "y'all would be

surprised where some women . . . and men . . . grow hair."

"You mean toes?"

The three women had laughed.

"Ya need to get out more, Marisa, bless yer heart," Tiffany had opined. "Yes, toe hair exfoliation is very popular t'day, as well as nose and ear hair removal, but the sign was directed more to back yonder." Tiffany had giggled and patted her curvy butt in the sparkly dress she had just donned for the cocktail party.

Okaay!

Another popular attraction at the beauty salon was a procedure call vajazzling. Think vagina. Think dazzle, as in crystals and sequins, *down there*. The places some women would place jewelry!

Also in the Oasis complex was a massive exercise room, Hurts So Good, with all the most modern equipment. It promised, "We provide the pain, you get the gain."

There wasn't enough time in Marisa's days on the island for her to test that promise. The most exercise she could hope for was the occasional swim.

The spa, Feels So Good, where Marisa worked the morning shift, starting at six a.m., offered nine different types of massages, all of which she had been trained to perform. But there were also salt scrubs, body wraps, saunas, and a steaming mineral Jacuzzi.

Marisa was taking a break at about ten-thirty when Hedy, the spa supervisor, joined her in the employees' lounge.

Hedy eased her ample body down into the comfy leather chair, and sighed. Turned out Hedy was a competitive bodybuilder. Her burgundy hair was teased into an old-fashioned beehive, giving her further height.

Like the other spa employees, Hedy wore the revealing white, tank-top jumpsuit, but she'd disdained the red high heels for a pair of athletic shoes. "Executive privilege," Hedy had explained to Marisa when she arrived at six that morning. "Or flat feet. Take your pick."

Somehow, Marisa couldn't reconcile this image with the clown-sex husband. And she didn't really want to know more.

Marisa was wearing the jumpsuit as well, with high heels (no executive privilege for her, or flat feet . . . not yet anyhow), but she'd donned a thin red sweater that covered her breasts, butt, and bare arms. "I'm allergic to air-conditioning" she'd lied. Thus far, no one had complained, but then she hadn't run into Mr. Vanderfelt yet.

"How's it going, sweetie?" Hedy asked.

"Great. I've done a Swedish massage on two customers—a movie producer's wife and a boat captain. A deep tissue massage on a ditzy female porno star, who threw her back out during some anatomically impossible sexual position. And a relaxation massage on Mitzi Dolan, the PR director for this whole shebang. Talk about hyperactive."

Hedy smiled, having heard worse, Marisa was sure, especially with two other massage therapists, Sonja Ingram and John Ferguson, both of whom weren't as picky as Marisa about the type of massages they were willing to do.

"How are the tips, honey?"

"Good, actually. Hundred-dollar bills, except for Ms. Dolan, who seemed to think I work gratis."

Hedy rolled her eyes. "Sonja got a five-hundred-dollar tip from one customer this morning."

Marisa's jaw dropped.

Before she had a chance to ask what Sonja had done to earn such a bonus, Hedy said, "Don't ask."

Marisa insisted that her clients' private body parts be covered with a sheet, and she made it clear up front (pun intended) that she was a therapist, not a prostitute. Not even for "a little bit of touchy-feely," as one man once coaxed her. That didn't mean that the recipients of her massages didn't get turned on occasionally, both male and female, but she just ignored their physical reactions and chatted away about everyday things to distract them. "How about them Marlins? Did you see what Miley Cyrus did on that MTV special? I hear the weather will be good all week." It usually worked.

Not everyone liked to talk during a massage, and Marisa respected that. Usually, she played it by ear, and if she sensed they didn't want to talk, she just put on some soothing music and did her work. She was versatile.

"Tell me about your little girl," Hedy said. "Eleanor told me you're here to earn extra money for her treatment."

"Isobel . . . Izzie . . . has a terminal brain tumor. Except that there's an experimental operation being tested with some success in Switzerland. Because it's experimental and being done in a foreign country, my insurance won't cover the cost."

"How much?"

"One hundred and seventy thousand."

"Phew!"

"Tell me about it. I've managed to raise a hundred thousand through various fund-raising drives and grants and such, but time is running out, and . . ." She let her words trail off.

"How much time does she . . . do you have?"

Marisa shrugged. "It's hard to say. Less than a year. But the longer we wait, the less chance there is that the operation would succeed."

"And you expect to earn that kind of money here, massaging and waitressing?" The look of pity on Hedy's face pretty much said that Marisa was being hopelessly optimistic.

Marisa dabbed at her eyes with a tissue and laughed. "No, I don't expect to earn seventy thousand dollars." *Unless I do something really drastic.* "But I will earn a substantial sum to put toward that goal, lots more than I could earn at home. And I'm hoping to meet someone who could help me raise the cash. The Internet is where it's at today, for everything. Millions of people can be reached with one tap of a computer key. The right person might be able to set up a website that could save Izzie's life."

Hedy cocked her head to the side, and her heavily lacquered hair went with her. "Haven't you tried that yet?"

"I have, but only on a limited basis. I don't really have the knowhow to do it in a big way, and, frankly, thousands of other people with equally needy medical situations are vying for the same dollars. I need a creative, Internet-savvy person to put a new angle on her case and create a buzz. Someone told me that some of these porno sites are among the most sophisticated and creative, and that's why they're so profitable. Makes sense that some of these Web designers would be here."

"I hate to break it to you, sweetie, but the computer nerds I've met here so far are just self-centered young twits who care about nothing except lining their pockets, or hacking some super-secret government operation."

"Guess I'm looking for a miracle."

"Or a sugar daddy?" Hedy guessed, but there was no judgment in her voice.

"If all else fails . . . maybe," Marisa admitted.

Hedy reached over and patted her forearm. "We'll both pray for a miracle."

Hedy urging prayer? She sounded a lot like Marisa's mother. "Why are you here, Hedy?"

"Same as you. Money. I want to open my own

women's gym and spa in Jacksonville . . . that's where I'm from . . . and even though I've always worked and earned a good salary, my louse of an ex-husband emptied our bank account when he took off for the circus." She rolled her eyes and laughed heartily.

"You don't seem angry or bitter."

"I'm not. Oh, I was a little, at first, but I'd been trying to get rid of the runt for years. Good riddance to him!"

Before they got up to return to work, Hedy said, "I can put a donation jar for Izzie on the front counter, if you don't mind."

Marisa wanted to object. She hated being the object of pity, making herself and her problems so conspicuous. But where her little girl was concerned, she couldn't afford foolish pride. And every dollar counted toward that seemingly impossible goal. "Thank you. Izzie and I would be grateful."

Her next client, Yolanda Dupre, a sex toy entrepreneur, wanted a hot stone massage, one of Marisa's specialties. While Marisa used the smooth, round stones that had been heated in hot water as extensions of her hands, she massaged the tension out of the woman's neck, shoulders, arms, back, and thighs.

The whole time, Yolanda talked. All it took was a single question from Marisa: "How did you get started in your business?"

Yolanda was probably about fifty, but looked forty, thanks to some expert plastic surgery. (Marisa could recognize the signs at twenty paces and knew where to look for the hidden stitches.) Her neat cap of black and white waves bespoke an expensive hair salon. She wore diamond studs in her ears. Probably Cartier or Tiffany. When she'd first arrived, Marisa recognized a Chanel suit, and it wasn't a knockoff, either. The real deal! Which had to cost at least a thousand dollars.

Speaking with a cultured British accent, Yolanda

said, "I first got into the sex toy business on a small
scale, just bits and bobs, vibrators and dildos for home
parties, that kind of thing, when my twin sons were
sophomores in high school, talking about going to college. We had moved to the States by then. I met my husband when he was a visiting prof at Oxford University;
I divorced him when he was going for his fifth master's
degree in yet another liberal arts major at NYU. I tossed
him to the dust bin and never looked back. I was never
on the dole, but my sons had to pick Stanford, one of the
most expensive schools, of course. Oh! Oh! That feels so
good. Try to work that area a little more."

Marisa had been massaging the woman's nape. It
was a stressed area for many women.

"Anyhow, I was in the right place at the right time
when the sexual revolution broke out. Not the wom-
en's lib revolution, but the one in the nineties with the
Internet explosion. It started with that website that
sold soft porn novels for women. In the past, women
hesitated to buy such literature openly in their local
bookstores, but the Internet allowed them to make
purchases without anyone ever knowing. The bloke
who started that erotica website became an instant
millionaire. I saw my opportunity and jumped right
in, or you could say, I vibrated right in."

"How do you find new products? I mean, there can
be only so many variations on a vibrator or . . . or . . ."
She hated to say that D word. " . . . male appendages."

Yolanda smiled at her seeming prudishness. She
was on her back now, with her arms crossed under her
nape, staring up at her. Marisa was working her feet
and calves. A sheet covered her from breasts to upper
thighs.

"You'd be gobsmacked. There's always something
new. Inventors come to my company with ideas, unin-
vited, or I attend trade shows."

"Trade shows. You mean, like car shows?"

"Yep. Sexual electronics. I pick up most of my new products at these events. That's where the Whirly-Girly was discovered."

Marisa wasn't about to ask what a Whirly-Girly was.

But Yolanda sensed her confusion and said, "I have one in my purse. I'll leave it for you at the front desk." She laughed at Marisa's heated face.

Inga and Tiffany are right. I don't get out enough.

"Right now, I'm looking for a good nipple product, something that simulates warm, moist male lips and tongue, with the proper suction, rhythm, and the feel of a real, semi-abrasive tongue. Thus far, all we have are these suction cup thingees that don't do diddly, if you get my meaning."

Okaaay!

Yolanda grinned impishly at Marisa, enjoying her discomfort.

"I don't mean to be offensive, but you seem like a woman more accustomed to the country club than the porno club. Don't you find this a bit . . . well, embarrassing?"

"Oh yeah. I blush all the way to the bank."

Well, she told me!

"What one person finds grotty, another one finds perfectly normal." She shrugged. "And I'll tell you something that will surprise you. I feel as if I'm doing a service to women. Not every woman has a man to shag in her life, by choice or fate. They deserve pleasure and satisfaction, even if it's at their own hands. I also feel as if I'm doing my bit to liberate women about sexuality. It's all right for women to be randy, too. I'm so knack-ered of folks who still think it's a man's world."

Now I've done it. Damn, damn, damn! "Honestly, I didn't mean to be insulting. I have a tendency to be sarcastic."

"You weren't snarky, at all. I don't hesitate to tell people to sod off when they cross the line. That was just my usual podium spiel," Yolanda said with a smile as she sat up lithely on the table. "What's your story, Ms. Lopez? What brings you to a porno conference?"

"Don't you mean FOE?"

"Bugger that!" Yolanda said with a grin.

Marisa gave the short answer, "Money."

"There you go!"

Marisa wanted to ask Yolanda about her Internet website and how she'd found someone to help her. It was unprofessional of her to want to pursue her own interests with a customer, but then she once again set her pride and good sense aside. "How important is a good website to your business?"

"Essential. It's everything."

"Who does it for you?"

"White Cloud Designs from Los Angeles."

"Are they expensive?"

"Unbelievably expensive. In fact, with this dodgy economy, I'm trying to talk at least one of my sons into an Internet design major so they can take over that aspect of the business when they graduate, but the idiots are more interested in becoming doctors or lawyers. Can you imagine?" She grinned at Marisa, then turned serious when she noticed the crushed expression on Marisa's face. "What is it, dear?"

Marisa bucked up then and waved Yolanda's concern aside. "Nothing important," she said. "It's been very nice chatting with you."

To her disappointment, Marisa got only a twenty-dollar tip from Yolanda, which would have been considered good back in her regular job. She expected more here. However, when she went out to greet her next customer, she saw a little gift from Yolanda wrapped in plain brown paper. The Whirly-Girly? She also saw several hundred-dollar bills stuffed in Izzie's jar. Hedy told her they were from Yolanda. Once again, Marisa had made a rash judgment about someone, only to learn perception was not reality.

That theory was tested when her next client arrived . . . none other than Lance Rocket.

"Ms. Lopez?" he asked, sauntering into the room, thankfully wearing an oversize white towel to cover his generous endowments, not that she was looking below his hairless chest. Seeing as how he had thick, dark brown hair, he'd probably been waxed.

"Mr. Rocket," she said, leaning forward to shake his hand. "We met briefly last night at Mr. Goldman's party."

"Right. Call me Lance." He shook her hand. "That was something with Farentino keeling over like that."

"Yes, but I understand he's going to make it. Thank God! Please sit." She motioned toward the massage table.

Some people's legs dangled over the side, but because of his height, about six-foot, his bare feet were planted on the tile floor. He was a handsome man, but up close she could see by the fine webbing at the corners of his eyes and mouth that he was older than she had thought. Possibly forty. You wouldn't know it by his body, though, which was lean and well-muscled.

"What kind of massage are you interested in, Lance?" She pointed to the sign on the wall, which listed seven different types that she gave.

"Pfff. I could probably use them all, but it's my thighs and hamstrings that are killing me."

"Oh?"

"I work on my knees too much," he told her with an absolutely straight face, assuming she knew what he did for a living.

"Are you a priest?" she asked, just to tease.

"Huh?"

"On your knees. Praying a lot."

He grinned when understanding seeped in. "I pray at the love altar," he said, still with a straight face. "However, I don't practice celibacy."

She barely stifled a groan. She'd stepped right into that one.

"I had numerous knee injuries when I played football in college. As a result, my knees are shot, especially the left one. To relieve the strain on my kneecaps, I tend to work more in a squat position or leaning back. Try doing that for hours at a time, and your hamstrings would scream, too."

No way was Marisa going to picture that.

"Have you consulted a doctor?"

"Yeah, but I don't have time for knee surgery and lengthy rehab. And I can't take off work for six months, either, like one doc suggested. The best I can do is cortisone shots every three months."

"Okay. Well, let's see what I can do. Lie down, face first."

He did, but had to adjust himself more than usual for obvious reasons. The towel was still draped over his behind and his face rested on the small pillow at the top of the table. Still, he squirmed around. Muttering, "They oughta have donut holes cut in these tables to accommodate us men. Big, padded donut holes."

What could she say to that? Nothing. Instead, she busied herself with gathering some towels until he was settled.

"I'm putting warm oil on my hands, and then I'm going to try to work these hamstrings. Okay?"

"Just take it easy."

She tested the muscles on the backs of his thighs, which were indeed tighter than over-wound springs, first with soft presses of her fingertips, then deeper presses by the knuckles and heels of her hands.

"Sonofabitch!" he groaned.

"Does that hurt?"

"Hell, yes!"

She could see that his hands were fisted, the knuckles white.

"But don't stop," he quickly added and exhaled whooshily several times until she could feel the tendons loosen and lengthen. "There, that's the spot. Damn, but that feels good. *There*. Right frickin' there."

Since he was more relaxed now, she changed her massaging to longer, firmer strokes from the tops of his thighs down to the backs of his knees, and even his calves and the arches of his feet. When he moaned intermittently now, it was from the lessening of pain.

"I'm going to massage your shoulders and biceps, too. Often, to compensate for the pain in one place, we tighten up other parts of our body."

"Whatever works, babe."

Some women would find that term offensive, but she could tell he didn't mean it that way.

"So you played football in college. Where?"

"Penn State."

"Whoa, that's big-time college football."

"Yep. Division One."

"When did you get involved in . . . um, adult movies?" She found it difficult to say "freedom of expression" movies. It just didn't fit.

He chuckled, perfectly aware of her hesitation to mention the word *pornography*. "After college. I graduated with a degree in American literature, and—"

Holy moly! A porno poet!

"—the only job I could get was substitute teaching high school English—"

What did he expect, with that major? Really! She constantly ran into people who said such things as, "I got a 4.0 in French medieval history, and I just don't understand why I can't land a job." She was tempted to tell them, "Get a reality check, buddy."

"—even though I had imagined myself the next Ernest Hemingway."

Really? Okay, a writer then. But did he have a clue what most writers made? Think barely more than minimum wage.

"I barely made enough to care for my wife and baby girl."

Bingo. "You have a wife? And a daughter?"

"Hah! I have three daughters now. And, before you ask, I've been married to the same woman for eighteen years."

Call me naïve, but why do I find it so hard to reconcile a wife at home and a husband boffing dozens of bimbos?

"An old college girlfriend, who had just starred in that Internet sensation *Mandy Does Manhattan*, mentioned me to her director. You've seen that one, right?"

"Uh, no." She didn't want to say that she'd seen at most three adult movies in her lifetime and then only parts of each before either laughing herself silly, or being so disgusted or embarrassed she refused to watch more. Instead, she told him truthfully, "I was only about ten years old back then."

"Oh," he said, "but it's a classic. Most people I meet have seen that one."

Obviously, I'm not most people, and I'm no longer sure if that's good or bad. "So you didn't need any acting experience to move from the classroom to the big screen . . . or little screen, in the case of TV?"

"No acting experience. In fact, I didn't have a lot of sexual experience, either, believe it or not. Yeah, I'd always carried this junk around with me, but I didn't have a clue what to do with it. Time to profit from what had been an embarrassment before, I decided." He was lying on his back now and waved a hand toward the bulge down below. The grin on his face belied just how embarrassed he was, or had been. "That was fifteen years ago, and I'm still going strong." More big ol' grinning. "Except for these damn knees."

"Can't you take a break for a while? Get the operation and do a few months' rehab?"

"Are you kidding? My wife would have my ass in a sling if I did that."

She wanted to insist that surely a wife of eighteen years would want her husband to get better, but by now she knew she'd said too much. Surprise must have shown on her face, though, before she could mask it with a polite change of subject.

"Carla's become accustomed to a certain lifestyle. We just bought a vacation home in Costa Rica, not that I've gotten to spend more than a weekend there so far. Plus, my oldest daughter is a freshman at Harvard. Do you have any idea how much tuition is there? And I have two more daughters coming up for high school graduation. Ka-ching, ka-ching."

Another porno player getting into the game because of higher education expenses. None of that "The devil made me do it." Nope. "My kids made me do it."

I wonder if I'll ever have to worry about paying for Izzie's college education.

I can't think about that now. I just can't!

"Well, then, I suggest that you find a reputable physical therapist, or a licensed masseur, who can work on you weekly, or twice a week, if possible."

"How about while I'm here on Grand Keys? I could barely crawl out of bed this morning."

"You can come in every morning, if you'd like, but I should probably alternate the types of massage. Deep tissue one day, hot stones another. Regular Swedish massage, of course. Even relaxation massage or aromatherapy could help."

"Sounds great to me."

"And, by the way, you should drink lots of water today to wash out the toxins I loosened up for you."

"No prob. I drink lots of water anyhow." He gave her a two-hundred-dollar tip when he left, but she noticed that he never once asked about her life, or her family. His only interest was in himself. That was not unusual. Lots of folks were self-centered that way, and not just "celebrities."

It was one p.m. by the time Marisa cleaned up from Lance's appointment. She had time for only one appointment before she had to leave for the bungalow, where she would grab a quick sandwich for lunch and do her best with a travel sewing kit to make her waitress uniform presentable, or at least minimally modest. Her dinner shift at the Phoenix Restaurant started at five p.m. and ran until midnight. No early-bird servings on this island.

With only ten minutes to spare, she tossed the sheet and pillowcase in the laundry basket, wiped down the table with disinfectant, and laid out clean linens. Then she ran into the bathroom for a quick pee and repair of her makeup. When she came back out, her next client was already coming through the door of the customer dressing room.

Dr. Sig! Six-foot-four of blond-haired Norse yumminess.

"What are you doing here?"

"Someone got up on the wrong side of the bed furs this morn. Are you wearing anything under that garment?"

She glanced down, realizing that she'd forgotten to put the sweater back on when she'd been in the bathroom. Raising her chin haughtily, she barely restrained herself from grabbing a towel to cover herself. Even worse, she felt her nipples pearling just from looking at Sigurd.

Wearing nothing but a towel!

And, though he didn't display Lance's particular type of assets, he had plenty of his own. Wide shoulders, slim waist and hips, long, long, lightly furred legs leading down to narrow, well-formed feet. Today, his dark blond hair hung loose to his shoulders with those thin braids on either side of his sharply sculpted face.

"No. Are you?" she snapped, and immediately regretted her hasty reply.

"Not a thing," he said, adjusting the knot on the low-riding, hip-hugging towel. Even his belly button was attractive. *Darn it!* His lips twitched with a knowing almost-grin—*Darn him!*—which he quickly replaced with a frown. "You ask why I am here? I am here because we have a problem."

"We? There is no 'we.'"

"For my sins, there very definitely is a 'we.'"

"Forget the 'for my sins' crap. What are you doing here? My next appointment was with a Mrs. Kervanjian."

"Um. Mrs. Kervanjian had a change of plans." A light blush colored his sharp cheekbones.

"Oh really? Did you flash those cute fangs of yours at her?"

"My fangs are not cute." The blush deepened.

Fascinating! She put her hands on her hips and tapped a foot impatiently, then immediately folded her arms over her chest when she noticed his eyes about to bug out with gaping at her breasts.

"What do you want, Sigurd?"

He gave her a look that pretty much said, *Are you serious?* But then he shook his head as if to clear it and asked, "Have you been with Harry Goldman?"

"*Been with?* Are you crazy? When would I have time to 'be with' anyone? I left the party last night and was in bed by midnight. I got up at five a.m. to arrive here for my first appointment at six a.m."

"Does that mean that you have not been with Harry?"

She rolled her eyes. "What is it with your fixation on Harry Goldman? He's no different from any other man."

"I beg to differ." Sigurd was walking around the room, picking up and examining various items. Like the hot stones, which he dropped from one hand to the other before rubbing his palms appreciatively over their smooth surfaces. "As soft as the skin on a maiden's buttock," he murmured.

Oh Lord! He's not picturing my behind, is he? Not that I'm a maiden, whatever the hell that is, probably a virgin.

He examined a battery-operated Shiatsu massager, which he turned on and off before grinning at her.

"It's not that kind of vibrator," she insisted.

He put up both hands in surrender. "I have no idea what you mean."

Yeah, right.

Then he undid the stoppers on several vials of oil and sniffed. "This is my favorite. It reminds me of your essence."

She could read the label from where she stood on the other side of the table. It was the oil of rose honey, cut with a pinch of ginger to tamp down its sweetness. "The only essence I have is soap and deodorant."

"Whatever you say," he agreed, but his eyes said differently.

In fact, she could smell his orangey-evergreen cologne even through the other scents in the room, but she'd mentioned it to him before and wasn't about to get involved in that discussion again. "What did you do to Mrs. Kervanjian?"

"Do? Nothing. Well, I might have mentioned that they are giving away free sex toys in the hotel lobby, until the supply runs out. She decided to reschedule her appointment."

She narrowed her eyes at him.

"They *might* be giving away such devices. In fact, your previous customer overheard my comment and went running out of here like a bat out of hell. And believe me, I know bats out of hell."

"Whaaat?" *Yolanda? Oh Lord! She must have thought someone was giving away her products while she was getting a massage. There goes a repeat customer!* "First, that 'for my sins' repeat nonsense, now bats in hell, I don't understand half of what you say." Just then, she noticed that his towel had slipped and was in danger of falling off. "Fix it," she gurgled, motioning toward his lower region.

"Sorry," he said, not at all sorry, if the grin on his face was any indication, as he redid the knot at his hip.

"Listen, are you here for a massage? If not, I have better things to do than—"

He hopped onto the table and swung his legs like a little kid. "I'm game if you are."

"Game? Game? My work is not a game. I'll have you know—"

"I pick number five. Full body massage," he said, pointing to the sign on the wall.

"Why?"

"Why not? Methinks I have a kink in my . . ." He waggled his eyebrows, then said, " . . . shoulders."

"Oh, just lie down. And shut up, I don't want to hear anything more about 'our' problems."

He lay down face first, his feet extending over the

bottom of the table, his face resting on his folded fore-arms, but then he raised his head. "Shall I take off my towel first?"

"No!" She gave him a very unprofessional shove to his fool head.

"This should be fun," he said.

At least he hadn't added, "For my sins!"

Chapter 11

Vampires and angels get aches and pains, too . . .

Michael was going to have a fit.

Sigurd's intentions had been noble—well-intentioned, leastways—when he'd come looking for Marisa this morning. He needed to end this whole situation regarding Marisa and Harry Goldman and cleanse her sin taint so that he could move on to other more demanding matters, like destroying demon vampires in paradise.

But what did he do instead? Set himself up for a massage. A massage, for the love of a troll! Angels did not get massages, nor did vampires, as far as he knew. Vikings, on the other hand, would be game for anything with even a hint of sex. And the rubbing of bare skin betwixt a man and woman implied sex, in Sigurd's sex-deprived opinion, no matter what Marisa claimed.

First thing this morning, he'd resolved to seek out the bothersome woman and explain in alarming detail if need be that she was in dire danger and must get off the island. Barring that, he must remove her himself.

To his dismay, she was already gone from her sleeping quarters when he arrived just past dawn. At work, massaging, he was told by her Norse friend, Inga, with a wide yawn. He'd awakened the woman from a sound slumber by transporting himself into the bedchamber and just barely prevented her from shrieking her head off by clamping a hand over her mouth. Furthermore, Inga had informed him, once he'd calmed her down by stating emphatically that he meant no harm to her or her friend, that Marisa would go from massaging to waitressing, all day long.

"Is there no time when Marisa will be free?" he had asked.

"Not if she can help it," was Inga's irksome answer.

Well, if Marisa wouldn't fit into his schedule, he would fit into hers. With a massage! Not that he really intended to get a massage. Just the thought of it turned his blood hot, and he had been thinking on it a lot since the idea had first entered his fool head hours ago. He'd performed routine medical duties in his office all morning, and this was the first chance he had to get away. A lunch break, he'd told Karl, who snorted his opinion.

And now here he lay on her massage table, almost naked. His face rested on a small pillow, his arms dangling over the sides of the table. His raging enthusiasm was a painful lump under him, a reminder that this seemingly innocent activity was forbidden fruit to a long celibate vampire angel.

Still, he was tempted.

Behind him, he heard Marisa snicker and say something under her breath about donut holes. He had been thinking about fruit, *forbidden* fruit, not sweet treats, like donuts. Same thing, he supposed.

"Marisa, I did not really come here for a massage."

"You could have fooled me. You're lying on my massage table, naked except for a little towel over your butt, and about five miles of muscles waiting to be rubbed."

"Um," he barely choked out.

"What are those scars, or bumps, on your shoulder blades?" she asked. "Were you in an accident?"

He muttered something about "Run-in with an archangel. Would you believe me if I said that I might grow wings there someday?"

"Would you believe me if I said I was a mermaid and I forgot to bring my tail with me?"

"Sarcasm again!" he complained. "I need to talk with you about something important."

"Talk, talk, talk! What is it about your need for lecturing me?" He could hear her sigh from the other side of the room where she was fiddling with the dials on a sound system that burst into the most inappropriate, or was it appropriate, song of all. "Sexual Healing." Hah! It would take more than the savage beats of modern music to heal his sexual needs. "You scheduled a massage, and that's what you are hot damn going to get. I'm tired of hearing about the need for talk."

"Marisa! If you lay your hands on me, just a little bit, my half cockstand will be standing tall. And you do not want to witness *that*."

"Oh puh-leeze! I don't know what a cockstand is, but I can guess. Do you think you're the first man to make a crude suggestion during a perfectly unsexual massage?"

Unsexual? She is demented. "All I know is, if you even breathe on my bare skin, I will be roaring my enthusiasm."

"Roar away! It won't get you anywhere."

"Are you really that daft to challenge me so? I tell you true, m'lady, if you stand close enough that those pointed nipples are anywhere near my face, I will surely take a nip, and I do not mean a fanging."

She came closer, the lackwit woman! "I do not have pointy nipples."

He turned his face on his still folded arms and opened one eye to stare at said breasts. "Definitely pointy," he concluded.

She shook her head as if he were a hopeless case.

He was. "If I inhale one more whiff of your honey-ginger woman scent, I will probably swoon like a girling."

He could swear she giggled. "You're teasing me."

"Teasing, am I? Woman, if this need I have of you grows any bigger, I will be compelled to lift you up onto the table, under me, and I will surely have to swive you three ways to Muspell."

"What is Muspell?"

"Norse Hell."

There was an extended silence in the room then. He turned his head this way and that and could not see her. So he sat up and saw that she was propped up against the door a short distance from the bottom of the massage table. On her face was an expression of . . . He could not tell for sure. Interest? Or outrage?

It did not matter. He could not stay in this small, confined space with her much longer without doing something he would later regret. Well, mayhap not regret so much as have to repent. Michael would know, and Michael would punish, sure as sin.

He stood and dropped the towel.

She swallowed.

"Do not worry. I am just donning my outer garments so you will no longer be tempted by my assets."

"Egotistical buffoon," she muttered, but he noticed that she did not turn her face away to avoid looking at his nakedness.

Once he was dressed in denim braies, an old Navy

SEALs T-shirt that Trond had left behind at the castle last year, and athletic shoes, he said, "Bottom line here, Marisa. You obviously need money, or you would not be here on this bloody island."

"Bloody?"

He waved a hand dismissively. "Bloody, blasted, damn, whatever."

"You know that I need money?"

"Of course. Why else would you consider spreading your thighs, your toes pointing to the high heavens, for such a man as Harry Goldman? And yes, nipples and toes can both point."

She bristled. "It's none of your business who I open my thighs for, you crude sonofabitch."

He was the one who bristled now, at her crudeness. He might be a Viking, crude as any man, but he did not appreciate such traits in his women. *I mean, any woman. Not mine. Definitely not mine. It was a slip of the tongue, Michael.* "If it is bloody lucre that will lure you away from this island, then I will get it for you," he conceded with ill grace. It went against the grain for him to bribe the woman.

Her eyes widened. "What?"

"How much? What would it require for you to go home?"

"Seventy thousand dollars."

That much? She prizes her body highly, I must say. But what he said was "A pittance."

"What?" she repeated. "You consider seventy thousand dollars a pittance? I thought you said that you aren't a wealthy man."

"I am not."

"Listen, this is a pointless conversation. I hardly know you, and I'm beginning to find your constant interfering in my life insulting, if not a bit on the stalkish side."

"I am a protector, not a stalker."

"Oh really? And what would you expect for that amount of money?"

Under normal circumstances, everything. But it has been a long, long time since I was normal, if ever I was. "Nothing."

"Bullshit! At least with Harry, I would know the cost. With you, it would be an open-ended nightmare."

"That is a ridiculous assumption. Even if you are right, why would a deal with Harry be more palatable than one with me?"

"I don't know. It just feels that way. Do you really have that kind of cash on hand?"

"Well, not on hand, precisely . . ."

"That's what I thought."

" . . . but I could probably get it."

"Probably?" She laughed. "This conversation is over."

"This conversation has not nearly begun." He inhaled and exhaled for patience. Time for the hard truth. "If you must know, I am not really a doctor."

"Surprise, surprise. I told you from the beginning that you didn't look like any doctor I've ever met."

"Well, I *am* a doctor, but more important, I am a vampire." He flashed his fangs, just for emphasis.

She should have jumped away, or shrieked with shock. She did neither. "Ho-hum! That trick is getting old."

He crossed his eyes at her stubbornness. "A vampire angel, to be more precise."

"Is that a fact? No offense, big boy, but you are the farthest thing from an angel I have ever seen. Not that I've come in contact with many angels."

"I'll give you facts, you stubborn wench. This island is teeming with demon vampires. Lucipires. We call them Lucies, for short."

"You named a demon vampire Lucy. Like, *I Love*

Lucy? Is there a Ricky demon, too, and how about Ethel and Fred?"

"No, you witless female. Lucies, as in L. U. C. I. E. S."

She crossed her eyes, just to mock him, he supposed.

"You jest, when this is a dead serious matter. There are demon vampires, I tell you. Big, monstrous creatures with scales and red eyes, and tails and, yes, sharp fangs. Creatures that seek out sinners, such as you are determined to be." There! Let her muse on that for a moment. Let her realize the danger she faced on this island.

She just stared at him for a long moment, and then she burst out laughing.

Not the reaction he was hoping for.

Sometimes you get a lemon, sometimes a peach, and sometimes a Garden of Eden apple . . .

Marisa blinked, then blinked again.

She was back in her bungalow, lying on her bed. How she had gotten there, she had no idea. A second ago she'd been in the massage room with Sigurd and . . . *Sigurd!*

Jumping up, she stomped into the living room. Sure enough, there was the doctor himself, bent over, examining the interior of their small fridge. The seat of his jeans stretched tight over a butt that was beyond spectacular.

Holy Levi Strauss!

"You have no beer," he said, straightening.

"No kidding. We have no food, either, and I'm starving. I didn't have a chance to eat breakfast, and—" She glanced at her watch, "Yikes! I have only two hours to shower, alter my waitress uniform, make a phone call to my daughter, and . . . What are you doing?"

He was speaking into his cell phone. "Calling for lunch."

"They don't do room service to the employee bungalows."

He arched his brows at her, as in *Watch me!* and continued placing an order. "Don't forget the beer, Tillie. Yes, Sam Adams will do. Or Heineken. Sure, send both." Placing a hand over the phone, he asked her, "What do you want to drink with your sandwich? Beer okay with you?"

"No, a diet soda. And I don't want a sandwich. I want a salad. A Caesar salad with dressing on the side. No anchovies," she said, just to be contrary.

To her surprise, he repeated the order into the phone, then concluded, "Thank you. A half hour will be fine. I owe you." Followed by a sexy laugh.

Marisa could only imagine what the person at the other end of the call had suggested. She tilted her head to the side in question.

"That was Tillie—Matilda Thorsson—head chef in the hotel kitchen. I did a favor for her this morning. She forgot to bring her migraine prescription."

A likely story. "Thorsson? Another Viking? Are you people everywhere?"

"'Twould seem so."

"And are all of you vampires or demons or angels?" she inquired mockingly. *And drop-dead gorgeous?*

"Hardly. We will continue that particular discussion, and perhaps you will be less inclined to make jests."

What particular discussion? Oh. He means that nonsense about the danger of fangy creatures on the island. She'd been distracted by his leaning his wide shoulders against the wall, extending his long legs out, and crossing his Adidas 550–clad feet at the ankles. They were really big shoes. *And, no, I am not going to make that clichéd extrapolation.* "I'll give you ten minutes, and then you're out of here." She glanced pointedly at her watch.

"Pfff! I would only need five minutes if you would listen with an open mind."

"Pfff! If my mind were any more open, I would be afraid of rain."

"More jests!" He shook his head at her, then sat down in one of the wicker chairs, despite its being too small and uncomfortable for his large size. He wore a drab green, Navy SEAL T-shirt tucked into jeans that were faded to a pale blue, almost the color of his compelling eyes . . . eyes that were flashing with irritation at her.

Hah! I'm the one who has reason to be irritated. "How did I get here?" She motioned with her hand to indicate the bungalow. "Last thing I recall was you telling me some ridiculous story about vampires. Did you knock me out or something?"

"Or something. You were laughing so hard I was afraid you would wet your panties. You *are* wearing something under that wanton garment, *aren't* you?" His eyes locked on her lower region in the revealing white jumpsuit she still wore, where a discerning person could see there was no panty line. And he was obviously very discerning.

"Of course I'm wearing an undergarment," she said, and walked behind the wicker sofa, which shielded her, somewhat. She wore a thong. Not that he needed to know that. "But you still haven't answered my question. How did I get here?" She rubbed the back of her head and noticed no bumps that would indicate a sharp blow; nor did she feel any particular ache in her neck. As a doctor, he would know just where to pinch in order to obtain unconsciousness, wouldn't he? It couldn't be a drug because she hadn't drunk anything in his presence. *If he slipped me a roofie, I'm reporting him to the medical board. The Viking medical board. A joke? Me? He's right. I'm becoming a regular comedian. Must be hunger.*

"Teletransport," he answered succinctly.

"Huh?"

"I have certain abilities," he told her, rather hesitantly.

Men and their bragging! Though what that has to do with how I got here . . .

"One of them, teletransport, is the transfer of matter from one point to another without traversing physical space."

Say again? "Well, that's as clear as mud." She thought a moment, then laughed. "You mean like 'Beam me up, Scotty' teletransport?"

He made a tsking sound of disgust. "This is not *Star Trek*. This is another type of wars. Demons against angels. Vampire demons, called Lucipires, to be specific, against vampire angels, called vangels."

I am getting a headache.

"Zeb, whom you met last night, is a Lucie. Me, I am a vangel, for my sins."

That "for my sins" crap again. I wonder if I remembered to bring aspirin? "You're beginning to scare me."

"You should be scared. That is why you must leave this island."

We're back to that same old song again. "I didn't mean that kind of scared. I meant scared of you. You, my doctor friend, are a bit of a loony bird. Did you escape from an asylum?" She rolled her eyes, then pointed to the logo on his T-shirt. "And are you a Navy SEAL, too?"

"No, that is my brother Trond."

She set that news aside for the time being. "Are you even a real doctor?"

"How many times must I tell you that I am in fact a

licensed physician? But that is only my job when I am not called on to be a vangel."

"A doctor only when he doesn't have better things to do? That's a new one."

"Why do you continually missay me? And I have told you afore, and it bears repeating, your cynical tongue ill-suits a lady."

At least he regards me as a lady. I'll give him that, and not an inch more. "Your constant harping on me to leave Grand Keys ill-suits you."

"Sit down and stop pacing. Do you deliberately distract me with that revealing garment? Up, down, up, down your arse cheeks go. And I do not care what you say, I can see the dimples in your buttocks. You are *not* wearing panties."

Marisa stopped dead in her tracks, having been unaware that she'd been walking nervously (*What woman wouldn't be nervous in close confines with a gorgeous Viking who claimed to be a vampire?*) back and forth between the kitchen and the sliding doors to the patio. Even worse, she'd forgotten that she was still wearing the revealing bodysuit *without* the sweater cover-up. She plopped down into a chair opposite him and put a floral throw pillow on her lap. "I'm wearing a thong, for heaven's sake!" she said before she could bite her loose tongue. Now she was giving him new images of her bare self to imagine.

And he was imagining, all right. With a grin, he said only, "Aaah!"

"And I do not have dimples there."

"Mayhap my vision is blurred by your female scent clouding the room."

The female scent nonsense again! Before he had a chance to remark on her breasts, as well as her butt and her body odor, she raised the pillow higher.

His grin grew wider.

He was a very good-looking man when he wasn't scowling, his usual expression. Around her, anyway.

"Talk. Get it over with. I have things to do before getting to work. What exactly do you want from me?"

"I want you to leave this fucking island." He was clearly getting exasperated with her.

She was exasperated, too. "Nice language for an angel!"

"We are permitted to use bad language, well, not permitted precisely but excused, as long as we do not use sacrilegious expletives, as in using the Lord's name in vain."

She blinked at the convoluted logic in that explanation.

"So will you leave the island?" he asked with a patience he clearly did not feel.

"Not going to happen. Not until my work commitment is completed. Ten days and not a day less. Next?"

"Then you must let me fang you. No, no, let me finish. It will not hurt. I will suck a little blood from you to remove the sin taint. Then I will inject a little of my own blood into your bloodstream through my fangs. The result? You will lose the inclination to commit the great sin you are contemplating." He smiled as if that explained it all, and she should be happy to comply.

Not bloody likely! "Are you nuts? First of all, I am not a bad person, and—"

He raised a hand, interrupting her. "I did not say you are bad, only that you are about to be bad."

"People do bad things all the time. It's not the end of the world."

"It is if Lucies are in the vicinity."

She inhaled and exhaled for patience, waiting for him to explain.

" 'Tis true that Lucies go after only the most evil of humans, except sometimes when they sense a person about commit a great sin, they fang them enough to plant a sin taint. Then the inclination becomes a compulsion."

"Like me, I suppose?"

"Precisely."

Marisa tried to recall anyone biting her, and couldn't. Except for that one time when they'd first arrived and she'd gotten that mosquito bite on her neck. The only person nearby at the time had been the blond-haired, surfer-looking guy signed up to be a scuba instructor. When she'd rubbed her neck, he'd told her that she ought to have that looked at, that "bites" could get infected. Then he'd smiled at her, and was it revisionist memory, but had he had slightly elongated incisors? She wasn't exactly sure.

While her mind had been wandering, Sigurd had been continuing to talk. "Once the grievous sin is committed, the demon vampires arrive to drain the person until the human body disappears, and then he or she will re-form into bodily shape back in the torture chambers of Horror, the main palace of Jasper, king of the Lucipires."

Drain? Yuck! This is like a bad vampire novel: Interview with a Crazyass Vampire Angel.

"Usually, the victims are kept in 'killing jars,' large-size, clear glass containers similar to those used by butterfly collectors—"

Butterflies now? Angel wings, butterfly wings, I suppose it makes sense. No, it doesn't. I am getting thoroughly confused with all these ridiculous analogies.

"—where they are kept in a state of stasis until they agree to become demon vampires. Usually, it takes some horrendous torture to help that process along."

Marisa's jaw had dropped lower and lower with each fact Sigurd fed to her. But the only torture she could imagine at the moment was being annoyed to death by incessant, impossible-to-believe chatter.

"Now do you understand?"

"You do tell a great story."

He threw his hands out in frustration. "Just humor me then. Let me take a little bite of your neck, and I will leave you alone."

For some reason, that bothered her . . . that his only interest in her was her potential hookup with Harry Goldman. *Isn't he interested in me as a woman? Not that I'm interested in him as a man. Hah! Who am I kidding? I'm so interested I'm probably drooling.* She licked her lips to make sure.

He groaned.

"What?"

"You have the lips of a harlot."

He is interested, she thought with inordinate pleasure. "First, you call me a lady, and now a harlot. Make up your mind."

"You are both, and that is the best combination. To a male, leastways. To this male, certainly."

"Look, it's been fun talking with you"—*not!*—"but I really need to alter my waitress uniform, take a shower, and get ready for my first shift at the restaurant."

"We still need to finish this conversation."

"As far as I'm concerned, the subject is closed."

"Not even close. What is wrong with your uniform?"

"I'll show you." She went into the bedroom and came back out with the black nylon dress and the travel sewing kit she planned to use. Holding it up against her, she said, "I've got to let the hem down two inches; that's all the fabric there is, but I haven't stitched it yet. And I want to sew up some of this cleavage, too. Otherwise, I'll be flashing my customers."

She thought he would make some crude comment, but instead he said, "I can do that for you. Go, take your shower. The food should be here shortly, and then we can finish our conversation."

"You can sew? Good Lord, you are a man of many talents. A seamstress now, too."

"I'm a physician. I need to know how to stitch a wound with precision. How much different can a hem be?"

"Go for it," she said, heading for the bathroom. It was the quickest shower in history, followed by an equally quick blow-dry of her hair and application of makeup. She came out in a long silk Donna Karan robe to find Sigurd speaking on a cell phone. Her cell phone!

"Yes, there is a beach here.

"No, I have not made any sand castles yet. Maybe later.

"Uh, I will see if there are any seashells and send one home for you. Of course, a biiiig one. They are the best kind.

"No, your mommy is not having nearly enough fun, but she makes lots of jokes. No, I do not know what is the difference between an alligator and a fish.

"You can't tuna fish? Oh, that is a good one.

"You know another joke. What is it? How do you make a tissue dance? I cannot imagine. Magic?

"You put a little boogie in it? Miss Izzie! Shame on you!" He laughed.

"Izzie?" Her five-year-old daughter loved silly jokes, and she told the same ones over and over, forgetting that the receiver already knew the punch lines. "You're talking to my daughter?" Marisa gasped and tried to grab for the phone.

Sigurd held it away from her and spoke into the phone again. "Your mother is here now. Yes, I will remember about the seashell. Buh-bye to you, too."

He handed the phone to Marisa and, to her surprise, sat down to continue sewing a neat hem on her dress. He really could sew!

She walked out to the patio and sat down. "Izzie, honey, how are you?"

"I called you, Mommy, all by myself. Buelita told me the numbers and put them in. And that nice man answered. Is he your friend?"

"Um, yes." What else could she say?

"Like Buddy Dalton is my friend?" Buddy was a next-door neighbor roughly Izzie's age. Occasionally, they played LEGOs together. Buddy was a LEGO fanatic.

"Sure," she said, and could only imagine the kind of playing a Viking like Sigurd would engage in. "How are you feeling today?"

"Good. I slept a long, long time. I dint get up 'til really late this morning. Buelita sez it's 'cause I got so much sun at the pool yesterday."

"Did you have fun?"

"Yes! You dint tell me you was going to the beach, Mommy," Izzie complained.

Sigurd must have mentioned that.

"Why can't I come and be with you? I would be a good girl. I would even eat my scrambled eggs." Some kids hated vegetables, Izzie had an odd repugnance for eggs. "Please, please, please."

"Not this time, sweetheart. I'm working all day and evening, but I promise you, we will go to the beach after I get home." *Please God, let that be a possibility.*

"And get a whole bucket of seashells."

"For sure! Let me talk to your grandmother now."

"Okay," Izzie agreed, then yelled, "Buelita!"

Marisa cringed. "Love you bunches, peanut."

"Love you more," Izzie replied happily.

"Marisa, dear, how are you?"

"I'm fine. This is my first day of work. I made four hundred dollars in tips this morning at the spa, and I'll be starting a waitress shift later this afternoon."

"You work too hard. Be careful you don't burn out, sweetheart."

Marisa couldn't afford to burn out, but she didn't want to be so negative with her mother as to point out that fact. "The spa director put an Izzie jar on the front desk."

"That's nice. Every little bit counts."

"How's Izzie doing?"

"Remarkably well. She had a wonderful time at the pool. Yes, I remembered to slather her with sunscreen, and we made sure she didn't overdo the swimming. The girl does swim like a little fish, doesn't she? Like you, sweetheart."

The warmth in her mother's voice was such a gift to Marisa. There had been way too many occasions when there had been tears and distress. Marisa vowed in that moment to do whatever was necessary to make sure Izzie got the operation and there would be happier times not just for Marisa and her daughter, but for her whole family.

"We got a letter from Steve yesterday."

"Oh?"

"He sent you a check for Izzie. For five hundred dollars."

"Where would Steve get that kind of money in prison?"

"He said he earned it from working on the prison farm."

Marisa knew for a fact that the prison inmates were paid twenty-five cents an hour for their work. He was probably gambling. She sighed deeply. "That was nice of him, Mom."

"Yes, it was. Marisa, baby, I worry about you."

"Me?"

"Yes, you work too hard. You do not pray enough. At some point, we all must 'Let go and let God.' It is the only way."

"I promise, Mom. I'll pray," she said, and she did after ending the call, except her prayer wasn't exactly what her mother had in mind.

"Dear God, help me to do this thing I must to save Izzie."

When she went back inside, Sigurd was holding up the uniform. "What do you think?"

He had indeed lengthened the hem and stitched the bodice. It remained to be seen how it would look. "Thanks for your help."

"Now we will have time—"

A knock on the door interrupted whatever Sigurd had been going to say. No doubt the same old/same old refrain about leaving the island. It was a waiter rolling a trolley with their lunch.

She shouldn't have been surprised to see that there was enough for a small army. Five kinds of sandwiches (chicken salad, roast beef, cheeseburger, a Reuben, and a turkey club), the Caesar salad, a fresh fruit plate, crème brûlée, and chocolate cake. Bottled water, two kinds of diet soda, and three bottles of beer. "Expecting company?"

"No. Why?"

The waiter set up the spread for them and left with a smile when Sigurd slipped him a fifty-dollar tip.

Marisa tied the belt on her robe tighter and sat down. She should have reached for the salad, and she would, but first she grabbed the chicken salad sandwich on whole grain bread. Her favorite kind, with big chunks of white meat chicken along with crunchy grapes and walnuts. "Mmmm," she said after taking her first bite.

Sigurd was watching her, as if mesmerized.

"What?" She wiped her mouth with a napkin.

"If you swive like you eat, sex with you must be spectacular."

She was pretty sure that *swive* was an archaic Norse synonym for the F word. She should have been offended, but she wasn't. Instead, she felt a little tingle in her girl parts . . . all of them. "You sure have a way with words. Strange words." She motioned for him to eat, too. Which he did, with gusto, prompting her to wonder, to herself of course, if he swived like he ate.

He must have guessed what she was thinking because he said, "Yes, I do," and winked at her.

She felt that wink all the way to her toes, and, yes, the girl parts in between.

"Tell me about your daughter," he urged as he helped himself to a cheeseburger, chips, and half her salad, after having already consumed the Reuben and drunk one of the bottles of beer.

In between bites of the chicken salad sandwich, which was as delicious as it had looked, she told him, "I'm a single parent. Izzie was born five years ago. I dropped out of college to take care of her. At first, I was able to manage working as a massage therapist while continuing my education. I always intended to get a degree in physical therapy. But then, two years ago, Izzie . . . got sick." Her voice choked up, and she cleared her throat. "After that, I quit school altogether and added a waitress job at a salsa bar. I also moved back home at that time to save money. Izzie and I live in an apartment over the garage. Mom and Dad help a lot in caring for Izzie while I'm at work. That's it. The whole story," she concluded, and picked at her half of the salad.

"Your friend Inga told me that your daughter has a tumor. What kind, specifically?"

"Grade III brainstem glioma. It started with headaches and vomiting and unusual drowsiness. Moved on to moodiness, muscle weakness, seizures. We have most of those conditions under control now, but there has already been some respiratory and heart function impacted, which will get worse as she and her brain continue to grow. Doctors tell me that the tumor is inoperable because of its location."

He nodded and said, "I'm not a brain specialist, but I understand the problem. If it's inoperable, why are you trying to raise money by . . ." He was probably going to say something about her prostituting herself for the money, but instead he let his words trail off.

"There's a clinic in Switzerland that has been having luck with a new type of laser that can more precisely kill tumor cells, but it's experimental, and outside the country, and not covered by my medical insurance. In other words, very expensive."

Sigurd was picking out the peaches from the fruit plate and licking the juice from his fingers as he ate. A disconcerting action in light of the serious news she was imparting to him. To his credit, he was also listening intently to her every word. "I have a passion for peaches," he said with a shrug when he noticed her watching him eat.

"You are such a little boy," she observed, but his use of the word *passion* gave her other ideas.

"I do not think I was ever a little boy," he countered enigmatically. "But back to your daughter . . . have you tried prayer?"

Shocked that a medical person would offer such a suggestion, she just gaped at him for a moment. "Not you, too!"

He arched his brows.

"My mother. That's her remedy for everything."

"It can't hurt," he said with a shrug.

She recalled then that he'd told her he was some kind of angel. A vampire angel, of all things. It made a warped kind of sense that he would suggest prayer.

"Not that I'm saying the operation should not be done. Like my brother Trond always says, 'Trust in God but bring your gun.'"

"The SEAL?"

"Yes."

"You're not really helping, you know."

"I do not have that kind of money on hand, but I might be able to get it from . . . someone," he said tentatively.

"And what would I have to do in return?"

"So suspicious," he said, wagging a forefinger at her. "I would expect you to trust me by letting me fang out your sin taint and leave the island."

He is like a broken record. She shook her head. "I can't do that. It's my problem. I'm responsible. I can't just walk away and trust that someone else, a virtual stranger, and a weird one at that, will take care of us." She patted her heart. "Furthermore, when a child is sick, family members do everything, *everything*, to heal them. Don't you agree?"

He looked at her with a strange expression on his face, then said in almost a whisper, "Not always." Taking a long draw on his beer, he turned to her again and said, "I could make you leave, you know. In fact, I could teletransport us back to your home in a second. 'Twould not be easy, and it would drain my energy for a day, but it can be done."

"Not that I believe you, but don't you dare! If you find a way to make me leave, and I lose the opportunity to save my daughter, I'll blame you. Do you really want the death of a child on your conscience?"

"It wouldn't be the first time," he revealed. The expression on his face was serious.

"What?" she asked.

His jaw was clenched tight, and there was a slight tic at the side of his mouth. He was probably gritting his teeth. He refused to elaborate.

She assumed he meant that he'd been unable, as a doctor, to save some children. A totally different matter.

"Why would you accept money from that evil Goldman but not from me?"

"Having sex with Harry would be distasteful, but done for a good cause. I don't think that counts as prostitution when there is a good reason for it, do you?"

"I hardly think God makes that distinction."

"Whereas sex for money with someone with whom you might conceivably have a relationship feels sick to me."

"We do not have a relationship," he said with horror.

She was rather offended by his horror. Still, she said, "Yeah, but we probably could under the right circumstances. I'm not saying we will. But there is always that possibility."

"I never said that I would require sex in return for any cash I might be able to garner."

"Doesn't matter. Taking money, a large amount of money, from a potential lover would be icky."

"Lover?" he choked out. Then, "Icky." He shook his head at her, "That is the finest example of female illogic I have ever heard."

"Said by a professed vampire angel. Talk about illogic!"

"Well, then, you will have to at least let me fang the sin taint out of you."

"Do you never give up?"

"Never. Well, hardly ever."

"And don't you dare think about holding me down

and doing . . . that thing you said." She shivered with distaste.

"I cannot force you. Removal of the sin taint must be voluntary."

"You have rules and everything for all this crap?"

"Believe you me, it is not crap. It is very serious life-or-death, Hell-or-Horror business."

She glanced at her watch and let out a little squeal of dismay. She had to be dressed and back in the hotel to waitress in a half hour. "Finish up. I've got to get dressed." Ten minutes later, she came out and saw that all the food was gone. All of it! Lordy, the man must have a big appetite, but he didn't have an ounce of fat on him. If she ate like that, she'd be a blimp. Clearing her throat to get his attention, she asked, "What do you think?"

She wore the same black nylon dress with the red belt and her red high heels. Sigurd had indeed lengthened the hem by two inches, but it was still three inches above her knees. Worse, though, was the buttoned front that was now sewn strongly right up to mid-breasts. But the result was a very tight-fitting bodice from under her breasts to her waist, much like a bustier, causing her breasts to jut out. That, in combination with the belt cinching in her waist, made her look like one of those Playboy Vargas models.

Sigurd's mouth dropped open, and the only thing he said was, "Lord. Have. Mercy!"

And he wasn't praying.

Just then Sigurd's head shot up and he sniffed the air. Turning, he stared at a waiter approaching on the path leading to the bungalow. Not the same one as before. But nothing unusual in that. The young man was probably coming to remove the cart and dirty dishes.

In the blink of an eye, Sigurd had pulled a long knife from a hidden pocket in his jeans and moved toward the patio. Without looking back at her, he said, "Lock the door after me, and do not open it under any circumstances."

"Huh?" Her puzzlement was multiplied when she saw the waiter seem to recognize Sigurd and smile. And then . . . and then, oh Lord! . . . the waiter began ripping off his clothing.

A flasher? Criminy! I shouldn't be surprised, being here on Porno Island. But that's all I need. How am I going to get by him? And only a half hour until my shift!

But, no, it was much worse than any half-wit getting thrills by sporting the junk in his trunk. No, the young man was evolving—like that Michael Jackson *Thriller* video where he morphs into a vampire—to become some kind of beast. Taller, about seven feet, with claws and a scaly body oozing some kind of slime, red eyes, and long fangs that extended almost to the chin. And he . . . it . . . suddenly had an even bigger knife than Sigurd's.

Holy frickin' hell! And she meant that literally if this was indeed one of the demon vampires Sigurd had mentioned.

She noticed that Sigurd's fangs had elongated, too, by some magic trick, she hoped. Because, frankly, this whole scenario of vampire demons and angels was freaking her out.

They were going at each other now, like warriors. Skilled, for sure, as they sliced and stabbed, lunged and swerved. It was over almost before the strange fight began. Sticking out a long leg, Sigurd tripped the beast, causing it to fall forward on its ugly face. Before it could rise again, Sigurd kicked it hard so that it rolled over. In that brief moment of surprise, Sigurd raised his knife high and stabbed the monster through the heart.

Before her very eyes, Marisa saw the beast dissolve into a pile of what appeared to be slime. With an expression of distaste on his face, Sigurd took a pair of disposable gloves from his back pocket. She supposed doctors carried the things around all the time in case of some emergency, or was it the vampire angels who needed them in case some demon vampire happened to pop out of the bushes. *Ha, ha, ha! I'm losing my mind.*

In any case, Sigurd donned the gloves and picked up the clothing the waiter had worn, dropping the items onto the fire pit, which he immediately lit with the fire starter wand sitting on a nearby table. Then, with the efficiency that bespoke his having done this numerous times before, he went over and turned on the landscape hose coiled onto a bracket attached to the bungalow. He hosed the slime off the flagstones, then returned the hose to its holder. He removed and tossed his gloves onto the fire as well, which was soon dying down.

Only then did he turn and notice her standing at the door, gaping at him with horror. Even as she watched, she saw his fangs retract until they were the normal, slightly longer incisors.

Normal? Hah! There was nothing normal about this guy.

She should be frightened. She was certainly frightened of that beast he'd just destroyed. But for some odd reason, Sigurd himself didn't scare her. Though she was a little repulsed by what she'd just witnessed.

Sigurd seemed to sigh, then walked purposefully toward the door and her. Only when he was inside and the door locked behind him did he speak.

Raising his chin high, as if he sensed her revulsion, he said, "Now do you understand why I must fang you?"

Chapter 12

The Good Book says . . . what? . . .

$\mathcal{S}$igurd sat alone on the deserted end of the beach, waiting for Marisa's waitress shift to end.

Despite being scared spitless after what she had witnessed, the stubborn woman had insisted on going to work.

She still wasn't convinced that vangels and Lucies existed. "It must be some kind of magic. A mirage or something," she had said, hoping he would agree.

"What further proof do you need?"

"None!" She'd backed away from him, as if he was the monster, not the devil he'd destroyed.

Now he had other things to ponder.

"Michael!" Sigurd called out.

Silence.

"I need to talk with you," he yelled, looking upward.

More silence, except for the shush of the waves that hit the shore in a foamy spill and the occasional gull overhead *caw-caw*ing in its flight over the waters, searching for fishy food.

The stars blinked above. The moon shone brightly, bouncing off the water like celestial sparks. But, as usual, Michael didn't come when summoned in a flash of wings and a graceful landing. In fact, most times, he appeared when least expected, when least wanted. Although Sigurd surely wanted him now, as evidenced by his having the balls to summon an archangel. Leastways, Michael would view it that way. Sigurd couldn't be concerned about the repercussions now. Surely more years added on to the already expanded original penance.

Pressing his palms together, fingertips pointing upward in a prayerful position, he pleaded, "Please come."

"What now?" Michael somehow managed to be sitting next to him on the sand, staring out toward the ocean. He was wearing denim jeans and a T-shirt, just like Sigurd, except his were white, all white, and his feet were bare. His long, dark hair hung loose to his shoulders. Sigurd was not a man given to admiring the looks of other men, but Michael was truly glorious in appearance, even in modern clothing. Besides that, there was an aura of light around him, and the essence of some divine perfume, like sandalwood or frankincense. Essence of angel.

My brain is falling apart, bit by bit. Really. Me, speculating on what kind of cologne an archangel exudes!

"Is God's creation of this world not wondrous?" Michael sighed with appreciation at the scene before them. "The oceans, the skies, the moon and stars. Like a fine painting, His brushstrokes created—"

"I need a favor," Sigurd interrupted. When Michael started on a discussion of all the wondrous things the Lord had done, he could go on for a long time. Not that the Lord hadn't done all that Michael tended to drone on about, but time was of essence to Sigurd. "A *big* favor."

"Oh? And thou art deserving of favors . . . why?"

"The Bible says, 'Ask and you shall receive.' So I thought I would ask."

"Thou darest quote the Bible to me? Verily I say, as I have always said, you Vikings are thickheaded fools."

Sigurd felt his face heat. He would like to argue with Michael over that overused insult, but he needed to get in his good graces.

"Furthermore," Michael continued, "the Bible also says, 'Remember, nothing happens but what God wills.'"

"Are you saying that the child is destined to die?" He didn't bother to explain which child. Michael knew. Michael knew everything, if not instantly, then eventually.

"Idiots! I am always having to deal with these idiots." Michael rolled his eyes heavenward. "How true that proverb, 'There is more hope for a fool in Heaven than for someone who speaks without thinking'!"

I am not about to get into a Bible quotation debate with Michael. I would lose before I began. "All I need . . . all she needs . . . is a little bit of money."

"How much?"

"Seventy thousand dollars."

Michael arched his brows.

"To you, that is a small amount."

"How do I know you will not go out and buy a big boat?"

Caught! Michael knows that I was envious of Goldman's yacht. "I wasn't going to kill the man over the boat, which truly was a work of art, though I probably will have to kill him in the end." Even he could recognize how lame his defense sounded.

"Or buy a vintage automobile with angel wings?"

"I was only admiring the damn . . . uh, vintage vehicle. And they are fins, not wings." He referred to the restored, classic 1956 Cadillac Coupe de Ville driven by his hospital director. "Dr. Morgan doesn't deserve such a car."

"And you do?"

"Well, yes. I have been working hard. Do I not deserve a reward?"

He recognized the mistake of his thinking when he saw the stern expression on Michael's face. "When will you learn that envy is your great sin, one you must continually work to conquer?" Michael shook his head as if Sigurd were a hopeless case. "As a dog returns to its vomit, so a fool repeats his folly."

What a picture! "I wasn't going to steal the car or anything. And I certainly don't have the funds for a yacht. Jeesh!"

"Did thou just use the Lord's name in vain?"

"All I said was 'Jeesh!'"

Michael narrowed his eyes at him.

He hadn't thought about it before, but he supposed the word was just a softened way of saying Jesus. "Sorry."

"Sorry carries no credence with me, fool. Besides, should thou not be more concerned about your mission here on this island? What news have you for me?"

"I met with Karl, Svein, Jogeir, and Armod earlier this evening. We spread out and searched every part of the island we could access, and it is our belief there are at most a dozen Lucies here, in addition to the five we have destroyed so far, two of them my kills."

"So few?"

Sigurd shook his head. "There are undoubtedly some on the boats anchored off the island, and Jasper is expected to arrive tomorrow on his own yacht."

"Pfff! It does not surprise me that Satan's comrade would array himself in splendor, as if the fine trappings of an opulent ship could hide his stink. Jasper ever was a vain man, even when he was an angel."

Sigurd did not want to go off on that tangent. Michael liked nothing more than to talk about the fallen angels—Lucifer, Jasper, and the lot—whom Michael had expelled from Heaven. "In any case, according to Zeb, Jasper intends to use only about fifty Lucipires on this mission, his goal being a low-key operation that would garner little attention."

"And how is Zebulan doing?"

"Doing . . . how?"

"Does he show signs of remorse for his sins?"

"He has always shown that . . . as long as I have known him, leastways. Are you really going to turn him into a vangel?"

Michael shrugged. "The Lord's ways are not for me to fathom."

Sigurd wanted to say, *Bullshit!* That Michael had tremendous influence with the Almighty. But that rude expletive would gain him nothing.

Time to bring the subject back to his request. "Will you give me the money to help the child?"

"No."

Would it be a sin to punch an archangel? Probably. "That is all, just no?"

"When wilt thou learn, Viking? That is not the way of our Father. If it was, more people would be winning lotteries, passing exams, getting a new car"—he gave Sigurd a meaningful scowl at that last—"having babies, not having babies, getting miraculous cures, and so on."

"Then why say, 'Ask and you shall receive'?"

"Because when you pray, God always answers your prayer, but not always in the way you want. He guides you toward what is best for you, in the long run."

That was as clear as the water in a Norse fjord on a cloudy day. And Sigurd did not like the sound of that "in the long run." There might not be time for a "long run" for Marisa's child.

"Why dost thou care so much about this child? You have worked with many children losing the battle with cancer. Oh. Could it be that it is the mother you care about?"

"Of course not," Sigurd said quickly. Probably too quickly by the looks of Michael's suspicious eyes.

"Remember my admonition when your brother Mordr married that human last year. No. More. Wives. For. Vangels."

"Hey, I'm not as dumb as you think I am. I got the message loud and clear. I do not even know Marisa all that well, let alone be considering marriage." He might be considering other things, though. Like that old Viking adage: "Bed her, not wed her." He looked directly at Michael to see if he'd read his mind. He hadn't. This time. "And that is your final word? You will not give me the money?"

"I will not."

"I don't suppose you would toss out a miracle for the little girl? No? I didn't think so. I know, I know. 'That is not the way of the Lord.'"

"I trust that you will find a way," Michael said, patting him on the thigh.

"What does that mean?"

But Michael was already gone.

Bite me! ...

Marisa ended her shift at the Phoenix Restaurant shortly after midnight. She was tired to the bone, having worked since five p.m., but it had been a successful night in terms of tips. A whopping thousand dollars.

But that thousand dollars, along with any other money she earned this week, would be gravy. She hoped. The money for Izzie's procedure would come from another source. She hoped.

It was almost with a warped sense of relief that she had made a decision about Harry Goldman. He had been dining in the restaurant with several bigwigs, including Martin Vanderfelt. When Harry had approached her privately as she came out of the kitchen, she had agreed to a late dinner with him on his yacht the following evening. Very late, because she would have to shower and change after her night shift.

A woman did what a woman had to do, Marisa had decided. But she was not dumb; there would be terms set before she, as Sigurd had so crudely put it, "spread her thighs" for the man. She felt queasy at the thought, but not at all guilty, even if Sigurd did claim it to be a grievous sin. Izzie's clock was ticking and Marisa had spent enough time searching for solutions.

Her only goal at the moment was to return to her bungalow, where she hoped to get five hours of much-needed sleep. One of the best things about being so busy was that she hadn't had time to dwell on the gory scene that had occurred earlier that night on her patio.

Vampires? Hah! Didn't matter that they were angel or demon vampires, they were still vampires.

She had a sneaky suspicion, though, that this involved porno flicks in some way. In fact, she'd mentioned to Sigurd first time they'd met in that line outside the Purple Plum Hotel that she'd read an article in *People* magazine about a new porno film series called *Sucked!* But how would Sigurd the Viking Doctor be involved? He'd denied knowledge of the series then. Still . . .

Even more alarming was the possibility that he might have slipped some hallucinogenic drug in her food or diet soda that produced that horrific, imaginary scene. But what would be the purpose of that?

Her head hurt just trying to figure it out.

Exiting the restaurant into the lobby, she was not surprised to see the man himself leaning against an opposite wall, waiting for her. He must have showered and changed because his hair, which had earlier hung loose with thin braids framing his face, was now pulled back in a long ponytail. He wore an unbuttoned, long-sleeved denim shirt over a white T-shirt tucked into button-fly jeans. Well-worn Nike hightops on his big feet. No designer duds for this dude. He didn't need them.

And, yes, she noticed the button fly, even as she tried to tamp down her irritation with the guy. He couldn't seem to take a hint that she didn't want him hanging around. Forget about the protection he promised against some unseen and unbelievable threat. She hadn't needed protection until she met him.

"This is getting old," she said on a sigh, walking toward him.

When she got closer, his head shot up and he sniffed the air. "What have you done, Marisa?"

"Huh?" She felt herself blush. He couldn't possibly know about her date with Harry. Could he? "I have no idea what you mean. And stop sniffing me like I smell or something."

"You smell, all right. Like a bloody damn lemon. I could turn you upside down, dunk you in a fountain, and we'd have lemonade for a hundred people."

"You sure know how to compliment a girl."

"That wasn't a compliment."

"No kidding."

"Sarcasm again! Truly, a quarrelsome woman is like a constant dripping," he told her. "So the Bible says, and I agree."

"I thought that verse referred to a nagging *wife*."

"Same thing," he muttered, and grabbed her by a forearm, steering her across the lobby.

"Hey, we're going the wrong way. My bungalow is that way."

"We are not going to your bungalow."

Uh-oh! "Where are we going?"

"To my hotel room."

"I don't think so!"

"I *do* think so, you willful, irksome wench."

"I'm not going to have sex with you."

"Mayhap you should wait until you are asked."

She felt herself blushing again. Especially since he'd practically frog-marched her into the elevator, where several people were listening intently to their conversation. He pressed the button for the fifth floor and stared straight ahead. His left hand held her right hand, tightly.

"I could scream," she said under her breath.

"Go right ahead. I might even enjoy sticking my tongue down your throat."

"That was crude."

"I am crude."

"I thought you were a doctor."

"Can doctors not be crude?"

"Don't you even care that we have an audience?"

Sigurd didn't even glance at the two men and one woman pretending not to listen to them. "They are vangels."

"They are not!" she said, indignant that she wouldn't know the difference between abnormal beings, like vampire angels, and other beings at this porno conference, who were also abnormal, in her opinion. The woman was all tarted up with high hooker heels, a huge mass of blonde hair, thanks to extensions, and a skin-tight, low-cut, red dress. And the two men, with thick locks slicked back off their faces and wearing slim black pants and garishly colored polyester shirts unbuttoned to the waist, thick gold chains, resembled blond-haired John Travoltas from *Saturday Night Fever*. Someone's idea of what a male porn star would look like, she supposed.

The three of them smiled at her, displaying slightly elongated incisors, just like Sigurd's. The woman gave her a little wave.

Oh my God!

"Convinced?" Sigurd asked, staring straight ahead. Clearly, he was angry with her.

Well, she was angry with him, too. "Did you slip angel dust into my drink this afternoon?"

Someone snickered, but it wasn't Sigurd.

"What?" He turned slowly to look at her.

"That hallucination or whatever it was this afternoon—you know, the woo-woo, I-am-a-fierce-Viking-warrior-fighting-off-scary-demon-monsters . . . Well, I'm thinking you must have given me some kind of drug, like angel dust. Since you claim to be an angel of some kind, it makes perfect sense—"

"Woo-woo?" he asked her with an incredulous expression. "Do not be a lackwit."

"Along with being a willful, quarrelsome wench?"

"You said it!"

The elevator pinged and the doors opened on the fifth floor.

Sigurd said something to the other three in some foreign language and they nodded before heading down the hallway to the right while Sigurd pulled her in the other direction.

"What language was that?" An irrelevant question, but she was so tired she wouldn't know relevant from irrelevant.

"Old Norse."

"Of course it was."

"Your sarcasm is going to cause your death if you are not careful."

"Death by Viking?"

"You said it!" he repeated again. Tugging a key card out of his jeans' pocket, he inserted it into the door, opening it, one-handed. She had trouble making the darn things work with two hands.

Sigurd dropped his death grip on her hand and urged her ahead of him. The door locked ominously behind her, but, for some reason, she wasn't afraid. As long as she didn't accept any drink or food, she should be okay.

Sigurd's hotel room was nice, but not overly large or luxurious, as some of the rooms or suites probably were. A small sitting room held a desk, love seat, and chair facing a flat-screen TV on the wall. The bedroom, seen through a wide archway, had a king-size bed and two bedside tables, along with another flat-screen TV above a triple dresser. Lamps provided soft lighting in both the sitting room and the bedroom.

Sigurd must be a neat freak because there wasn't an item of clothing lying about, or a dirty glass, or even loose change on an end table. In fact, through the open closet door to her immediate right in the little hallway inside the door, she could see his clothing hung neatly on hangers, each equally distant apart, including what appeared to be a full-length cloak.

She touched the cloak and remarked, "Planning on going to a masquerade ball as Zorro while you're here? Or, I know, you really are trying out for a part in that vampire movie series *Sucked!*"

He muttered something.

"Did you actually say that you would like to suck me?"

"No," he said, a grin twitching at his lips, "I said, 'I'll give you *sucked*.' In other words, I intend to do just that."

Moving forward into the other room, she sank down onto the luggage bench at the bottom edge of the bed and sighed. "Listen, I'm exhausted. I need to get some sleep. Say what you have to say so I can go home."

"The time for saying is over. Now is the time for doing." Turning away from her, he took the cell phone off his belt clip, placed it on the dresser, and pressed a button for the voice mail. Belatedly, he realized it was on the speakerphone and he had an audience. He seemed to consider turning it off, then shrugged, as if it didn't matter if she overheard.

"Hey, Sig. Vikar here. Harek and Cnut should arrive tomorrow, along with a dozen more vangels to help you out. I understand that Jasper intends to use only fifty of his Lucies on this mission. The bastard is getting wiser in his old age, unfortunately for us. Anyhow, even fifty kills for us would be a good haul."

"Aren't you afraid to let me hear your secrets? Then you might have to kill me? Ha, ha, ha," Marisa said.

"I'm considering it. Ha, ha, ha."

"They should arrive about dawn," the man named Vikar continued on the voice mail. "There's a supply boat anchored offshore that they'll use as a control center."

Even as he listened, Sigurd took off his denim shirt and folded it over the back of the chair, thus revealing a back shoulder holster. He unbuckled the straps and placed both the holster and pistol carefully on the dresser.

"Cnut and his men will target Jasper's yacht," the voice mail continued. "Harek is concerned about that ship of youthlings that is rumored to be on its way. Let him handle that, and you can focus on the island."

"Ship of youthlings? Huh? What's a youthling?" Marisa asked.

Sigurd, still seething with anger at her—*Big deal!*—ignored her question and lifted the hem of his right and left pant legs, withdrawing throwing stars that had been placed somehow inside the athletic shoes. These, too, he put carefully on the dresser. Or maybe they'd been in some kind of ankle sheaths.

"And who is Vikar? And Harek and Cnut?"

"My brothers. Shh."

"Mike said I'm not to give you any money, if you ask," the Vikar person said with amusement in his voice.

"Pfff! As if I would ask you. Every cent you earn goes into that bloody castle," Sigurd muttered to no one in particular, since the person on the other end of the voice mail couldn't hear him.

"Why do you need seventy thousand dollars anyhow, bro?"

Marisa's lolling head shot up. *Had he asked someone for money, for me? And been denied?* Well, that put the last nail in the coffin of her upcoming "deal" with Harry.

Yanking his T-shirt from the waistband of jeans, Sigurd crossed his arms and drew it up and over his head. From some hidden pocket or slit on the right leg, he removed a long knife, similar to the one he'd used this afternoon in that "imaginary" fight with a demon vampire. It joined the other weapons.

"Call me when you get a chance," the Vikar person was concluding. "Alex was talking to Armod a bit ago and now she's humming the Wedding March. Any idea what that's about?" The sound of a chuckle could be heard clearly over the speaker. "Bye."

Sigurd made a snorting sound of disgust.

"Who's getting married?"

"No one. 'Tis just an example of warped vangel humor."

She didn't see what was funny about someone getting married. But then she'd been so disconcerted by the speaker on the phone and the array of weapons that Sigurd was unloading that she belatedly realized Sigurd was down to bare feet and bare chest, and was about to unbutton his jeans.

"Whoa, whoa, whoa. What's with the striptease?"

"No teasing," he said, leaving the top button undone, which revealed his belly button and a light pelt of hair pointing down, down, down, toward low-riding briefs. Not to mention his wide shoulders and narrow waist and ridged abdomen.

Holy happy trails!

He stared at her then with eyes that were now more silver than blue. The same way they'd gotten when he'd killed that monster in the mirage today, the same way they'd looked when he'd kissed her on Harry's yacht.

It must be a sign of high emotion.

Or arousal.

Oh boy!

"If not a striptease, then what?"

"Time to get down to work. Vangel work."

"What kind of work requires you to be nude?"

He arched one eyebrow, looking meaningfully at his jeans.

"Half nude," she corrected.

"Seduction."

Chapter 13

To seduce or to be seduced? That is the question . . .

"**M**uch as I like those red, swive-me-silly shoes, and much as I picture them in my dreams, kick them off," he suggested. "I would hate to imagine you wearing them in Hell, or even worse, in Horror."

Mayhap later you can model them for me, wearing naught else but the skin God gave you.

If someone doesn't interfere with my plans.

Not that I have any specific plans, someone.

I am just playing this game by ear . . . or is that by cock?

I did not just say . . . think . . . that!

What was her reaction to his demand . . . uh, request that she remove her shoes, the start of her own striptease?

She yawned. The wench actually yawned whilst he stood before her "half nude." Well, she wouldn't be yawning for long.

"You dream of me?" she asked, homing in on the least relevant part of what he'd said.

Instead of chastising her for minimizing the importance of Hell or Horror, he thought, *Only every night since I met you.* But answered with a lie, "No. That was a jest."

"I thought you never jested . . . uh, joked."

I didn't. I don't. "It is a defense weapon I am perfecting since making your acquaintance because . . ."

". . . . because . . . ?"

"Because, you persistent wench, if I do not laugh, I will have to kill you."

"Ha, ha, ha. I thought you were going to say that if you didn't laugh, you would cry."

"That, too." *But not because of some bloody joke. Because I am so horny, I am no doubt growing antlers.* "Take off the damn shoes," he snapped, then tamped his temper down and offered with consideration, which was not usually one of his strong points, "You will be more comfortable."

"For your seduction?"

Screw consideration. "Yes."

"Seduction, huh? Because you are so crazy hot to have me?"

"Well, lukewarm, but with a little encouragement, I could no doubt simmer." *Think boiling blood and steam heat rising off my favorite body parts.*

She arched her pretty brows at him, clearly not buying his enchantment with her.

"If you must know, I have to seduce you in order to gain your consent so that I can fang the sin taint from you." *There! Any plainer and a six-year-old could understand.*

"Are you saying that you seduce everyone you fang? I don't recall you telling me that."

Are you taking notes now? Dost think I tell you everything? There are things that would curl your . . . Never mind. "Of course not." He tried to imagine seducing that pimply-faced, expletive-spewing teenage gang member he'd come across last week in a Miami alley, and shivered with distaste. He had saved the idiot youthling, though, and sent him on his buttocks-exposed, braies-dragging way to sin no more. With a sigh of exaggerated patience, he explained to Marisa, "Victims of a sin taint, or those dreadful sinners on the verge of being taken by the Lucipires, are offered a choice when we vangels find them. They must consent. We cannot fang them otherwise. Do they repent? Do they agree to a vangel's bite to remove the sin poison? Or not?"

"Why am I not being offered a choice?"

He felt like tearing out his own hair, strand by strand. "Because!"

"That was mature!"

For a woman who claims to be exhausted, she sure can talk. Blather, blather, blather. "Because there all kinds of fangings. Betimes a vangel must fang a Lucie, during battle." *Yeech!* "And betimes a vangel fangs his partner during sex." *Not so yeech!* "It enhances the pleasure a hundredfold, I have been told. Sex fanging happens only with a life mate, not in the casual mating, such as modern-day one-night stands."

"I still don't understand."

I don't understand, either, truth to tell. I just know that I must save you. I must. Besides, the less you understand, the better, my dearling. Just say yes. "If I cannot make you agree willingly, then I will seduce you into compliance."

"And that is acceptable according to the vangel rule book."

"Vangel rule book?" He almost smiled. "I do not know what the 'rule book' says in that regard. Since we are at cross wills on this issue, I can only try to convince you to my way of thinking without actually clubbing you over your stubborn head." *And enjoy myself in the process.*

"I'm so tired. Can't we do this some other night?"

A ploy to stop me altogether. I am not so thickheaded that I cannot see that. "No, we cannot forestall the inevitable. I have too many other responsibilities weighing on me without worry over you." *Plus I have an enthusiasm that is becoming more enthused by the second.* "I'll do all the work. Just lie back and let me fang you."

"Men have been telling women that for centuries, but they say 'bang,' not 'fang.'"

"You deliberately missay me. And crudely, too. Just lie back and let it happen. It will be over before you know it."

"Just lie back and dream of England, huh?"

England? What has England to do with this? The bloody Saxons! Even during sex, they stick their big noses in Viking affairs. "Or sugarplums, or whatever little girls dream of," he suggested, instead.

She gave him a pointed, unconsciously sultry look. "I'm not a little girl."

"I know." *Lord, but I bloody hell know!*

He went down on one knee and removed first one high heel, then the other. He hadn't expected the gesture to feel so intimate. But, by the heavens, it did. Monumentally so! She felt it, too. However, instead of enjoying the experience, she would have kicked him if he hadn't surprised her before that thought entered her head by holding on to her ankles. "Wha-what?"

He considered pushing his luck and sliding his palms up her calves and over her thighs, but if there was anything a Viking warrior knew about battles it was: Timing is everything. Marisa wasn't nearly ready for such a direct assault.

That didn't mean he could wait for something to happen. What was that modern adage: "You snooze, you lose." Or as Sorkel the Skald used to say, "He who hesitates has an axe in his head."

He placed his hands on her waist and rose to his two feet, taking her with him. For just one second, he placed a kiss on her stunned lips as she dangled above the carpet like a limp puppet. Then he tossed her up and onto the middle of the big bed and crawled over her before she regained her senses and attempted to get away. Or walloped him with a pillow.

"Get off me, you big baboon." She yawned again.

"Not a chance."

Yet another yawn.

It was insulting, really. Vikings did not bore women. And, no matter what else he was, he was still a Viking.

"I can't breathe."

"Liar." His arms were levered over her, his lower body pressing her to the bed. He was not suffocating her, no matter what she implied. Still, he put his mouth close to hers and blew softly between her lips. He had no idea why he did it. A reflex, mayhap.

She gasped, and, to his surprise, she blew back into his mouth.

He gasped, too.

Soon, they were exchanging breaths in an even, rhythmic fashion. He was breathing for her. She was breathing for him. They were breathing as one.

He had never done such before, and he doubted she had, either, by the stunned expression on her face. At least she was no longer yawning.

"What are you doing to me?" she whispered.

"What are you doing to me?" he countered.

"This is the sorriest seduction I've ever experienced," she said, though he could tell she was intrigued. In fact, she was licking her lips as if to retain the taste of him, even though they hadn't actually kissed.

He imagined that he felt every lick of her tongue on a certain part of his body. "I have not yet begun," he rasped out.

"Begun what?"

She's confused. Good! Every Viking knows a confused woman is halfway to the bed furs. "Seduction. I have not yet begun my seduction." He paused. "A sorry seduction, you say? Get seduced a lot, do you?"

"Every other day at least."

He started to smile and then corrected the action because his fangs were already starting to elongate with arousal, and he didn't want to scare her. Yet. Forget scaring. Another part of his body was elongating, too. The one that imagined licking. He could tell the exact moment she noticed the hardened rod aligned perfectly betwixt her parted thighs because her squirming stopped, abruptly. And it wasn't fright at all he saw on her face now. The exhaustion had left her eyes and was replaced with . . . interest?

"Consider me seduced," she said, and wiggled her bottom so that she rubbed herself against him like a cat against a catnip pole.

He felt like purring. Or swishing his manly tail. "No, no, no. You cannot be seduced so quickly. You must needs be writhing with want, begging for me to . . . take you." What he really meant was "bite you," but 'twas best not to remind her of that until the perfect moment.

"I could writhe," she said, and did in fact do just that, placing her arms overhead and thrashing her body about sinuously like a harlot in heat. She gazed up at him through half-slitted, sultry eyes. Then concluded, "Seduced!"

Is she playing me at my own game? Is the witch trying to seduce me? Does she dare make mock of me? "You cannot be seduced so quickly. Seduction takes time and talent."

Sure enough, when she thought he was relaxed with her seeming consent, she gave his chest a mighty shove and attempted to slide out from under him. He let her, but then caught her with an arm about her waist and rolled so that she was on top, straddling him, the hem of the dress having ridden up practically to the bridge of her thighs . . . a bridge he was dying to cross. In the process he slid the back zipper of her dress from her neckline to the belt, which he unbuckled and tossed aside.

Caught by surprise, she fought to crawl off him and, at the same time, keep her dress from falling off in front.

Accommodating fellow that he was, he helped. Lower the dress, that was.

Holy frickin' clouds! Her hair, which had been clipped neatly atop her head with tortoiseshell combs, had come undone on one side and hung loose to a bare shoulder. The waitress dress, which he had sewn so expertly for her that afternoon, fell forward, catching at her elbows. She wore a blush-colored lace undergarment that cupped her full breasts and raised them up like ripe peaches, and he did love a good peach.

He rolled so that she was under him again. "Dost yield, wench? Dost repent of the sin you are contemplating? Dost welcome my bite? Dost agree to stay away from Harry Goldman and other men who pay for services?"

"Dost, dost, dost!" she mimicked. "Dost that 'men who pay for services' apply to you, too? You mentioned that you might be able to get the money for me."

His heart sank down to his navel. *Oh, the unfairness of it! To be reminded at this moment that I am here for a higher calling, not to take advantage of a wench's weakness.* "Now you would couple with me for money?" *The sin taint must be getting stronger.* "You said that you would prostitute yourself with Goldman but not with me."

"I never used the word *prostitute*."

"I have no patience with word games." *Certainly not*

now when my brain is blurred with the possibilities of other kinds of games.

"This is no game to me." When he did not respond to that remark, she prodded, "Well? Show me the money."

He shook his head. "The . . . uh, person from whom I might have obtained the funds, declined."

"If there ever was such a person to begin with!"

"I do not lie." *Much.*

"So you're poor as a church mouse. Just like me."

More like a rat. Leastways, that is how I am feeling in my failure to convince Mike. "You could say that."

"Then I don't agree to anything, you big oaf."

"So be it," he said with mock resignation. Mock, because he was beginning to enjoy this verbal sparring and its inevitable outcome. "Seduction it is, then."

"Do your best," she snarled, and there was definite challenge in her voice.

His elbows were braced on either side of her head, but his hands were free, and he used his fingers to brush the loose strands of hair behind her one ear. Then he laved a line with his tongue from the center of her upraised chin to the lobe of her ear, which he nipped with his teeth.

She stiffened.

His moist tongue traced the inner whorls of her shell-like ear. Then he blew the wetness dry.

She shivered.

He used the tip of his tongue to stab into the center of her ear in a cadence matched to the beat of his pounding heart. At the same time, his hands had moved under her and lifted her silk-clad buttocks, exposed by the rising hem of her dress, in his palms, and guided her hips in a rhythmic counterpoint to the thrusts of his tongue. Multitasking at its finest!

She moaned.

Or mayhap he was the one who moaned.

His head spun as a strange fog of sensuality seemed to be swirling about their bodies. Not quite a fog, actually. More like wisps of cloudy sensations wrapping around them like a cocoon, teasing, tempting. The tendrils of the mist were caressing his body, like fingers. Or was it Marisa's fingers? No, her arms were braced tightly against her sides as she attempted to resist his charms.

And the air, ah, it was filled with the scent of honey and ginger. It occurred to him in that moment that the most delicious meal in the world, one he was going to try first chance he got, was peaches drizzled with ginger honey. Was there such a dish? If not, he would invent one.

Mayhap she had eaten something with those flavors, and that was why he smelled them so strongly. He would taste her lips, just to make sure. Leastways, that's what he told himself as his lips swooped down to take succor from her parted lips. This was no sweet, tentative kiss. More like a hungry, devouring search for . . . something.

He nipped her lips and tongue. He wet her lips. He sucked and thrust and pressed and thrust and thrust and thrust.

Somehow, sometime, in the process, she'd wrapped her arms around his shoulders. Her bare legs twined about his thighs. And she was answering him, kiss for kiss.

It was no longer a question of would she yield? Would he?

Sigurd had never intended to take this "seduction" to the level of actual intercourse. Fool that he was, he'd planned the "near-sex" that his brother Trond had claimed to invent. All the touching and feeling and pleasure of bedplay without the sinful outcome . . .

well, sinful in Michael's eyes for unmarried couples, and, since marriage was forbidden, sinful, period, for vangels. Trond claimed it was almost as good as the real thing, meaning actual intercourse. This would be Sigurd's first walk down that path.

Who am I kidding?

A lose-lose situation.

And I am definitely losing.

Or winning, some might say.

Aaarrgh!

He panted for breath as he raised his head to look down at her.

She stared up at him, and while she held his eyes, she undid the front clasp on her bra and drew the fabric apart.

He was truly lost then.

Her breasts were full, even lying down—*some women's breasts went flat as oatcakes when on their backs, a definite prick to the balloon of unrealistic male expectations*—and not peach-colored at all. More a dusky olive tone to go with her Spanish heritage.

In that moment, Sigurd decided that he liked olives, almost as much as he did peaches.

The areolas were a dusky rose, the nipples pointed nubs of paler pink.

He touched them, just touched them with the tips of his fingers, and she arched up off the bed, keening her pleasure in a long wail. "Aaaaaahhhhh!"

Temptation reared its head, and he succumbed without a shred of resistance to the desire, nay the compulsion, to sample the feast laid afore him. No tentative licks of the tongue or sweet kisses from his lips now. Instead, he took one breast into his mouth, areola and all, and sucked rhythmically, his tongue pressed against the hardened nipple.

As if he'd flicked the switch on her motor, she began

to buck against him. With a keening wail of "Oh, oh, oh, oh, oh . . ." she began to climax. Just from his ministering to her breast! What would she do if he employed any one of the dozens of other talents he had in his centuries-old arsenal?

Her peaking triggered his orgasm as well, and even as he continued to suckle her and thrust his denim-clad hips against the vee of her legs, he did something he had not done since he was an untried youthling back in the Norselands. He spilled his seed inside his braies. And it felt so damn wonderful!

He raised his head and saw that she was as stunned as he at the short bout of ecstasy that had overcome them. He probably could have gained her consent then for a sin fanging, but he wanted more now. Much more. Instead of being sated, his appetite was whetted. The sensual fog still surrounded them, in fact was growing stronger. Resisting temptation was no longer an option, if it ever had been. Especially since underlying it all was the faint scent of lemons.

With a speed honed over the centuries, he eased out of his jeans and small garment, wiping the wetness off himself with the dry part of the briefs. Then he tugged her loosened dress down over her hips and legs, leaving only a blush-colored scrap of fabric covering her clearly damp mons.

He put a hand over the dampness, then leaned down to sniff her musk. What a heady, heady scent to an already aroused male! And, yes, he was growing hard again. It had been so long, and she was so very fucksome.

His touch there caused her to rouse from her sex stupor, and she blinked several times before murmuring, "What? What did you do to me?"

He was not about to let her regain her senses. Yet. Nor would he argue who had done what to whom. Yet.

The silk briefs joined the waitress dress, his jeans, and briefs in a pile on the floor. Not daring to put his body over hers, skin to skin, for fear of embarrassing himself, again, he instead lay on his side, propped on one elbow, and gazed down at her. No time to admire his handiwork in the kiss-swollen lips and budding nipples, or the sex flush that covered her face and upper chest. He placed a hand over her dark curls and urged, "Open for me, sweetling. Let me bring you to paradise."

"Been there. Done that. Waiting for the T-shirt."

"Huh?"

"Listen, Sigurd. It's been a long time since I've had sex, and—"

"Not nearly as long as me, sweetling."

She tapped him on the chin in chastisement for his interruption.

He nipped at the forefinger before she yanked it back.

"As I said, I've gone without for a long time, and that's my only excuse for coming like a locomotive at your mere touch."

"Loco-locomotive," he sputtered. "Mere?"

She scowled at yet another of his interruptions.

He played with one of her breasts to make up for his rudeness.

She slapped the hand away. "Let me finish."

He rolled over onto his back and put his hands up in surrender.

"As I said, twice now, I haven't had sex since dinosaurs roamed the earth, practically, and I certainly didn't plan on doing so tonight, but now that I'm here, I don't believe in playing games," she informed him.

"Which means?"

"Let's just do it and be done."

Huh? What did she say? "Just do it," he repeated dumbly. "No. See, the thing is, I never intended for us to actually do it. More like near-doing-it. Ha, ha, ha! Wait. What are you doing? Oh! Oh crap! Oh no, no, no! Oh yes, yes, yes!"

She had thrown a leg over him and levered herself up to a sitting position. *On him!* Before he could blink or say, "Sweet swiving sin!" or some such nonsense, she took his rampant erection in hand and was guiding him home.

He might have seen stars then.

"Hol-y mol-y!" she said, gaping at him as her body adjusted to his size, the inner muscles rippling and clutching like an erotic glove. A perfect fit!

"Do. Not. Move!" he ordered, and put his hands on her hips to make sure she obeyed his command. If she shifted even one little bit, he would be the one making locomotive sounds. And not the *chug-chug-chug*ging sounds, either. More like the *toot-toot* whistling ones, heralding a big train on the way! *My brain has turned to porridge.*

She stared at him for a long moment. "So. You never intended to actually do the deed with me? Just tease me?"

"Seduce you," he corrected, "but instead . . ."

"Instead . . . what?" she asked when he failed to finish his sentence.

"Instead you seduced me."

She should have been outraged at his suggestion, but no, this wench just smiled a little Mona Lisa smile, and Sigurd, having met the model for the Mona Lisa at one time, knew good and well what that smile meant. She was pleased with herself.

"And now what?" she purred, leaning forward so that her breasts touched his chest hairs. Holding his eyes with her unblinking ones, she used her breasts like pendulums, back and forth, back and forth.

He felt the reverberation of her action all the way to

his cock, which grew even larger inside her. Without any direction from him! Not that he ever had much luck "directing" that fool appendage.

She felt the reverberation, too, he could tell, because her vaginal muscles quivered around him. She sat up abruptly, stunned.

He impaled her still. Sweet heavenly skies! Did he ever!

Neither of them moved, down there, and yet there *was* movement. Subtle and excruciatingly, torturously exciting shifts where they were joined.

Something strange and mystical and wonderful was happening. The ginger-honey fog swirled about him, turning him nigh intoxicated like the most intense ale-head madness. The fine hairs all over his body stood to attention like erotic antennae. What the fuck was going on? He didn't have a clue, and, frankly, for his sins, he didn't demon-damn care.

"You ask what happens next?" he asked in a voice he scarce recognized for its rawness. *I haven't a clue.* He flipped her over and under him and ever so slightly lifted himself up and back inside her. "And now the seduction begins."

"About time!"

Chapter 14

Drac had nothing on him! . . .

"About time, is it?" Sigurd shook his head at her. "Keep daring me, you wanton wench, and you will be sorry."

"I'm already sorry, but that doesn't mean I want you to stop."

Did I just say that? Who am I? Who am I becoming? Wanton . . . that about says it all. Next I'll be twerking.

No, I won't.

Marisa didn't recognize the person behaving in this manner. She was no virgin, true, but she didn't have all that much sexual experience, either, other than Chip the Dip(shit) back in college, and two other short-term affairs since then. Very short. But being the sexual aggressor was beyond anything she'd ever done before.

Not that I started this whole shebang.

But I succumbed so-o-o easily.

You could say I put the she in the bang.

I was certainly the one who put him inside me.

Where he still is.

Boy, is he ever!

She-bang, she-bang, she sang to herself, doo-wop style.

"Do you blush now, Mar-is-a?" Sigurd drawled. "Troll's breath! You do!" He hooted with glee.

It was enough to make her want to pull the blankets over her head with humiliation. Except that she was already covered. By the man himself.

She-bang, she-bang, her inner slut crooned.

She blamed it on the fog that seemed to envelop them. An orangey-evergreen mist with tendrils that swirled and touched all the secret places on her body, exciting her to the point of madness . . . or wanton behavior. In fact, even her scalp felt stimulated with sexual tension. The sensations were—she hated to use the word, but no other would suffice—heavenly.

Sigurd had her pinned to the bed with his "impalement," but her upper body was relatively free, with his upper body braced on his elbows over her. So she took advantage of the freedom to arch her breasts up off the mattress against his chest with her head thrown back. The fine hairs there, along with the foggy threads of carnal mist, abraded her nipples with such sweet torture that her inner muscles spasmed around him.

She saw the surprise on his handsome face. "You are killing me," he groaned.

"I thought you were already dead."

"I am. You are killing me again."

A sudden, uncomfortable thought occurred to her. "You're not going to impregnate me with some monster seed, like *Rosemary's Baby*, are you? I mean, some people say I look like Sophia Loren, but Mia Farrow? No way!"

"Sophia Loren? Isn't she an elder movie star? Nay, I do not see the resemblance." He was huffing slightly, as if he was trying to get his arousal under control. Fat chance! The huffing reverberated down to where they were joined and gave her a few little jolts, like electric shocks.

Marisa got so sick of the Italian actress comparison some times. Harry Goldman was the most recent man to home in on the resemblance. In fact, he seemed obsessed, like she was a doppelganger or something. It was refreshing to be just herself. "I could kiss you for that," she told Sigurd.

And she did just that, with lips and tongue and teeth, to his obvious surprise, though he shouldn't be all that surprised. After all, she'd practically impaled herself on him without an invitation.

"That was a demon in *Rosemary's Baby*," Sigurd told her when she ended the kiss. "I am an angel, remember?"

"How can I forget? A *vampire* angel." For emphasis, she reached up and did a quick hit-and-run lick of one of his exposed fangs.

If the tongue-kiss had startled him, the fang-lick had a different reaction. He was the one spasming inside her then, before he stiffened and got himself under control. And she meant the other parts of his body stiffened, not *that* part, which was already stiff, of course.

Interesting, though. That fangs are especially sensitive. Like my nipples. She stored that information away for later. And the fact that his fangs tasted like the sweetest, most delicious oranges.

"Besides, I could not impregnate you, even if I wanted to, which I do not." He was back to the *Rosemary's Baby* subject, which she'd already moved on from . . . to nipples. Much more interesting. "Except for my brother Ivak, all vangels are sterile. He recently had a baby, named Michael. Ivak ever was a suck-up!"

"Good thing about the sterility because I totally

forgot that you aren't wearing a condom." And that was a monumental mistake she never made. A sign of just how strange this whole encounter was. "Um, do I have to worry about STDs?"

"Marisa! I am a doctor." He shook his head at her asking such a question. "I get tested all the time, even though I have not been active sexually in a long time."

She found that hard to believe, that a man as virile as he was could go without for more than, oh, let's say, a week, but that was a question for another time. "So, back when you were a Viking—"

"I will always be a Viking."

"Okay, back when you were a human Viking," *Lord, that sounds so dumb.* "Did you have children?"

"No. None that I know of."

"Do you care that you can't have children now?"

"Not much," he said. "Enough with this chatter. You are distracting me, and I must concentrate lest I explode from overarousal."

That was exactly the point. She was trying to make him lose control. He'd teased her enough. Time to give him a taste of his own medicine. "Is there such a thing as overarousal?" She put her arms on his shoulders and raised her knees on either side of his hips, feet firmly planted on the bed. A clear signal, if there ever was one, that she was more than ready for him to move, that she was the one in control.

"I am depending on it," he said, and withdrew himself inch by inch from inside her, then inch by inch put himself back in again, to the hilt. Definitely an impalement. Of the best kind.

She looked down, with fascination, at the picture they made there. His silky blond hairs blending with her coarse black curls, a tapestry of sex. Forget that classic combination, ebony and ivory. This was onyx and gold.

"Pretty," he said, and she saw that he was looking at the same place she was.

Then, to her chagrin, Sigurd withdrew from inside her, every excruciating drag a pleasure-pain path. She grabbed his hips to hold him in, but he was stronger than she . . . and determined. And in control. Dammit!

"No, no, no!" she protested.

"Shh," he said, placing her hands above her head, "we do it my way."

"But—"

"This time."

"Oh boy!"

Sigurd laughed and then used what seemed like two hours, but was probably only twenty minutes, to demonstrate just what a master of seduction he really was. Marisa had been outclassed in that game from the get-go. And she no longer cared. What hormone-packing woman would?

He caressed her skin and murmured his approval of everything he saw and touched. The smoothness. The naturally tan, olive tones. The dips and swells. He was especially fascinated by her breasts, "the perfect size to fit a big man's hands," and her butt, "firm but deliciously ample." She would have been insulted, except he made "ample" sound like the highest compliment. Truly, there wasn't any part of her body that escaped his attention, including her toes, "like succulent figs." At first, she thought he said "pigs," as in "This little piggy . . ." and almost giggled. Almost. But he'd already moved on to her belly button, "Satan's well." That last wasn't such a great compliment, either, in her opinion, but Sigurd explained that he meant it was "sinfully tempting."

Okaay!

He was also vocal in his appreciation of her taste as he explored her with his mouth. And there wasn't anyplace forbidden to this man's wicked lips and tongue and teeth, and, yes, fangs, which she'd discovered added a new dimension to a kiss. A little extra friction. A little extra bite of pleasure. Oh, he never broke the skin. That he was saving for when she gave her full consent. Frankly, at this point, she would agree to swinging on a trapeze, or a cloud, if he would just damndamndamn-move-dammit inside her.

"Do you like this?" he murmured, as he sucked softly against the sensitive skin of her neck.

"Yes. Can I touch you now?"

"Not yet. How about here?" He was kissing the underside of one breast.

"Yes, but higher," she demanded.

"Here?" His lips moved over to her underarm, which, to her surprise, was an erotic spot on her body she'd been unaware of. Still, it was not where she wanted . . . needed . . . to be touched. "The underside of a woman's arm, where it meets her body, is especially sensitive on some women. Do you agree?"

"Talk, talk, talk. I would agree that the moon was made of blue cheese if you would just move."

She felt laughter rumble in his chest, reverberating right down to his penis that was embedded even tighter inside her, if that was possible.

"You know that I can feel your penis laughing, don't you?"

"What?" That certainly got his attention. He raised his head. He had been licking the curve of her elbow. "It does not," he said indignantly, as if a laughing male appendage was the last thing on earth he would want.

"Oh yeah, it definitely does. You laugh. It laughs, too."

"That was another deliberate attempt to distract me," he decided, then used his nose to nuzzle her underarm. He was back to that territory again. "You never answered. Dost like me here?"

"Yes. No. Maybe. Aaarrgh! You know good and well where I want your mouth. Either put yourself there now or I'm going to grab on to those angel wing knobs of yours and guide you there." She'd already discovered that just the mere brush of her fingertips over that scar tissue caused him to practically jump off the bed. She started to lower her hands to do just that when he grabbed her wrists and raised them on high again, pressing them down onto the mattress above her head, and holding them in place with just one hand.

He suckled her then, with an expertise that was beyond anything she'd ever experienced or imagined. He drew on her hard, then soft. Setting a rhythm that alternated with flicks of his tongue and the grating of teeth against her nipples. Her breasts seemed to throb. Her nipples hardened even more and were almost painful with the intensity of his ministrations. The expression "Hurts so good!" came to mind.

Then, he withdrew his penis from inside her and used his hand to guide its tip in a strumming fashion across her engorged clitoris. Once, twice, and she began to keen, "Oh, oh, oh . . ." The prelude to her orgasm. He slammed back inside her.

And stopped.

Again.

She moaned.

Again.

"Stop your climax," he ordered.

"What? How?" she stammered through the haze of the overwhelming excitement rippling over her body.

"Stiffen your body. Look at me." When her sex-hazy eyes were unable to focus, he demanded again. "Look. At. Me." But his voice was so raw and raspy with his own arousal that she could hardly hear him.

His eyes were more silver than blue now. His long hair was thrown back over his shoulders. And he could no longer hide his fangs, which should have been frightening, but for some odd reason were just the opposite.

"I like your fangs," she whispered.

He nodded, as if that had some meaning.

"Do you agree to my removing the sin taint, Maris-a?"

She nodded. She would agree to anything he asked of her now, her body was so thrumming with need.

"Do you repent of the sin you are contemplating? Will you deny Harry Goldman your body? Will you let me fang you?"

"Yes, yes, yes!"

"So be it!" He licked his lips and put his mouth to her neck. The piercing didn't hurt at all. In fact, she rather liked the feel of his fangs breaking her skin. When he groaned deep in his throat, she sensed the moment that her first drop of blood trickled into his mouth.

But then, she lost all sense of what was happening where. His fangs at her neck. His hands everywhere, always on the move, caressing and arranging her body this way and that to intensify what his erection was doing inside. Because he was finally, finally, moving.

In, out, in, out, he moved with incredible slowness.

Suddenly, he wasn't moving slowly at all. He was pounding into her. Slam, slam, slam. Each wet, slick sound of him hitting her just there was causing the most incredible, hard, convulsing climax of her life. And it was never-ending.

Somehow, her knees were over his shoulders. When had that happened? She took advantage of the opportunity and used the backs of her calves to rub against his angel wing scars.

He roared, he actually roared, when she did that

and she felt some warm liquid eject from his fangs into her neck and, like the headiest, most potent aphrodisiac, her entire body went on humming, mind-blowing red alert.

Good Lord! Do fangs ejaculate? And do they ejaculate some sex drug or something? Should I be alarmed? Hah! Too late for that!

And speaking . . . thinking . . . of ejaculating, he was certainly doing that below at the same time. A torrid stream was hitting her vaginal walls. Talk about multitasking, she thought, which was amazing that she could even put two thoughts together in the midst of this mind-blowing sex.

Even more amazing, she could swear she was doing the same. She'd heard that some women ejaculate during orgasm, but it had never happened to her before. It hot damn was now.

Even her breasts seemed to be throbbing convulsively. A breast climax? That was a new one. If she ejaculated there, she would be mortified, not that she wasn't mortified by the other ejaculation. She lowered her hands and touched her breasts. The only moisture was what remained from Sigurd's mouth. *Whew!*

Finally, he withdrew his fangs from her neck with a tiny pop, threw his head back, his arms extended like virtual tree limbs, and groaned long and hard as he continued to twitch inside her, and her body continued to spasm around him.

She thought she heard him mutter, "Holy Heaven and Viking Valhalla!" before she passed out.

Love me, love my fangs . . .

Marisa slept soundly, and Sigurd let her. For now. After revealing her earthy, passionate side to him

(*Viking men did appreciate an earthy woman!*), Marisa had another thing coming if she thought he was going to be satisfied with just one taste. (*Viking men were known for their appetites, and his long-deprived hunger was immense.*) He would need at least two or three or twenty bouts of sex play with her and feared even that would not be enough. (*This Viking man knew a good thing when it hit him in the . . . face, if not other body parts.*)

This was the best sex Sigurd had ever experienced, and he was going to have to pay for it in additional vangel years. He knew it sure as boars snort and bears bellow. But at the moment, he was more than willing to pay the price for ecstasy of this monumental nature.

At first, Marisa had lost consciousness from the shocking intensity of their mutual climax. And, yes, it had been shocking, even to a man with almost twelve hundred years of experience in the bed arts. He might have gone light-headed himself for a few moments.

But now she slept, because of the bone-melting satiety, as well as the well-earned exhaustion from over-work. The poor woman was deluded if she thought she could keep up this pace of hours on her feet, even if she was young and healthy, even if only for ten days. On the other hand, needs must, and her need for money was a driving factor. He envied those who had wealth in abundance, even as he recognized the truth of that adage about money being the root of all evil.

At least he'd removed the sin taint from her, and she'd agreed to abandon plans for sex with Harry Goldman for money. He realized, though, that she hadn't agreed to leave the island, which continued to be dangerous with all the Lucies in residence or just arriving.

He lay on his side, propped on one elbow, looking down at her. One arm was thrown over her head in abandon. The hand of the other arm was splayed over her flat stomach in a protective manner, which he found interesting. Was she reliving in her dreams all they had done? He hoped so. He certainly would for years to come.

Damn, but Mike is gonna have my ass.

Her hair had come loose from the combs that had held the long strands atop her head. He would look for the combs later. Bed-mussed hair . . . was there a greater turn-on for a man? Well, yes, there was, actually. Her breasts were full, the nipples still erect, like bruised rosebuds, from his ministrations. He liked that he'd marked her in that way. A secret he would have of her once she was clothed again, out and about.

Although she was slim and leggy, her waist was uncommonly small, thus giving her a voluptuous appearance. Her stomach was flat, leading down to a thatch of dark curls. Many women waxed themselves there, but he much preferred the mystery of the female body the way nature intended. When spread wide to a man's eyes, 'twas like opening a gift. Different every time, and yet essentially the same.

He leaned down and sniffed her. Her musk, along with his seed, made a compelling scent that caused his cock to twitch. Who was he fooling? His cock had scarce left her inner channel afore starting to twitch. A nonstop sex twitch.

I will have to tell my brothers about this new talent.

Or not.

She squirmed in the bed and made a snuffling sound, as if she might be awakening.

He immediately drew back to his position at her side, knowing without a doubt that she would be repulsed by his smelling her intimate parts. Women were strange that way. He, personally, would not mind her sniffing him, as long as he was clean at the time. Cleanliness was an attribute most Vikings favored.

Back in the day—*Did I really think that? Back in the day? Am I becoming a graybeard?*—the cleanliness of a Viking man was why women of so many countries welcomed them to their bed furs. That and their virile good looks, of course.

The air conditioner in the room kicked on, and that slight noise caused her eyes to open suddenly and stare at him in shock.

"Oh my God! It wasn't a dream." She glanced down and saw her wanton pose of nudity. The hand above her head shot down to cover her mons while her other arm pressed over her breasts. They did little to hide anything.

"I've seen all your bits, sweetling," he told her with a grin he didn't even try to curb. "Nothing to hide now."

She groaned. "Where's the sheet? Give me the sheet."

He was lying on the sheet and not about to budge.

"This should not have happened." As if some memory just came to her, she put a hand to her neck. "Did you . . . ?"

"I did."

"Is it . . . the thing you keep harping on . . . gone?"

"The sin taint? I don't know. You tell me. Do you feel any different?"

"I am supposed to have a date with Harry tonight, but the thought makes me nauseous. I think I would throw up if he touched me."

"Good," he said.

She glanced at the luminous numbers on the bed-side clock and squealed, "One-thirty. I have to go. I'll never be able to get up at four to go to work at the spa." She threw her legs over the side of the bed and sat up, all in one motion.

"You're not going anywhere." With a growl, he took her by the waist and tossed her up and over his body to the far side of the bed, the one against the wall. Arranging himself over her, he said, "I am not nearly done with you."

She paused in her squirming attempt to escape his embrace. "Is there more you need to do . . . related to the sin taint?"

"No." He licked at her lips, which were swollen from his kisses. Just before thrusting his tongue into her mouth, he informed her, "This time is for me."

Then, rolling her again, onto her belly, he raised her up on her knees, her face pressed into the pillow, and took her from behind, a position that allowed him to fondle and stroke her breasts and female bud at the same time.

She screamed. Eventually.

He roared. Eventually.

Life was good.

Chapter 15

Sex, Viking style! Holy Valhalla! . . .

Sigurd was insatiable.

She was insatiable.

He fanged her.

She f— nailed him.

He took her doggie-style.

She invited him to shower with her. His suite might be modest, but the bathroom was not. Multiple heads, rainforest shower, and a Jacuzzi bathtub. Enough said!

He showed her the Viking S-spot. With his tongue!

She showed him how to salsa dance. In the nude.

Finally, when every bone and muscle in her body ached with fatigue, she fell into a deep sleep, only to awaken abruptly several hours later at the sound of a food cart being rolled into the room. She hid under the duvet until the amused waiter left.

"You can come out now," Sigurd said with a laugh. "The boy has left. You made his day, by the way."

"What time is it?" she asked, sitting up, the duvet held up over her breasts.

"Ten o'clock."

She tossed the bedspread aside and jumped out of the bed, uncaring now of her nudity. "This is bad, really bad." She scrambled to find her clothing and discovered it folded neatly in a pile on the dresser, her underwear and the uniform. The high heels were tucked side by side against the wall. She was too distraught to be embarrassed over Sigurd handling her underwear. "This is bad, really bad," she repeated. "Late for work my second day. I had five appointments lined up for this morning. I'll be fired."

"Slow down, Mar-is-a. You do not have to be at work until five. I made some . . . uh, arrangements with the spa director. By the by, Hedy is a very nice woman. Didst know she took a fjord cruise to the Norselands on her vacation five years ago?"

"Aaarrgh!" She found a hotel terry-cloth robe and put it on before confronting him, hands on hips. "What kind of arrangements?"

Color bloomed on his face.

Not a good sign.

"Sit down and eat. We will talk."

"I don't want to eat." She glanced at the mirror over the dresser, then did a double take. "Oh. My. God!" Her hair looked like it had been pulled through a keyhole, backward. Her face and neck and the vee of skin on her chest revealed by the robe were whisker burned, or was it a sex flush? Same thing. Her lips were bee-stung swollen, better than Botox any day. There was a slight bruise on her neck that might be a fang mark. She could only imagine the condition of the rest of her body. A slight memory of Sigurd sucking on her inner thighs came to mind. "Oh. My. God!" she repeated.

"You really should not use God as an expletive," he told her, sitting down on one of the two chairs that had been arranged about the table, picking up a piece of toast, which he proceeded to butter.

The last thing she expected from him was a lecture on her morality, especially after the night they'd just spent together. She moaned softly just thinking about it, especially . . . No, she couldn't possibly have done *that*.

She plopped down into the chair facing him. "What arrangements?" she asked again.

"Hedy was very accommodating when I told her you were indisposed."

"Indisposed." She put a hand to her aching head.

"Unable to do massages in the spa this morning. Instead, you are doing personal . . . uh, therapy on me this morning in my hotel room. I paid her the spa fee, from which you will be paid, and if you would not be offended, I will give you a generous tip. No, no, no! Do not dare put that outraged expression on your face. This is not money for services rendered. This is just a friend helping you out."

"Friend?" she scoffed.

"Lover. Angel. Whatever. I forced you to come with me last night, and I am responsible for your sleeping in this morning."

"You didn't force me to do anything," she admitted, and sighed with resignation. "But if you dare to leave me a tip, I'm going to cut off your favorite body part with a butter knife. No. I take that back. It better be a really big tip."

He grinned.

"I thought you didn't have any money."

"I never said I have no money. I said I do not have seventy thousand dollars in ready cash."

"How come you're not working? Don't you have to be in your doctor's office for walk-ins?"

"Karl is handling any routine patients. If there is a serious problem, he will alert me."

"Very efficient," she said with what was becoming her usual sarcasm.

He didn't seem to mind. "I like that you do not whine and complain endlessly about having succumbed to my charms."

"Don't flatter yourself," she said, helping herself to Eggs Benedict and small dish of fresh fruit, in addition to black coffee laced with two spoons of sugar. "I behaved out of character . . . and, believe me, I never do what I did last night . . . because it's been so long since I had sex."

"Not nearly as long as me," he said, not for the first time referring to a long bout of celibacy, which she still found hard to believe, especially after his performance with her. While he spoke, he spread peach jam on his buttered toast, then licked the remaining sweet preserve off the knife.

She felt a throb of awareness between her legs at that unconscious gesture.

"How old are you, Sigurd?" she asked, then sighed with pleasure at the excellent taste of poached egg topped with hollandaise.

"Twenty-seven human years. One thousand, one hundred, and sixty-five vangel years. So almost twelve hundred years total."

She choked on the coffee she'd just swallowed and put a napkin to her mouth. "Say again."

"I was twenty-seven at the time I was turned vangel in the year 850."

More of his impossible-to-believe story! Maybe he's crazy. I should be careful. Hah! Too late for caution when I've screwed him six ways to Sunday. Or he screwed me six ways to Sunday. Whatever. We're both screwed. "So you live forever, and stay the same age? A good gig if you can get it. Did you take a swig from the Fountain of Youth?"

"Not forever," he said, taking her verbal jabs with total seriousness. "Originally, my seven brothers and I were given seven-hundred-year 'penances' as vangels, but being Vikings and tending to sin on occasion"—he grinned at that admission—"we have had more years added on with each transgression." He shrugged and began to butter and spread peach jam on another piece of toast, having eaten the first one as he talked. "At the rate I am going, I expect I will be a vangel until the final Judgment Day. The Lord only knows how many years Mike will add for last night's pleasures."

"What did you do that was so wrong . . . in the beginning?" She wasn't about to ask him what was so wrong about last night's "pleasures."

"Each of us Sigurdsson brothers was guilty of one of the Seven Deadly Sins in a big way. Vikar's was pride. Vikar is my oldest brother and keeper of the castle in Transylvania. Trond, a Navy SEAL, sloth or laziness. Ivak, a prison chaplain, lust. Mordr, a military man, wrath. Harek, greed. Cnut, a security expert, gluttony. And me, for my sins, envy."

"Holy creepin' cow! That is some story."

"If only it were a mere story!" He spooned some scrambled eggs and bacon onto his plate. "And that is why I have not had sex for thirty years."

Her mouth dropped open.

"What is your story, Marisa? Why have you been celibate? And for how long?"

"Six years since I was involved with Izzie's father. Two years since my last partner."

"Pfff!" he said. "Two years is naught in the scheme of things."

"I suppose so if you're counting by centuries," she scoffed, still not buying his thousand-plus-year-old age.

"Is your daughter's father helping to raise funds for her operation?"

She shook her head. "Chip is married with two kids of his own, one of whom is autistic. He can't afford to help Izzie," *if he wanted to.*

Sigurd chewed thoughtfully on his bacon. "I have an idea," he said, wiping his mouth with a napkin and laying it over his plate.

"How to raise money for Izzie?" she asked hopefully.

"No. I will have to think on that. Mike seems to think I will come up with a solution on my own," he told her. He didn't sound very confident.

"Mike? Oh, you mean Michael the Archangel." This was a bad sign when she was beginning to understand his references.

"The very same. In any case, the idea I mentioned is of a different nature." His eyes practically smoldered at her.

"Seems to me you have way too many ideas."

"That is one of my talents."

"So what's your big idea?"

"We need a bath."

"We?"

"Definitely we."

It was a devilish situation . . .

Reynaldo Muniz was a high haakai Lucipire, recently raised to that rank by his master, Jasper, and he aimed to make a good showing on this first mission since his promotion.

If he did well, Jasper might appoint him to the elite council of his advisers. There had been an opening since that bitch Dominique Fontaine expired a few years ago. Evil was all well and good for a demon, but Dominique had been a nasty, sly-tempered woman who enjoyed getting her fellow Lucipires in trouble, himself included. Satan had the dubious pleasure of her company these days. More power to him!

Even though Reynaldo was only two hundred and ten years old, he was a powerful devil, having been taken when he was a thirty-year-old, Spanish-born wrecker living off the Florida Keys. Which made this new mission on Grand Keys Island especially suited to him because he knew the region well. Before he died and went to Horror, he had made a prosperous living plundering the many shipwrecks along the two-hundred-mile chain of reefs and shoals from Key West to the Dry Tortugas, no matter that hundreds and hundreds of sailors and passengers died in the operations. One of his favorite tactics had been to tie lanterns to donkeys' necks and lead them slowly along the shorelines, leading distressed ships to believe they were lights on bobbing ships anchored at some port. In other words, a safe harbor, but were in fact rocky cliffs and beaches, rich pickings for Reynaldo and his men. In his heyday, Reynaldo had witnessed one ship a week go down.

Those were the days! Reynaldo mused now as he paced the small office of the yacht where Jasper's assistant, the French hordling Beltane, had led him a half hour ago. Reynaldo was here at his master's command, but he would have come, anyway. He had news to report.

It was not easy pacing in the limited space, seeing as how he was in his full demonoid form. Seven feet tall with a tail that would do a dinosaur proud, or a large alligator. More than once, he'd almost knocked over a porcelain jardinière that held a miniature palm tree in the corner. He was nervous.

Jasper came striding into the room then, and Reynaldo almost swallowed his fangs at the sight. *For the love of Lucifer!!* Today his master was in humanoid form. He had a red scarf tied around his head, pirate style, with a gold hoop in one ear. His puffy-sleeved shirt was unbuttoned to expose his dark chest hairs and tucked into slim black pants and swashbuckler-type boots up to his knees. A long sword hung from a scabbard at his side. He looked and was attired exactly like that actor Johnny Depp in his pirate movies. Except for one difference. Jasper was sporting such a big cock that the ridge was evident almost up to the wide leather belt.

Zebulan had warned him earlier that Jasper had been attired as Clark Gable from the movie *Gone with the Wind* when they had met. Apparently Jasper was trying out different personae to blend in with the island setting. Though what *Gone with the Wind* had to do with an island, Reynaldo wasn't sure, possibly the smoldering temperatures, tropical suit, and such associated with a Southern plantation. Whatever the cause, the costume was something else to witness in person. Reynaldo schooled himself not to show his amusement.

"Reynaldo! Good of you to come so quickly!" Jasper said, sitting down behind a desk, where he lit and then puffed away on a thin cheroot. "Make yourself comfortable." His master waved a hand toward the straight-backed chair sitting in front of the desk.

Reynaldo contemplated the chair, then his size and inconvenient tail. Without hesitation, he morphed into the humanoid form he was taking for this mission. A six-foot-tall Internet entrepreneur, using his own name, Reynaldo was about to launch a website that would offer cheap sex films, mostly homemade by depraved couples with a taste for exhibitionism. As an incentive, monthly prizes ranging from one thousand to five thousand dollars would be given to the best entries. In the weeks since he'd set up his site and since coming to the island, he was already awash with five hundred offerings. It was amazing what folks would do for a few thousand dollars, and they were so clueless as to sign away their rights with the entries.

Knowing how much Jasper appreciated a well-groomed demon, Reynaldo wore a designer suit of beige summer-weight wool, which practically matched his dirty-blond hair, arranged today in a neat ponytail low on his neck. A white silk T-shirt hugged his body and was tucked into his slacks with a leather belt. His skin was almost pure Castilian olive. You'd never know he had been born in a poor Madrid slum.

Sitting down, Reynaldo crossed one ankle over the opposite knee, wondering with what was probably hysterical irrelevance if he should have worn socks with his brown loafers.

"Cigar?" Jasper inquired, shoving an open desktop humidor toward him, where there were big, fat Cuban cigars, as well as the thin cigarillos.

Reynaldo shook his head. He was so nervous he would probably shake ashes all over himself.

"Tell me how things are going," Jasper said.

"This island was the perfect setup for this mission, and not just because of the decadence of many of the conference attendees, who are ripe for our picking. Like the proverbial fruit. Ripe, as in rotted souls." He flashed Jasper a fangy smile at his witty comparison.

Jasper fang-smiled him back.

Demons ever did like to dwell on the original forbidden fruit and how Satan had succeeded with Adam and Eve.

"That is to say," Reynaldo continued, "geographically, set apart from the mainland, the island is somewhat free from the eye of authorities. People coming and going. So that, when they go missing, it is assumed that they returned back to Key West for business or home emergencies. It will be weeks before the number we have taken registers with law enforcement. Even then, they will be unable to prove anything. The island will be empty once again, and the conference organizers scattered hither and yon."

"Zebulan thinks we should limit this mission to a smaller harvest, to avoid detection. One hundred, at most. Do you agree?"

"I do. These hit-and-run operations in the end will garner more for our side than massive operations that result in all-out warfare once the vangels know we are about. Not that they don't already know we are here on Grand Keys Island." Reynaldo paused for emphasis. "That is my good news for you today, m'lord. Not only are there vangels here already, but I recognized one of the VIK."

Jasper straightened and almost dropped his thin cigar. Placing it carefully in an ashtray with fingers that nigh trembled with excitement, he asked, just to be sure, "One of the Sigurdsson brothers?"

Reynaldo nodded, pleased with himself to have brought such pleasure to his master.

"Holy brimstone! You continually surprise me, Reynaldo." He paused. "Which one?"

"Sigurd Sigurdsson. The doctor."

"Ah! He is the one guilty of the sin of envy."

"Envy? That is all? Envy does not seem such a great sin to me."

"It can be, and it is and was in Sigurd's case. He killed a child, his own younger brother, out of envy. Envy eats at a sinner's soul, like a cancer. A great sin, truth to tell, because it can lead to so many other sins."

"I discovered his presence by accident, actually,"

Reynaldo admitted. "I was following this young woman I fanged a day or so earlier, just to plant a sin taint. Of Spanish descent like myself, she was not yet 'rotten' enough, ha, ha, ha, to be taken, but she is contemplating some great sin. I was just helping her along with my initial bite, but last night I watched for her to leave the restaurant where she is working. My intent was to check on the course of her contemplated sin, but then I saw a man waiting for her. It was the doctor."

Jasper rubbed his scaly hands together, creating a raspy sound. Even when they were in humanoid form, a Lucipire's skin tended to be dry and flaky. Reynaldo would send Jasper a tube of his favorite skin cream later.

"Shouldn't you have stayed and waited for an opening to pounce?"

"They went into his hotel room and after waiting for hours, I realized the VIK was nailing the wench. And you know those Vikings. Once is never enough. Though I thought sex was forbidden to vangels."

"Pfff! They are Vikings, as you say. Do you think they can stay away from a wet twat for long?"

"Of course not." Reynaldo loved when his master shared such crude conversation with him. It implied a closeness he hoped to nurture.

"This is perfect," Jasper said, smacking his lips, which was not easy to do with fangs. "Even if we only take a hundred humans, one vangel—bloody hell, one VIK—would make the whole mission a success. Satan might even celebrate with us!"

And I would get the promotion I want. Reynaldo bowed his head with a humility he did not feel. Instead, he wanted to crow with triumph.

"I'm surprised that Zebulan didn't know about this."

"I am, too." Reynaldo had always been a little suspicious of the Hebrew Lucipire. Always missing at certain times, always in his face at others. But he would not dare speak of those suspicions without proof. Zebulan was a known favorite of Jasper.

"This is what we will do," Jasper said, down to business now. "You will concentrate entirely on Sigurd, and the woman if she helps you nab the VIK. Let the others harvest regular sinners."

"Your wish is my command." *Hallelujah and here comes the council seat!*

Jasper rang a little bell, and in slipped Beltane on silent feet to stand near a console table holding glassware, an ice bucket, and bottles of beverages. "A drink to celebrate?" Jasper arched a brow at Reynaldo.

Reynaldo nodded.

"Scotch and blood on the rocks?"

"Perfect!"

Soon after, as they sipped their delicious drinks, Jasper made a toast, raising his crystal tumbler to clink with Reynaldo's. "Here's to sin!"

Chapter 16

It didn't take long for her bubble to burst . . .

Marisa couldn't stop grinning.

It was barely one p.m., and the sun was high overhead as she lay in her bikini on the patio chaise, basking in a bit of rare relaxation, waiting for her hair to absorb the conditioner she'd applied a short time ago. A stone statue of a dolphin streamed water into a small fountain. A soothing, splashing sound, mixed with that of the ocean waves in the distance. The tropical plants and flowers that flourished in abundance were aromatherapy at its best. This island truly was a paradise.

If she wasn't careful, she would fall asleep, and she had too much to do. Canceling her date with Harry being priority number one. She'd realized after parting company with Sigurd that she didn't have a phone number for Harry, and she doubted information would have a listing for a boat. So she'd stopped by Martin Vanderfelt's office, knowing full well they wouldn't give out such private information, but instead left a message with the secretary, asking that Harry contact her on her enclosed cell number.

Her roommates were at work, where she should be under normal circumstances. But she'd stopped at the spa after leaving Sigurd's hotel room, and Hedy had assured her that she'd been covered for the morning, thanks to Sigurd's intervention. If Marisa wanted to come in at three, she could get in another couple of appointments before her restaurant job, Hedy had said. Fortunately, Hedy hadn't asked any questions, but she probably guessed where Marisa had been.

Inga hadn't been so discreet when Marisa had met up with her on her "walk of shame" home that morning. "Somebody got laid!" she'd hooted. Tiffany and Doris were working, but Inga didn't need to report for her shift until this afternoon. So Inga had been off to soak up some rays by the pool before doing some shopping for toiletry items in the hotel gift shop.

At the moment, Marisa couldn't care less if Inga or anyone else knew what she'd been doing all night, and this morning, too. Besides that, by what she'd witnessed on her walk back in the hotel corridors, open meeting rooms, even by the pool, the tone of this conference had been amped up considerably on the freedom of expression meter. Couples could be seen half-naked making out in public. On the leather lobby sofa, against the wall next to the elevator, on the sink vanity of the unisex restroom.

Eleanor Allen, the woman who'd interviewed Marisa initially for her job here and was now working the front desk, had noticed Marisa's gaping mouth and told her as she passed, "Not to worry, the maintenance staff uses disinfectant spray by the gallon, or in some cases they just hose everything off nightly."

"That is disgusting," Marisa had said.

"You have no idea," Ms. Allen said with a grimace.

Continuing down the corridor, Marisa had seen, through the open double doors, a packed meeting room. The sign on the door had read "How to Masturbate on Camera." Becky Bliss and two other actors, one male and one female, were holding a panel discussion complete with demonstrations on a twenty-foot screen behind them.

"It's important to look moist there all the time to give the appearance of arousal. I usually have the stagehand spray me with cooking oil," Becky said with a giggle.

The other woman, a young redhead with torpedo-shaped breasts practically falling out of a tank top, had piped in with "I doan need ta do nothin' down yonder. I'm slicker'n spit on a doorknob durin' a love scene. I love sex and it shows."

The guy, who turned out to be Lance Rocket, had made a rude gesture rubbing his crotch and said, "Hell, I'm always ready," which caused the audience to burst out with laughter.

Becky had glared at them both, then put the other actress in her place, "Let's see how spitty you are when you've done the same love scene ten times, honey."

When Marisa had reached the outdoor pool, she saw four couples playing nude volleyball.

"Winners get to screw the losers," Tiffany had informed Marisa. Tiffany was sun-bathing, topless, with her legs dangling in the water.

Marisa didn't think she'd be swimming in that pool anytime soon. She needed a shower. Another shower! "Holy frickin' cow!" had been her only comment. Tiffany had probably thought she'd been referring to the volleyballers and not her very large breasts, which stood up perkily all by themselves. God bless silicone!

But now Marisa was back at the bungalow, having showered, and was letting the conditioner do its work.

She rarely had time for such personal pampering back home.

Lying there, her body practically hummed with satiety, despite aches in some intimate places. Muscles she hadn't used in years, if ever, had been exercised. The best possible workout, better than any gym. She would go inside shortly to soak in the bubble bath she'd purchased at the spa. Peach-scented.

She grinned some more.

Maybe Sigurd would join her. No, he wouldn't. He was off holding office hours. She would see him later tonight, though. "Rest up, dearling," he'd told her after kissing her good-bye two hours ago. "I have some ideas."

She loved the Viking endearments he used with her . . . sweetling, dearling. She loved the way he kissed. She loved the way he made love. She loved his ideas.

More loopy grinning.

Oh, she knew she had lots to worry about. Izzie still needed an operation, and Marisa was still short on the funds to pay for it. But for this moment at least, she was going to leave it in someone else's hands. Not Sigurd's. She was not that foolish. But somehow, with the calmness that seemed to have seeped into her soul following Sigurd's fanging out the sin taint, the oddest refrain kept shifting through her brain: "Let go, let God." And she wasn't even a religious person, not outwardly anyhow, and especially not after all the ungodly things she'd done with Sigurd.

She found herself grinning again.

Good thing no one could see her.

But then someone did, or soon would. Marisa heard voices approaching.

"Yikes!" She shot to a sitting position and grabbed for a towel to cover her skimpy suit.

Doris was walking up the path, prodding a young man forward in front of her with a pistol pressed into his back. It was Armod, the young friend of Sigurd's, the one with the Michael Jackson fixation. He was arguing with Doris over his shoulder.

"I was guarding Mar-is-a, I tell you."

Who? Me?

"Against what? Lizards?"

There were a lot of lizards around. Harmless, but creepy creatures.

"Against evil forces. Put the weapon down, m'lady. I do not want to hurt you."

"Hah! As if you could—"

Spinning on his feet, Armod knocked the pistol out of Doris's hand and it flew up and into the small dolphin fountain. He couldn't have been more accurate if he'd aimed for it. Maybe he had.

Tackling a flailing Doris to the ground, face first, Armod held her hands behind her back and knelt over her. "Stop struggling and let me explain."

"I'll explain you, buster. I'm with the FBI, and you are in big trouble."

What? Doris is with the FBI? Well, that made sense, Marisa supposed. It explained the pistol and Marisa's original suspicion that Doris was not the cleaning lady type.

Oh no! Was it possible the FBI knew about Steve's secret stash of knockoffs in the garage? Was it possible that Doris had recognized all of Marisa's clothes and shoes and jewelry as counterfeits? Reflexively, she hid her wrist with the Tiffany watch on her lap. With a barely stifled groan of despair, Marisa wondered if she was going to "take the fall" for her brother? Was she going to be charged as an "accessory" to the crime? She'd learned those terms on *Law and Order*. But, really, was she going to be called an accessory for wearing knockoff accessories? No, she answered herself. The FBI didn't go after such low-level criminals, did they?

"I do not care if you are FBI, AFT, CIA, or AB-frickin'-C. That is no excuse for hitting me over the head with a hard object," Armod snarled, raising a leg to straddle Doris's back. He then sat on her rump and held her joined hands in his when she refused to stop struggling. With Doris being about five-foot-two and Armod about six-foot-two, and with Doris bucking and snorting her anger, they resembled a giant sitting on a small pony, or something out of a Monty Python comedy.

"It was only a small rock. And it didn't even break your skin."

"There will be a big bump, though."

"How else was I going to stop you from attacking Marisa?"

"I was not attacking her. I was guarding her, you lackwit."

Aaarrgh! Enough is enough!

Standing, Marisa went over and chastised the two of them. "Are you two nuts? You're going to have hotel security here in a few minutes if you don't stop raising such a ruckus. Doris, I know this young man. He's a friend of Sigurd's, the hotel doctor. And Armod, Doris is my roommate. I don't know about this FBI stuff, but I'll find out."

They both stilled and looked up at her, though Doris was still flat on her belly and Armod was still straddling her.

"Let her up, Armod. And, Doris, control yourself. We're going to sit down and discuss this, without violence."

A short time later, the three of them sat around the patio table, drinking Tiffany's sweet tea in plastic glasses. Doris had changed from her hotel maid uniform into shorts and a T-shirt. Armod wasn't wearing his usual Michael Jackson duds today—white socks, lone white glove, etc,—but he did have on a black T-shirt with the logo "Thriller" under an unbuttoned Hawaiian floral shirt with blue jeans and sneakers.

"Who are you?" Doris demanded of Armod. "Are you on the hotel security staff? You look about sixteen years old."

"I am twenty-one," Armod declared indignantly, but his face flushed with color.

Marisa wondered idly how many vangel years he was besides those human years. Then chastised herself because she still wasn't buying all that vampire angel/demon crap.

"I am a dancer in the Michael Jackson revue in the nightclub," Armod informed Doris, his chin raised proudly.

Doris frowned. "Why would the hotel doctor hire you to guard Marisa?"

Marisa felt the need to intervene before Armod said something he shouldn't. "Sigurd is sort of my boyfriend." *After one night? My boyfriend? It sounds so high school-ish, but what else can I say. "He's my vampire angel lover who needed to fang me"? Hardly.* "He's being overprotective." *Well, that's the truth.*

"You can't tell anyone that the FBI is here," Doris told them both.

"Who would I tell?" Marisa asked. "It's not like I know any bad guys. Besides, I don't know why you're here."

Armod, still affronted over the age insult, promised nothing. He would be blabbing as soon as he got back to Sigurd was Marisa's guess.

"Just suffice it to say, there is suspicious crap about to come down on this island."

For some reason, that strange creature thing she'd

seen on this very patio the day before came to mind. But that couldn't be what Doris was referring to. "Are you talking about demon vampires?"

Armod shot her a glance of shock, whether at the fact that she knew about those supposed creatures or that she was mentioning them out loud.

"What? You mean those dumbass actors in that porno flick *Sucked!*? No. Hell, no. Have you ever seen anything more stupid than those folks walking around with fake fangs?"

Armod immediately clamped his lips shut tight.

"Terrorists?" Marisa asked then, realizing how stupid she must have sounded, mentioning vampires. "You think these pornographers are terrorists?"

Doris shrugged.

"What would be the point of bombing an island or whatever it is you think they're planning?" Maybe Sigurd was right. Maybe Marisa did need to go home.

"That's some jump in conclusions, Marisa. I never said they were planning a bombing."

"What exactly are you saying? Who are they?"

"There are some bad characters here. Ones who've been on our watch list for years." At the frown of confusion on Marisa's face, she added, "Money laundering. Sex trafficking. Prostitution. That kind of thing."

"Oh," Armod said, clearly relieved that his cover wasn't blown.

"Anyone in particular?" Marisa asked. Was Harry engaged in any of that stuff? Probably. Would she take that kind of dirty money if it meant saving Izzie? The moral dilemma kept getting more and more complicated. Good thing she wasn't going to have to face that question since she'd agreed to cancel her date.

"That is information I cannot divulge. I've already said more than I should have." Finishing her tea, she plunked her glass on the patio table and rose to go inside. As she opened the door, she turned to Marisa for one last warning, "It would be a good idea for you to go home before all hell breaks loose."

"Why does everyone want me to leave the island?" Marisa muttered then.

Armod was still there, shifting nervously, and Marisa suspected he was anxious to get back to Sigurd and relate all that Doris had told them. "Go ahead and report back to your boss," Marisa told him, not sure where she got the idea that Sigurd, a doctor, was the head guy on this island for the vangel gang, but there was no doubt in her mind. About that, at least.

"My orders are to watch you like a bloody hawk until you start your waitress shift."

"Don't you have work yourself? At the nightclub, I mean."

"Well, yes. There is a rehearsal a hour from now, but—"

She waved at him in a dismissing fashion. "Go. I'm going to take a bath, then nap for an hour. Besides, Doris is here to protect me. From whatever. Criminals or demons. Take your pick."

Armod didn't smile at her little joke. "If you think it would be all right?"

"I do." She waved him off again.

Marisa did take her peach bubble bath, and then, passing Doris's closed bedroom door—the woman was probably on the phone with her FBI supervisors—Marisa went into the room she shared with Inga, whose clothes were scattered about in her usual disarray. Marisa was too tired to care at the moment. In fact, she just recalled that she hadn't heard from Harry yet. She would have to find another way to contact him about canceling their date. Maybe Eleanor would know his number. Or Tiffany, who seemed to know everyone and everything about this conference. Later, she thought with a wide yawn. She would do all that later. For now, she had scarcely set her alarm and crawled under the sheets when exhaustion took its toll. With the rhythmic hum of the overhead fan and the sound of the ocean through the window, she fell into a deep, deep sleep.

And she dreamed.

Not the erotic dreams she would have expected, reliving the events of the night before. No, these were strange dreams with strange people saying strange things.

There were two men standing in her bedroom. One of them looked remarkably like Clark Gable from *Gone with the Wind*, and the other was some well-dressed Spanish dude in a designer suit, who looked vaguely familiar.

Marisa tried to sit up, but she seemed frozen to the bed with invisible ties. But she wasn't panicked. Yet. It was just a dream.

"Are you sure she is the one?" Clark asked.

The one what?

"Yes, master."

Master? Who calls anyone master today? Am I dreaming that I'm living in a different time? The Civil War era, maybe. But wait, that can't be. The other guy is wearing Hugo Boss, or I don't know my designer labels.

"The sin taint is gone, Reynaldo," Clark said with disgust.

Boy, is it ever!

"We can't fang her now. Innocents cannot be turned," Clark pointed out.

"I know. The VIK must have removed the sin taint I planted in her earlier. I should have returned earlier to finish the job." Reynaldo's fingertip trailed raspily, like a claw, along the skin of her neck on the left side, where she no longer had any bite mark. She knew because she'd checked in the bathroom mirror when she'd returned to the bungalow.

Then how did this Spanish creep know about fanging and sin taints? She struggled against her invisible ties. Were these demons in her room, or were they vangels? No, vangels wouldn't be disgusted that she was pure again. Well, pure as a woman could be after being screwed every which way but and including loose. She tried to scream for Sigurd, but no sound came out of her wide-open mouth.

Now she was scared. This was no dream. It was a nightmare, one of the worst kind, so vivid it felt like it was actually happening.

"It would not have worked," Clark pointed out. "She had not completed the great sin she was contemplating."

"Still, I should have fanged her again, to increase the compulsion."

"Woulda, coulda, shoulda," Clark said with a laugh. "Don't you love some of these modern sayings?"

Ignoring the question, Reynaldo went on, "But she *has* been fornicating with the VIK. I can smell the sex on her. Is that not a sin?"

"Christians frown on illicit sex, but it does not rise to the level of high crime. It was not even adultery. Or sex for hire. No, she would have to become much more sinful before she would be ripe for Lucipiredom."

Thank you, God!

"So we cannot take her with us now?"

"No."

"Can I fuck her?"

"If you wish, but later. Use her as a lure for Sigurd first. You do think he is enamored enough to come back to her for more, don't you?"

"Definitely."

"And she . . . is she still receptive to the VIK's attention?"

"Hah! The two of them are so lustsome for each other, the air fair reeks around them."

"Good, good."

"I wonder, though . . ."

"What?"

"The woman has a sick child, and I wonder how long she would welcome the vangel to her bed if she knew what you told me about Sigurd . . . you know . . . that he killed a child, his own little brother."

"Actually, it wasn't the only time. He was about to throw a baby, King Haakon's newborn child, over a cliff when Michael intervened. To my mind, though, some of the sins he has committed due to his grievous weakness for envy are even worse than that. Still, you could be right. Perhaps we could plant the idea in her head. Child killer."

No, no, no! It's not possible. Sigurd is a doctor, a healer, not a killer. And definitely not a killer of children.

"Shall I take Sigurd now? He is in the hotel medical office, I believe. I have a mung and two hordlings standing guard."

What? I have to go warn Sigurd.

"No, he is too strong, and the setting is too public. Watch the woman. He will come to her. When he does, bring him to me. This will be a glad day in Horror if you accomplish this task. And, Reynaldo, you will be rewarded accordingly, if you get my meaning."

"Yes, Jasper."

Jasper? Jasper! Criminy, the king of all the Lucipires is standing here in my bedroom.

Even as she stared, aghast, the two "men" morphed into these huge, scaly beasts with red eyes and fangs and tails, then disappeared into thin air. The only thing that remained was the faint, sulfurous scent of rotten eggs in the air.

A short time later, Marisa awakened to the loud ring-ing of her alarm clock. Blinking awake, she was able to sit up and stare about her. Nothing had changed. And everything had changed.

Was it all a bad dream? Or reality? She was having trouble distinguishing between the two, and not just because of what she'd just "witnessed."

She jumped out of bed and quickly pulled on a robe. She had to contact Sigurd as soon as possible. She had to warn him about the Lucipires.

But when she called Sigurd's office on her cell phone a few minutes later, and Karl called him to the phone, the first thing she said was: "Are you a child killer?"

Chapter 17

**The you-know-what was about
to hit the celestial fan . . .**

Sigurd stared at the phone in his hand, his heart
hammering against his chest walls. "Marisa? Is that
you?"

"Yes, it's me, dammit. Answer me. Are you a child
killer?"

When he hesitated, she did not wait for an answer,
but he did hear her gasp before she clicked off.

Who would have told her about his past? The only
one he could think of was Armod, whom Sigurd had
assigned to protect her. The boy did tend to let his
tongue run loose betimes, but this was a breach of the
highest confidence.

"Karl!" his voice boomed out as he opened the door
to the reception room. His nurse had taken a lunch
break, and Karl was handling the reception desk for
the few patients who waited for Sigurd's services.

Several patients jumped in their chairs, their charts

having revealed to him on earlier inspection a migraine, an infected paper cut, and a yeast infection. Nothing critical. Karl just raised his brows.

Sigurd motioned for Karl to come into his office, and he closed the door after him. "Where is Armod?"

"He was waiting to talk to you, and he just went down the hall to get a Pepsi."

"I told him to guard Marisa," Sigurd said through gritted teeth.

"He says that he has important news to impart to you, and that Marisa is safely sleeping under guard of her pistol-packing roommate."

"I find no amusement in this situation, Karl. So stop smirking. Which roommate? Surely not the twittering one with the bosoms."

"Nope. The short FBI one with no bosoms to speak of."

"What FBI?"

"Is there more than one?"

Sigurd growled.

"I'll let Armod explain."

And he did. After being excoriated by Sigurd for failure to stick to his mission of guarding. The boy would not fail to obey his orders to the letter in the future, that was for sure. But more important, if Armod had not spoken to Marisa about Sigurd's past, who had?

The possibilities were beyond frightening, even to a vangel.

After directing Karl to cover for him in the office, Sigurd sent a chastened Armod off to his dance rehearsal (apparently, a new member of the company was a Lucipire imp creating chaos, though why Armod had failed to tell him before this was hair-pulling frustrating). Sigurd then teletransported to Marisa's bungalow. He told Svein to follow discreetly after Armod to make sure the youth didn't get himself killed by a mere imp demon.

Marisa was standing in the small kitchen, wearing naught but a white terry-cloth robe, making a cup of coffee in the microwave. She smelled of peaches. He almost smiled, but cut himself short when he noticed the glare she directed his way.

"I won't ask how you got here so quickly," she said. "I've had enough creepy stuff for one day."

Was she calling him creepy? Was this the warm . . . nay, hot woman who'd left his bed hours ago? The one who'd welcomed his caresses and promised more when they met later this evening?

He moved closer and opened his arms, about to embrace her. Forget about waiting until tonight. He'd like to pick up where they'd left off, and do lots more. Lots. Mayhap he could love the anger out of her.

She ducked under his arm.

Or mayhap not.

She took her cup to the living room, where she placed it on the low table and turned on him. Arms folded over her chest, she tapped one bare foot impatiently.

"Sweetling?"

She put up a halting hand. "No more endearments."

"Heartling?" he coaxed, trying a new endearment, one he rarely used because it seemed too intimate. He held his arms out to her again.

She waved him away. "Sweetling, dearling, heartling . . . enough with the meaningless love words! Why not say it like it really is . . . fuckling?"

He grimaced at her coarse word, though it was an apt description for some women he'd known in his time. Not her, though. "What has happened?"

"Have you ever killed a child?"

"Who told you that?"

"That's not important. Just answer me."

"Yes, for my sins, I have."

She flinched and backed away from him, as if he were suddenly repulsive to her. "Get out!"

"I can explain."

"I doubt that, and I don't want any explanation. You know my situation. You know I have a child that needs saving, and you have done just the opposite. How many children have you killed, by the way."

He felt his face fill with color. "Just one."

"*Just.*"

"One," he corrected.

"How about the baby on the cliff?"

He was shocked that she knew about that. He had thought that only he and Michael were aware of what he'd been about to do that long-ago night. "I did not do it, and probably would not have."

"Probably? Probably?" she nigh shrieked.

"Marisa, I need to know who told you."

"Get out. I don't want to see you ever again. Please, just go." There were tears in her eyes that tore at his soul.

"I will go, but you must tell me who told you. Was it Michael?"

She shook her head, slowly. "It was a dream, or nightmare, or something. There were these two men. Jasper and Reynaldo, I think they were in my bedroom, and—"

"*What?* Jasper was here? *With you?* He dared . . . He tried . . . Oh my God!" With a roar of outrage, he raised his eyes and hands upward and called for help, "MICHAEL!"

With a whoosh of flapping wings and flying feathers, the archangel landed in the little bungalow between him and Marisa. Even Sigurd, who had met the celestial being on hundreds of occasions, was impressed with the visage he presented today. White robe, gold linked belt, shining halo, feathered wings the size of small airplanes when extended.

"You called? *Again?*"

Uh, maybe he should have waited to seek Michael's help in private.

"Maybe?" Steam nigh rose from Michael's nostrils. "I have more important places to be, things to do, than be at the beck and call of a mere Viking."

Sigurd was about to explain himself, but Michael raised an arm and pointed a forefinger at him. "You and I will definitely speak, and you will not like what I have to say."

Then Michael turned and pointed the same forefinger at Marisa, who was staring at the archangel as if he was a heavenly apparition, which he was. "And you, oh doubtful daughter of Eve, need to have more faith."

Marisa was unable to speak. At the sight of an archangel in her living room, she was as frozen as Lot's wife when she turned into a pillar of salt.

"Vikings! The bane of my life!"

On those words, Sigurd was teletransported out of the room so fast that he lost his breath and fell flat on his arse when he and Michael landed on the top of a mountain. Sigurd had no idea where. Mount Everest, for all he knew. In fact, he stood and peered over the edge, then jumped back. There was about a hundred-thousand-foot drop, with no bottom in sight, and him not having earned his wings yet.

Sigurd had heard the expression "Sink or swim." Was Michael going for a new one, "Fly or fall"? Was this the way a vangel finally got his wings? If so, he'd rather not.

"Idiot!" Michael muttered. Then, "Now! *What* have you been up to, Viking? Seduction to remove a sin taint? Tsk, tsk, tsk!"

Archangel tsking was not a good sign. Sigurd knew in that moment that rewards were the last thing Michael had in mind for him. Sigurd was in big trouble, only a small part of which was due to Jasper's presence on Grand Keys Island, the reason he had called on Michael.

For a few lackbrain moments he'd forgotten that he was the one who summoned Michael. Again.

Walking the wobbly line between good and evil, and she wasn't even wearing her designer stilettos . . .

Marisa was beginning to think she might be having a nervous breakdown of some sort.

Really, the things that had been happening to her didn't make sense. Not the man who claimed to be a vampire angel, not the beast he'd fought out on her patio, not the two men who appeared so life-like in her dream, and now an archangel in her living room. She was becoming delusional, that was the only explanation, and she just couldn't afford to get sick, mentally or physically, with all that she needed to do for Izzie.

And speaking/thinking of Izzie, she was not surprised when her cell phone rang, and the caller ID said it was her parents' home line.

"Hello."

"Marisa, honey . . ." her mother began.

Marisa's heart tightened. She knew right away that it was not good news. "What? What's happened? Is Izzie okay?"

"Izzie is all right. Well, she hasn't wanted to get out of bed today. Claims she's sleepy, and her head hurts, but—"

"That's not like Izzie." Her daughter got up at the

crack of dawn, even when she wasn't feeling very well. And her head hurts? Marisa didn't even want to think about the implications of that.

"I know. I called Dr. Stern, and he said to keep taking her temperature and blood pressure every couple hours. It's probably nothing. Just a low-grade fever that won't go away."

It was not nothing, Marisa just knew it wasn't.

"But that's not why I called, not entirely. You are to call the clinic in Switzerland as soon as possible. Here's the number." Her mother rattled off a long list of numbers.

"Why? What did they say?"

"They have an opening in less than two weeks. Otherwise, you might have to wait another six months if you're still interested."

And have the money. Always it comes back to the money. "I'll call right now. Let me know if there's any change in Izzie's condition, good or bad. I'll get home right away if you need me."

"I know that, honey."

"Tell Izzie I love her."

"I will. All she can talk about is the really big sea-shell that your friend promised her."

"My friend?" Marisa's brow furrowed. *Oh. She means Sigurd. The really big child killer. He won't be bring-ing my daughter anything now, that's for darn sure, if he ever was.* "Tell her Mima will be bringing the really big shell."

It took some time to complete the international call, and then a further delay connecting with Adrian Sorrel, the clinic's administrative assistant in charge of scheduling. She'd never met the woman in person, but she felt like she knew her well; they'd spoken on the phone so often.

"Marisa, I'm so glad you got back to us so quickly. I

have good news. Dr. Frankel's schedule has a sudden opening. He can do Isobel's operation on July 27."

"That's only ten days from now." *Three days after my work here on the island is completed. If I stay that long.*

"Shall I put your daughter on the schedule? If so, she'll have to be here the day before to start pre-op procedures. We already have your hundred-thousand-dollar deposit on file, but we'll need the remaining seventy-thousand dollars on the day of the procedure. Will that be a problem?"

Marisa was about to tell her that she didn't have the money yet, but Adrian knew her situation well. With a sigh of resignation, Marisa knew what she had to do. "We'll be there, Adrian. With the money. E-mail me the details, and contact me by phone if there's any change."

No sooner did she click off than the phone rang again. The caller ID said "private number." She answered, figuring she could hang up if it was Sigurd.

"Mar-is-a, darling, you were trying to contact me? Please, don't tell me you are going to cancel our dinner date."

It was Harry Goldman. What perfect timing! She girded herself with resolve. She could do this. She had to do this. "No. I'm looking forward to seeing you. In fact, I'm going to take off early this evening. Would nine o'clock be all right, instead of twelve?"

"Perfect! I'll send a hotel cart to pick you up at a quarter 'til." There were golf-style hotel carts that operated among the various paths for the paying guests.

"I can walk. You don't have to do that."

"Of course I do. I treat my women well," he said in an insinuating manner.

Well, she guessed she'd given him the right by agreeing to the date.

"I'll go put the wine on to chill right now."

"So that's it. I'm definitely going to do it," she said to herself after saying good-bye. Suddenly, she smelled lemons. Raising a forearm up to her face, she sniffed. It was as if she was exuding the lemon scent from her pores.

Could Sigurd have been telling the truth?

Did demon and angel vampires really exist? Did a big sinner or someone about to commit a big sin turn lemony? Had that apparition in this very room been a high-ranking angel? St. Michael himself?

She shook her head in dismissal, not because she refused to believe—it was hard not to believe with all the facts being stacked in Sigurd's favor—but because it no longer mattered. She had an ill child, and she no longer had any choice for helping her.

Whoa, whoa, whoa! she could swear she heard a voice in her head say. *There is always a choice.* It was probably just her conscience.

Screw conscience! Screw the devil. Screw angels flying too close to the ground. Screw Sigurd. Wait a minute. I already did that. A giggle escaped her then, a sign of her crumbling sanity, no doubt.

Besides, committing a sin for a good cause should count for something.

Sin is sin. Sex for money equals prostitution.

Yeah, but sex for money to save a life is a good kind of prostitution. Isn't it?

Am I crazy? Good prostitution?

It's not like I would be enjoying the sex. In fact, eew!

Eew! is not an excuse for sin.

Surely the gravity of sin is mitigated by the circumstances. Like Robin Hood stealing from the rich to save the poor. Or murder in self-defense. Or—

Am I seriously attempting to negotiate with God? Really?

Not God. My conscience.

Same thing!

Aaarrgh! Bottom line: A mother does what a mother's got to do. And I certainly can't rely on Sigurd anymore. A child killer, for heaven's sake! Her head ached at the thought, and she refused to think there might be an explanation. There could be no justification for murdering a child.

The inner voice countered, *Forget Sigurd. What happened to "Let go, let God"?*

God is apparently busy. I have to help myself.

She waited for thunder to clap outside and the skies to open with outrage at her sacrilegious thought.

Nothing happened.

Her die was cast.

The consequences of sin . . .

"Seduction to remove a sin taint. Fifty additional years as a vangel!" Michael proclaimed Sigurd's punishment as he paced around him. Sigurd was still leery of the sharp drop off the mountain where Mike had taken him. Besides, a sharp wind had picked up. His luck, he'd be blown away. He backed up and sat down on a big rock.

But then he thought about what Michael had said. *Is that all?* Sigurd thought. *If I had known I could get so much pleasure for so small a penalty, I would have—*

"Five acts of fornication. Five hundred years."

Oh. I see. He's going to draw this out, one bad act at a time.

"Disobedience. Twenty-five years."

Should I ask disobedience to what? No! That will just give him an excuse to pick me apart, one little indiscretion at a time.

"*Little* indiscretion? You exceed yourself, Viking!" Michael roared at him. "Calling on an archangel as if thou were a superior, and not a lowly vangel."

"Marisa was going to commit a grave sin. I had to help her."

"By fornication? Save your weak explanations!"

"And this latest time. I called on you today for an urgent matter. To inform you that Jasper is on the island."

"Pfff! Dost think I do not know of Jasper's whereabouts? Why do you think you were sent on this mission?"

"Uh."

"To save a handful of misbegotten miscreants bent on sexual perversions?"

"Uh."

"Nay, this was your chance to destroy the strongest of all demon vampires."

"You could have told me that!"

"That is not the way it works, and you know it well and good. Or you should. After one thousand, one hundred, and sixty-four years, one would think you had gained a brain. Did you think I had sent you to this paradise . . . this Garden of Eden . . . to be the new Adam?"

"Of course not."

"Was the apple so sweet?"

You have no idea.

"Was it worth the 'worm'?"

What worm? Oh, the sin? Probably. "How come Vikar and Trond and Ivak get to be with women? Why not me? Why do they always . . ." His words trailed off as he realized his mistake.

"Envy again, Sigurd. Will you never learn? What am I going to do with you?"

Sigurd bowed his head, then raised it with determination. "Give me a second chance to complete my mission on Grand Keys Island."

Michael paused and studied him closely. "As you

ask!" he finally conceded. "Vangeldom is all about second chances, is it not? But there are conditions."

"Like what?"

"Thou shalt stay away from the woman."

Uh-oh! When he starts with the shalts, *he means business.* "But what if she—"

"Not your concern."

"And the child?"

"Who appointed you this child's savior?"

Sigurd felt as if he were trapped in an impossible situation. If he refused Michael's conditions, he would no doubt be sent in shame back to Transylvania, or somewhere worse. If he agreed to Michael's conditions, he would be abandoning Marisa to a possibly horrible fate. Leastways, it felt that way to him. And what about the innocent child?

"I will try." It was the best he could offer.

Michael stood and folded his arms over his chest, glaring at Sigurd.

"So be it then. Your wish is my command."

"Hah! Humility has ne'er been a Viking trait. Why do you not you say what you really mean?"

"What I'd really like to say is fuck, fuck, fuck!" Sigurd blurted out.

"At least that was honest," Michael said, to Sigurd's surprise, but then he added, "Rude expletive to an archangel . . . twenty-five years."

Chapter 18

A lesson in being a tart, and not the fruit kind . . .

Inga and Tiffany were helping Marisa get ready for her big date.

And Marisa was thankful for any help she could get. She was so nervous she could barely comb her hair, let alone hold a mascara wand.

Marisa had already showered and perfumed up. Before she could stop her, Tiffany had spritzed Marisa with enough of her sweet Shalimar to choke a goat—*or a vampire . . . and, yes, there is a vampire I would still like to choke*—even in some places where the sun would never shine. Spraying her pubic hair wasn't out of line for a woman getting ready for a heavy date, she supposed, but when Tiffany aimed for her butt, as well, Marisa put her foot down. "Enough!"

Now Marisa sat on a straight-back chair in the bathroom, wearing nothing but a towel wrapped around her sarong-style. A black Sorrentino sheath with a modest cleavage in front, and a shocking cleavage in back hung from a nearby doorjamb. She would need to forgo a bra to wear the dress, which was a wrinkle-free number Inga had brought, along with a pair of silver, open-toed, Louboutin slingbacks. Luckily, she and Inga wore the same size. Her only jewelry would be a pair of silver chandelier earrings.

Inga was sitting cross-legged on the floor painting Marisa's toenails bloodred, while Tiffany stood behind her, teasing her hair into bouffant bimboness.

"I still don't think teased hair is the 'in thing' today," Marisa continued to protest.

"It is ta men," Tiffany insisted.

Marisa looked at Inga to see if she agreed. Inga just shrugged. Tiffany had way more experience than either of them, despite her younger age.

"Besides, we have a sayin' in the South. The higher the hair, the closer ta God," Tiffany said with a giggle.

"I don't think God has anything to do with what I'm about tonight," Marisa said.

Thankfully, neither Inga nor Tiffany was being judgmental with Marisa. She needed all the support she could get. From the moment Marisa had explained what had happened, not about Sigurd having killed a child but about the operation being imminent, Inga had understood perfectly why Marisa had made the decision to keep her date with Harry. Inga had given her a big hug and whispered against her ear, "Go for it, sweetie!"

Inga repeated her encouragement now, sensing Marisa's reservations, "You can do this, Mar. Fifteen minutes of 'ick' and you'll have the money for Izzie's operation."

"What if he wants more than once?" Marisa asked.

"He undoubtedly will. Fifteen minutes at a time . . . heck, you can probably hold your breath that long."

Bless Inga for her unflagging optimism. "I wish you could come along, and be my personal cheerleader!"

"Now, that would be perverted. Honey, Harry is sixty, if he's a day. I'd be surprised if he can still get it up, even once," Inga declared.

But then Tiffany disagreed with Inga. "Hah! Some sixty-year-old men have got more wick in their candles than younger men, even without the little blue pills. My aunt Maybelline usta say, 'The older the bone, the harder the marrow.'"

"Marrow?" Marisa choked out.

"Tiff, you are not helping," Inga chided.

"Sor-ry! It's just that you two're such sad sacks, bless yer hearts, lookin' at this lak a fate worse'n death, when it could be a wonderful opportunity."

"It's the only opportunity I have," Marisa admitted.

"There ain't nothin' wrong with gettin' yerself a sugar daddy. Us wimmen have gotta take care of ourselves."

"We are women, hear us roar," Inga said under her breath.

Tiffany ignored Inga's sarcasm, if she even recognized it as such. "Aunt Maybelline had five different sugar daddies after Uncle Beaufort died. One would go ta his Maker, and she'd find her 'nother one. She died in bed when she was eighty-six, if ya get mah meanin'."

"Good Lord!" Marisa said.

Inga had just finished with the first coat of polish, and she looked up at Tiffany with interest. "Maybelline, huh? I don't suppose she was related to the Maybelline cosmetic family?"

"Doan Ah wish! Anyways, it doan matter diddly-squat if Harry's a bit older and a little soft aroun' the middle, as long as the equipment still works. Heck, even if it doan work so good," Tiffany continued as she teased away. "In fact, Ah can give ya some pointers on what ta do ta make his willy more willin', if ya want."

"No!" Inga exclaimed.

"Please don't," Marisa said at the same time.

"Heah's one thing Ah know fer certain. Ya gotta make sure ya get somethin' in writin' before ya drop yer panties."

"*What?* I can't do that. It's too cold-blooded." Marisa cringed at the thought of carrying some kind of legal document before she let Harry have his way with her. "I might as well ask for the cold hard cash up front."

Inga surprised Marisa by saying, "Not a bad idea."

"Inga!"

"Do you trust Harry?" Inga asked.

"Only as far as I can throw him." He must weigh two hundred pounds. "Can I have another glass of wine?"

They'd all had a glass of wine when they'd started this makeup procedure. It hadn't helped to calm Marisa's nerves so far.

"You better not," Inga advised. "You're already going to be wobbly on those stilettos."

Soon, dressed and ready to go, Marisa got her first look at herself in the full-length mirror on the back of her bedroom door. "Yikes!" she exclaimed.

"It's wonderful, isn't it," Tiffany said. "Lordy, Ah do love a good makeover." She hugged Marisa and went off to take a long bubble bath.

"Help," Marisa pleaded weakly with Inga, who was bent over with silent laughter.

"Okay. While Tiffany's in the bathroom, let's see what we can do."

They went to the small kitchen, where Inga helped Marisa to comb out and shampoo her hair. Once clean of the two pounds of lacquer, and towel-dried, they arranged her damp hair into a tight chignon low on her neck, pinned tightly in place. Then they went back into their bedroom where the two of them used cotton balls and baby oil to remove some of the eye shadow and rouge. Marisa still had a crimson mouth and eyelashes so heavy they drooped sexily of their own accord, but she looked a little better.

"What do you think?" she asked Inga.

Inga shrugged. "You no longer look like a street-walker."

"Are you sure?"

"Now, you're more like a high-price call girl."

"Great! Just the image I'm going for." Marisa and Inga high-fived each other.

Marisa couldn't help but wonder, though, as she walked toward the hotel cart that waited outside to take her to the dock, *What would Sigurd think of me now?*

Fighting devils or terrorists, it's all in the planning . . .

"All hell is about to break loose, and I mean that exactly how it sounds," Sigurd told Karl, Jogeir, and Armod, along with Sigurd's three brothers, Vikar, Cnut, and Harek, who were crowded into Sigurd's hotel suite for an emergency meeting.

Svein was off guarding Marisa, at Sigurd's direction. Michael had ordered Sigurd to stay away from the woman, but that didn't mean he couldn't delegate his protection. Did it? In any case, she would probably keep her dinner date with Goldman. He assumed they would go to Calloways, the luxury restaurant in the hotel. She couldn't get into too much trouble there, in his opinion.

In the meantime, several operations appeared imminent that would endanger his vangel mission. So he'd called on his brothers for help. In all they had sixty vangels here ready to work once given the order.

"Harek, what have you discovered?"

Harek was seated at the desk with his usual laptop computer in front of him. "The FBI will be ending their investigation with a number of high-level arrests later tonight. Tax evasion. Money laundering. Sex trafficking. Credit card fraud. A whole slew of charges. Any number of offenses, just to get these criminals behind bars, even when they can't get them for other crimes."

"How many targets are involved?"

"At least a dozen. They're not looking for the lower-level culprits at this time."

"Is Harry Goldman one of them?" Sigurd couldn't help but ask.

Harek studied the screen, then nodded. "Money laundering, but there's also a suspicion of . . . Holy clouds!"

"What?" The fine hairs stood out on Sigurd's nape with alarm.

"Did you know he owns a string of Mexican brothels?"

I knew it, I knew it! Dirty as bathwater after a Norse battle. But, oh Lord, what has this to do with Marisa? Please, God, let it be that he is just attracted to her personally. Not that that isn't bad enough. Oh shit! I better warn Svein. After tonight, I am going to set Marisa straight, Michael or no Michael. She needs to know that Harry isn't just bad, he's dangerous.

"Are you listening, Sigurd?" Cnut inquired, a knowing grin on his face.

"Of course," Sigurd answered, then, "What were you saying?"

Vikar tsked his opinion of Sigurd's wandering mind. Vikar was an expert tsker, a trait he'd picked up from Michael. Irksome, really.

"I was saying that Jasper has big plans for this evening, too. He and his haakai minions have pinpointed the most evil of the folks here at the conference, and they intend to take them out tonight."

"At the same time as the FBI will be at work," Armod pointed out. Apparently, he and Doris had become great pals. A match made in lackwit heaven.

"With the federal agents muddying the waters, this might turn into one of Jasper's usual SNAFUs, as Trond would say. Situation Normal, All Fouled Up." This from Jogeir, who'd been involved in the Lucipires' dragon-fuck at Angola Prison last year.

"We can only hope," Vikar said, "but we have to plan for the worst. What's the word from Zeb?"

"Last I heard from him, this afternoon, Jasper is still going with a low-key mission here. Slow and easy. No big hit-and-run mass killings," Sigurd explained. "However, they want to get some of the more evil characters tonight. They don't want to risk losing them by waiting until the end of the conference when they might somehow be redeemed."

"When does it end?" Cnut inquired.

"Six more days."

"Which means that the FBI and the Lucies will be targeting some of the same sinners tonight," Vikar concluded.

"Along with us vangels," Cnut pointed out. "We'll all be butting heads for our own purposes."

"A SNAFU, for sure," Sigurd said. "All right, here's what we have to do. Harek, you cover that yacht that's arriving tonight, supposedly carrying some very young prostitutes."

Harek nodded.

"Svein will be covering Goldman. Cnut, you patrol the grounds. Armod, the nightclub. Jogeir, there's a party in the penthouse that may very well be moved out onto one of the yachts. The movers and shakers, some of the most vile purveyors of smut, will be there.

Vikar, you should investigate any other boats of a suspicious nature in the area. And I'll do surveillance in the hotel rooms and corridors. There's some kind of conference special event being held in the ballroom. Each of us should have a team of at least six vangels. Any questions?"

When no one spoke up, Sigurd added, "Our goal tonight is to save sinners, where possible. Barring that, we would prefer the evil ones be taken into custody by the FBI, rather than by Jasper. Agreed?"

"Agreed," they all said.

"Here's hoping that by morning, we all have deep tans," Vikar quipped.

They all joined hands then, and Sigurd prayed, "Lord, help us this night to conquer evil forces. Amen."

As his brothers and fellow vangels scattered to their various positions, Sigurd added another prayer. "And please protect Marisa since I cannot. Don't let her be alone with the bastard."

Date with a devil, or so it seemed . . .

Marisa had managed to make it through wine cocktails (she had three) and a wonderful dinner of oysters Rockefeller, fresh flounder, baby parsleyed potatoes, and cherries jubilee (none of which she tasted for all her nervousness), and was sipping at a coffee liqueur when Harry said, "I want to show you something."

Marisa nodded. This was it then. She could no longer pretend she was having a friendly dinner with an older gentleman.

He stood and extended a hand to her. "You can bring your drink with you." He picked up his dirty martini (his fifth of the evening, by her count) in his left hand, and laced the chubby fingers of his right hand with her left. She was taller than him in her four-inch heels. He didn't seem to mind. In fact, some men liked taller women. It empowered them, or something, according to a *Cosmo* article she'd read one time. Something in the vein of, "See. I'm short, but I can still get me an Amazon of a woman." Caveman Napoleon Complex, or some such thing.

He led her out the doorway of the small salon where they'd dined and toward the sleeping quarters. He'd given her a tour of the sumptuous yacht when she first arrived, boasting that it had cost a cool five million dollars (disgusting, really, when you considered how little she needed for something so important, and he frittered away millions on his toys), but he hadn't shown her any of the ten staterooms. Yet.

She was being too hard on the man. Really, she was, and she had to stop if she was to get through this night. Harry had been a polite and charming date, thus far, she had to give him credit for that. Other than kissing her cheek initially and touching her bare arm or nape on occasion, she couldn't criticize him for being overly familiar, let alone jumping her bones, as she'd expected.

In fact, he'd spent most of the time telling her about growing up in a Newark, New Jersey, housing project, and how he'd built his fortune one job at a time from age fifteen when he'd dropped out of school. She suspected a bit of larceny from the get-go, from what he insinuated unapologetically. He'd also told her he had a wife of thirty years, estranged, of course, and two grown children, who were also estranged. She didn't ask for details, and he didn't offer them. But, bottom line, she would have to add adultery to prostitution . . . for her sins, as Sigurd would say.

She probably smelled like a bloody lemon by now, despite Sigurd's removing her sin taint. Harry certainly did. Even over his heavy dousing of Aramis, the scent of lemons was strong on him. It must mean he was a particularly bad sinner, or about to be. Like her. Funny, she'd never noticed that lemon phenomenon until Sigurd pointed it out to her.

No, no, no, she was not going to think about Sigurd now. The prick! The baby-killing prick! She had to put him out of her mind or she would never survive this night.

More important, as to Harry, the man had asked about Izzie, her condition, her prospects for getting better, what needed to be done. Without the words actually being spoken, he knew that Marisa was there because she needed money. A lot of money.

The whole time, his staff had been very discreet, almost invisible. As soon as they served a dish, they disappeared. Even now, as Harry led her down the teak-paneled hallways to what she presumed would be his stateroom, there wasn't a person in sight. That she could see, anyway.

He released her hand to open the double doors of his stateroom, a large bedroom and sitting room suite, and stood back smiling at her as she entered. "What do you think, my dear?"

What she thought was that she'd landed in crazy land.

She had expected a large, Playboy-style bedroom, complete with satin sheets and overhead mirrors, and this enormous suite had that in spades. What she hadn't expected was all the framed posters of Sophia Loren movies that covered all the walls. Arranged on chairs underneath some of them and hanging in the open closet were replicas of the costumes Sophia had worn in each of those flicks, everything from a sophisticated sheath to a sexy white sundress to a skimpy bathing suit to a transparent negligee that left nothing to the imagination. There were *El Cid*; *Houseboat*; *Desire Under the Elms*; *Man of La Mancha*; *Yesterday, Today and Tomorrow*; *Two Women*; *The Black Orchid*; *It Started in Naples*; *Arabesque*; *Legend of the Lost*. Each with its own ensemble, complete with shoes, hosiery, and jewelry. Even wigs on faceless heads sat on the closet shelf.

"What do I think?" she finally responded. "I think you have a thing for Sophia Loren."

"I do. I told you that before, as I recall. In fact, you could even say it is an obsession of mine. My wife certainly thinks so." His face, gentle and kind so far, turned hard. "Do you have a problem with that?"

She shook her head slowly. "I just . . . don't understand." She chugged down the last of her after-dinner drink and set the stemmed glass on a dresser.

He'd already put his martini on a bedside table and sat on the edge of the bed. He patted the mattress next to him, indicating she should sit, too, which she did, with even more foreboding than she'd felt all evening.

His face softened then, but only a little. "Here's the deal, and, yes, I know that you need a large amount of cash, so we must deal. I will pay for your daughter's operation, and in return you . . ." He shrugged, glancing about the room.

I'm afraid to ask. "And I . . . ?" she prodded.

"Will be my Sophia Loren."

Oh boy! Nuttier than a fruitcake.

"Every night, you will wear a different outfit, and you will be my Anna Cabot, Cinzia Zaccardi, Filumena Marturano, Natascha, Cleopatra, Rose Bianco, Dulcinea . . ."

One flew over this cuckoo's nest, for sure. "But . . ." She stood and walked around the large bedroom and sitting area, quickly counting. "There are twenty posters from twenty different movies."

He laughed, and it was not a nice laugh. "You

thought I would pay seventy thousand dollars for one night with you? No offense, darling, but even Sophia Loren herself would not be worth that much."

"Of course I didn't think that, but I can't be away from my daughter for twenty nights, especially during this time of her operation nine days from now." In fact, once he gave her the money, she intended to leave the island, possibly as soon as tomorrow.

"Let your mother go with her. You want the money, those are the conditions." He scooched himself up onto the bed so that his head was propped against the pillowed headboard and his short legs extended and crossed at the ankles.

Would he consider an IOU? Probably not.

She hated him in that moment for the power he held over her. And for the evil that seemed to ooze out of him along with the lemon scent. Frozen in place at the foot of the bed, she said, "I still don't understand. This conference will be over in a few days."

"You will travel with me until the terms of our contract are concluded."

In public? Everyone would know? This is a nightmare, an absolute nightmare. "Contract?"

"Verbal. I would not sign anything that could be used against me in the future."

Of course he wouldn't. "How long? How long would you expect me to stay with you?"

"One month."

She shook her head. "I can't do that. Sorry. It's just too long an absence from my daughter."

"Two weeks then. Twenty-four/seven. Whatever I want, whenever I want."

A trophy mistress on his arm in public, a trophy sex slave in his bed.

She couldn't speak over the lump in her throat, but she nodded.

"However, I'm not doing anything until the money is in the hands of the clinic in Switzerland. I know that sounds crass, but I have to be hard for my daughter."

His face went stone hard and downright mean. "You are in no position to dictate."

"Maybe not, but it's my daughter's life at stake here. I have to be firm on that, at least."

His hands fisted and unfisted at his sides before he agreed. "The money will be transferred in the morning. In the meantime, take down your hair. And do not wear it up like that again. Style it like Sophia did in most of her movies."

She nodded. "I can't take my hair down tonight, though. I put it up wet. If I unpin it now, it will be just a flat mess."

He was about to protest, then seemed to take her word for it. "At least show me the goods."

No more Mr. Nice Guy, apparently.

But then, two could play that game. "Show you the goods, huh? How about, show me the money. Bottom line: No money, no sex."

If he had been standing, he would have struck her, she could tell. This was becoming a more and more impossible situation. *How do I get myself in these messes? How can I get out? Do I want to get out? No, I want the money. I need the money. Oh Lord!*

"Lose the dress, honey. Slowly. Give me something."

She could do that.

Turning, she gave him a good look at the low back cleavage on her dress as she walked to the stereo system built into a wall unit and pressed play. Immediately, Frank Sinatra began crooning something about strangers in the night. For sure! This night was getting stranger by the minute.

She undid the side zipper on the dress and looked at him over her one shoulder, about to shrug out of the tight sheath, when the bedside phone rang shrilly. With a grunt of disgust, he grabbed for it and yelled into the receiver, "What? Didn't I tell you not to disturb me? What? From Brazil? When? Where are they now? Oh shit!" He got up from the bed and told her, "Stay right here."

"Maybe I should come back tomorrow."

"No! I'll be right back."

"But—"

"This is an urgent matter. A . . . shipment . . . that arrived earlier than expected. Turn on the television, or take a little nap," he suggested, coming over and giving her a short kiss on the lips, followed by a run of his palm over her rump. He grinned lasciviously. "Maybe masturbate a little to get yourself in the mood."

What? No way! "I told you, there will be no sex tonight."

"There's sex, and then there's sex," he said ominously, and was gone.

"Now what do I do?" she murmured to herself, turning.

"Get your sweet arse out of here as fast as possible," said a blond-haired, blue-eyed man standing near the open door of the bathroom. It was Sigurd's friend . . . fellow vangel . . . whatever. Svein.

"Oh my God! You scared me. How did you get in here?"

He arched his brows as if to say that she knew the answer to that question.

"*Why* are you here?"

"Sigurd ordered me to protect you."

"He has no right—"

"Michael has forbidden him to go near you, forbidden fruit and all that," he informed her with amusement, "so he sent me in his stead. He thinks you are in the restaurant, by the way. I think his head may very well explode once he finds out you are out on a boat alone with Goldman. You're supposed to be under Sigurd's shield."

"I don't need protection and I sure as hell don't need Sigurd's frickin' shield."

"Hah! I have ne'er seen a woman in more need of protection. Did you know that everything in this room is being filmed and recorded? Every lascivious act you engage in will no doubt be on the Internet one day, or for sale in some video venue."

"I haven't done anything lascivious." *Yet.* She glanced around quickly to see if she could recognize a hiding place for a hidden camera. She couldn't, of course.

"Not to worry. I have disengaged them. But you must be more careful of your virtue, m'lady."

"This is the craziest night of my life."

"And it is not yet over."

She rezipped her dress and straightened the shoulders. "I have to leave a message for Harry."

"Even knowing what a devious fellow he is?"

She didn't bother to answer, just pulled out a drawer of the desk to get some stationery. She wrote a short note telling Harry that she'd gone home, knowing he was busy, and for him to call her in the morning. "I'm taking the Anna Cabot outfit with me for tomorrow night," she told him.

Then she gave her full attention to Svein, who was waiting impatiently for her to finish. He glanced meaningfully at the dress and heels she carried with her, but she didn't bother to explain.

"Well?" she snapped. "Protect away."

He laughed and opened the door, looking this way and that before motioning for her to follow him. He put a forefinger to his lips, cautioning silence. "I have a boat waiting up ahead. Can you crawl down a ladder in those shoes?" he whispered.

"Needs must," she replied, also in a whisper.

Just before they turned a corner, Svein put up a halting hand.

Harry was standing arguing with a man who looked Mexican and spoke with a Hispanic accent. Something about "blonde ones" and "more money" and "too much trouble."

Svein grabbed her hand and led her back the way they'd come, then across the ship and along a circuitous route so that they were back on the original side of the vessel but on the other side of Harry and his still arguing companion.

"What was that about?" she asked once they were in the motorboat, which Svein was rowing until they got far enough away not to be heard.

"You don't want to know."

It could have been no more than an hour later, but seemed like days, when Marisa was back in the bungalow. There was a big conference party tonight, and her roommates were absent. Thank God! She had a lot of thinking to do.

Although she hadn't done the deed with Harry tonight, she still felt dirty. A good scalding shower and a loofa sponge would do the trick, but she was so exhausted physically and mentally that she just dropped down onto the bed, fully clothed, without removing her makeup, something she never did.

Oh well. Tomorrow is another day, Scarlett, she told herself. *Too bad there is no Rhett on the horizon to come save me, or Izzie.*

Chapter 19

Work, work, work! . . .

$\mathcal{S}$odom and Gomorrah had nothing on this. In fact, this *was* Sodom and Gomorrah. The Grand Keys Island S&G Party, to be more specific.

Despite the FOE organizers' attempt to change the image of pornography, there was no subtlety in this event. Sigurd suspected that what had started out as a "cute" idea proposed by Vanderfelt and his cohorts had snowballed into "grotesque," thanks in part to the influence of the Lucies. Of course, "grotesque" was in the eyes of the beholder, and his eyes, personally, were wide with shock. And it took a lot to shock a Viking.

Sigurd had witnessed decadence in all its formats throughout the centuries, including Caligua's famed orgies, and this shindig ran a close second. The hotel fair reeked with sex, alcohol, drugs, and in some cases unspeakable perversions. After spending hours working to save sinners and destroy Lucies, discreetly so as not to alert Jasper to their presence, in the corridors and private rooms of the hotel, he and Vikar were now standing in a darkened corner of the large ballroom, taking a brief rest before the heavy business of the evening would commence.

They were both dressed in black denim pants and shirts, covered with long black cloaks to hide their weaponry. In this strange crowd, no one gave them a second look, not for their attire, anyway. They had been propositioned, however. By women *and* men. Multiple times.

It was almost one a.m., and a live band still performed, providing a loud, pounding beat of music with provocative lyrics. One particular song kept repeating a refrain about wanting to do bad things to a woman. Very appropriate to the scene before them.

Naked and half-naked men and women were dancing in lewd movements simulating copulation. Some of them were Lucies.

Vikar turned his head this way and that, trying to figure what one writhing female was doing in the name of dance.

"It's called twerking," Sigurd told him.

"Huh?" Vikar shook his head at Sigurd. "You have been hanging around with Armod too much."

Three bars offered drinks and other illicit substances. On the sides of the ballroom, on extra-large pillows provided as decorative seating, actual copulation was taking place, sometimes with multiple partners.

"I did that one time in the midst of alehead madness," Sigurd confessed.

Vikar glanced at him with surprise. "Really, Sigurd? You? Ivak, I would not be surprised at, but you?"

Sigurd shrugged. "As I recall, it was an unsatisfying experience. I do not see the pleasure to be gained in sharing the swiving."

There was even a dungeon-like booth where people

were whipping each other. Some women were so drunk or drugged out they had to be held up by their partners. Sex toys were offered for sale, along with every type of condom imaginable, at a booth in a far corner. *A man worth his testosterone would want a talking condom?* Skin piercings were being done in another booth, mostly in intimate places.

"Ouch! Did you see that?" Vikar was staring at a young man who was having an industrial-size bolt implanted through his balls. "Why would any man submit to such?"

"Ivak told me one time that it supposedly enhances the swiving, for the woman."

"Ivak is a fool," Vikar concluded. "Am I getting so old that I am shocked by this? Am I turning into an angelic prude?"

Sigurd laughed. "No chance of that. But, yes, you are old. All of us vangels are."

Vikar jabbed him in the upper arm with a fist. "Vikings love a good party. Many an ale-flowing feast have we both attended where the bed furs shook, but I find this rather disgusting."

"You said it!" Sigurd glanced at his watch. It was one-fifteen.

"Is it time?" Vikar asked.

"Almost. Wait here a minute. I have to do something." He'd just noticed Tiffany, Marisa's lackwit bungalow mate, struggling against a man who was attempting to tug her outside the room. It was a Lucie who was doing the tugging.

The woman was a Lucie target if there ever was one. He'd heard her proclaim her dreams of wanting to be an adult movie star. He'd seen some of the lowlife film producers she'd been associating with while here at the conference. He'd even seen her come out of one of their hotel rooms earlier this evening, disheveled and clearly having been compromised. If she was even capable of being compromised.

Still, she was a sinner, and he had to offer to save her.

In a darkened corridor marked "Employees Only," the Lucie was attempting to back Tiffany up against a wall. "Ah don't want to. Ah changed mah mind. Let me go," she was protesting. Surprisingly agile, despite her very high heels, she ducked under his arm and danced away.

The Lucie went after her, doggedly pursuing his prey. "You can't change your mind now, bitch," said the young man dressed in surfer shorts, a tank top, and flip-flops. His blond hair was spiked. His fangs barely showed, yet.

"Did you call me a bitch?" Her eyes were darting this way and that, looking for an exit.

"No. I said 'witch.' Like 'sweet witch.' Come here, witchie, witchie. Come here now." The Lucie, whose eyes were turning red and his skin starting to scale, was beckoning Tiffany with a forefinger. Soon he would be in full demon form and unable to hold off pouncing.

"Uh, not today," Sigurd said, already drawing a long-handled knife from an interior sheath of his cloak.

The Lucie was a low-level hordling, and not all that old. Only two hundred or so years. Thus not as strong as Sigurd, not even close. The demon spun on his heels and morphed into full demonoid form. As it raised a clawed hand, Sigurd thrust his specially treated knife into the beast's heart. Before his eyes, and those of a stunned Tiffany, the demon dissolved into a puddle of stinksome sulfur.

"Give my regards to Lucifer," Sigurd said, wiping his knife against his pant leg, "because you will no longer be answering to Jasper, my friend."

Now that he'd dispensed with the Lucie, Sigurd turned his eyes to Tiffany, who was gazing at him with the same fear as she had for the Lucie. No wonder. His fangs were out and fully extended. And he'd just killed a monster, without hesitation. She probably thought she was next.

"Here's the deal, Tiffany, and we don't have much time. You are a sinner who has been bitten by a demon vampire. You can either change your ways by agreeing to a fanging by me to remove the sin taint, or you can go on your merry way. But this I guarantee, you will be a Lucipire by morning unless you change your ways."

"Ah doan . . . Ah doan understand," she stammered in a deep Southern accent, cowering against a vending machine in the hallway. "Who . . . what are you?"

"I am a vampire angel. One of the good guys."

She was weeping silently, her eye cosmetics running rivulets in dark tracks down her face. Like a girling she appeared now, a girling in harlot attire. "What do you want?" she sobbed.

" 'Tis not what I want, but what you need. Do you wish to continue on your sinful ways? Is this really the life you want?"

She shook her head. "Ah wanna go home."

"Then you must agree to let me remove the sin taint from you by sucking a small amount of blood from your neck. It won't hurt much, if at all, but it must be your choice."

She nodded reluctantly.

He performed the ritual, quickly and painlessly, for the most part. When he was done, he told her, "Go and sin no more." *Or at least try not to sin too much.*

Smelling sweet and not at all lemony now, she swiped at her eyes with a handkerchief he handed her. "Thank you fer helpin' me. Ah'm goin' back ta mah room ta pack. Ah'm gonna call my boyfriend and tell him Ah'm comin' home. Maybe Ah kin get mah job back at the hair salon."

"Good," he said. "You might want to try convincing Marisa to go with you."

He knew from Svein's call that Marisa was back at the bungalow, having ended her date with Goldman. He'd almost had a heart attack when he learned that her dinner date had been out on Goldman's yacht. The woman was too stubborn by half. The hard-headed witch hadn't ended her relationship with the evil man totally. Of course, she didn't know just how evil he was. Still he shivered with distaste at what Svein had told him about Goldman's perverted sexual tastes and what he had asked of Marisa, but that was not the old man's most evil side. Turns out he was heavily involved in the sex trafficking, and that was what had called him away from his encounter with Marisa on the yacht. The boat carrying new "goods" had arrived earlier than expected and the procurer had wanted Goldman to take custody sooner than he had planned.

In any case, it was all moot now. Goldman was heading for the slammer, if all went according to plan.

The FBI was making arrests out on the boats right now. Helicopters and law enforcement boats had them surrounded. Sigurd had decided to relinquish any of the vangel targets on those boats so that the federal agents could take over. Yes, they lost some converts and Lucies in the bargain, much to Harek's displeasure—he had wanted to take those particularly vile miscreants down himself—but this way the FBI's attention would be diverted away from the vangel mission here on the island. Which was about to take place in full force any minute now.

It horrified Sigurd to realize that Marisa might have been out on the yacht in the midst of all this. He'd given Svein orders to take any steps necessary to keep her in the bungalow for the rest of the night.

Coming back to the ballroom entrance, he gave a nod to Vikar and the two of them began to stroll slowly and openly across the vast space, deliberately attracting attention, something they normally avoided. Along the way, he could see heads shoot up, male and female Lucies sniffing the air, getting the scent of not just vangels in the room, but members of the VIK. Any Lucie who caught one of them would be rewarded greatly by Jasper.

By the time they left the building and were on the grounds, several dozen Lucies were on their tails. Not to worry. Cnut and Harek and a troop of vangels were spread like a net. If any of these Lucies escaped tonight, it wouldn't be for the vangels' lack of trying.

A half-dozen vangels were stationed at the various exits of the hotel, as well, to prevent any humans from coming out and witnessing the battle to ensue, especially with the Lucies in full, frightening demonoid form. If even one human pulled out a phone camera, all the news media in the world would pounce on the story. Secrecy was important.

And it *was* a battle that ensued. There were imps and hordlings galore, who were dispensed quickly, those being the weaker of the Lucies. But the huge mungs and the much stronger haakai stood their ground with swords and knives flashing. Screams of death. Roars of outrage. Shouts of triumph. Grunts of defeat.

Near the end, Sigurd recognized Reynaldo, one of Jasper's haakai du jour, a new favorite that was being considered for promotion to the Lucipire council of commanders, according to Zeb. Reynaldo recognized Sigurd, too. "Ah, the VIK who stole the woman from me."

Woman? What woman? Oh. Sigurd realized that this

must be the Lucie who'd fanged Marisa, the one who'd stood with Jasper in Marisa's bedroom "dream."

He pulled his switchblade sword from its special scabbard at his back. By pressing a button, the weapon doubled in length. In his other hand, he held the long knife he'd used earlier on the Lucie attacking Tiffany. Guns were to be avoided, whenever possible, because of the noise. "Where is Jasper?" he bellowed.

"Nowhere you VIK can find him," Reynaldo said with a grunt when he lunged with his long sword and just missed Sigurd's thigh.

"We will. Eventually," Sigurd countered, feinting with his sword but then swiping his knife in a wide arc.

Reynaldo, who was a formidable opponent, ducked and swiveled, coming back at Sigurd with another lunge, which hit home, slicing across his upper arm. Luckily, it was his left arm. The demon beast smiled. Not a pretty sight with its four-inch fangs, drooling mouth, and red eyes. "Hah! You assume good will conquer evil."

"Of course."

"I will have great fun toasting you in Horror tonight, and I do not mean with an alcoholic beverage," Reynaldo boasted.

Enough of this baiting! Sigurd pitched his knife directly at the Lucie's heart, and his aim would have been true, except that two things happened at once. He heard his brother Vikar yell, "Sig! Watch your back!" At the same time, there was the most piercing pain in his right shoulder.

Then, the blackness came over him. Total, all-encompassing oblivion.

It was like no other morning after . . .

"Marisa! Wake up. How can you sleep through all of this? Wake up, for heaven's sake!"

Through bleary, half-slitted eyes, Marisa saw Inga standing in their bedroom, next to the queen-size bed they shared. It was still dark outside, but a bedside lamp provided enough soft light for her to see. Her alarm clock said three a.m.

"What?" she asked, sitting up. Her head felt like an axe was embedded in it. Too much alcohol on top of stress equaled one pounding headache.

"All hell is breaking loose on the island and out on the boats. Didn't you hear the sirens? Doris is away on her FBI work. All her stuff is gone. She left, without a word, even. And Tiffany is packing up to go home. We should probably be doing the same. I can't imagine that this conference will continue after tonight."

Whoa! She must have slept through something momentous. "Make some coffee while I get dressed. Or undressed," she said, looking down at the black sheath she still wore. She staggered off to the bathroom, where she took three aspirins and then let out a shriek of fright when she saw herself in the medicine cabinet mirror. Her hair and smeared makeup were a sight to behold, and not a pretty sight, either.

It took her ten minutes just to get a comb through the tangles, and she had to soap and rinse her face three times before she got all the foundation and mascara off.

"Where were you so late, Inga? Partying?" she asked first thing, after taking a long sip of the black coffee.

"No partying, thank God! Oh, Marisa! I met a man. I think I'm in love. I think I've finally met 'The One.'"

Marisa arched her brows at Inga. Her friend liked to

party, and she dated a lot. But *The One* was not a term she used loosely.

"Rob Lowry. He's thirty-five years old. Divorced. No children. He owns a water taxi service out of Key West with six boats that travel back and forth to the various islands. He went to West Point, served six years in the Army, was honorably discharged as a captain when he had to come home to take over the family business after his father's death. His mother still lives, and acts as book-keeper for the company. He has no brothers or sisters. He's tall, well-built, bald as a golf ball, has one chipped front tooth, kisses like a pro, and is sexy as hell."

Marisa had to smile. "You learned all that tonight?"

Her friend blushed, and she almost never blushed. "We spent the night on one of his boats, just talking and drinking wine, but mostly talking. Seemed like we had so much to say to each other. Like we had to catch up on all the years we'd been waiting to meet each other. That sounds corny, doesn't it?"

"No, honey, it sounds just perfect," Marisa said, putting her cup down and squeezing her friend's hand. "I'm happy for you."

Just then, the sound of helicopters flying low could be heard.

"This has been going on for the past hour. FBI and Coast Guard choppers coming and going from the mainland to some of those yachts out there. Rob says people in town have been aware that something big was going to come down."

"Drugs?"

Inga shrugged. "No one knows."

"Oh my God! You mentioned yachts. Was Harry's one of them?"

"I really don't know. Good thing you got out of there, just in case, huh?"

In more ways than one, she thought.

"But, honey, there's much more. That big party that was to be held at the hotel tonight . . . whoa, boy! What a dirtbag affair it turned out to be. For all of Vanderfelt's hype about FOE and pornography is not all that bad, this was the worst of the worst." Inga went on to explain some of the amazing happenings, which would be disgusting to most sane people. "Even worse . . ." Inga began.

"There's more?"

"Oh yeah! There appeared to be some kind of fight that took place outside between Sigurd and his guys and some dragons."

"Dragons? C'mon! Really?"

"Well, no one really witnessed the fight firsthand. But supposedly there were these beasts the size of buses with tails and claws."

Marisa would have laughed, except that she recalled the waiter turned beast who'd appeared on her patio, the one Sigurd had destroyed into a puddle of slime. This nightmare kept getting more nightmarish.

"I'm beginning to think it was a mistake for us to come here," Inga said.

"Ya think?" Marisa couldn't be angry with Inga, even though she was the one who'd pushed Marisa into coming.

Something occurred to Marisa then. "Tiffany? Oh my God! Where was she in the midst of all this crap? Do you think she got hurt? You mentioned she was packing, but . . ."

They both stood at the same time with alarm.

Marisa knocked on the other bedroom door. "Tiff? Are you in there? Are you okay?"

There was a mumbling noise from inside.

"Can we come in?"

"All right," Tiffany said sleepily.

Marisa opened the door and clicked on the wall light switch. She and Inga stepped inside.

Tiffany, under a thin blanket on the bed, blinked against the sudden light. "What?" Her luggage was packed and sitting next to the door. She'd probably gone to bed until the morning boats would operate back to the mainland.

"Are you all right?" Marisa asked.

Tiffany sat up and began to weep.

"What's wrong? What happened? Were you at the awful party tonight?" Inga asked.

The weeping turned to bawling.

Marisa sat on one side of the twin bed, and Inga sat on the other, each holding one of Tiffany's hands.

"It was awful," Tiffany wailed. "First, Ah was at the party up at the penthouse. Ah think Ah musta had a funny drink, ya know what Ah mean. Ah had sex with the movie director Ah tol' ya 'bout, but mah brain is fuzzy 'bout the rest. Ah mighta had sex with some others."

"Oh, Tiff!" Marisa said, leaning forward to give her a quick hug.

"After that, Ah somehow got ta the party down in the ballroom. Ah've never seen anythin' so disgustin', not even in some of the bad adult videos, and y'all know Ah'm no prude when it comes ta that stuff." She shivered and pulled her hands free to tug the blanket up over her shoulders.

"This man tried to force me . . . Ah said no, but he kept following me, but then Sigurd saved me. Ah don't want to talk about it anymore." Before she pulled the blanket over her head, Tiffany held Marisa's gaze for a moment, and Marisa understood the horror she saw there. The rapist had been a Lucipire, in demon form, and Sigurd had destroyed it in front of Tiffany. "Ah jist wanna go home," Tiffany whined under the blanket.

One last thing Marisa needed to know. She tugged the blanket down slightly and saw what she'd suspected. Fang marks on Tiffany's neck. "Oh no!" Marisa said, putting her fingertips to the marks.

"It's okay," Tiffany told her. "Sigurd removed the . . . Ah mean, he saved me."

Marisa could tell that the girl didn't want to say more. Heck, she probably didn't really know what Sigurd had done, especially if she'd still been under the influence of drugs. But Marisa did. He'd removed Tiffany's sin taint, just like he'd removed hers. Not that it had done her much good, since she went on her date with Harry anyhow. And still would, truth to tell, if he was around tomorrow. After all, nothing had changed regarding Izzie.

"Ah'm leavin' first thing in the mornin'," Tiffany told them, after she blew her nose loudly into a tissue. "Tee-Beau is gonna drive up from Georg-ah and meet me in Key West ta take me home. Ah'm never gonna leave him again, Ah swear."

"I'm leaving in the morning, too." Inga patted Tiffany on the arm and stood. "We can take the water taxi back to the mainland together."

They both looked at Marisa, who stood, too. "I'll decide tomorrow."

"Marisa," Inga protested.

"Tomorrow," Marisa insisted.

The next day, the choice was taken out of her hands.

Chapter 20

His wings were clipped . . .

Sigurd was lying, pain-ridden and stiff as death, in a castle bed in Transylvania when he regained consciousness.

Last thing he recalled was his encounter with Reynaldo, the haakai Lucipire, and someone coming up to stab him in the back. Vikar had called out a warning to him, but too late for Sigurd to escape injury. Even so, Vikar must have saved Sigurd from a fate worse than death for a vangel—being taken to Horror and tortured into becoming a demon vampire—by killing the Lucipire who had come up behind him. Otherwise, Sigurd would be in Tranquillity, not a castle bedroom. Tranquillity was the place vangels went, those who died before their time. It was a holding place until Judgment Day, much like Purgatory.

"Infection" was always a problem when anyone was injured by a Lucie weapon, which would have been treated with poisonous mung. Even if a fatal blow hadn't been made, the slime itself in an open wound could cause death. That must be what happened to him.

He tried to sit up but fell back weakly onto the bed.

"Whoa, whoa, whoa. You are not ready to get up yet," Karl said, rising from an overstuffed chair where he had been reading a paperback book, probably one of the mystery novels he devoured. Karl leaned over him, adjusting a blanket and straightening the PICC lines that ran from an IV pole beside the bed into his arm.

"A PICC?" he asked, his voice a dry croak that hurt his throat. Usually, a peripherally inserted central catheter was only used for patients with long-term care, as compared to a temporary IV line.

"Here. Take a sip." Karl handed him a bottled water with a straw in it, like he was an invalid or something.

His eyes went wide, even as he took several sips of the icy fluid. "Heavenly," he whispered in appreciation as he sank back further into the pillow.

"Not quite, good buddy," Karl said. "Heaven, I mean."

Sigurd studied the bags hanging from the pole. A saline solution for dehydration and probably antibiotics, he recognized. But there was also a bag containing blood.

"I bled out?" He didn't recall a wound that would have bled so profusely, but then he'd passed out right after the last blow.

"No, but you've needed good vangel blood to dilute the toxins from the Lucie's blade. Your brothers have been donating a pint a day."

"My brothers?" *As in plural?* "Here?" He was so confused. Yes, Vikar would be here at the castle, but . . .

"Yep. All six of them are here. Sitting vigil. They're down in the chapel as we speak, praying for you."

Sigurd tried to laugh at the image, but it came out as a cough. "I have been that bad off?"

"Oh yeah. Here's the funny thing, if you can find humor in any of this. Guess what saved you? Your angel bump. The Lucie's knife hit that hard bone, harder than any of us realized they are, and skittered off to the right. All you got was a superficial slice on your upper arm. Mike says that if you ever get your wings now, you'll probably fly lopsided."

Ha, ha, ha. That is just great. Archangel humor. "How long . . . ?" He waved his hand weakly over the bed, words coming hard for him.

"You've been dead to the world for four days now. It was touch and go there a few times, my friend."

"Four days?" his raspy voice exclaimed in alarm. "The island? The mission?" And something else equally important nagged at his mind, but he couldn't quite grab the thought.

"You're not to worry. The island operation was a success. Almost all the Lucies were taken down. The only ones who escaped were on the yacht."

"Jasper?"

"Got away."

Sigurd said a vile expletive that vangels were forbidden to use and sank back into the blessed blankness. Karl was wrong. The operation had not been a success. Sigurd had failed to take out the master demon, which had been his primary mission. Mike was going to be so pissed with him.

The next day, when he awakened, he recalled what had been niggling at his mind. He jackknifed to a sitting position and said, "Marisa?" Even though his head pounded like a bloody drum and his upper arm felt like a molten knife was in it, being twisted to and fro, he managed to stay upright until he got his bearings. "Marisa," he said again. "I need to see—"

"Lie back down, Sig." It was his brother Vikar now. He was standing next to the bed. "Marisa made it off the island, just fine."

Out in the hallway, he heard a child's voice say, "I wanna see Unka Sig." It was Gunnar, Vikar and Alex's adopted son.

"Not now, Gun," Alex said. "Maybe later. Now come away from there."

"Doan wanna."

"Gunnar, do as your mother says," Vikar yelled, even though the door was closed.

The yell reverberated through Sigurd's head like an echoing bell, and he winced.

There was silence for a moment as Gunnar tried to decide if his father meant business or not.

"I mean it, boy. I can still paddle your little butt."

As if he ever would!

"I'm gonna read *Goldilocks* ta Unka Sig. That'll make him feel better. It's his favor," said another child's voice. Gunnar's twin, Gunnora. He suspected her face was pressed up against the keyhole, trying to look in.

"Nora! You can't read *Goldilocks*," Gunnar protested. "You can't do the bear growls like I can. Grow-ell!"

"Can, too! Grrrrr!"

Alex interjected, "Why don't we go down to the kitchen and see if Lizzie will let you make peach tarts for when Uncle Sig wakes up."

The thought of food made Sigurd's stomach roil, even the fruit sweets he usually devoured.

"Yippee!" the two young voices said, and clattered away down the hall, hitting each step downward with a loud thud. He felt each thud in his pounding head.

The door opened a crack then and Alex peered in. "Welcome back, Sig. You better be up and about soon or the kids are going to drive us nuts, trying to keep them away."

"I'll try," he said. When she was gone, he turned to Vikar, who'd pulled a straight-back chair up beside the bed. He noticed idly that the blood bag was gone, though the saline line was still in place. "Tell me everything," he demanded. "From when I got hit."

"It was mostly a matter of cleanup after you went down. Harek and Karl teletransported you back here to the castle and began immediate medical procedures. The rest of us stayed to handle any remaining Lucies."

"How many?"

"Forty-seven, including six haakai and eight mungs. As far as I could tell, none of the Lucies on the island escaped."

"But Jasper did?"

"He did."

"Then the mission was a failure."

"Why do you say that?"

"Because Mike told me that destroying Jasper was my primary goal."

"Sig! That is the goal in any of our missions, and none of us has been able to take him down yet. It does not mean we failed."

"It feels like failure to me." He shrugged. "Tell me more."

"You never saw so much slime in one place. It took us an hour to clean up the mess, and even then there was enough left behind to raise questions. The news media was on the story of the island doings like a hog on slop. Not just the FBI arrests for sex trafficking, tax evasion, money laundering, and so on. That in itself was a huge story. But then, there was the disappearance of so many folks who'd attended the conference, or the seeming disappearance. I'm referring to those that had been taken by the Lucies. So far, it's just speculation because most folks didn't want their attendance at such a sordid event to be known. Tracking them down would be difficult even under normal circumstances."

"Did they cancel the remainder of the conference?"

Vikar nodded. "Oh, they tried to resume, as if nothing had happened. But folks were scared. From the top, it was like rats jumping ship. I refer to those investors and filmmakers and Internet entrepreneurs who did not want the media light to shine on them. They were gone by dawn, escaping by yacht or helicopter or seaplane, whatever means available. As for the average attendee, the shame of having participated in that orgiastic party we witnessed had many of them hiding in their rooms the following day. Of course the first boats onto the island were news media, and soon there were more of them than the attendees."

"Goldman?"

"Arrested. Sex trafficking. Probably out on bail already. His kind always manages to escape punishment."

"And Marisa? I know you said she managed to leave the island, but did she return home? And what about her daughter? Please don't tell me she is still involved with Goldman in any way."

"I do not know, Sig. We've been too worried about you and unable to do much except . . . What are you doing?"

He was tearing the gauze bandage off his arm, about to remove the PICC line. "I have to see Marisa. I have to see if there's anything I can do to help."

"But Sig, you are not strong enough to leave your bed yet." Vikar gave him a slight shove, and it was enough to have him flat on his back again, panting for breath against the pain. "Besides, Mike said to tell you to stay put until he can come talk with you."

"About frickin' what?"

"I have no idea. Maybe your next assignment. Maybe he'll be sending you back to Johns Hopkins. Maybe the Mayo Clinic this time. Maybe he is just concerned about your well-being."

"Maybe, maybe, maybe. Vikar, I have to know that Marisa is safe. I have to do whatever I can to save her child. I have to!"

"Why is she so important to you, Sig? Could she be your life mate?"

"I don't know. I truly don't. I was only with her one time."

Vikar arched his brows at him.

"Well, one long, memorable night," he amended. "All I know is that my heart hurts when I think of life without her."

"Sounds like a life mate to me."

"But Michael said no more life mates, in fact no more relationships of any kind with humans. I am lost, Vikar. I am lost," Sigurd said on a groan as the black sleep began to overtake him again.

"You need to focus on yourself now, Sig. Take care to heal your body."

"The only thing I care about is Marisa, and I fear for her."

"Maybe you need to trust in a higher power working on your behalf."

"More maybes! Maybe you need to leave me alone. Misery does not love company."

And he *was* miserable. Bone-deep, heart-sick miserable. Despite all the odds, despite all the warnings that it could not be, Sigurd suspected that Vikar was right, that he had found his life mate, and lost her, and that hurt more than any Lucie blade.

But he was a Viking, as much as he was vampire or angel, and as such he could not just lie back and do nothing.

He waited in his half-dead state for his brother to leave, and when he did, Sigurd fought the blackness and agony to sit up, then stand. With professional expertise, he removed the cath lines and then the PICC itself. He staggered at first, but then was able to pace the room several times to get his bearings.

Sitting on the dresser was the large conch shell he'd picked up on the island as a gift for Marisa's child after talking with her on the phone that one day. It must have been in his luggage, which Alex had undoubtedly unpacked.

He should dress, he decided then. He was wearing only a pair of plaid sleep pants that Alex must have found somewhere for him. No matter. He hadn't the strength to pull on a shirt or bend over to put on a pair of shoes.

In fact, he had to focus hard to teletransport himself out of the room and through the ether to his destination.

Miami, here I come.

When angels pray . . .

Sigurd landed flat on his back on a soft surface, but it was painful nonetheless. Without rising, he gazed around him and realized by the dim light of a princess lamp that he was in one of two narrow beds in a little girl's bedroom. Pink walls, pink curtains, pink bedspreads, pink, pink, pink.

Rising on the elbow of his uninjured side, he gazed over at the other bed where a little girl in a ruffled nightgown—pink, of course—was staring at him, wide-eyed and wide-awake. She had a cap of short, dark curls on her head, and her nose was different, and she had a rosebud mouth rather than fulsome lips, but still she looked like a little version of Marisa.

To his surprise, she was unafraid of him, a stranger in her bedchamber in the middle of the night. In a whisper, she asked, "Are you an angel?"

"I am." *Sort of.*

"Did you come ta take me ta Heaven?"

A vise clamped over his heart at her words. What a brave little soul she was! "No, sweetling, I am not that kind of angel."

"Oh. You mus' be my guardian angel then."

He shook his head, hardly able to speak over the lump in his throat. "Not that kind, either. I'm just an angel friend come to visit you."

"I don't have very many friends 'cause I'm sick."

And he saw then that her condition was not good. She was very thin and her eyes were ringed with deep shadows. "I know a little boy and a little girl who would like to be your friends. They're my nephew and niece, Gunnar and Gunnora. They're three years old."

"I'm five," she said as if that were so much older, "but I could still be their friend."

"They would like that."

"What's that?"

He glanced down to where she was looking. He'd somehow brought the conch with him. "I promised you a large seashell. Remember?"

She nodded and reached out a hand, weakly, for it.

He stood slowly so as not to alarm the child and laid it on the bed beside her head. "If you are very quiet and hold it up to your ear, you can hear the ocean," he told her.

"Really?"

He nodded and showed her what to do. Even a

conch shell was too heavy for her little hand to hold up without support.

"Wow!" she whispered.

"I'll put it over here where you can see it." He placed it on the bedside table next to the dim-bulbed lamp.

He could feel the heat coming off her body before he touched her forehead with his fingertips. She was warm but not alarmingly so. "Don't mind my touching you, Izzie. I'm a doctor." He sat on the edge of her bed as he examined her lightly, taking her pulse.

"An angel doctor?" She giggled. "Didja hear about the banana that went to the doctor?"

"No," he said tentatively.

"It wasn't peeling well," she said with more giggles.

Was there anything more precious than a child's giggles? he thought suddenly. Especially a sick child's giggles. "Good one!" he told her. "Did you hear about the bear with no teeth? No? He was a gummy bear!" He'd heard Gun telling Nora that joke one day. He couldn't believe he even remembered the kid joke.

"Silly!" Izzie smiled at him.

Silly was the last thing a Norseman wanted to be called, or so he'd thought. Until now. He brushed some curls off her face, then used his fingertips to examine her skull.

"Are ya lookin' for my bad lump? It's inside my head."

"I know that, dearling. Let me feel, anyway." He combed his fingertips through her curls 'til he found the exact spot on her scalp. How he knew the lump was under there, he couldn't say for sure, but he knew. Massaging softly, he prayed silently, *Lord, help this child. She is pure of heart. Too young to die. Take me instead for I am old and black of heart. Please, Lord. Please!*

Sigurd was shocked at his own words. He'd always considered himself more vampire than angel, more Viking than anything else. And he rarely prayed, except to mouth the rote words on certain occasions. He hadn't come here to pray over this child.

Still, there was a peace that came over him as he prayed, and an odd jolt of heat that tingled at the edge of his fingertips, like little electric shocks. When he drew away, he saw that Izzie's eyes were closed, and she was sleeping evenly. He kissed her on the cheek and rose, feeling suddenly pain-free. He arched and stretched. No pain. Not so surprising, he supposed, since vangels tended to heal themselves quickly. His lengthy illness had been the anomaly because Lucipire toxins had been involved.

Tiptoeing across the room, he looked out a window, then realized he was in an apartment over a garage. He went to a door that was partly open. On the other side was an adjoining bedroom. Marisa's?

Yes, it was she. Lying on a double bed, wearing naught but a long shirt that proclaimed: "I salsa! Do you?" With arms thrown over her head, she was deep in an exhausted, almost unnatural slumber. He could tell she was exhausted by the dark shadows under her eyes, like her daughter's. Even in sleep, she seemed to be frowning with worry. It was a wonder she hadn't heard him in her daughter's room.

Not wanting to startle her, he slipped into the bed beside her, covering them both with a light blanket. He was going to awaken her, soon, carefully, so she would not scream with alarm, but she was so warm, and smelled so ginger-honeyed, and his body was beginning to recall all it had been through these past five days, that he found himself snuggling close to her, but not touching, and fell asleep himself.

What he did not see, or hear, was the black-haired archangel standing hands on hips over him, tsking. Nor did he notice the celestial fog that swirled about and settled over him and Marisa, providing a cocoon of peace.

Then the fog and the angel left. And went into the other bedroom.

Chapter 21

Dream lover . . .

Marisa was dreaming, and in her dream she was not surprised to smell oranges and evergreen. A citrusy tart pine scent that belonged to only one person. Sigurd.

Without opening her eyes, she turned into the open arms of the man lying beside her. How had that happened?

It's a dream. That's how it happened, fool.

Smiling, she nuzzled her dream lover's neck and inhaled deeply.

"Marisa," he said on a sigh, tugging her closer so they both lay on their sides, facing each other. "I have missed you, heartling."

"I didn't want to, but I missed you, too . . . sweetheart," she admitted, and rubbed herself against him.

He moaned and used one hand on her lower back to align their bodies to his satisfaction, and hers. His other arm cradled her head. "I tried to stay away."

"I'm glad you didn't."

"I was afraid you might have gone with Goldman, after all."

"I was tempted when he called once he was out on bail, but I just couldn't do it. Izzie's fate is in God's hands now." She laughed when she saw the expression on his face. "I didn't mean you. It was wrong of me to ask for your help. Izzie is not your responsibility. I just meant that I've stopped trying to control everything that happens in my life. I realized that I'm a control freak. I had to let go. What will be will be."

"Oh, Marisa. I wish—"

"Shh. Let's not dwell on that now." Her one hand was caressing his bare chest and shoulders, but halted when it came to a large bandage. "What's this?"

"I was wounded. I've been ill," he said, and leaned in to kiss her. It was a gentle kiss, but long and long and long. His breath became her breath, her breath became his. They needed each other to live.

She was disoriented when it ended, but still she was able to ask, "How sick have you been?"

"Very sick. Did you think I could have stayed away otherwise?"

"I don't know," she answered truthfully. Nothing had changed since Sigurd had admitted to the child killing, and yet everything had changed. She somehow sensed that it didn't matter. She somehow sensed that he was not a bad man. There must be an explanation. She trusted that there was. But she no longer needed details.

He tapped her chidingly on the chin. "Woman, don't you know I love you?" She could tell he was surprised by his own words. But then he laughed and repeated the words, "I love you. 'Tis true. I love you. I have nothing to offer. I don't even know where I will work after this. Or even if I will continue to be a doctor. For all

I know, I will be a farmer. My life is not my own. No future. Just now. But I hot damn love you."

And that was enough for her. For now. Because now was all she had in this dream. She rolled over onto her back and pulled him over her. "Show me. Show me how much you love me."

"Demanding woman!" he said with a grin.

"The demanding woman who loves you back," she said, putting her hands to his nape and drawing him down. His long hair was loose and hung down over her head like a silky curtain.

"Ah, that makes all the difference then."

Somehow he was naked, and so was she—the magic of dreams, she supposed—and when he entered her it was with the slow, excruciatingly slow strokes of love. Over and over and over again, he told her with his body how much he adored her. The words had been said. The body spoke now.

Sigurd's lovemaking back at the island hotel had been raw and lusty. This was different. Still expert. Still bespeaking a deep hunger. But it was like riding a sensual wave, each escalating to a more intense level. When he fanged her neck near the end, she didn't protest. It seemed a natural part of this undulating ride she was on. She could only hold on for the peaks, and there were many of them, before they both crashed into a bone-melting orgasm.

"Love you. Always," he said against her neck. She thought she felt tears.

She slept deeply then, and it was full morning when she finally awakened, feeling more rested than she had in weeks. Well, who wouldn't after a dream like that? It must be what men referred to as a wet dream.

Normally, she got up often during the night to check on Izzie. She'd been surprisingly quiet last night. That caused Marisa's eyes to shoot open and she jumped out of bed to check on her.

Izzie was sleeping peacefully. Her complexion was almost normal, not the pale, somewhat yellowish tint of the past weeks. And she seemed pain-free, although she hadn't had any meds since midnight. A quick digital thermometer on her forehead showed no elevated temperature at all.

Strange.

"Mommy?" Izzie said, opening her sleepy eyes slowly. "Can I have butter toast fingers for breakfast. With peach jelly. And orange juice."

Izzie hated orange juice, and Marisa wasn't aware that her daughter had tasted peach jelly ever in her young life. Strawberry, yes, and grape, but never peach.

Very strange.

That was when Marisa noticed the object Izzie was cradling in her arms.

A seashell.

And it wasn't even his birthday . . .

Sigurd should have been surprised, but was not, to find himself back in his bedroom at the Transylvania castle. He took off his pajama bottoms and put on some denim jeans and a T-shirt with athletic shoes. Then he lay on the bed, his hands folded behind his head, waiting. For something, he wasn't sure what.

It was a mystery how he'd gotten back to the castle. He didn't recall teletransporting back. Well, not so much of a mystery. He had a sneaky suspicion—

"Sigurd! What the hell are you doing out of bed? And the IV lines? Tsk, tsk, tsk!" Vikar stepped into the room and scowled. His oldest brother did a lot of scowling, except at his wife Alex, and the two children, of course. Maybe it was just Sigurd who brought out his sour side.

"Mike wants to see you. He's coming up here now. We thought you were still connected—"

"I can speak for myself, Viking," Michael said, stomping into the room. And he really was stomping today, wearing a plaid shirt, jeans, and cowboy boots.

"Yippee-ki-yay?" Sigurd inquired with a grin.

"Get along little dogies?" Vikar added, also grinning.

"Very funny! I have serious business with some vaqueros in Mexico that are about to have their spurs trimmed. I need to slip in without being noticed."

Sigurd had news for Mike. A plaid shirt? He'd gotten his cowboys mixed up. But then, Michael was going to be noticed, no matter what he wore.

"You are feeling better. Good," Michael said. "Come with me then. I have something to show you." Without waiting for a reply, he turned on his heels and left the room. *Clomp, clomp, clomp,* he went down the hall.

Sigurd arched his brows at Vikar.

Vikar shrugged.

Sigurd rose, and the two of them followed Mike along the corridor and down the wide staircase to the first floor, then out the front door.

"A little gift for you, Sigurd, to show that We are well pleased with the job you did on the island," Michael said and stepped aside.

Sitting on the front driveway was a shiny new— well, restored vintage—red Corvette Stingray. A real man's wet dream, though he wouldn't say that to the saint.

Sigurd's jaw dropped. "For me?" The vehicle must be worth more than a hundred thousand dollars. Maybe two.

Michael smiled. "For you. I know how envious you

were of that doctor at Johns Hopkins. This is a different type of automobile, but We thought—"

"It's great. It's fantastic. I just can't believe . . ." He walked up and ran his fingertips over the warm surface of the roof. If a man could make love to a car, this would be the model.

"Hey, how come I don't get a kickass car like this?" Vikar complained. "I've completed lots of successful missions. More than Sigurd, I wager."

"Vikar, Vikar, Vikar. You have a wife and family. Do you begrudge your brother this small pleasure?"

"Well, no."

Sigurd understood then what the car represented. No wife or family for him, but instead a material item to feed his sin of envy. It was called giving with one hand and taking with the other.

Well, bull-fucking-shit!

He was about to turn on his heel and go back into the castle to sulk, but then he had a second thought. "Is the title in the glove box?"

Michael nodded hesitantly. "It is. And it's in your name."

"Well, thanks for the gift, then. I think I'll give it a spin."

"Do you want me to go with you?" Vikar asked.

"No!" Sigurd said, way too loudly.

It was only as he'd left the castle grounds and was cruising down the turnpike, heading south, that he phoned Harek and asked, without preamble, "Where's the nearest classic car sales company?"

Miracles really do happen . . .

Marisa called Dr. Stern to see if he could see Izzie that afternoon.

Her daughter had been acting surprisingly well

since she awakened that morning. Eating a hearty breakfast. Begging to go to the pool. Chasing the neighbor's new puppy around the yard.

Even her mother noticed, especially when Izzie said, "Abuela, can we make *torticas de moron* t'day?" The Cuban shortbread cookies with guava and lime centers were time-consuming and took more energy than Izzie had been capable of for a long time.

Sometimes terminally ill people had sudden bursts of good health before they died. Marisa was very much afraid that Izzie was dying.

Therefore she was stunned when Dr. Stern called her into his office following hours of first, consultation, then testing, then further testing. He'd told Marisa's mother to take the child out into the waiting room while he spoke to Marisa. She and her mother had exchanged worried looks, expecting the worst.

"I don't believe it. I just don't believe it," the sixty-something doctor said, taking off his eyeglasses and cleaning them with a tissue. "In all my years of practice!" He appeared to have tears in his eyes.

Oh, this is bad. I don't know if I can bear it. But I must. I must. For Izzie. "What? What's wrong? Is it even larger than you expected?" Tears were already brimming in her eyes, too.

He shook his head. "Marisa, my dear, the tumor is gone."

She had been standing, but she sank down into a chair. "How can that be?"

"Who knows? A miracle? Izzie must have a guardian angel," the doctor quipped.

Marisa knew exactly what had happened then.

Sigurd.

He really was an angel. She was in love with an angel. A hot-as-sin angel.

The tears streamed down her face then. Tears of joy.

How could she ever thank Sigurd?

For now, she jumped out of her chair and ran out into the waiting room, where she hugged Izzie and then her mother and then Izzie again.

"Let's go home and make cookies," Marisa said suddenly.

"Yippee!" Izzie said, dancing around. Her mother looked at Marisa as if she'd lost her mind.

"But instead of the guava, let's use peach preserves. I think I know someone who deserves a cookie."

He knew he was good, but that good? . . .

Sigurd sold the car for a cool one hundred and fifty thousand dollars, a bargain for the Philadelphia dealer, who pounced on Sigurd's offer. Apparently, the Stingray was worth at least fifty thousand more. Sigurd could not care less.

While he was in the bank later that afternoon, having a cashier's check drawn, he called the clinic in Switzerland where Izzie was to have her operation. After some phone tag, he was finally connected with a woman named Adrian. He explained that he had the money for Izzie's operation and asked to what account he should wire the funds.

"Uh, Ms. Lopez called today and canceled the operation."

"What? Are you sure?"

"I'm sure. She did. An hour ago."

"Why? Oh no! Did Izzie . . . Did she . . . ?" He couldn't say the word *die*. He just couldn't. After all his efforts, surely God would not be so cruel. No, he couldn't think like that.

"I'm sorry, but I cannot discuss one of our patients with you. I appreciate the gesture you were going to make, and I'm sure Ms. Lopez would, too. Perhaps you should contact her."

He hung up without responding.

Now what? If Izzie had passed, Marisa would be devastated. Should he go to her? Or should he wait?

Teletransporting used up lots of energy. With that, on top of Sigurd's recent illness, he would probably look like an albino when he next saw Marisa, despite all his saves on Grand Keys Island. The hell with that! He teletransported, anyway. And landed on his arse in the backyard of Marisa's home in Miami. What was it with the landing on his arse lately? Probably some warped archangel idea of funny.

Thus he was standing, dusting off his behind, when Marisa opened the back door. "What took you so long?"

"Huh?"

She threw herself into his arms, and, yes, knocked him on his arse. Again.

She didn't seem to mind. She was kissing his face and neck, and crying, and laughing, and saying, "Thank you, thank you, thank you."

He was laughing then, too, but he had no idea why.

Finally, he recalled his reason for being here. Izzie. Something had happened to Izzie.

But wait. Marisa wasn't acting like a grieving mother. Maybe her sorrow had pushed her over the edge. "Marisa, heartling," he lifted her up off him and still sitting, legs extended, placed her on his lap, "I am so sorry about Izzie."

"Sorry? Why are you sorry?"

"Because she . . ." He paused. "Why were you thanking me?"

"Because you saved her, you wonderful man, you!"

"Me? I did? How?"

"A miracle. You cured my baby. You really are an angel, aren't you?"

"Yes, but I've never done any miracles before. Marisa, are you sure?"

"That she's cured? Or that you're responsible?"

"Both. Where is she?"

"Inside. Taking a nap. My mother and father went to the grocery story. He came home from work early to celebrate. They'll both want to thank you, too."

"Marisa, I don't think—"

"C'mon inside. I'll show you." She jumped off his lap and stood, holding a hand out for him to stand.

When they entered the kitchen, he was hit with the sweet smell of cookies . . . and peaches. That on top of Marisa's ginger-honey woman scent was enough to intoxicate him. He *was* feeling a bit woozy.

"Izzie made them for you," she said, pressing one of the cookies against his mouth. It was delicious.

After creeping into Izzie's bedroom and seeing that she did indeed appear to be sleeping normally, he went into Marisa's bedroom with her. They closed the door.

Before he made love to Marisa again, he wanted to clear the air first.

"Marisa, I killed my little brother a long, long time ago."

"How?"

"By neglect."

She made a scoffing sound.

" 'Tis true. I had healing talents, even back then, but I was envious of my brother Aslak, who was only five years old. Like your Izzie. When he became ill, I did nothing to save him."

She winced, but then she asked, "Sigurd, how old were you?"

"Ten."

"Oh, Sigurd!" She hugged him. "As you said, it was a long time ago."

"I am a grave sinner. Always envious of others. And

I am selfish, too, so selfish that I want you to marry me."

"Why is that selfish?"

"Because you have a child. You would stay the same age, as I would, as long as I remain a vangel, while Izzie would grow older, as humans do. But then, if I should die, you would, too. What would happen to Izzie then?"

"What would happen to your brothers' children if they should die?"

"We care for each other. We are all one large family."

"See. If my parents weren't still alive, your family would care for Izzie, right?"

"Right. You make it sound so simple."

"It is, if we love each other. Will Michael approve of us being married?"

"I think so. I think it's why he offered me the big temptation, as a trick."

"What big temptation?"

"I'll explain later. Suffice it to say, I have a hundred-and-fifty-thousand-dollar check in my pocket," he said, picking her up, her legs wrapped around his waist, and spun several times before dropping them both down to the bed. It was surprising the bed frame didn't break, with that falling on his arse nonsense again. "But first, I want to pledge my troth to you, Viking-style."

And he did.

Vikings did it better than anyone.

Vikar said so.

Marisa said so, too.

Much later.

Epilogue

And the vangel beat goes on . . .

Sigurd and Marisa were married a month later in a
Miami church by a visiting clergyman named Father
Michael. They would have been married at the castle,
which Marisa and Izzie had already visited, except it
would have been impossible to have Marisa's parents,
her newly paroled brother Steve, her friend Inga, and
others as guests where there were always dozens of
vangels in residence.

Even so, all of Sigurd's brothers were in attendance
along with Vikar's wife, Alex; Trond's wife, Nicole;
Ivak's wife, Gabrielle; Karl and his wife, Faith; Gunnar
and Gunnora; and the new baby, Michael. Izzie had
already made great friends with Gun and Nora as they
raced around the reception hall after the ceremony.
You'd never know the little girl had been sick.

Marisa was beautiful in a long, cream-colored
wedding dress by Nicole Miller, the real deal, not a
knockoff. Inga, her maid of honor, wore Vera Wang,
and that's all she would say on the subject. Steve had
offered to get Hugo Boss tuxes for the men, but Sigurd

had politely declined. He and his brothers wore plain black suits. "You're lucky we aren't wearing cloaks," he told his fiancée when she suggested a visit to a downtown tailor.

Marisa's parents had gone all out in arranging a traditional Cuban wedding reception with exotic foods and rum punches, although many of the Vikings preferred their beers. There was a cooler of Fake-O in a back room for any vangels in need of emergency sustenance. The band played nonstop salsa, except for the occasional Michael Jackson song requested by Armod.

"Just out of curiosity, why did you give in so easily?" Sigurd asked Father Michael during one of the breaks. The archangel was holding a sleeping baby Michael in his arms. *Did I mention that Ivak was a suck-up?* "I mean, you didn't even raise a protest when I told you I wanted to marry Marisa."

"I gave up. It has become a losing battle with you Vikings. I am thinking I should just marry off the rest of you VIK and be done with it, except I would do the choosing this time. There is this ex-nun in Poland, a pretty girl, despite the unfortunate warts. Or how about Regina? Two vangels together might be a good partnership."

Harek and Cnut overheard those remarks and gasped with horror, seeing as how they were the only VIK left unwed. They were seen leaving the party early for parts unknown.

"By the way, I've decided what you can do with that check that's burning a hole in your pocket," Michael continued. "Along with Marisa's hundred thousand."

Sigurd had been hoping that Michael had forgotten about that.

"A down payment on an island."

"What?"

Marisa came up to stand beside him, and he reflexively put an arm around her shoulders, tugging her close to his side. She fit perfectly.

"I was just telling Sigurd about his new assignment. Both of yours, actually, since you are now partners." Michael smiled, and it was not a nice smile.

Marisa stiffened slightly. She was not yet accustomed to being dictated to. She would learn.

"You will buy Grand Keys Island and begin a renovation of the hotel."

"Another renovation!" Sigurd exclaimed. "First Vikar with that crumbling castle and then Ivak with that run-down plantation."

"As I was saying, you will renovate the hotel. It will be another vangel headquarters, though we probably should be expanding into other countries. Later. In any case, your cover will be that it is a clinic for very ill children. A place where families can come to recover, along with the sick. I haven't thought out all the details yet. I am sure you will come up with something wonderful."

"But . . . but I'm not that kind of a doctor."

"You will be."

"I think it's a great idea," his traitorous wife said.

He squeezed her tight to show he was not amused.

"I do think it's a good idea," she insisted. "There are all kinds of possibilities."

"Smart lady," Michael said as he walked off. Then he yelled, "Someone come take this baby. It just did something very unangelic."

"Do you really think you could live on an island?" Sigurd asked her later that night after demonstrating some new Viking bed tricks. Norsemen were ever inventive when it came to loveplay.

"Are you kidding? Me. A vampire. In paradise. What else could any woman want?"

"Don't forget angel. And Viking."

"An excess of riches," she declared.

And he showed her just how much excess he had in him.

She later said her cup runneth over. He wasn't sure how she meant that, but he chose to take it as a compliment.

Reader Letter

Dear Readers:

Vampire in Paradise is my fifth Deadly Angels book. I hope you liked Sigurd's story. Did you know that there really are X-rated conferences like the one depicted in this book? Maybe not on a tropical island, but similar just the same. Who knew!!! I didn't.

So far, I've taken my Viking vampire angels to Transylvania, Pennsylvania (*Kiss of Pride*), Navy SEAL land in Coronado, California (*Kiss of Surrender*), the bayou with that rowdy Cajun LeDeux family (*Kiss of Temptation*), Las Vegas (*Kiss of Wrath*), and now an island off the Florida Keys (*Vampire in Paradise*).

Next up will be Harek's story. He's the Viking brother who is a computer genius, the one guilty of the sin of greed. Mike (that would be St. Michael the Archangel, the vangel's heavenly mentor) wants Harek to set up a website for him on the Internet. Meanwhile, Harek's trying to hide the huge bundle of money he made on the stock market, but every time he tries to "lose" it, he makes even more. He is stuck in Siberia. But not for long!

There will be even more vangel books coming, of

course. After all, there is one more Sigurdsson brother, Cnut, left with his story to tell. And, hey, you have to check out my novella, *Christmas in Transylvania*, in which Cnut shows up with a Ragnor Lothbrok hairstyle. If you've been watching *The Vikings* on the History Channel, which is wonderful, by the way, you will know what I mean. Travis Fimmel could float any lady's boat, Norse or not, if you get my meaning. That's who I'm picturing as I write Cnut's book. <grin>

And then, of course, Zebulan, the good demon, intrigues me with his tragic past. Don't you think he would make a good hero? And I have a sinking feeling that Regina, the vangel who used to be a witch, deserves her story to be told.

In addition, there are still a few Vikings dying (forgive the pun) to tell their stories in a historical setting. Alrek the clumsy Viking, Wulfgar the Welsh knight, Jostein the somber Viking with an estranged wife, Jamie the Scots Viking, Finn the Vain, or Tykir's brothers, Guthrom, Starri, or Selik. Or how about the Viking Navy SEALs? So many choices! Do you have a preference?

Please keep checking my website, www.sandrahill. net, or my Facebook page, Sandra Hill author, for more details on all my books and continually changing news. There are often special promotions with bargain prices on books. I periodically have great Viking or angel jewelry giveaways on my Facebook page. Also, signed bookplates are available for any or all books by sending a SASE to Sandra Hill, P.O. Box 604, State College, PA 16804.

As always, I wish you smiles in your reading.

Sandra Hill

Glossary

Above the salt—In medieval times, salt was a valuable seasoning. It was placed in the middle of the table. And those of noble status or favored guests were placed "above the salt."

Abuela—Grandmother.

Braies—Slim pants worn by men.

Buelita—Grandmother.

Café con Leches—Coffee with steamed milk.

Ceorl (or churl)—Free peasant, person of the lowest classes.

Drukkinn (various spellings)—Drunk.

Fjord—A narrow arm of the sea, often between high cliffs.

Frisian—Refers to a Germanic coastal region along the southeast corner of the North Sea.

Haakai—High-level demon.

Hersir—Military commander.

Hordling—Lower-level demon.

Imps—Lower-level demons, foot soldiers so to speak.

Longship—Narrow, open watergoing vessels with oars and square sails, perfected by Viking ship-builders, noted for their speed and ability to ride in both shallow waters and deep oceans.

Lucifer/Satan—The fallen angel Lucifer became known as the demon Satan.

Lucipires/Lucies—Demon vampires.

Mead—Fermented honey and water.

Mima—Mom.

Mungs—Type of demon, below the haakai in status, often very large and oozing slime or mung.

Muspell—Part of Nifhelm, one of the nine worlds in the Norse afterlife, Muspell is known by its fires guarded by Sert and his flaming sword.

Natilla—A flan.

Ropa Vieja—Cuban dish whose literal translation would be "old clothes."

Skald—Poet.

Stasis—State of inactivity, rather like being frozen in place.

Sword dew—Blood.

Teletransport—Transfer of matter from one point to another without traversing physical space.

Thor—God of war.

Tia—Aunt.

Trifle—A dessert made with layers of custard, fruit, and cake, and sometimes wine or fruit juice or jelly.

Tun—A cask or measure equal to roughly 252 gallons.

Valhalla—Hall of the slain, Odin's magnificent hall in Asgard.

Vangels—Viking vampire angels.

VIK—The seven brothers who head the vangels.

Whelp—Puppy or young offspring of a human.

Read on for a sneak peek at

Even Vampires Get the Blues

the next book in the

DEADLY ANGELS SERIES

from *New York Times* bestselling author

SANDRA HILL

Available in print and ebook
from Avon Books
August 2015

PROLOGUE

Hedeby, 850 A.D.

You could say he was a Viking Wheeler Dealer . . .

Everything he touched turned to gold, or least-ways a considerable profit, and thank the gods for that because Harek Sigurdsson was a brilliant Viking with an insatiable hunger for wealth and all its trappings.

It didn't matter that he had vast holdings in the Norselands, an estate in Northumbria, several hirds of warriors who served under him when called to battle by one grab-land king or another (Harek was a much-sought battle strategist), amber fields in the Baltics, trading stalls in the marketplaces of Hedeby, Kaupang, and the Coppergate section of Jorvik, a fleet of twelve longships and two knarrs, and numerous chests filled with coins, jewels, and rare spices. It was never enough! Not to mention two wives and six concubines . . . or was it seven?

Not that he wanted or needed any more wives or concubines. Like many Viking men (Hah! Men of all lands, truth to tell), he was betimes guided by a body rudder known for its lackwittedness when it fancied a woman. The Wise Ones had the right of it when they proclaimed: A cock has no brain. Well, at the ripe old age of twenty and nine, he had finally taken a sip from Odin's famed well of knowledge. In future, when he came upon a comely woman, he would bed her, not wed her, then send her on her merry way with a pat on the rump and a pouch of gold coins. Cheaper that way and lots less trouble!

Harek had just completed a meeting with Toriq Haraldsson, his agent here in Hedeby. Toriq had once been a hersir overseeing Harek's Norse housecarls. Unfortunately, the fierce swordsman had lost an arm in battle. Harek had no qualms about hiring the handicapped man as his business representative. Loyalty and honesty were more important in that role than fighting skills. Besides, Toriq had once saved Harek's life in battle at a time when Harek had been young and not yet so adept in fighting. A berserk Dane had been about to lop off Harek's very head. Suffice it to say, the wergild for a man's head was enormous.

As they walked side by side on the raised plank walkways that crisscrossed the busy market center, men and women alike glanced their way, not just because of their impressive Norse height and finely sculpted features. Their attire . . . fur-lined cloaks, gold brooches fastening shoulder mantles, soft leather halfboots . . . could support a tradesman's family for years.

Unaware or uncaring of the attention, Toriq scowled

and grumbled under his breath. Toriq was not happy with Harek today.

"Spit it out, man. What troubles you?"

"This latest venture of yours . . . it ill-suits a man of your stature," Toriq said, but then he had to step aside to accommodate a crowd that had gathered to watch a craftsman blowing blue glass into a pitcher. Other artisans were hammering gold and silver into fine jewelry. In fact, Harek noticed an etched armband he might purchase later. In other stalls, workers could be seen carving wood and ivory, or firing clay pots in kilns behind the trading tables.

Hedeby was an exciting city, always something going on. To Harek, the bustle of commerce, the sounds of money being made, were like music to the ears. There wasn't anything that couldn't be purchased here, from the prized walrus rope that was cut in a single spiral strip from shoulder to tail to . . . well . . . to his latest venture.

"Slave trading, that is what rubs you the wrong way?" Harek asked, now that he and his agent could walk side by side once again.

"Yea, and it should rub you the same, boy." Toriq always referred to Harek in that way, even though Harek had long since been blooded in battle and thirteen years since he'd saved his bloody head. Toriq himself had not yet seen forty winters.

"'Tis just another way of amassing a fortune." Harek shrugged, not taking offense. After all, Toriq was a free man, welcome to voice his opinion. Still, it did not hurt to remind him of certain facts. He glanced pointedly at the massive gold ring that adorned Toriq's middle finger, a writhing dragon design with ruby eyes, worth a small fortune. "My ventures helped make you a wealthy man, Toriq."

"That they have, and most appreciative I am."

"And your eight children, as well?" Harek mentioned, trying to lighten the mood. "How else would you dower all those daughters?"

Toriq was always complaining about how expensive it was to support females, much as he loved his six daughters and his lone wife, Elsa. "All boys need is a sword and occasional change of braies and boots, but girls want gunnas and hair beads and slippers and brooches for every occasion and all the household fripperies that are a seeming necessity," was Toriq's usual refrain.

Not today, though. He just shook his head sadly at Harek.

"I am always looking for new ways to earn still more gold. Slave trading is no different than trading in amber or money lending, both of which have been our mainstay. I'm only surprised I haven't tried it afore."

"There is a vast difference, Harek."

"How so? In every country, there are thralls. You have thralls yourself."

"Nay. I have indentured servants. Due to their own circumstances, some folks are forced to sell themselves, but only for a time. Then they are free."

"You are splitting hairs, my man. Vikings are known to free thralls if they are well-pleased. Some even wed their thralls or take them as concubines. Slavery is a fact of life. Why should I not profit from it?"

Toriq threw his arm out in frustration . . . and almost knocked over a plump maiden. After apologizing profusely, he turned to Harek once again. "You have riches enough to buy a small kingdom. Why can you not be satisfied with what you have?"

Harek was approaching frustration himself now, and he bristled. Criticism, even from a friend, could go too far. "A man cannot have an excess of gold. All the sagas say 'tis best to save for rainy days."

"Pfff! It could rain for forty days and forty nights, like it did for that Noah character the Christians babble on about, and you would still stay afloat. On the other hand, you would probably fill your Ark . . . rather longship . . . with gold, and it would sink from its very weight. Then, where would you be? Sunk by your own greed."

Realizing the inadvertent humor in his remark, Toriq laughed and squeezed Harek's forearm. "Peace, my friend. You gave me back my life when I thought I no longer had worth as a man. You know I will do whate'er you ask."

"Even if it leaves a bad taste in your mouth?"

"Even then."

They had almost arrived at the harbor when a horn blared, announcing the arrival of yet another sea vessel. Hopefully, it would be *Silver Serpent*, Harek's largest longship, which was expected any day from the eastern lands. With its human cargo.

Anyone entering or exiting Hedeby, located at the junction of several major trade routes, had to do so by foot or horse or cart through one of three gateway tunnels built into the massive, semi-circular ramparts of the fortified city. Once they passed through into the bright light onto the wharves, Harek surveyed the seventy or so ships and boats with flags of many colors, denoting family, business, or royal allegiance, tied at anchor or beached farther on for repairs.

The new arrival was indeed Harek's slave trader. To his dismay and Toriq's horror, they could practically smell the "cargo" afore the passengers even alighted.

And what a motley bunch they were! More than fifty men, women, and children of various nationalities, from ebony to white skin, wobbled on shaky sea legs over the wide gangplank onto the dock. There should have been a hundred. Harek shuddered to ask what had happened to the others. Even a dimwit could see this was a disaster that meant money lost. The most tight-fisted farmer knew you did not starve a pig before market.

As a whole, the starvling group, wearing raggedy garments, was filthy, some covered with dried vomit and other body emissions. Scabs, bruises, and lice were in clear evidence. Their eyes as they passed by him were dead, except for a few in shackles that held his stare with murderous intent.

"The reeking ship will have to be scrubbed down with lye afore used again for any purpose," Toriq noted, as if Harek had not already come to the same conclusion.

"I want these thralls bathed, fed, and clothed. A healer will have to be called to treat some, I warrant," Harek told Toriq.

"It will be a sennight or more before any of them are fit for the auction block."

"And time wasted means money lost," Harek repeated one of his favorite proverbs.

"Precisely."

"Meanwhile, I have a thing or two to say to the captain of this floating cesspit."

"Where shall I take them?" Toriq studied the individuals, some of whom were shivering despite the summer heat. Obviously, they could not be housed in the slave quarters where goods and persons were stored before auction, not in this condition. If naught else, there would be fear of contagion. Odin only knew what diseases bred on these sorry bits of humanity.

"I have no idea where to house them. To Muspell, for all I care, at this point."

Toriq tapped his chin thoughtfully, then said, "I will take them to the storage building behind the amber trading stall. It is mostly empty now. Elsa will know what to do about delousing these people and fattening them for market, though she will not thank me for the task." That was as close as Toriq went to taunting him with I-told-you-so's.

"Buy her a new gold neck torque with my regards," Harek advised.

"You do not know women if you think that will suffice," Toriq told him.

"Do whate'er you must then."

It was, in fact, three sennights before Harek returned to Hedeby from a brief trip home to his Norse estate where he'd been summoned to handle a crisis involving a neighboring chieftain with a land dispute. The lackbrain Viking would think again afore trying to steal property from Harek in his absence, especially in his present mood.

His first wife, Dagne, resided there, and what a shrew she'd turned out to be! Now that the first bloom of youth had passed Dagne at twenty and five, Harek could scarce bring himself to give her a conjugal duty-swive. 'Twas hard to find her woman place in all that fat, Dagne now being as wide as she was tall. But did she appreciate his husbandly attentions? Nay! She was too busy complaining:

"There is not enough wood for the hearth fires."

It is summer. You do not need to keep all the hearth fires burning.

"The cook is too mouthy and disrespectful."

Probably because you invade her domain too much.

"One of the privies needs cleaning."

Then, clean it.

"Why can't we have a beekeeper in residence?"

Because you would tup him, as you did the blacksmith, the shipwright, the horse breeder, and the monk.

"The rushes in the great hall are flea ridden."

Um, I can tell you where we keep the rakes, my dear.

"Your mustache is too bristly."

Then stay away from my damn mustache.

"I heard that Queen Elfrida has a new silver fox-lined cloak. Why can't I have one, too?"

Because a dozen foxes would have to die to cover your bulk.

"There is a black bear in the north wood needs killing."

I can think of something else that needs killing.

"I might be increasing again."

And yet I have not been home for nigh on ten months. How do you explain that, my halfbrained wife?

There was a good reason why Norsemen went a-Viking so much.

In the end, Harek left his Norse estate, with good riddance, vowing to himself not to return for a long while. And renewing his vow never to wed again.

To his relief, Toriq had already handled the thrall situation in his absence. Not only cleaning and feeding them, but selling them at the slave mart the day before. "Four thousand mancuses of gold for fifty slaves! That is wonderful!" Harek exclaimed, doing a quick mental calculation. "Even with expenses . . . initial purchase price to the slavers, sixty seamen's wages for one month, food and clothing for the thralls during the voyage, medical care where needed, the auctioneer's commission, and a goodly bonus for you . . . there has to be a clear profit of at least twenty-five hundred mancuses."

Toriq nodded. "A few of the skilled slaves . . . a carpenter, a farrier, a wheelwright, a weaver, and a beekeeper . . . brought a goodly amount by themselves."

Good thing Dagne, with her sudden yen for honey, did not hear of the beekeeper.

"And, of course, the younger, more attractive women raked in considerable coin. I saved one especially nubile Irish wench from the bidding block. For your bed play, if you choose. Otherwise, my Elsa says she must go." He waggled his eyebrows at Harek.

He slapped Toriq on the shoulder in a comradely fashion. "A job well done, my friend! Already I can see the possibilities for the future. Longships sent to different ports to gather new cargo. The Rus lands, Byzantium, Norsemandy, Jorvik, Iceland. With more selective purchases and better treatment, I guarantee there will be even better returns on investment."

"Cargo? Cargo?" Toriq sputtered. "You are speaking of human beings, Harek. Many of whom are stolen from their homes."

"You still object?" Harek was surprised. "I thought . . . I mean, you did such a good job. I thought you now accepted the wisdom of slave trading as a side business."

Toriq shook his head vigorously. "I mean no insult, Harek, but you will have to find another man to handle this trade. I did it this once, but no more."

"No offense taken," Harek said, but, in truth, he *was* offended. Perhaps that was why he was so dissatisfied with the Irish woman in his bed furs that night. Beautiful, she was, but Toriq had failed to mention that she could not stop weeping for her young son who had been sold to a Frankish vintner and a husband who had been left behind on a poor Irish farm. Never mind that it had been the husband who'd sold her and his youngest son into thralldom.

Disgusted, Harek made his way to the sleeping quarters on his largest knarr anchored at the docks. There, instead of celebrating a new, successful business venture, he succumbed to a long bout of sullen mead drinking which led to alehead madness. Leastways, it had to be madness for the *drukkinn* apparition that appeared to him out of the darkness was not of this world.

A misty, white shape emerged. Ghostlike.

"Harek Sigurdsson!" a male voice yelled out of the mist, so loud that Harek jerked into a sitting position and almost rolled off the small pallet built into an alcove. He blinked and tried to see the hazy blur standing in the open doorway leading to the longship's deck. The only light came from the full moon outside.

At first, he was disoriented. Who wouldn't be with a head the size of a wagon wheel, with what felt like a battle axe imbedded in his skull?

A man . . . he could swear it was a man he saw standing there, and yet at the same time, there was no one there. Just a swirling fog.

"Who goes there?" he yelled out, thinking it must be one of the crew stationed on board overnight.

Silence.

Now he was starting to be annoyed. "Present yourself, man, or suffer the consequences."

No one answered. Good thing because he realized he had no weapon in hand. Should he go back inside? What kind of weapon did one use with a ghost?

He shook his head to clear it, to no avail. He was still under the influence of ale. Or something.

He could see clearer now and it was a tall, dark-haired man wearing a long gown in the Arab style who beckoned him outside. The gown in itself was not so unusual but the broadsword he held easily in one hand was, especially since it was his own pattern-welded blade. Then, there were the huge white wings spread out from his back.

What? Wings? Huh? It couldn't be possible. He closed his eyes and looked again. Definitely wings.

Was it even a man? Or some kind of bird?

He had heard of shivering men suffering from wild dreams of writhing snakes or even fire-breathing dragons, but usually it was men trying to wean themselves away from years of the addictive brews or opium. Harek rarely drank to excess and never had an interest in the poppy seed.

But Harek had a more important issue at the moment. His bladder was so full he would be pissing from his ears if he didn't soon relieve himself. Making his way through the now empty doorway, he staggered over to the rail. Undoing the laces on his braies, he released himself and let loose a long stream of urine. When he was done . . . shaking his cock clean, then tucking it back into his braies . . . he breathed a sigh of relief, then belched. Which was a mistake. His breath was enough to gag a maggot.

Which cleared his head enough to let him know he still had company. The man-bird stood there, scowling at him with contempt. The wings were folded so that you could scarce tell they were there.

"Who . . . what are you?"

"Michael. The Archangel."

Harek knew about angels. In his travels, he had encountered many a follower of the Christian religion, and a pathetic religion it was, too. Only one God? Pfff! "I am Norse."

"I know who you are, Viking."

He did not say "Viking" in a complimentary manner. And, really, Harek needed to get to his bed and sleep off this alehead madness. Best he get this nightmare over with as soon as possible. "And you are here . . . why?"

"God is not pleased with you, Harek. You are a dreadful sinner, as are your brothers, as are many of your fellow Norsemen. 'Tis time to end it all."

"End it? Like, death?"

"You say it."

"All of us?" he scoffed.

"Eventually."

"That requires an explanation. Are you threatening me and my family?" He inched backward from the looming figure, hoping to reach a nearby oar, which he could use as a makeshift weapon. But he felt dizzy and wobbly on his feet. "I need to sit down."

"What you need, fool, is to pray."

What a ridiculous conversation! He could not wait to wake up and tell his friends about this strange dream. It would be fodder for the skalds who ever needed new ideas for their sagas. "Pray? For my life?" he scoffed.

"No. For your everlasting soul. Your death is predetermined."

Enough! This madness had gone on long enough! "Speak plainly," he demanded.

"Thou art a dreadful sinner, Harek. Dreadful! Your greed is eating you alive, and you do not even know it."

He must have appeared confused. Bloody hell, of course he was confused. "What have I done that is so bad?"

The man-thing . . . an archangel, he had called himself . . . shook his head as if Harek were a hopeless case. "Your most recent activity is so despicable. How can you even ask?"

"Oh! The slave trading! That is what this is about." Harek was disgusted up to his very gullet with all this sanctimonious condemnation of his business dealings. First, Toriq. Now some angel with flea-bitten wings trying to lord over him.

"I do not have fleas."

That was just wonderful. The creature could read minds.

"And I am not a creature."

Harek inhaled deeply for patience and almost fell over. He reached the rail for support. "In truth, what is so wrong with thralldom? Your own Biblical leaders . . . Abraham, David, Moses, had slaves."

"You dare to compare yourself to such great men!" He pointed a long forefinger at Harek, and he felt a jolt of sharp pain shoot through him.

"I only meant—"

"Silence! For your sins, you will die, leaving your mortal form behind. For the grace of God, you are being given a second chance to redeem yourself."

That caught Harek's attention, but he was an astute businessman. He knew no great prize came without a price. "And what must I do to redeem myself?"

"You will become an vangel . . . a vampire angel . . . one of the troops being formed to fight Satan's evil Lucipires, demon vampires."

"I am a Viking. I hardly think I am the material for saintly angelhood."

"You will not be that kind of angel."

"For how long would I be required to fight these . . . um, demons?" He was still not convinced this wasn't just a bad dream.

"As long as it takes. Seven hundred years at first. Longer, if you fail to follow the rules."

"Now there are rules?"

"No great prize comes without a price," Michael told him, repeating his own thoughts back at him. Again. "Do you agree?"

"Do I have a choice?"

"There is always a choice."

What did he have to lose? Harek nodded, and before he had a chance to change his mind, the archangel pressed the tip of the broadsword against Harek's chest, causing him to lean backward, farther and father, until he fell over the rail into the water.

It should have been no problem. He was a leather-lunged swimmer when need be, but his body was suddenly riddled with excruciating pain. His jaw felt as if it were being cracked, then forced back together with an iron vise. In fact, it felt as if he had long fang-like incisors now. And his back! His shoulder blades seemed to burst open. The place where wings should go, he presumed, but instead, the skin healed into raised knots. All this happened in the matter of sec-onds as he sank deeper and deeper into the murky depths. Choking on the briny water. Fighting to swim upward against a force determined to hold him down. Drowning. He no longer fought his fate.

Even so, Harek had time and brains enough left to realize that he'd forgotten to ask one question:

What exactly was a vangel?

She stunk, all right, and not like a rose . . .

Camille Dumaine was dragging her feet as she walked from the beach at the Coronado Navy SEAL training compound . . . her thirty-year-old bones feel-ing every bit of her just completed five-mile jog in heavy boots on wet sand under a bright, ninety-degree California sun. Didn't help that she was sweating like a pig or that one of the swabbies in the newbie class had barfed all over her during "sugar cookies," a par-ticular exercise designed to punish. Also didn't help that she heard a male voice call out, "Yo, Camo! You're wanted in the commander's office."

It was Trond Sigurdsson, whose Navy SEAL nick-name was Easy. All SEALs got appropriate, and not-so-appropriate nicknames when they first entered BUD/S training, Basic Underwater Demoliton SEAL. Trond was a mite lazy, known to always look for the easy way. Same nicknaming was true of the elite WEALS, Women on Earth, Air, Land, and Sea, the sister unit to the SEALs, of which Camille was a charter member, two years of training and five years on duty now. Thus, Camille's nickname of Camo, which wasn't a play on her name, or not totally, but her ability to camouflage herself, no matter the setting. Being invisible in a crowd could be invaluable for a special forces operative, male or female, she'd learned on more than one occasion. It was one of the prime reasons she'd been recruited to begin with.

A chameleon, that's what she would put on her resume, if she had one. Who knew, growing up in New Orleans' Garden District, that being of average height and weight, with plain brown hair and eyes, and just a touch of Creole coloring in her skin would be such an asset? Certainly not her, and definitely not her mother and father, Dr. Emile Dumaine and Dr. Jeannette Fortinet, world-renowned heart surgeons, or her over-achieving brother Louis Dumaine, who was a rocket scientist. No kidding! But she had learned early on that, with the aid of make-up, clothing, a wig, even something as simple as posture or hand gestures, she could change herself into whatever she wanted to be

"I need to shower first," she told Easy.

"I think Mac means *now*. They've been holding off the meeting 'til you got back from your run." He sniffed the air and took a step back, even as he spoke, and then grinned. Easy knew well and good that SEALs and WEALS had to work just as hard, physically, after they'd earned their pins to keep in shape. Smelling ripe was not so unusual. "The more you sweat in training, the less you bleed in battle," was a familiar mantra.

A meeting? He mentioned a meeting? She went immediately alert. Rumors had been circulating for weeks about a new mission. One that involved taking down those African scumbags who had been kidnapping young girls for sex slaves. Camille felt passionately about what was being done to these innocent children in the name of religion, and she wanted in on this mission. Partly she was infuriated as a women's rights issue, but it was also her history as a Creole that fueled her fire. Camille's grandmother many times removed had been "sold" at one of the famous pre-Civil War Quadroon Balls when she was only fifteen.

Just then, she noticed another man with Easy. He had stopped to talk with SEAL Justin "Cage" LeBlanc and was now approaching her and Easy. The similarities, and the differences, between the two men were immediately apparent. Both were very tall, probably six foot four, lean and well muscled, but whereas Easy's attire . . . athletic shorts, drab green SEAL t-shirt, and baseball cap, socks, and boots . . . said military to the bone, this guy wore a golf shirt tucked into khaki pants with a belt sporting an odd buckle in the shape of wings, designer loafers without socks, and a spiffy gold watch. Whereas Easy looked as if he was about to work the O-Course, the other man carried an over-the-shoulder, high-end, leather laptop case. The most dramatic difference was between Easy's dark, high and tight haircut, and the new guy's light brown hair, spritzed into deliberate disarray. The pale blue eyes they both shared were the gravy on this feast for the eyes.

Camille wasn't drawn to over-endowed men, especially ones who were so vain they moussed their hair in the morning, especially since she worked in testosterone central where muscles were the norm, but Holy Moly! This man, probably no more than thirty, was the epitome of sex on the hoof.

She licked her lips and forced herself to calm down. *I look like hell*, she reminded herself. *On a good day, this superior male specimen wouldn't give me a look. After two failed near-marriages, I do not need another complication. Wash your mind, girl. I better check to make sure I'm not drooling.* "Your brother, I presume?" she said to Easy.

"How could you tell?" Easy said with a laugh. "Camo, this is my brother Harek Sigurdsson. Harek, this is Camille Dumaine, the female Navy SEAL I told you about."

Why would Easy be discussing me with his brother? Definitely not proper protocol for secretive special forces members to be made known to civilians, even a family member. She frowned at Easy, who just grinned. The idiot! Even if he was married to a fellow WEALS member and a good friend of Camille's, Nicole Tasso, his charm was wasted on her.

His brother, on the other hand . . . whoo boy!

She took the hand that Harek extended to her as he said, "I've heard so much about you that—"

They both froze, extended hands still clasped. A sensation, like an electrical shock, except softer and coming in waves, rippled from his fingers onto hers, then rushed to all her extremities. It was like having world class sex without all the bother.

"What is that odor?" Harek asked, as if stunned.

Talk about an instant lust destroyer! "Vomit," she disclosed.

He shook his head. "No. Roses." He closed his eyes, leaned forward slightly and inhaled deeply. "Hundreds and hundreds of roses."

Turning to his brother, he asked, "Can't you smell it?"

"Are you demented? She smells like she's been rolling in . . ." Easy's voice trailed off as something seemed to occur to him. "The mating scent! Finally! You've been bitten! I can't wait to tell Vikar and the others."

"No! That's impossible!" Harek was staring at her now like she was some strange, repulsive creature.

And what was it with those slightly elongated incisors of his? She hadn't noticed them at first. Not that they looked bad. It was just that today, with all the modern orthodontics, folks, especially male ones pretentious enough to get designer haircuts, would have corrected the imperfection.

"What scent? What bite? I need to get to the meeting." She tugged her hand out of his continued clasp and was about to walk away.

Easy, who had been bent over laughing, raised his head and said, "'Tis the musk men and women in my, uh, family give off when they meet their destined life mates."

Well, that was clear as mud, especially since Harek was muttering, "No, no, no! Not now. Not her! I just got back from Siberia. I haven't thawed out yet."

"What the hell is a life mate? And why not me? Forget I asked that." As for thawing out, if he was any hotter, he would combust. She gave the obviously distressed man a glare and turned on Trond. "In case you need a reminder, Easy, I am not a member of your family."

"Yet," Easy said ominously.

Harek looked as if he was going to throw up.

Welcome to my life, Camille thought.

At Avon Books, we know your passion for romance—once you finish one of our novels, you find yourself wanting more.

May we tempt you with . . .

- **Excerpts** from our upcoming releases.

- Entertaining **extras**, including authors' personal photo albums and book lists.

- Behind-the-scenes **scoop** on your favorite characters and series.

- **Sweepstakes** for the chance to win free books, romantic getaways, and other fun prizes.

- Writing **tips** from our authors and editors.

- **Blog** with our authors and find out why they love to write romance.

- **Exclusive content** that's not contained within the pages of our novels.

Join us at
www.avonbooks.com

AVON

An Imprint of HarperCollins*Publishers*
www.avonromance.com

FTH 1013